All That Really Mattered

J. A. Barker

ALL THAT REALLY MATTERED

This is a work of fiction. All the characters, names, incidents, organizations, and dialogue in this novel are either the products of the author's imagination or are used fictitiously.

iUniverse books may be ordered through booksellers or by contacting:

iUniverse
1663 Liberty Drive
Bloomington, IN 47403
www.iuniverse.com
1-800-Authors (1-800-288-4677)

Because of the dynamic nature of the Internet, any web addresses or links contained in this book may have changed since publication and may no longer be valid. The views expressed in this work are solely those of the author and do not necessarily reflect the views of the publisher, and the publisher hereby disclaims any responsibility for them.

ISBN: 978-1-4917-8620-8 (sc)
ISBN: 978-1-4917-8655-0 (hc)
ISBN: 978-1-4917-8621-5 (e)

Library of Congress Control Number: 2016901909

Print information available on the last page.

iUniverse rev. date: 5/4/2016

To my beloved son
John Hamlett Barker

Love looks not with the eyes, but with the mind,
And therefore is wing'd Cupid painted blind.

—Shakespeare, *A Midsummer Night's Dream*

All That Really Mattered

Prologue

My dearest Andrew,

It breaks my heart to say it: our marriage is over. I have agonized over our situation ever since your operation. I was fearful the experimental transplant would be certain death for you, but I knew you preferred death to the depressed, paralyzed life you were living. As hard as it was, I came to accept your longed-for end to your suffering. Neither of us was prepared for your survival. Now your sixty-year-old brain is in a thirty-year-old body so unlike yours you hardly know how to manipulate its sturdy young muscles, and I now have a husband whose body is thirty years my junior that I cannot recognize in the slightest. What a tragic pair we have become.

Where does the essence of a person reside? You have always said you are essentially your brain—that every other part of you can be replaced with transplants or artificial parts or simply amputated, and as long as your brain remains intact, you are present. But you are wrong, Andrew. You say you are still the same person because your brain is here with all of its knowledge and memories and feelings, but I cannot see you, nor hear you, nor feel you. I hear your words, but they come from the voice of a stranger. I see your smile, but it is not the smile I always loved. I look into your new dark brown eyes for some small trace of the familiar, but they are not as expressive as your old, liquid blue ones I adored. Your body is hard and muscular, not long and lean like the one my hands have caressed and memorized over our many years together. You are all new, a stranger in my bed. The husband I have cherished for thirty-five years is gone. You are as dead to me as if you had not made it through the operation. Dead! Gone! I cannot have a thirty-year-old stranger for a husband, Andrew. Surely your new eyes can see we are mismatched now, and your brain must tell you we no longer have a viable marriage. You are just too loving and kind to admit it. So, I am saying it for you.

I have loved you thoroughly, Andrew. You have made my life rich with happiness and little joys. Your love and gentle ways sustained me through the heartaches I have suffered over the years: the loss of my parents, the four miscarriages, and the bitter news that I would never be able to have a child. And it was the strength I gathered from your steadfast love that sustained me through your tragic accident and through the agony of seeing you suffer every single day physically and mentally for five long years. I railed at the Fates for ruining your body, but I thanked God every single day for sparing your mind.

But you were more than a brain to me, Andrew. It was the whole package I loved. Even crumpled in a wheelchair, it was still you, my wonderful, brilliant, kind husband. I have always thought of us as kindred souls. I was sure my love for you was complete, perfect, absolutely unconditional, and yet I find to my surprise that there are limits after all. Except for God, I cannot love someone I cannot see.

And I wonder about your soul. Surely you have one, but whose soul is it now? Is it still the one you had before the operation? Does a person's soul convey with the brain? Or is your soul mixed up with the one whose body you inhabit? Or worse, do you now have that poor deceased young man's soul? I sometimes detect a difference in your personality, an impatience or an irritability that wasn't there before. Do you even know what sort of person he was? Even though I know you don't believe in souls and consider these kinds of questions silly, you know they matter vitally to me. I do pray for your sake, that your "friendly agnostic" soul, as you have always called it, is still your own and God, who gave you the strong scientific power of doubt, will pardon your inability to do otherwise.

I am so sorry, Andrew. Please forgive me. I simply am not strong enough to handle this, to live the life we now face. I cannot be your wife anymore because I cannot have who you are now as a husband. When you think about it rationally, you will realize that by virtue of your operation, I am now old enough to be your mother. You need a young wife who is vigorous like you are now, who can give you the children I couldn't.

So I am filing for a divorce, if in fact one can divorce a man who has been officially declared dead. As you know, I have adequate assets to live comfortably for the rest of my life, so I want you to keep the house and farm and everything for your new life. Just send any personal items when you get to it.

Please don't try to stop me, Andrew; do not come here to try to change my mind. I am absolutely resolute. I cherish the memories of our life together. I want to remember you as you were, as we were. We were very happy once, just one unit in this world. That is how I want to remember us. I never want to see this new person who calls himself my husband again.

I know you still love me, as I do the memory of you, but I pray that in time you will find someone younger and better suited for the person you have become. Now is your chance to start over and have the family you always wanted. And you will be able to get back to your lab and continue your important research.

Andrew, please, I beg you, make the most of this blessing, this miracle. I truly wish you a happy and fulfilling new life. As for me, I am going to stay out here in California with my sister. We will be two widowed sisters, really, because my husband is now dead too.

My dearest, dearest Andrew, I am so sorry. I am heartbroken. I mourn the loss of the only man I have ever loved, and I always will.

Margaret

chapter 1

Andrew

*A*ndrew read the letter again, folded it carefully, put it in his desk drawer, took it out again, ripped it to pieces, threw it in the fireplace, and watched it burn. He didn't feel any better. He paced back and forth, agitated, trying to make sense of it all. And why did he just throw her letter away instead of keeping it in his drawer? He was not normally the impulsive sort and was already sorry that he destroyed the last communication he would ever have from her. Andrew noticed several pieces floating away from the fire onto the hearth. He quickly retrieved them and smoothed them out to see what he managed to save: "cannot see," "tragic pain," "Dead! Gone!" Well, that pretty much summed it up. He stared at what was left of their marriage for a few minutes more and carefully put the charred pieces back in his desk drawer. He was utterly devastated.

No one would have ever called Margaret beautiful, but she was a natural blonde with a slender, athletic build and attractive enough to catch Andrew's attention. In fact, Margaret was the first and only woman Andrew had ever loved. She was a poet, a painter of words whose aesthetic approach to life enabled her to enhance reality or create a different one. She was the architect of their marriage, building and shaping it into a richness Andrew could not imagine living without. Even after the accident, she plied her magic to make the most of it she could. She added the spirit, the spice, the seasoning to his otherwise cerebral existence. Without her, he would be too literal, too dry, too much a scientist.

In the first few years of their marriage, he made love to her passionately and often, the way all young people in love do. Later, after a difficult endometrial cancer surgery and treatment, sex was often too painful for her. His violin became the most effective means by which he could communicate his love and appreciation for what she brought to his life. He could explain his love, but he had trouble expressing it. His words never had the depth of his music.

Andrew had always let her take the lead, and she had done it again just now. How strange, though, that Margaret could see so many things in her mind that did not exist in reality, and yet she could not see her husband, who actually did. He wondered if this was just an excuse she had made up to set him free. He knew it would not be beyond her to make this kind of a sacrifice for his sake. He hoped this was the case, because he could not handle the thought of her total rejection. And now she was gone. He had not even been able to tell her good-bye.

"A blessing, Margaret? A miracle? Really? So far, it's been nothing but a goddamn curse!"

The initial euphoria of waking up to live again as a healthy, whole man spurred Andrew on through the rigorous, grueling year of rehab in Walter's clinic. After being in an induced coma for a considerable length of time while the stem cells regenerated the vital nerve circuitry, Andrew was like a newborn baby testing out each muscle to see what it could do. Learning to coordinate his new body's muscles was far more arduous than Andrew had anticipated. Balance and walking came relatively easy, but developing his fine motor skills was slow, frustrating, and ongoing. The most difficult challenge for Andrew, however, was learning to control the residual part of his body donor's brain. Walter's research on primates had shown better outcomes when a third of the right anterior frontal lobe of the body donor was left in place. Unfortunately, in addition to some executive functions, this portion of the brain is also where personality primarily originates. Although Andrew's full brain would be dominant, Walter had to develop a cocktail of drugs that would suppress the body donor's personality as much as possible. Still, chemical imbalances produced by stress and alcohol could cause the stronger emotions of the body donor's personality, like temper and irritability, to become accentuated. Keeping it in check would present a lifelong challenge for Andrew.

Andrew winced in disbelief when he first saw a young, handsome Italian staring back at him in the mirror. An Italian! It was a good thing his Boston Brahmin parents were not alive to see him like this! He wished Walter had found a body more suitable to his age and stature and ancestry, but he knew Walter had to take what was available. Still, the freedom of movement and the sense of vitality after so many years confined to a wheelchair trumped all his misgivings. He liked his new body's muscularity, its lower center of gravity, and the warm sexual stirrings he thought were gone forever. He was beginning to feel good. He wanted to jog and play tennis. He wanted to make love. But most of all he wanted to play his violin again.

From the age of six, the violin had been Andrew's best friend, his muse, his comfort. Shy and reserved, he had always used his violin to express his most deeply felt emotions. He became so proficient with his playing that on his sixteenth birthday his father gave him a highly prized eighteenth-century Guarneri violin—not one of the very best, of course—but still one to be envied. It had a wonderfully full, rich tone that Andrew loved, and so did his audiences when he gave recitals. He had missed his violin terribly over the years of paralysis and was eager to start playing again. Walter kept telling him he needed to be patient.

Andrew's high spirits took a major dive when Walter lifted the quarantine and Margaret was allowed to visit for the first time. Although Andrew and Walter both tried to prepare her emotionally for what to expect, the wide-eyed, startled-deer-in-the-headlights expression on her face and the loud gasp as her hand flew up to her mouth was an image Andrew would remember for the rest of his life. This was not the joyous reunion he had envisioned, anticipated, dreamed of night after night. As handsome as he was, he could feel her recoil at the sight of him. She didn't even so much as touch him that first meeting. Her visit was so painful and awkward Andrew was relieved when she left after only fifteen minutes. He told himself that this was only a temporary setback, although he immediately recognized that the age difference would be a huge hurdle for both of them. Still, he hoped he would soon have his beloved Margaret back in his arms, arms with which he could once again hold her, as he had longed to do for the past six years since the accident.

Subsequent visits were better but not by much. They made small talk, avoiding the obvious topic. Andrew managed to hug her and hold her hand, but she seemed as reserved and shy as a schoolgirl on a first date. He did not know how to reach her, how to get back to where they used to be. He needed his violin. She had always loved to hear him play. He would win her back with his music. She would see, despite his appearance, nothing else had really changed. He might look younger, but that was just his covering, skin deep. Inside he was the same Andrew she had always loved. And he was the same Andrew who loved her.

After much pleading and cajoling by Andrew, Walter acquiesced and let him have his violin. When Margaret brought it on her next visit, Andrew gently lifted the violin out of its case and held it to him for a few minutes, stroking the neck and body lovingly. He knew he would be a little rusty after so many years, but he tuned his instrument and optimistically started to play Elgar's "Salut D' Amour," one of Margaret's favorites. His fingers couldn't even handle the first few measures. After a lifetime of practice, he was playing like a first grader. He tried again to no avail. Embarrassed and frustrated at his ineptitude, he was almost afraid to look at Margaret, and when he finally did, she quickly looked away. Now he understood why Walter had been reluctant to let him have his violin. He should have known! His new body could not possibly do what it had never been trained to do. He sounded like a beginner because, as far as his new body was concerned, he was one. Andrew's frustration soon slipped into full-blown anger. He felt like throwing his violin across the room but wisely threw his music instead. He turned back to Margaret just in time to see her slipping out the door. He noticed she had tears in her eyes.

———

When Andrew was finally released from Walter's clinic and the operation became public, things went from bad to worse. He was a freak, a sideshow, and the media circus around Walter and him was unnerving. Walter was on the covers of *Newsweek, Time,* and *Scientific American* and had made the headlines of the *New York Times,* the *Wall Street Journal,* and the

Christian Science Monitor. The *St. Louis Post Dispatch* gave its hometown celebrity a full half of the front page above the fold. Dr. Walter Rubin had accomplished the unthinkable, the impossible! He had performed the first successful human brain transplant. The brain belonged to his friend and former colleague Dr. Andrew Hamilton, the paralyzed professor emeritus of neurosciences at the medical school. The recipient body was that of a local thirty-year-old Anheuser Busch truck driver named Anthony Costello, brain-dead from a hit in the head with an errant baseball bat during a pickup game with some of his work buddies.

You can imagine the discussions and debates that followed on the evening news and Sunday talk shows. Fox News featured several prominent members of the religious Right who insisted Dr. Rubin was a murderer and should be arrested for killing Dr. Hamilton who, although paralyzed from the neck down, was still a live and lucid human being when his brain was cut out and given to Anthony Costello. They argued that physician-assisted suicide was morally reprehensible, against the will of God, and if brain transplants became sanctioned by our government, it was tantamount to legalizing murder by consent or convenience. Our most vulnerable citizens, children and the elderly, would soon be in grave danger of having their lives taken from them because they were too deformed, too ill, too old, too mentally incapacitated, too costly to care for, or unwanted. If Dr. Rubin was allowed to go unpunished, Americans would see the start of a slippery slope that would end in the government forming "death panels" to decide when it was time for each of us to die. "God says death is at a time of His choosing, and we have a moral imperative not to interfere with His will. This is another case of science and the godless left tromping on the right of the American people to have a God-fearing country free of moral decay."

A panel representing the Far Left on MSNBC declared it totally unethical to use a prime young man's whole body to benefit a single sixty-year-old rich man in no danger of dying when the various organs could have been used to save a number of dying individuals desperately in need of those organs. "If a person wants to die because life is unbearable, the answer should be euthanasia or physician-assisted suicide, not brain or body transplants. The religious Right needs to stop trying to legislate morals for the whole country and allow Congress to pass a law giving such a person the right to a dignified, physician-assisted death." They pointed out that insurance companies were unlikely to ever pay for such expensive procedures. That meant only the rich would be able to afford them, creating yet another case of special treatment for the privileged few, causing more resentment and widening the divide still further between ordinary hardworking Americans and the elite 1 percent. "Furthermore, the inhumane treatment imposed by Dr. Rubin on an unknown number of animals, including chimpanzees, in pursuit of his research should make this surgery especially repugnant to all decent, caring Americans. At least, thanks to our new endangered species law covering captive chimps, it will be illegal for him to use them so inhumanly in the future."

Disagreeing with the Right and the Left, a group of neuroscientists on CNN hailed this successful surgery as an exciting landmark in brain research with enormous ramifications for the future of medicine and its potential benefits for mankind. "What if such an operation had been available for Einstein when he was dying of heart failure? How much longer might he have lived and what of further importance, such as the grand unification theory, might he have been able to add to our understanding of the universe? Some of our badly mangled veterans and terminally ill children facing cruel, untimely deaths could have normal lives again with body transplants. In no way should we allow such research to be prohibited by groups on both ends of the spectrum trying to legislate morals and promote social and political agendas. If the United States prohibits this research the same way it has tried to restrict stem cell research, it too will move to the research centers of Europe and Asia, and the United States will miss out on developing some of the most important and revolutionary advances in medicine."

Legal experts debated whether this was a brain transplant for Mr. Costello or a body transplant for Dr. Hamilton and wondered, since one body was declared brain-dead and the other body was declared dead after the brain was removed, were not both men legally dead, and if so, what was the legal status of the person now alive? Should a new identity be issued? A new name? A new social security number? If not, who is he? Would the doctor's credentials and other records accrued during his life follow this new person, even if he was declared to be Mr. Costello? Would traffic records, police records, if any, and credit ratings for Costello follow along with his body to Dr. Hamilton? Or should all be expunged from both men because they were both legally dead? Furthermore, what was the legal status of these two men's wives? Were both women widows due survivors' benefits, or was only one wife a widow and one still a wife? If so, how would one determine which is which? There were many interesting unprecedented legal issues to decide. Unsurprisingly, the lawyers could not reach a consensus on any of them.

Philosophers posed an interesting counterargument: "Since the body of one man has been kept alive, and the brain of the other man has been kept alive, has anyone's death actually occurred? Clearly, both men are in some sense still alive even though there is only one physical being now present. So what is the identity of this individual? Is he now someone quite different from either of the persons involved, or is he like any other human being who has had, say, a heart transplant? What makes us human anyway? Beyond having conscience, self-reflection, empathy, and compassion, we also have an ephemeral essence (some might call it the self, others the soul). This defining essence is the one constant in a sea of variables. It is who we know ourselves to be, and it is expressed through our values, beliefs, innermost thoughts, and deep-down emotions. This sense of self is a moral compass and is exhibited through the interplay between the mind and the physical attributes of an individual, not as they exist in isolation but rather in the context of family, society, and the world. The various perceptions of an individual's mental and physical characteristics and capabilities, his ethnicity and cultural habits, are also profound factors in shaping personality, but personality is an unreliable reflection of the self because it is subject to the vagaries of countless outside influences, including the chemical environment of the brain at any given time. Still, the self, raw intelligence, knowledge, and the specific bibliography of experience of an individual and the interplay between them remain the dominant factors of personhood. Who this person is should be evident. Despite the presence of a small piece of Mr. Costello's frontal lobe, without Dr. Hamilton's full mind-generating brain to think, reflect, love, create, be inspired, worship, and orchestrate the music of life in its own particular way with its own free will (if there is such a thing), there can be no humanity present as we understand it and certainly no personhood. It therefore follows that the surviving individual cannot be Mr. Costello. Without question, the now existing person is Dr. Andrew Hamilton."

Geneticists, on the other hand, begged to differ. They argued that although the dominant brain belonged to Dr. Hamilton, the body—including the face, the fingerprints, and, more importantly, the DNA—belonged to Mr. Costello. "The ethnicity belongs to Anthony. If Andrew ever fathers children, their biological father will be Anthony, not Andrew. Predispositions to any diseases or illnesses will be those of Anthony, not Andrew. Personality, to some extent, will also be affected when stress, alcohol, and other chemical stimuli disrupt Andrew's chemical equilibrium and bring Anthony's personality to the fore. The pheromones and age will be Anthony's, not Andrew's. Every aspect of this individual, except the brain with its knowledge, memories, and habit of mind, is contributed by Anthony. It therefore stands to reason that this person is far more Anthony Costello than Andrew Hamilton. The gene pool, the DNA, should be the ultimate determination of identity. Therefore, the individual in question is definitely Anthony Costello."

Psychologists and sociologists found Andrew irresistible subject matter for their particular brand of research. Their curiosity provoked an endless barrage of questions. "What are his physical and emotional responses to his new body? Has he adjusted to the difference in age, stature, and body type? Has he noticed any personality changes, memory loss, or emotional instability? Is he suffering from depression? Does he find that people react differently to him as an Italian than as his Anglo-Saxon (WASP) former self? How do his friends and colleagues react to him? More importantly, how does his wife react to him? Is he sexually recharged, and is he still attracted to the same kinds of women now that his pheromones are different from the ones he had? For example, would Andrew find Anthony's wife more appealing now than his own? And why is he so certain that he is Andrew when he looks like Anthony, walks like Anthony, talks like Anthony, and sometimes acts like Anthony? How will he react if a court decides that he is Anthony with a brain transplant and not, as he maintains, Andrew with a body transplant?"

Andrew considered some of these questions off base and even ridiculous. There should be no question whatsoever as to his identity. His mind as he knew it before the surgery was still intact. His knowledge, experiences, and memory belonged to him alone, as did the particular way he looked at the world. Having no patience for such personal lines of inquiry, he put the psychologists, sociologists, and reporters off, saying he hadn't had enough time to adjust to the new realities yet. That also happened to be the truth of the matter. Andrew just wanted to get back to his normal, quiet, former life.

And so on, week after week, the talking heads were having at it. In addition to the interviews, there were book offers and movie rights to consider. Margaret had refused to be interviewed and had fled to her sister's in California to get away from it all. Anthony Costello's wife and his ailing mother had fought bitterly and publicly in court with each other over the disposition of Anthony's body and now seemed to have gone into hiding and hadn't been heard from since. But Andrew had no place to hide; he had to be seen. He was Walter's proof that the operation was a success. It was part of the original bargain. Never expecting to be alive for Walter to collect, Andrew had readily agreed to it.

Walter's success was the culmination of decades of relentless research. As jogging partners discussing their projects over the years, Andrew had followed Walter's progress with interest. He had marveled at Walter's ingenuity in building a modified heart-lung machine that could circulate an oxygen-enriched liquid to a severed brain in order to keep it from going bad during the long, intricate operation to reconnect it. The two of them had speculated over numerous cups of coffee on how to concoct this special oxygen-rich liquid that would feed the brain but be otherwise neutral to the body's blood supply. Walter's research had shown that the body and the brain needed to be kept below eighteen degrees Celsius for a prolonged period of time beyond that needed for him and his team to painstakingly reconnect. To rebuild the nerves, Walter had used a special accelerated stem cell rejuvenation technique actually developed by Andrew in his research on optic nerves before his accident. So Walter insisted that Andrew share in his success and cooperate with the media. He had to be seen and heard, however repugnant he found it to be.

And Andrew found it exceedingly repugnant! When he had asked Walter to take him to a state or country where assisted suicide was legal, Walter had countered with a proposition. Having performed successful brain transplants on primates, the next step was to try it on a human. Consenting to be the first human brain transplant case would give Andrew the best of all possible outcomes. If the operation was a failure, he would be dead as he wished; if it succeeded, he would have a healthy new body and have every reason to want to live. Either way, he would be making a huge contribution to this important research. The fact that he was a neuroscientist made him the perfect candidate if the operation was successful. Walter told Andrew that he had secretly been hoping that he would have the opportunity to present this option to him.

Andrew didn't need any persuading. He had known Walter since coming to St. Louis to join the faculty at the medical school some twenty years ago. They lived down the street from each other off of Wydown Boulevard and jogged almost every morning at five o'clock until that fateful winter day Andrew was hit by a car. When the university's Human Subjects Committee refused his request to pursue brain transplant research ten years ago, Walter left the medical school and opened his own private lab with the help of a few wealthy donors, including Andrew. He had been working quietly under the radar in pursuit of his goal. In anticipation of his eventual success, Walter had already resolved the legal issues involved with such an experiment, especially permission to perform what could amount to an assisted suicide on a terminally ill or paralyzed volunteer if the experiment failed. His and Andrew's good friend and lawyer, Charles Wilson, had handled the case, but it took a long time, a lot of money, and considerable legal maneuvering to keep the case and its results away from the press and out of the public domain.

Although Andrew had every confidence in Walter as a brain surgeon, he calculated it to be a number of years down the road before Walter would be able to perform a successful human brain transplant. Never for one moment had Andrew believed that the operation would succeed on this first try. He had wanted to die and saw the experiment as a sure way to end his suffering and miserable life dependent on Margaret for absolutely everything. He had not bothered to consider the consequences of waking up alive in some other person's body. The odds were against it. The science was against it. It was totally inconceivable to him.

He had endured so much this last year. He was exhausted. All he wanted was to get back to some semblance of his normal life.

And now this letter from Margaret.

chapter 2

Cullen

"*M*ommy! Mommy! There's Daddy!"

Cullen dropped the dishtowel and ran into the den. Shawn was pointing to the television. Cullen looked at the man being interviewed and froze.

"Oh my God," she whispered, "Oh my God. What have I done?"

Her cell phone rang. "Cullen, quick, turn your TV on to CNN. It's Tony! I didn't really believe you when you told me last week. I simply couldn't imagine that he is still alive even when it was in the papers. But seeing him sitting there talking like nothing happened … how weird is that?"

"It isn't really Tony, Meghan, and I'm staring at him right now. Can't talk. Call you later."

"Mommy, you said Daddy had gone to live with God. How did he come back? Why didn't he come see us first before he went on TV? When is he going to come home?" Cullen could hear the excitement in his voice.

"That isn't Daddy, Shawn. This man just looks like him."

"It is too Daddy! I see him. I hear him. It is too him. I want Daddy to come home." Shawn was crying now and ran out of the room. "I want my daddy," he sobbed, just like he had done every night for a full month after Tony died.

Cullen was crying too, but she couldn't force herself to turn off the television. It was so strange to see her dead husband sitting there with Dr.

14

Walter Rubin and talking to Dr. Sanjay Gupta, looking and sounding the same but so different somehow from the man she had known. He had on an expensive-looking three-piece suit for one thing, something Tony had never worn, but that couldn't be the difference. It was the demeanor and the vocabulary. Yes, that was it. This man seemed older, smarter, more sophisticated. It was absolutely fascinating to see Tony, not as a struggling, undereducated, and unambitious man flailing around on the emotional surface of life but rather as he could have been with more opportunities and ambitions and, she had to admit, more brains. It was also very sad. It wouldn't have been just the looks and the sex. She could have loved him then.

Cullen had seen the news when it came out. How could she have missed it? It was everywhere. Although Tony's name was mentioned briefly, mercifully there were no pictures of him, just pictures of the brain surgeon Dr. Rubin and, once or twice, pictures of the neuroscientist Dr. Hamilton as he was in his wheelchair before the operation. Several reporters had done enough homework to find her and called asking for comments and interviews, but she had said no, she had her nine-year-old son to protect. She didn't answer her landline after that. Cullen already knew that against all odds the experiment had worked, and there was someone walking around in her dead husband's body. As promised, Dr. Rubin had called to inform her of the final outcome before going public. She had intellectually come to terms with it. But actually seeing it was something else entirely. And her son had seen! She had planned to shield him from all this until he was old enough to better understand, or until she could find the right time and words to tell him. She should have known that sooner or later he would find out, at school, at a friend's house. It was a risk she had been willing to take because she simply didn't have the energy to broach the topic with a son who was still grieving. How was she going to deal with the situation now? And what about her mother-in-law, Louisa? Thank God she was at church this morning and didn't watch the news. She'd go absolutely crazy if she saw Tony. She would be certain that this man was her son, that God had answered her prayers after all and brought him back to her. Not back to Cullen. Not back to Shawn. Back to her. Cullen's emotions were reeling.

Tony's mother had insisted that he be left on life support. The doctors were wrong. Her son could not be brain-dead. He would wake up, come back. She believed in miracles. She had been praying for a miracle ever since the day he was taken to the hospital.

Cullen did not believe in miracles. She had all but lost her faith when her parents were killed by some drunk in a car accident eleven years ago, leaving her with nothing but a burial policy and rent paid through the end of the month. She won a full four-year scholarship to St. Louis University because she graduated first in her class, but she still had to take out a student loan and get a part-time job modeling to live in campus housing and pay for what few extras she allowed herself. At the beginning of her second year of premed, a classmate introduced her to Tony, a night student two years her senior who lived at home and drove a beer truck during the day. He was quite handsome, and she was lonely and vulnerable. Whatever last veneer of faith she possessed evaporated when she lost her virginity and found herself pregnant with this smooth-talking Italian's child.

She had no money for an abortion, and she couldn't ask her one close friend, Meghan, for help because, unlike Cullen, she was a devout Irish Catholic. She could go to one of those agencies that paid to go full term and give the baby up for adoption, but Cullen wasn't sure if she went full term she would be able emotionally to give her baby away. And if she had the baby and kept it, she would have to quit college and get a full-time job, which probably wouldn't pay enough for childcare and a place to live. She had heard of medication abortion, but it was illegal in Missouri and not easily obtained, and it too cost money. Tony insisted that she marry him. He lived with his ill and aging mom in a small house on The Hill. There would be room for the baby. He opposed abortions. He let her know in no uncertain terms that he would not allow her to kill his baby. It was a mortal sin. He told her it was not only against his religion, it was also an affront to his ego. No abortion. End of discussion. He said he knew she didn't love him, but he liked her well enough and was willing to take responsibility for his actions. He said he was certain that things happen for a reason and that over time she would grow to love him. Cullen knew herself well enough to doubt it, but she had always had a strong sense for self-preservation and survival, and after weighing the situation carefully, she saw marrying Tony as her most viable option.

So she gave up her scholarship, buried her dreams of becoming a doctor, got a job in the registrar's office, and married this man she hardly knew, out of gratitude and desperation. Mostly desperation. She was angry: angry at the situation, angry at him but mostly angry with herself. This was not a case of date rape. He had not raped her. Lots of guys told her she was beautiful, a perfect ten, but Tony told her she was the most interesting person he had ever known and the smartest. No one had ever said that to her before. To him, so she thought, she was not just another pretty girl. He said he liked her for her brains. Cullen was seduced by her own vanity. She was seduced with the idea that she was brilliant. How smart was that? Pregnant, angry, and full of regret—not a good way to start a marriage. Only Meghan and Tony's mother were present at this flowerless, music-less, joyless event. Never mind the dress and the dreams, Cullen didn't even get to walk down the aisle.

No, Cullen did not believe in miracles. She believed in medicine. And she believed that Tony's senseless death could at least be put to good use if his body was given for medical research. At first she had thought to donate all his organs to the organ bank. Publicity over the court battle with her mother-in-law had caught the attention of Dr. Rubin, who approached her about his need for a young, healthy, brain-dead body for his extremely important research project. He assured her that what would be learned about the brain would benefit many individuals in the future, not just the few needing organs now. He said she would have to give her consent without knowing the details of his experiment because it was both complicated and controversial. Dr. Rubin had already had a lot of trouble with the PETA crowd when his experimental subjects were rabbits and chimps. They almost destroyed his lab twice. And the Nonhumans Rights Project group was building a case against him on behalf of his chimps even though he no longer needed them for experimentation. If word got out that he was going to experiment on a human subject, there would be those on the religious Right who would try, probably successfully in the conservative state of Missouri, to obtain a court order to stop his research altogether, groundbreaking brain research that had taken so many years to bring to this point.

Dr. Rubin explained that he did not want to expend the time and energy necessary to defend the legitimacy of his research all over again. He told her that the likelihood of success on his first attempt at this experiment was very small but that even its failure would give extremely useful information. And since the body would be kept on life support during the process, if his experiment failed, the organs could still be distributed for use by those in need. If it succeeded, a brilliant neuroscientist would have a new lease on life, and there would be hope for thousands of others in the same condition. This was all he could say, and she must say nothing to anyone until he reported the results publicly. He promised to personally keep her informed, but the whole process could take up to a year or more if the operation was a success. The patient could still die anytime during the early stages of recovery because of organ rejection. And, of course, there would be a long adjustment period before the patient could be presented to the public and resume a public life. Cullen liked Dr. Rubin. She instinctively trusted him. He was persuasive and persistent.

Luckily for Cullen, Louisa knew nothing about the experiment, but she had been vehemently opposed to having her son's body torn apart and given in pieces to strangers. She cried and pleaded with Cullen: where was her wake for him, his Christian burial? She complained bitterly that Cullen was denying her the right to properly mourn the loss of her beloved son. She begged and wailed. She secured a pro bono attorney and took Cullen and the hospital to court. She accused Cullen of being a whore who entrapped her son and now wanted to kill him and strew his body parts God only knows where so that she could collect his twenty-thousand-dollar life insurance policy. Louisa threatened to throw Cullen out of the house. She threatened to take Shawn away from Cullen the way Cullen was taking Tony away from her. The battle had been public and ugly, but the law was clearly on Cullen's side, and Cullen knew that Louisa would not throw her out. Except for a small social security check, Cullen's paycheck was the only money Louisa had coming in now that Tony was gone.

In the end, Cullen gave Dr. Rubin her consent. Living under the same roof was extremely difficult for a while, but Cullen was at work most of the time, and eventually Louisa gave up the fight, at least openly.

———

Louisa wasn't the only one Cullen had to worry about. Ever since Shawn had seen his dad on television, he had become increasingly withdrawn. His grades had plummeted, and he had lost interest in Little League,

Boy Scouts, and his model airplanes. Cullen had tried everything she could think of to explain what had happened and to reignite his interests, but Louisa, who was now aware of Tony's miraculous reappearance, had two hours each day before Cullen got home from work to fuel Shawn's suspicions that his dad was still alive, that it was indeed his dad he had seen on television. Cullen did not know exactly what Louisa was telling him, but she knew, given her mother-in-law's hostility toward both of them and her predilection for delusions and histrionics, it couldn't be good. Another worrisome sign was the fact that Shawn would not talk to her about it. Cullen could not afford a child psychologist, but there was someone at the university she knew well enough to approach for a favor. He was not one to resist helping a beautiful woman like Cullen, especially since he had been trying to get her attention for almost six months.

The psychologist told Cullen that Shawn was too young to make sense of the bizarre reality of what had actually happened. He simply could not believe it. He knew what he had seen and heard. His grandmother had convinced him his dad was alive and it was Shawn's fault that he wouldn't come home. Louisa told him that if he had not been born, Tony would have finished college, gotten a good job, and married a nice virgin Italian girl, not an Irish slut like Cullen. He would still be home with his widowed Mama Louisa like any good Italian son. At least this was what the psychologist managed after a number of sessions to pry out of Shawn. Shawn even asked him what the word "slut" meant. The mild antidepressant he had prescribed obviously wasn't working. The psychologist thought the best strategy would be to convince Shawn that Dr. Hamilton was not his dad, but it involved contacting Dr. Hamilton.

Cullen picked up her phone and put it down again. She was dreading this call, but the psychologist insisted this was the best way to help her son overcome his depression. She reasoned with herself that Dr. Hamilton really owed it to her to help. After all, she had fought all comers for the right to donate her husband's body for Dr. Rubin's research, and it was Dr. Hamilton's presence in that body that was causing her son so much anguish. Cullen rehearsed what she would say several more times with just the right amount of pain in her voice. She picked up the phone again and dialed the number that Dr. Rubin gave her after she explained to him what the psychologist recommended.

"Hello, Dr. Hamilton, this is Cullen Costello, Anthony Costello's widow."

There was a long pause before Andrew said anything. Cullen almost lost her nerve and hung up. After she heard him say, "Yes, Mrs. Costello, what can I do for you?" in a tone of voice warmer than she supposed Tony would have used under those circumstances, she began to explain her son's situation and why she had called. The psychologist said Shawn was a very bright, sensitive boy. If Shawn could spend a little time with him, Shawn would pick up on the subtle differences in mannerisms and tone of voice and vocabulary and realize Dr. Hamilton had no memory of Shawn's shared experiences with his dad. After a few encounters, he would grasp the truth of the situation and regain his sense of self-worth and know his mother was telling the truth. She was sorry for the imposition. She knew it was a lot to ask, but would he be willing to give her son a few Saturdays or Sundays of his time? She was desperate for help. It would be a wonderful gift to Tony's little boy and to her if he would consider it.

"I will be happy to help in any way I can, Mrs. Costello. I've never had children, though, so you'll have to help me in that department. What sorts of things does your son like to do?"

"He always loved to go to the Cardinal's baseball games with his father. There is a game next Sunday. Perhaps you could take Shawn to the game as an icebreaker. I would go too, of course."

"I've never been to one of their games, but that sounds like a fine idea. I'll read up on the Cardinals a bit between now and then so I can talk a little baseball with Shawn. He may wonder why I am taking him to the game if I don't know anything at all about it. What time should we leave to go?"

"Noon. It starts at 1:15. I'll text you my address and directions."

"Since you know Dr. Rubin, I will ask him to join us. It might make things less awkward for everyone, and I don't have a valid driver's license yet, so Walter can drive us down to Busch Stadium. See you Sunday, Mrs. Costello."

Louisa happened to be in the front hall when Andrew rang the bell. Because Louisa normally slept late and didn't come out of her room until after one, Cullen had not mentioned her plans. So when Louisa opened the door and saw her son standing there, she bellowed out in surprise, staggered backward, and almost fell into the hall table.

"Tony!" she cried and threw her arms around him like a drowning woman. "My son, my son, you've come back to me. You're home. God has answered my prayers." She kissed both of his cheeks and his forehead, tears of joy running down her face onto Andrew's neck.

At the sound of Louisa's voice, Cullen came running into the hall with Shawn. There was Andrew trying to extricate himself from Louisa's death grip. The last thing Cullen wanted was for Dr. Hamilton to encounter her mother-in-law or her mother-in-law to see him. Cullen had imagined a number of different scenarios when he came to the house. This certainly was not one of them. She had been so nervous about her own reaction to seeing him and his reaction to her, she had spent half an hour deciding what to wear and another half hour doing her makeup. Still, she had spent most of the morning trying to prepare Shawn for this outing with the man who was not his father but looked like him. She thought she had made a lot of headway getting him in the right frame of mind. Now all of her efforts were out the window. Shawn immediately ran, crying, "Daddy! Daddy! You came back!" and grabbed him around the one arm that Andrew had managed to free from Louisa.

Not knowing what to say to untangle this embarrassing mess, Cullen just stood there trying to keep tears from ruining the makeup she had so carefully applied. Andrew acknowledged her presence with a nod, but he continued to stand there without saying a word until Louisa and Shawn finally let go. *Now,* thought Cullen. *Make your move.* And miraculously, he did.

"We had better be on our way, Mrs. Costello. If we don't leave right now, we'll be late for the first pitch of the game."

Louisa started wailing. "Don't go! Don't go!" she begged, reaching out for Andrew like a supplicant. Cullen grabbed her purse and Shawn and hurried out the door, leaving Andrew to make his own getaway the best he could. The last thing she saw was Andrew picking up Louisa, who had collapsed in a puddle on the floor, sobbing hysterically. As Andrew came out the door, Cullen could hear her heart-wrenching plea: "Tony! Tony! My son! Come back! Don't leave me! Please don't leave me again. How can you do this to your poor old mama?"

Cullen dabbed at her eyes nervously and tried to regain her composure. She worried that Dr. Hamilton would never want to see her or Shawn again after what he had just been through. She also was worried that she might not be able to conceal the multitude of feelings she was experiencing right now about her deceased husband. Clean-shaven, in Brooks Brothers khakis and shiny loafers instead of old blue jeans and dirty tennis shoes, her former husband had never looked more handsome than he did right now. It seemed almost impossible that she was, in fact, looking at a complete stranger. If she had momentarily forgotten who he was, the gentle finesse with which he had handled the drama back at the house set him miles apart from Tony. Why had she not thought to warn him? Why had she not suggested that Dr. Rubin come to the door? How would Shawn process what he had just heard and witnessed? She couldn't think of a thing to say when Andrew got in the car except "I'm so sorry, Dr. Hamilton."

"Call me Andrew, please. No apology necessary, Mrs. Costello, Cullen, if I may call you that. The poor woman obviously misses her son. I felt badly having to walk out on her like that. Say, Shawn, do you know who the Cardinals are playing today?" Shawn did not respond. Andrew continued. "They're playing the Phillies. Who do you think will win?" Shawn did not respond. Andrew kept talking, impressing Cullen that he really did do his homework.

"I'm really excited that I'm finally going to get to see them play. Shawn, did you know the Cards have won eleven world championships? They've also won at least nineteen pennants. The team became the Cardinals back in 1900. I read that the old downtown Busch Stadium built in 1966 was replaced in 2006 by a new stadium that seats about forty-six thousand. Over three million fans go there every year." Shawn just looked out the window. Cullen told her son it was rude not to answer Dr. Hamilton, but Shawn just squirmed a little and bit his lip.

Great, thought Cullen to herself. *First Louisa and now Shawn. The chances of Andrew wanting to go out with us again are getting slimmer by the minute. I hope Shawn doesn't blow it completely.*

Cullen had not been in the new stadium with its Ballpark Village. She noticed the old Stan Musial statue right outside the third-base entrance, where she got her first look at the packed stadium with thousands of noisy, red-shirted fans and its light- and dark-green striped turf. It was exciting to have such good seats in the infield. Not only would they get a great view of the game, from this vantage point they could also enjoy the St. Louis skyline with an impressive view of the Arch. The gigantic Budweiser sign with the two cardinals on top and the big screen was almost straight across the field from them, so they would be able to see pictures and stats perfectly. Cullen heard Shawn utter a soft "Wow" when he saw where they were sitting. His dad had always bought the cheap seats in baseball heaven. Cullen thought maybe this would help Shawn loosen up a bit and show some interest.

Wearing the ball cap Andrew bought him, Shawn watched the game and ate his hot dog and french fries without saying a single word to anyone. With very little help from Andrew, Cullen tried to make small talk with Walter above the boisterous crowd. They talked about the game, the food, and the weather, hoping Shawn would chime in with at least some comment or request. But not a word was uttered until the bottom of the ninth with the Cards at bat. When it finally came tumbling out, Cullen wished it hadn't.

"Daddy, are you going to come home with us tonight? Will you stay this time and never leave me again?" Without waiting for an answer, Shawn came out with several more embarrassing questions. "Daddy, why did you change your name to Andrew? Did you do it so we couldn't find you?"

Cullen thought her heart would stop. Andrew looked down at his hands and shuffled his feet for what seemed like an eternity to Cullen. She could tell he was stalling because he didn't know how to respond. Tears started streaming down her cheeks, and she held her breath, bracing herself for what Andrew might say.

Just then, a Cardinal hitter nailed a grand slam over the right field wall for a two-run victory. The fans went wild—everyone on their feet, jumping up and down, yelling and hugging. Popcorn and confetti were flying everywhere. The music was loud enough to be heard in Illinois across the Mississippi.

When the roar subsided enough for conversation again, it was Walter who came to the rescue.

"Shawn, Dr. Hamilton is still recovering from a very serious operation. He tires very quickly. I am his doctor, and he still needs a lot of care from me and some very special medicine. I cannot let him go home with you until he is well, and I am not sure how long it will be. But he can still see you on Saturdays or Sundays and spend time with you. Maybe we can all go to the zoo next Sunday. St. Louis's zoo is one of the best in the country. I am on the board and have special access to restricted areas. We have several brand-new baby animals. How would you like to hold some of the new babies in the nursery? Would you like to do that next Sunday?"

Shawn did not respond, but there was a faint smile wavering at the edges of his mouth. To the relief of everyone, he didn't ask any more questions. Walter had knocked the ball out of the park. Everyone was home safe. At least for now.

chapter 3

Andrew or Anthony

"That is patently absurd! I tell you I *am* Andrew Hamilton. This is the license I had before my surgery. It clearly needs to be updated since I don't look like this anymore, and you're telling me you can't do it because you think I stole this license? That it isn't mine? This is preposterous!" His voice went up more than a dozen decibels. "Don't you people ever read the newspapers or watch television? I'm the man whose brain was transplanted into the body you now see." Andrew drew a deep breath before continuing. "You're crazy if you think I am going to take no for an answer and leave here without my new license." Everyone was staring now. The DMV clerk had a smirk on her face.

"With all due respect, sir, you're the one coming in here with another man driver's license, asking us to change the picture and vital statistics to match you. Now that's what crazy is! We're finished. I've got a lot of people waiting. Move on, please. Next!"

Andrew would not budge. The clerk signaled Officer O'Brien to come over and handle this loony. She gave him the license.

"Okay, mister, just calm down and come outside with me. I'm sure we can sort this out." The police ushered Andrew out of the building, holding on to him with one hand while calling headquarters with the other. When he got off the phone, he was all business. "Okay, buddy, where'd you get this license? I just ran a check on it, and this man died over a year ago."

"It's mine, Officer. I'm alive. I know it's hard to believe, but I'm Dr.

Andrew Hamilton, the man in the papers who had the body transplant. I'm in my new body."

"And I'm the pope masquerading as an Irish cop, wise guy. I know you Italians on The Hill don't think much of us from the Irish quarter, but you must take me for a total idiot! Let's go down to the station and see what the chief has to say about this."

Andrew bristled at being called an Italian. It took him a minute to remember he now looked like one. He knew it was useless to argue. He was sure he could clear this up with Officer O'Brien's superior. He got into the backseat of the car and buckled up.

The ride to the station in University City was a short one, but it was long enough for Andrew to get control of himself. He was amazed at how distempered he had become and how naive to assume that everyone was aware of his story. Evidently not that many people followed the news. He had never abraded his graduate students or postdocs when they displayed their ignorance. He would gently help them see their mistakes. That's why they always clamored to work with him and have him as a mentor. Today he had made an embarrassing spectacle of himself and had insulted that poor clerk mercilessly. Andrew was absolutely ashamed of his behavior now that he reflected on it. He had always been the quiet voice of reason who could defuse any argument with carefully measured responses. His colleagues marveled at his power of persuasion and his ability to overcome objections and counterarguments. Andrew was known among colleagues and students alike for his soft, even temper and his professional conduct. Walter had warned him to watch out for unexpected personality changes, especially under stress.

Andrew knew that preserving the personality was as much a part of Walter's research goal as preserving memory. To that end, Walter had made a thorough analysis of the chemical environment of Andrew's brain before the surgery so that, along with the antirejection drug, he could give Andrew the drugs he needed to replicate that same environment afterward. This would require regular doses for the rest of his life, but then so would the antirejection drug. It would be a necessary inconvenience. Still, the donor body's one-third piece of frontal lobe had its own chemical production that would modify that environment to some extent, and there was no way to know before the fact just how that would affect Andrew's personality, especially under various emotional conditions. Adjustments would need to be made as the differences became clear. This wasn't the first temper tantrum Andrew had had since the operation, but it was the first one on public display. His impulsiveness in going to the DMV, on the other hand, was something new for Andrew. He wondered if Mr. Costello was impulsive as well as short-tempered. It would be interesting to know.

"Well, well, another one," the chief said, looking at the license Officer O'Brien handed him. "Since all that ruckus in the media, you're the third perp we've had in here with a stolen ID claiming to have had a body transplant. I wish that doctor had stuck to his monkeys. If this kind of operation ever becomes readily available, we won't be dealing with just you crazies. The criminal element and the terrorists will use it to their advantage for sure. I hate to think!" The chief came around the desk and squinted at Andrew for a minute. "Say, you look familiar. What were you in here for recently? What's your real name?"

Andrew felt the heat rising in his face again. More stress.

"I haven't been here before. I look familiar because you've seen me on television. I really am the man whose brain was transplanted into another man's body. Andrew Hamilton is my real name. That's my old license I had before the operation. Now please let me call my lawyer. He will clear everything up and verify my identity."

The chief shrugged. "Okay, but while we're waiting for him, I want you to stand over here and face the camera. I'll run your mug shot against the files. I rarely forget faces. You must have priors."

It didn't take long. There was a certain satisfying glee in the chief's voice. "Aha, just as I thought! A hit. Says here you are one Anthony Costello, alias Tony, picked up twice in recent years for fighting in Mario's Pub down on The Hill, and once for drunk driving and assaulting an officer. A bit of a hothead, aren't you, Tony?"

With as steady and emphatic a voice as he could muster, Andrew stated that he was the former head of the neuro-ophthalmology lab at the medical school and indeed the man whose brain was transplanted into the deceased Mr. Costello's body. He said in as even a tone as he could manage, "I'm a doctor, a neuroscientist. I have never been in a fight in my life. Mr. Costello has been dead for over a year."

The chief smiled sarcastically. "Well, you're standing right here looking like the picture of health to me, Tony, and my records don't show you as dead. But Andrew Hamilton sure is."

At this, Andrew lost it; he was shouting now. "Can't you get it through your thick skull? I am not Costello!"

"Andrew, calm down. I've never seen you worked up like this before." It was his longtime lawyer and friend, Charles. "I called Walter. He's on his way now. We'll get this matter straightened out for you as soon as he gets here. Just relax. What in the world possessed you to go to the DMV in the first place? I warned you that you would have no legal standing until my petitions to the court are granted."

"I don't know, Charles. It was just impulse, I guess. Everything is taking too long. I'm getting tired of waiting for the bureaucrats to get around to doing their jobs. I'm tired of living like a recluse and of having you, Walter, and my housekeeper doing everything for me. I am almost as dependent on others now as I was in a wheelchair. Well, not really, but you know what I mean. I want to drive again and go wherever I want and do things for myself. I want my life back. Even all my assets are still frozen. I have to borrow money from you until I can get my estate back. I've been waiting long enough. It's been almost two years since the operation. Two whole years! Why does all this legal stuff take so long? My patience is wearing thin. I'm restless, unable to concentrate. Living like this is making me uncharacteristically irritable and frustrated. It's really getting to me, Charles. And all the media attention is nerve-racking. I just want my normal life back like any normal person."

"But you're obviously not a normal person any longer. Face it, Andrew. Your life will never be completely normal again. You know that. I understand your frustration, but we're in uncharted waters, and it's going to take a little time to get everything sorted out legally. No one has ever had to deal with all these issues before. How to restore a dead person's life and possessions after cremation and estate settlement isn't spelled out in any of the statutes or precedents. I will say I'm truly surprised at your strong emotional reactions. It's not at all like you. I know you understand all the ramifications of your situation, and I would have thought, with your background, you of all people would quickly adjust to the new reality and have the ability to cope."

"I do understand the new reality, Charles, but emotionally I'm having trouble. I'm not used to having so many strong roller-coaster emotions, especially negative ones, and I'm certainly not used to being treated so disrespectfully, called crazy, and a loony, and a perp. Things are bothering me now that wouldn't have before the operation. I seem to be torn in two directions at once and unable to control my reactions very well. I've become overly sensitive and emotional. Not good traits for a scientist."

"And you've become a little too impulsive, if you ask me, given your trip to the DMV." Walter had arrived. "You haven't stopped taking your meds, have you? No? Good. I told you to be on the lookout for personality changes. Back in my lab, you weren't confronted with the frustrations of daily life out in the real world. The drugs that worked in that calm, protective environment are not working for you now. I see I need to make some major adjustments in your medications. Some of Costello's strong traits are becoming dominant and are clearly irritating the hell out of you. But don't worry. It's a short-term problem. We'll play with the formula until we get it right."

"So, am I to understand that this Costello guy really is the one who had the brain transplant? How do I know I'm not being played? Wait a minute. Are you the doctor who performed the operation? I think I recognize you from the pictures in the paper and on television. I rarely forget a face."

"Well, you must have forgotten seeing Andrew on television. Yes, I am the surgeon, but you got the Costello part wrong. This man is Dr. Andrew Hamilton, who did, in fact, have a body transplant. And judging by the media parked outside the door who responded to my call a while ago, there will be some unwanted publicity on the evening news if you don't drop all charges against Dr. Hamilton right now."

The chief walked over and peered out the window at the small group of reporters and TV cameras outside the front door. "Damn it! That's all I need after the problems we've been having lately with false arrests and trigger-happy police. I don't give a damn who he is. Costello, Hamilton, your monkey's uncle. Just get the hell out of here and take this weirdo with you. There won't be any charges. Go on. Get out of here. And get rid of those damn reporters and cameras. No bad publicity, you understand? It was an honest, understandable mistake. Dr. Hamilton was disturbing the peace, after all, and O'Brien was just doing his job."

Andrew thanked Walter for coming and rode back to the house with Charles. "We have another problem, Charles. Costello has a criminal record. And their record shows he's still alive. Still alive! I'm dead, but he's still alive! How can that be?"

"Oh, I'm sure their records just need updating, Andrew. Don't worry. That's an easy fix."

———

When it finally came, Charles drove over to Andrew's house and gave him the bad news. Andrew escorted Charles to the den. It's where Andrew took everyone who visited. With its warm, cherry coffered ceiling, soft sage-green walls, and luscious oriental rug, it was easily Andrew's favorite room. He fixed Charles a scotch and soda while Charles explained the reason for his petition's denial. The court ruled that Andrew David Hamilton died and was cremated two years ago, and it was unprecedented for someone to take a dead man's identity along with his credentials, especially since the records showed that Anthony Giuseppe Costello was in fact still alive. Therefore, his legal records stood and could not be replaced as requested with the deceased man's records.

"It's not just a clerical error, Andrew."

Because of the unusual circumstances surrounding the uncertainty of the disposition of Anthony's body, he was never officially declared dead. First, the mother, certain that her son was not really brain-dead, refused to let the doctors pull the plug. Then the court issued a stay while the lawyers battled over Cullen's right to donate his organs or his body for medical science. And then Walter exercised the legal right he had earlier obtained from the court to have the body left on life support with all the organs intact and transferred to his clinic. Walter's surgical experiment succeeded, so he didn't take the body off life support right away or call the organ transplant agency to come get the organs. In the confusion surrounding this complicated and abnormal sequence of events, a time of death for Anthony Costello was never recorded, and no death certificate was issued. It was completely overlooked. According to the court, Andrew was officially Anthony Costello, now a thirty-two-year-old Italian male who had had a brain transplant. The organ donor was the deceased Andrew Hamilton. Walter had recorded his death at the time the brain was removed.

Andrew slowly sat down in his favorite green leather chair. "Damn! You've got to be kidding me, Charles. What do we do now? I need to go back to the university in a couple of weeks. I'm applying for a new grant. I need my new picture ID showing that I am Andrew David Hamilton, MD, PhD. I need a driver's license. I need my old social security number back. I need a passport, bank accounts, insurance, and all the other stuff for living a life. You have to fix this for me, Charles, and fast."

"Well, the only thing I know to do is to sue the hospital for not declaring Costello dead. This won't be fast though. It could take a while, but once we can prove he is indeed dead and that the hospital is at fault for not declaring him so, we can make our case for changing your identity back to Hamilton. Short of that, I can't think of anything else we can do at the moment. And that strategy may not work. Walter may have some idea. Surely he can help. I don't know about Anthony's widow. She is probably due some life insurance from Anheuser Busch, which I'm sure she hasn't received since there was no death certificate issued. Maybe she can join us in the suit."

"Cullen has enough on her mind right now, Charles. Let's not involve her."

Charles's eyebrows went up. "Oh, so it's Cullen now, is it? How do you know her?"

"It's a long story. I'd rather not go into it right now. I think we should get Walter over here and see what he can do to straighten out this mess. He was the last person in possession of both bodies, and he declared me dead. Maybe he was supposed to declare Costello dead instead of me."

"It was your body that got cremated, Andrew. You can't cremate a body without declaring it dead first."

"But it was only my body that got cremated, Charles, not me!"

"Hmmm, maybe we can have Walter file an administrative change declaring as the attending physician he forgot to enter time of death and file for a death certificate for Costello. Once that change has been made, he can ask the court for another administrative change stating he declared you dead in error. Maybe that will work. If it does, then we will petition the court to give you back your identity in your current body. It shouldn't take long at all for an administrative change. And that will also make it easier to handle the estate and other issues. With some luck, this strategy could make things go pretty fast."

And in fact it did work, and it didn't take too long. But just because the court gave Andrew back his identity doesn't mean everyone else did. He was still "Tony" to Louisa, he was still "Daddy" to Shawn, and he was still dead to his wife. He didn't know who he was to Cullen, but he was anathema to almost everyone else he knew. Dinner invitations didn't materialize. The casserole brigade of divorced ladies that usually descends on available men was conspicuously absent. Except for Walter and Charles, his old friends and acquaintances felt uncomfortable around him now. "It's all just too creepy," as one honest soul put it.

———

Andrew's journey back to academia was no less difficult. It had been seven years now since his accident ended his research at the lab. His grant and his project were long since terminated, and his replacement had been hired five years ago. Although he had kept up with the literature for the most part, thanks to Margaret, who read to him for an hour or two every day when he was paralyzed, he was still two years behind the curve with the advances so important to his research area. The technology in his fast-developing field could go through three generations in seven years. His postdoctoral students were now fully employed in labs scattered around the country, and all but a few of his colleagues had been hired away by other universities or industries clamoring for entry into this hot field. There were only a few familiar faces who remembered how the éminence grise Dr. Hamilton used to look, and they certainly did not view him as that now. A thirty-two-year-old with Andrew's credentials was seen more or less as a hotshot, certainly not as someone with the gravitas of a sixty-two-year-old with gray hair. They simply couldn't accept him as the same person. He now appeared to be the same age as many of the new postdocs, some of whom had invited him to join them for a beer at the local pub when he first arrived. No one would have dared be so presumptuous seven years ago.

None of the faculty in the department deferred to his judgment now. No one asked his opinion. No one dropped by to discuss ideas.

Uncomfortable around him, his colleagues gave him a wide berth and pretended to be too absorbed in their work or conversations to notice when he came their way. Postdocs working directly in his field knew of his important accomplishments, but many others in the department had never even heard of him. For all practical purposes though, Dr. Hamilton was presumed to have dropped out of the picture years ago. Wasn't he dead?

Andrew would have to wait until the news of his return reached next year's crop to have his pick of doctoral and postdoctoral students again. He would also have to wait until he could officially rejoin the faculty and get the grant money he needed for research. Right now the department was making some office space available to him as a courtesy.

Actually, a small office was all Andrew needed to write his grant proposals, but surprisingly, his heart wasn't in it. He spent most of his time there reflecting on the strange turn his life had taken. He didn't seem to have the same single-minded interest in his research he did before his accident. He lacked the laser focus he was known for in the past. Back then, if he was working on a specific problem in his research, a tornado could roar through, and he wouldn't even notice. At least that's what Margaret always said. Maybe the seven-year hiatus knocked the wind out of his sails. Maybe he had convinced himself when he became paralyzed that he had at least finished all his important work before his accident, giving him some sense of comfort, completion, and solace. On the other hand, maybe Tony's inability to focus was inserting itself into his habits. Whatever the reason, he now found it very hard to approach his work with enthusiasm or the sense of urgency the impending deadline demanded.

For the first time in his life, he was very much alone. He had lost his wife, he had lost his academic position at the university as a dominant player in his field, he had lost all his friends, except for Walter and Charles, and he had lost his image of himself as a man who was loved, an outstanding violinist, an excellent tennis player, a man who had lived well, a man who was respected. Before the transplant, Andrew was miserable, yes, but now Andrew suffered a more devastating kind of misery. The cost of gaining his new life was too dear; in the tradeoff, he had lost everything that ever mattered to him. He felt like Job.

chapter 4

Mission Accomplished

*C*ullen admired her new dress in the full-length mirror. It was the first one she had bought since Tony died. It was a summery yellow, the perfect color to complement her green eyes, auburn hair, and creamy complexion, and it was the perfect style to showcase her figure. Cullen knew her looks attracted attention almost everywhere she went because she could feel the eyes following her. She felt pretty certain she was having the same effect on Andrew. These Saturday and Sunday outings had become more important to her than just therapy sessions for Shawn. In a strange way, they were therapy sessions for her too. She dared to dream again. She imagined scenarios in which her prospects in life would suddenly change, give her a future again. She looked forward to being with Andrew all week long. Although Cullen was anxious for Shawn to become confident with the fact that Andrew was not his father, in her heart of hearts, she hoped it would not be too soon.

In the two years since Tony's death, Cullen had been too emotionally exhausted to consider becoming involved with anyone. She certainly wasn't looking for another husband yet, but when she was ready, she would be looking for someone special, someone who would rescue her from her current miserable existence and provide the opportunity for her to follow her dream of becoming a doctor. She hadn't met him yet, at least not until possibly now.

Cullen had experienced enough domestic trauma in her eight years of marriage to last her a lifetime. Everything was either *"grandissimo"* or *"pississimo."* There was no such thing as moderato with this very Italian family. If it wasn't Tony acting out his frustrations with his job and finances, it was Louisa recounting her toils and troubles like a nun saying her beads and just as often. Plates would fly; recriminations would end in shouting matches and slamming doors. Tears would soak the pillows at night. But when things were going well for Tony, not big things (big, good things never happened for Tony), just little things, like making ten bucks off the bookie, a good bowling score, hitting a home run on his company softball team, one would think he had won the lottery. Beer would flow, laughter would fill the house, and the sex would be great that night. All this drama was exhausting to Cullen, whose penurious family had been the quiet, long-suffering sort. She would have found a way to leave Tony long ago except for the fact that Shawn adored his dad, who adored him equally. When it came to Shawn, Tony morphed into the most gentle, loving man imaginable. He saved his temper and frustrations for Cullen and Louisa.

Despite the way Louisa treated Shawn and her, Cullen had a rather soft spot in her heart for Louisa. She felt sympathy and compassion for this pathetic woman who had endured a great deal of tragedy and hardship in her life and was now suffering from the onset of Alzheimer's. There was nobody who had ever loved her left to care. This made Cullen the self-appointed caregiver, a role Louisa grudgingly accepted. Cullen hated Tony's tirades, which could be especially vicious, even violent, when he had been drinking. She thought it particularly cruel the way he attacked his poor, defenseless mother, who loved him as only a mother could.

All this was ancient history now that Tony was dead, but the psychological scars of those tumultuous years of their marriage had hardened Cullen's determination to wait for the perfect mate. She knew she needed to take her time, not make another costly mistake. Tony's smooth good looks belied the rough, ugly streak inside. But Cullen detected in Andrew a gentle soul underneath that handsome sexy facade that had first attracted her to Tony. If Cullen had learned one thing from her marriage, it was to not trust appearances. She had discovered the hard way that one has to look beyond the physical in order to see the real person. She had been taking a close look at Andrew over the last few months. She knew for certain the person now inside Tony's body was a totally different man. The fact that he was undeniably brilliant, famous, and wealthy made him all the more attractive. Cullen decided Andrew was the one she had been waiting for. Her friend Meghan told her she was reaching too far and warned her not to get involved. Cullen had cautioned herself about the risks, but subconsciously she had already made her decision. She was twenty-nine. She was lonely. Now that she had found Andrew, she was impatient. She wanted a future worthy of her abilities. She had developed a keen sense of how to use her looks to her benefit, and she felt sure it would work on Andrew. Cullen was willing to take the risk.

———

Louisa was always waiting by the door to receive the big hug and peck on the cheek Andrew quickly dispensed as the path of least resistance upon entering the house. When she pressed him, as she always did to come home to her, he gave her the same excuse that Walter had manufactured for Shawn.

Shawn appeared in his ever-present baseball cap Andrew had given him. Cullen followed behind, looking absolutely fabulous in a yellow dress he hadn't seen. To Andrew, Margaret had been an attractive woman, rather pretty during her twenties and thirties, forties even, but never outwardly beautiful. Margaret was beautiful on the inside, and it radiated out for all to see. It was Margaret's contagious smile and enthusiasm for life, her creative spirit that caught Andrew's attention when they were in college. Cullen was another matter altogether. She caught his attention simply by walking into the room. He really knew very little about her, but it didn't matter. His excitement in her presence was automatic.

Today they were going downtown to explore Gateway Park and go up in the Arch. Andrew had never been there himself and wasn't sure how interesting it would be for Shawn, but Shawn seemed to like the idea, and it certainly beat Shawn's second favorite thing next to baseball … bowling. Andrew hated everything about bowling the one time they went. He was beginning to run out of options for their weekend excursions when the Cards weren't playing home games. They had been to the zoo, Shaw's Gardens, bicycling in Forest Park, Grant's Farm, the Science Museum and

Planetarium, and the St. Louis Art Museum (a real bummer for Shawn). He was not certain how many more times it would take for Shawn to realize Andrew was not his father, but he hoped it would be before the end of baseball season.

On the other hand, he wouldn't mind seeing more of Cullen and wondered how much it would complicate the situation if he asked her to dinner. It was only a hypothetical question in his mind; he doubted he would have the nerve to ask for an outright date. So far he had never been alone with her even for a few minutes. From the little he could tell about her, he was having a hard time understanding how in the world she could have married an abrasive, uneducated truck driver, no matter how handsome he was. Given her looks and sexual appeal alone, she was bound to have had other and better opportunities. He had long ago forgotten the rituals of dating and felt rather awkward at almost sixty-three asking a twenty-something to dinner. Oops! He wasn't sixty-two anymore. That was part of his problem, a mistake he kept making over and over again. He still thought like a sixty-two-year-old. He might have a thirty-two-year-old body, but he was still carrying a sixty-two-year-old mind-set around with him. He decided to approach Cullen in the guise of wanting a progress report. Actually, he did want to know if Shawn's grades and attitude were improving in summer school. He would wait until they got back from today's trip to ask her to dinner to discuss Shawn's progress.

"This is quite a spectacular view from up here, isn't it, Shawn? On a clear day like today, you can see about thirty miles in both directions."

"Wow, this is really cool! Look how big the Mississippi River is. I didn't know it was this big."

"Look over there. You can see the big bluffs still standing on the Illinois side of the river and miles and miles of floodplains. The Mississippi River is about a mile wide here, but it wasn't always that way. There is a big seismic fault down in the Missouri boot heel known as the New Madrid Fault. There was an earthquake in 1811 with a magnitude of over seven. It is thought to be the strongest one that has ever occurred in the continental United States so far. It was so strong that the church bells rang in Washington, DC, and Philadelphia. Lore has it that the river rolled backward for three days, but that didn't really happen. The river did widen significantly because large portions of the bluffs collapsed, and in several places the river actually changed course and created a number of lakes. There were areas where the riverbed dropped twenty feet, creating waterfalls that made travel impossible until the fast-flowing water wore them down to small rapids. Luckily, St. Louis was still a little frontier town at the time. It had very few people living there, and they were mostly Native Americans, so the damage wasn't catastrophic like it would be today."

"Could we have another earthquake here some day? Would it kill a lot of people like the ones we read about at school?"

Andrew was glad Shawn seemed to be interested in what he was saying for a change.

"Well, yes, we could have another big one someday. Some seismologists think we are long overdue. Actually, we did have another earthquake here in 1967, not nearly as big but big enough to get your attention, about a magnitude of five. The Arch was already here by then and a big tourist attraction. The Arch, like all really tall buildings, normally sways a few inches at the top. On a windy day, you can feel it slowly swaying back and forth. On the day of the earthquake, the people up here were really taken for a bumpy ride, especially the ones in the elevator. The tourists wondered why people weren't warned before going up to the top since it was so rough and scary. They didn't know there had been a quake until they got back down. If the Arch had not been built with that kind of flexibility, it would have fallen down. Building it was an amazing engineering feat for its time, especially putting in the last four foot section at the very top connecting the two legs. The legs are as wide apart as the Arch is tall, and the equilateral triangles they form is what makes the Arch stable enough to stand alone. There's a movie about it you can watch in the Arch museum, if you'd like."

Shawn turned away and stared out the window for several minutes. When he turned back around, he stared at Andrew for a minute more. He had a frown on his face, and he spoke in a challenging tone.

"How do you know all this stuff? Everywhere we go, you seem to know all about it. You didn't used to tell me stuff like this. Whenever I asked you questions, you always said you didn't know. You'd tell me to Google it when I got home."

Big tears were beginning to form in the corners of Shawn's eyes. He spoke in a softer, broken voice now.

"You aren't really my dad, are you?"

Andrew had seen the tears welling up and knew it was coming. He was ready for it.

"No, I'm not, Shawn. But I wish I were. I would love to have a son like you."

The tears rolled down Shawn's cheeks. He wiped them with his sleeve, but they kept coming.

They rode in silence down the elevator, out to the parking lot and back to The Hill.

As soon as the car stopped, Shawn jumped out and ran into the house. Cullen just sat there with Andrew for an embarrassingly long while without saying anything. Her outings had come to an unexpected end. It was a shame that the little trailers of future episodes she had been privately screening in her imagination were being sent to the cutting-room floor. She knew there was no reason for any more weekend excursions. Shawn now realized she had told him the truth. Andrew was not his father. Mission accomplished.

Cullen was certain that Andrew enjoyed being with her, but he made no moves to show an interest in seeing her again. *Maybe he is just shy and needs a little encouragement,* she said to herself and rummaged around for some way to start the conversation.

"I suppose I should thank you now for all the time you have given Shawn and me over the past several months. You have been more than kind and generous. And I will be forever grateful for the gentle way you handled breaking the truth to Shawn."

"You needn't thank me, Cullen. I was more than happy to be of service. Shawn is a terrific kid. I hope he will be all right now."

Cullen leaned in closer to Andrew so he could smell the subtle fragrance she was wearing and feel the warmth of her presence sitting next to him alone for the first time. She wanted him, and the way he was looking at her right now, she could tell he wanted her too. So why wouldn't he ask her out?

Cullen put her hand lightly on Andrew's arm and tried again. "I know you probably helped me because you felt some obligation under the circumstances to Tony's family, but you have gone way beyond what anyone could reasonably have expected. I can't begin to tell you how much I appreciate what you have done. I have enjoyed our outings so very much, Andrew." *There*, she thought, *surely he will pick up on this hint and suggest we go out.* When he didn't, leaving her hand in place, she leaned in a little closer and tried one last time in as alluring a voice as she could muster. "I know from Dr. Rubin that it had been your plan to commit suicide. I am so glad you didn't, Andrew. It gives me a very special comfort in knowing it was you Tony's body was able to save."

Andrew looked at her as if he were surprised that Walter had confided so much in her, but his expression softened, and his voice took on a warmth that showed he was genuinely moved by her comment.

"What a lovely thing for you to say, Cullen. I can assure you it has been a special pleasure for me to spend these weekends with you and your son. I have truly enjoyed every minute of it, except maybe the bowling."

Cullen gave a little laugh, remembering how awkward and out of place Andrew had seemed in the bowling alley. She waited a minute to see if he would continue, but he didn't. It seemed ridiculous that she had been unable to get Andrew to respond to her overtures, that her magnificently conceived future with him could end so pathetically, so abruptly, without cause. Meghan had been right after all. Andrew was too big a stretch for her. Letting herself out of the car before Andrew could get around, Cullen gathered up her dreams and went inside.

chapter 5

Elizabeth

"Elizabeth, do you have a minute? I would like to discuss your story." The creative-writing professor had handed back the critiqued short stories at the end of class and was leaning against the classroom doorjamb as the students filed out. This had been the first week's assignment, and he had given her a big A.

"You have a good imagination, Elizabeth, and a very interesting plot. I don't think I have ever heard of anything remotely like it. Surely you aren't going to end your story there, are you?"

"Well, Dr. Robbins, you told us to write a story between ten and twenty thousand words. I thought that was all I needed to do. Wasn't it enough? You gave me an A."

"That may have been the assignment, Elizabeth, but I don't think you're really finished. That isn't a satisfactory ending. It's rather lame actually. A story is never over until it's over, to coin a phrase, no matter how many pages it takes. Unfortunately, you chose a subject that doesn't lend itself well to a short story. There is so much more to tell. You certainly aren't through with Andrew, and you really haven't finished developing your themes. Too much is left in question here. You leave me unsatisfied, suspended. I'm thinking to myself, *What's the point of the story?* You've described a situation, but you haven't really told a story yet. I find myself waiting for what comes next. A story isn't like a TV drama that continues when you tune in next week. Where a story ends is all you get. But I know you know that."

"If it was that bad, why did you give me an A? Anyway, I wanted to be through with this story, Dr. Robbins. I thought this was as good a place to end it as any. Some peoples' stories are basically pointless, and even if they aren't, not all peoples' stories get to end satisfactorily or happily ever after. Some get cut short and end in medias res. Think of the various people on a plane, each with his or her dreams, ambitions, big hopes, little hopes. Then the plane crashes. All the hopes and dreams get wiped out right then and there. Same thing, 9/11, only many more people. Same thing in Iraq and Syria and everywhere else there is war. The bomb falls, the explosive device detonates, the gun fires. These people all had stories. None of them got to end satisfactorily."

"That's an interesting point, Elizabeth, but you're changing the subject. I hear the passion in what you're saying, but I don't believe that's what you're writing about."

Elizabeth was beginning to sense that he was trying to give her a hard time. She put up her defenses.

"Well, it's still part of it—decisions, choices, missed opportunities, zigs and zags, the vagaries of life, chance events that end or change lives irreversibly. In my story, Andrew had an accident that ended everything physically meaningful to him, and then he was physically restored only to be deprived of the two things most emotionally meaningful to him, his wife and his sense of self. Even though he was attracted to Cullen, he was too broken and too old psychologically to change. And Cullen's usual ability to use her sexual appeal to get what she wanted couldn't break through that psychological barrier. So they were at an impasse. It was over. End of story. Lots of relationships never get off the ground. It happens all the time for all kinds of reasons."

Dr. Robbins smiled at her, but it was clear he wasn't going to let it go at that.

"This is a graduate course in creative writing, Elizabeth, not Psychology 101. Now that you've chosen to write this particular story, I want to see what your creativity can do with it. I want to know what happens next and then what happens after that. For example, right where you ended, I was waiting for Andrew to give in and ask Cullen out to dinner while they were sitting there alone in the car, which, by the way, didn't explode at that point. He found her sexually exciting; she was trying to come on to him. It was the perfect opportunity. Why didn't you have him do that?"

"Like I just told you, because of who Andrew was. Even though that had been his intention, it seemed inappropriate, given what had just happened. Before the trip to the Arch, there was the expectation that their excursions would continue, and therefore a progress report would be in order. Now that Shawn understood the truth, such a report was superfluous. The psychologist said knowing the truth would cure him of his depression. Asking Cullen to dinner became a much bigger deal under the circumstances; it became a real date and an admission of interest. Andrew felt enough ambivalence about dating Cullen, given his love for Margaret, that he was not ready to admit too much interest and chance being turned down. His newfound sexuality was in conflict with his old habit of mind."

"Okay, I'll accept that, Elizabeth. But you should've said it. That point was hinted at, but it wasn't really clear. One of the striking things about your writing is your exceptional sense of who your characters are. I feel like they are people you have known and been close to. This is something very hard to teach in a creative-writing course. So many aspiring writers struggle with differentiating their characters' personalities and making them real. Developing good characters is one of the most important parts of the writer's craft. You seem to be well on the way to mastering this skill."

Dr. Robbins took the blazer he had folded over his arm and flung it over his left shoulder. This typical preppy gesture caught Elizabeth's attention. For the first time, she noticed how cute he was, boyish almost, with expressive blue eyes and brown curly hair. He looked neat and put together in a J.Crew and L.L.Bean kind of way, not like most of the younger professors, who wore the ubiquitous blue jean uniforms.

"Say, Elizabeth, have you ever read John Fowles's *The French Lieutenant's Woman*? In one of his chapters, 13 I believe, he says it was his intention to have Sara, who was staring out the window, wipe away her tears and tell us what was bothering her, but Sara just wasn't that kind of woman. He goes on to explain, as an author, you cannot have free reign to do whatever you want with a character. Once a character is created, you are limited in what the character can do or say. In other words, the character assumes a certain autonomy. It can't act out of character. I think you understand this concept well. What is interesting, of course, is your character Andrew does act out of character when his meds are out of balance and too much of Tony's temper and impulsiveness creep in. Andrew can't stop himself, yet he is always aware when it happens and tries to control it. I think you handle that part very well. By the way, if you haven't read Fowles's novel, you should. It's a real writer's book, the first half of which is written using nineteenth-century novelistic conventions and the second half early- and mid-twentieth-century conventions. It has three endings. It's a lot of fun. I think you would enjoy it."

"I appreciate the suggestion, Dr. Robbins. I'll take a look at it when the semester's over. Right now I want to concentrate on the next assignment."

"Actually, Elizabeth, instead of the next class assignment, I want you to keep writing this story, now that you've started it. You may have a novel here, or at least a novella. You've made a good start. Let's see what you can do with it."

chapter 6

Andrew and Cullen

"Hello, Andrew, this is Cullen. I just realized that I basically ended our weekly field trips when I thanked you last Sunday. I'm afraid I've created a big problem. Shawn showed up in the kitchen this morning dressed for the game. Not only will he be very disappointed if he doesn't get to go, I'm worried he will figure out the real reason you've been coming on the weekends. Right now, he thinks it's because you feel guilty for taking his dad's body. He said if you hadn't, God would have performed a miracle and brought his dad back to life. I tried to explain to him that his dad was brain-dead and beyond reviving, but his grandmother taught him to believe in miracles, and he had been praying hard for one. I don't want Shawn to find out that this was my idea, or rather the psychologist's, and not yours. He would be very upset with me. I hate to ask, but would you mind taking us to the game today? It will give me time to think of some way to handle the situation."

Andrew didn't care what the reason was; he was just glad for another chance to see Cullen. He had been kicking himself for not having the nerve to ask her out when they were sitting there alone in the car.

"Of course, Cullen. I was wondering what I would do with myself today anyway. Our outings can continue for as long as you want. It looks like rain though. Maybe for a little change of pace, if the game gets rained out, I could take the two of you to dinner. Nothing fancy. Some place where Shawn would be comfortable."

"That would be great, Andrew. There's a little family-style restaurant here on The Hill that has good food; it serves up a tasty plate of lasagna, or veal piccata, if you prefer. Shawn loved it the one time we went there for his dad's birthday. We only go to nice restaurants for special occasions, so it will be a real treat for both of us."

"I would ask Louisa to join us, but, quite frankly, Cullen, I find it difficult and embarrassing to be around her. Maybe I could send her a plate of something she likes home with you."

"That isn't necessary, Andrew, but I'm sure she'd be thrilled. Oh, the rain's already started. It's coming down pretty hard now, and it doesn't look like it's going to stop any time soon. I think we'll be eating Italian tonight."

Andrew arrived promptly at six o'clock. It seemed odd that Louisa wasn't standing guard at the door when he knocked. Then he remembered this was not his normal time. Cullen answered it, umbrella and bag in hand. She was wearing a soft green sweater. Andrew couldn't help but notice it matched her lovely eyes.

"Good evening, Cullen. Your carriage is waiting. Where's Shawn?"

"He's not coming, Andrew. He said it's his dad's birthday place, and he doesn't want to go there with you. I'm sorry."

"That's all right. We don't have to go there, Cullen. We can go somewhere else he likes."

"I told him that, but he's still bummed out because the game was canceled and doesn't feel like going. I fixed him some chicken nuggets and some oven fries. He'll be okay. Besides, I could use an adult evening out for a change."

Andrew could not believe his good luck. It was a date after all, without him having to ask.

There was so much he wanted to know about Cullen, like her background and why, with her exceptional good looks and intelligence, she had married a truck driver. Despite his abiding love for Margaret, he found Cullen to be a thoroughly fascinating woman. He wondered if it was his brain talking to him or his strong sexual attraction. He had never been obsessed with sex like a lot of men. Although not oblivious to the many attractive faculty wives and graduate students who made their presence known to him over the years, he had not pursued any of them. He had a wife, he had his work, and he had his violin. That was enough. It had always been enough. But then, he didn't have any of those things now. He felt empty and irrelevant, except for the last few months when he was needed by Cullen to help with Shawn. She had given him a much-needed purpose while he was waiting for his life to begin again. Being with her and with Shawn meant more to him than he cared to admit. It was a new feeling for him to be occupied with the lives of others instead of his work, his music, and other intellectual pursuits. And at sixty-two, he certainly didn't expect to be responding to Cullen like a teenager or the thirty-two-year-old inside of him now, or outside of him, or all through him, whichever. He wanted to hold her. He wanted to kiss her. He wanted to take her to bed. How was he supposed to handle those logistics? They were having dinner in a restaurant three blocks from her house with a son and mother-in-law waiting for her return. Well, anyway, the veal piccata was not bad.

"Have you ever been to the Trattoria Alfredo in Clayton, Cullen? I go there once in a while because it's near my house. The food there is excellent. It's not a place to take Shawn, but since you like Italian food, I'd like to take you there. How about next Friday night?"

When Cullen opened the door Friday night, she looked spectacular to Andrew. She had on a low-cut dress he hadn't seen before, and her luxurious hair had a drama all its own.

"Hi there. You look lovely this evening." He tried to make it sound casual, but his feelings sure weren't. "Tell Shawn and Louisa not to wait up. You'll probably be home late. Service there is very slow. They consider dinner to be a whole evening's entertainment." He was proud of himself for choosing a restaurant within five minutes of his house and giving her an excuse to be out that might allow for more than dinner. Just in case.

Andrew had made arrangements for his favorite table in the corner. He ordered a scallop appetizer for the two of them, followed by the veal piccata, all this accompanied by a marvelous bottle of Italian wine. Dessert was a ricotta pie Andrew had ordered early in the week as a special request.

It had been a favorite of his and Margaret's, and Andrew thought it would be a treat for Cullen to have something she probably had never tasted before.

As they lingered over the last of the wine, Andrew could tell it was beginning to have an effect on Cullen. She had that soft-focused look about her, and her voice was becoming deeper and a little slurred. She was also leaning over so far toward him that, in spite of himself, Andrew found himself looking at her cleavage as much as her face.

"Let's go back to your place, Andrew. You said it was near here. I'd love to see where you live."

Andrew couldn't pay the bill fast enough. He had been wondering how to get her in bed and couldn't believe she had just suggested it herself. It was a short drive back to the house and an even shorter tour when they got there. It ended, of course, in the bedroom.

How long had it been since he felt smooth, velvety skin and a firm, youthful body curving upward to meet his every thrust? How long had it been since he had entered such a deliciously warm, moist, welcoming environment? Not since Margaret was young and twenty-something. Had he appreciated it as much then as he did now, knowing the difference? *Stop analyzing, you fool. Just drown yourself in Cullen and enjoy.*

"Oh! Oh! Don't stop! Don't stop! Harder, Tony, please, harder!"

Oh my God! What did she just say? Andrew felt like he had just been thrown into an ocean of ice water at the moment of climax. He pulled away, stricken. How could he have been so stupid? How could he have allowed himself to get this involved with Tony's widow? How could he have deceived himself into thinking she could possibly be interested in a sixty-two-year-old man like him? He must have been temporarily out of his mind. She still loved Tony. That was clear enough. It was Tony she was seeing and wanting to be with. She didn't see Andrew. He wasn't visible. She couldn't be interested in him. Like Margaret, she could never love someone she couldn't see. Andrew was miserable.

"Oh, Andrew, I am so sorry. I truly am. I had too much to drink. I was out of control. It was just habit. Tony is the only man I have ever been with, and it felt the same, physically, and I had a momentary lapse. That's all it was. It didn't mean anything. I was emotionally engaged with you. Honestly I was. Please forgive me."

Cullen was crying now. She pulled the sheet up tightly around her, as if she were trying to hide or disappear. Andrew was already out of bed and headed toward the door.

"It's all right, Cullen. I understand. It's getting late, almost ten o'clock. Time to get you home. I'll take my things into the other bedroom so you can get dressed." And with that, he quietly closed the door and left Cullen to her weeping. *Damn it all, anyway,* he thought, thoroughly frustrated. *Damn it! Damn it!*

They rode home in dead silence. When Andrew walked her to the door, Cullen touched his arm lightly. Her voice was plaintive and soft. "Not that it matters to you anymore, but just for the record, Andrew, I'm in love with you. Not Tony. I never loved Tony. It's you I love. You."

"You needn't say anything, Cullen. I'm okay. I told you I understand. Let's just leave it at that. I don't like roller-coaster rides. Never did. I am too old for this, too old for you. Psychologically, I'm old enough to be your father. You need to find yourself someone else, some nice young man in his late twenties or early thirties. Good night, Cullen."

Before Cullen could say anything else, Andrew turned around and hurried back to his car. He pulled out from the curb and took off down the street going twice the speed limit. Luckily, no cop was around to see him run the red light. When he got home, he poured himself a glass of Chivas, gulped it down, and poured another one. He drank until he was totally wasted and spent the night in his green leather wingback chair. That was something Tony would do, not Andrew.

chapter 7

The Morning After

*W*alter rang the bell five times before Andrew answered the door. He was hungover, and his clothes looked like he had slept in them.

"Good Lord, Andrew. You're a mess. Things must not have gone too well last night. What happened?"

"Don't ask. Come on in, Walter. I'm making some strong coffee. You'll drink it strong this once, won't you? I'm not in any shape to jog this morning."

"That's easy enough to see. It was that bad, huh?"

"I'm not good at this dating stuff, Walter. I don't know how other men do it. They get divorced, date women half their age, have a great time, get married, start new families, have clandestine affairs with their colleagues' wives, live happily ever after or at least happily enough. All I want is Margaret back. She is the only woman I've ever loved and probably the only woman I ever will. I understood her feelings, though. I knew the second she saw me and I saw her, our marriage had to be over. I tried to hang on anyway because I love her so much and have always depended on her emotionally. Cullen, on the other hand, is a beautiful, captivating, sexy young woman, but I am Tony to her and too old. My interests are more mature. I want to sit and read in the evenings and go to bed early, not a twenty-nine-year-old's idea of a fun time. And besides, she's still in love with her deceased husband. It was his body that attracted her to me. That became obvious enough last night."

"I wouldn't be so sure about that, Andrew. From the conversations I had with her before she agreed to give me her husband's body, I understood her to say that she didn't love her husband. She couldn't be guided by her love. That was why she was having such a hard time deciding if it was the right thing to do, especially with her mother-in-law so opposed to doing anything except keeping her son's body on life support. I got the impression it was a forced marriage. She got pregnant, and he wouldn't let her have an abortion. Tell me what happened."

Andrew gave Walter an abbreviated version of his disastrous evening, trying at first to hide his wounded ego, but he was hurting too badly and getting all worked up again just talking about it.

"Can you believe it? She even tried to convince me she was in love with me. That's a laugh! My new life really sucks, Walter. You shouldn't have been such a good surgeon. You should have let me die on the table. If you were truly my friend, you would have done that for me."

"Aw, snap out of it, Andrew. I think you're wrong about Cullen. And even if you aren't, it isn't the end of the world. There are tons of young women out there who are dying to meet someone like you: good-looking, brilliant, cultured, filthy rich. Hang around the country club a little. They'll find you. Just wait."

"Huh, the country club probably would like to revoke my membership. I might as well quit anyway. I can't play a decent game of tennis anymore, and people who knew me before are so creeped out they're uncomfortable being around me. I'm a goddamned pariah, Walter."

"Maybe you should think about leaving St. Louis. With your credentials, most any university would consider itself lucky to get you. Duke is looking for someone right now. Maybe you should put the word out that you're looking. You might run into someone once in a while who knew the old you, but since you rarely went to conferences, most people know you by reputation only. A change of place would give you a fresh start."

Andrew poured the coffee as Walter continued. "Part of the problem, too, is you haven't made the psychological shift to your new age. You still think of yourself as sixty-two, but no one else is going to see you that way.

You aren't too old for Cullen or any other twenty-something. Looks like you aren't having any problems sexually. You need to loosen up and try acting your new age. Stop lamenting about your tennis game. Take up a new sport—golf maybe. Get some lessons with the pro. Lots of men don't have the money to start playing golf until they are in their thirties, unless they grew up playing at a country club, like you did tennis. It's okay to be a beginner. Instead of fretting over your inability to play your violin like you used to, take up the cello or something else. Try a new challenge. You like challenges. Stop waiting for your old life to start again, Andrew. Your old life isn't coming back. Try to enjoy a different new life. There are lots of wonderful things still left to do."

Andrew was relieved when Walter stopped lecturing so they could drink their coffee before it got cold. Walter always seemed to be lecturing him about something, and he always made it sound so simple and so reasonable. *Yeah,* thought Andrew. *That's easy enough for you to say. You aren't the one having to do it.*

"Andrew, I really think a big part of your problem is depression. We need to add an antidepressant to your regimen. Maybe that will help."

"No, Walter, no more pills! I'm already taking so many pills I don't have any room left for breakfast. I'm taking eleven pills a day as it is. Do you have any idea how long it takes to swallow eleven pills? I'm a walking apothecary. If anyone looked in my medicine cabinet and bedroom drawers, they'd swear I'm a drug addict."

"Well, you do have to have your daily fix." Walter chuckled.

"That isn't funny, Walter."

"Seriously, Andrew, I had to leave that piece of frontal lobe in place in order to ensure a good outcome. I'm sorry about the number of pills, but you needn't be so self-conscious about them. There are plenty of people walking around who take multiple medications on a daily basis for diabetes, multiple sclerosis, and on and on."

"Yeah, but I view it differently when it's for the brain. If it's for the body, it's Tony, but if it's for the brain, that's me you're messing with. Anyway, despite all the drug ads on TV for depression and anxiety, there's still a lot of stigma attached to people taking drugs to regulate their brains. Being sick in the body is perfectly acceptable. Being sick in the head, not so much. My antirejection drug is acceptable. Everyone understands its importance. But my meds to duplicate my old personality are not so well understood, and I wouldn't want anyone I'm dating to know I take them. They might think there's something wrong with me. Yet the meds are only changing my brain chemistry a little. What do people think alcohol is for? Why do they enjoy drinking? It's their brain-altering drug of choice. It has social acceptance, cache. Even cannabis is gaining status. But my drugs, with their long Latin names, no chance."

"I think you are overly sensitive about that, Andrew. Anyone you would want to date long enough for her to see you taking your pills would be intelligent and well educated enough to understand. You're worrying too much. Where's the confident, self-assured Dr. Hamilton I used to know?"

"I'm beginning to believe you did let that part of me die on the operating table, Walter."

Andrew poured some more coffee and settled back in his chair. He took a few sips while he was digesting what Walter had said.

"Getting back to your earlier comments, leaving St. Louis is an interesting idea. As much as I detest the looks and stares I get at the club and the university, I'm surprised I haven't thought of it. Moving away would solve a number of problems, not the least of which is extricating myself from Tony's family. Have you any idea how weird it is to have Tony's mother driveling over me and trying to get me to come home? Can you imagine me trying to play the role of his grieving son's surrogate father? Worst of all, can you imagine me entertaining a relationship with his widow, thinking she will love me for myself when all she can see is her deceased husband? It's totally idiotic! It's inconceivable even to me that I've allowed such things to happen."

"You didn't start this, Andrew. Cullen did. She asked for your help. You responded to her need the way you have always responded to those who asked for your help. That's just the kind of person you are. No way would you have turned her down. No way would you have been insensitive to her son's tender feelings. No way would you have destroyed her mother-in-law's belief that God had brought her son back. And as a young man with a healthy libido, no way could you have been in close proximity to a woman like Cullen for so long and not have been smitten. I'm half-smitten by her myself, in a fatherly way, more or less. And I still think you're wrong about Cullen. For God's sake, Andrew, the woman said she was in love with you. That was a brave, risky thing for her to do when you hadn't declared your feelings for her. There are a number of things she could've said to get you to keep seeing her son. She seems like a pretty articulate, straightforward young woman to me, too young and insecure to be manipulative. I personally don't believe she would have said she loves you if she doesn't in fact love you. And since she told me she did not love her husband, it has to be the you inside of him that she loves. At least that's the way I see it. As for her calling you Tony, that's just from habit, pure and simple. Hell, I called my third wife Shirley for the first five months we were married. Still do sometimes! Rose just laughs and calls me Sam. I think you need to man up and call Cullen. She might be the best medicine for you yet."

chapter 8

Cullen Again

Cullen was beside herself. She didn't know what to do next. She wasn't sure there was anything she could do. She really was in love with Andrew, but she certainly couldn't blame him for dismissing her sincerity and walking away after what she'd done. She had risked telling him because she was desperate to save the relationship. If he cared anything about her, it should have worked. Since it didn't, she clearly didn't mean anything to him. She had totally misread him and the relationship. He was not really interested in her beyond a little sex. She certainly couldn't blame him, given all the baggage she was carrying around like Marley's chains: a tarnished past, a deranged mother-in-law, a sullen, resentful son, and an ever-present phantom husband. It would take someone exceptionally tolerant or a little crazy to want to become romantically involved with her. Perhaps in her lonely desperation she had mistakenly projected onto Andrew the man she needed him to be, the man of her dreams. But somehow she knew deep down that he really was that person; he just wasn't interested in her.

And why would he be? Meghan had been right all along. Andrew was too big a stretch for her. How stupid of her to think that a sophisticated, world-renowned neuroscientist could have any interest in a college dropout like her. A good-looking woman might make it to bed with a man like Andrew, but he would quickly look past the cover for the content inside. And why would he choose her when he could have his pick of worldly, educated, accomplished women? And yet she felt certain that there was something between them beyond Shawn and physical attraction. How could she have destroyed her dreams with one word, one slip of the tongue? Was Tony's restless spirit punishing her for not loving him? Could Tony have made her utter his name at the worst possible moment? Where did those thoughts come from? Was it a bit of her old Catholicism creeping in, challenging her metaphysics again? She didn't believe in spirits, angels, saints, and God anymore. She didn't believe that there was a heaven or a spiritual realm. She did believe in purgatory though, because she was already living in it with Tony's mother. If Tony ever wanted revenge for being unloved by her, he had accomplished it well enough already by leaving her to cope with Louisa alone.

Tony was hardly the model husband himself. He had done his duty and married her for Shawn's sake. He figured that was enough, except where Shawn was concerned. If he loved her at all, he had a strange way of showing it. Tony treated Cullen like an indentured servant at home except when he wanted sex or when he wanted to parade her in front of his buddies as his trophy wife. What she hated most were the evenings he went out playing poker or baseball or bowling. The aftermath was unpredictably nerve-racking. If he won, he brought home a six-pack or two to celebrate. If he had a bad game, he would come home drunk and irritable, and, sometimes he was physically abusive. Once, he threw her to the floor so violently she went to the hospital with a concussion. Now that she thought about it, she believed in hell too. That's where she lived most of the time when Tony was alive. Now, with Tony gone, she was in purgatory with Louisa, an improvement of sorts. At least she would try to think of it that way.

Cullen had dared to think Andrew could be her ticket to get out of this mess of a life she had created for herself and Shawn. She wanted to finish her degree, make something of herself, fulfill the potential her parents and professors were sure she had, and do something important with her life. She wanted to become a woman of substance, a woman Andrew would want. Without any means of support except the little she earned working full-time, Cullen could wish and dream all she wanted. But she couldn't begin to hope.

What was wrong with having high standards and lofty aspirations, anyway? At least she wasn't simply opportunistic. She wasn't looking for just any man. She was looking for a doctor. At the university, several professors and graduate students clearly found her attractive. None of them were in the medical field, though, so she never considered any of them suitable. Even the divorced child psychologist she was taking Shawn to had made a number of overtures, and while she had considered dating him, it was for his sexy body rather than anything else.

Andrew was the first and only man to really get her attention, and it wasn't solely because of the weird circumstances. There was something very special about him. Seeing him in Tony's body brought into high relief who Andrew was, his very essence. She could see him clearly because what he brought to this physical shell was everything Tony lacked. It was Andrew she loved and wanted. Of that she was certain. Cullen remembered seeing the newspaper picture of Andrew when his successful operation became public. He was shown in his former body in his wheelchair. Cullen had thought to herself then that he was a strikingly handsome, distinguished, kind-looking man with a wonderful smile and beautiful, wavy silver hair. She wondered what it would be like to have been his wife before his accident, to have had the opportunity to live with him and be loved by him so thoroughly he loved her still. Andrew had not told her he still loved his former wife, but Walter had hinted at it, and Cullen could tell. If Cullen had a phantom husband, Andrew had a phantom wife. Very different, of course, but still …

What was hard for Cullen to understand was how Andrew's wife could love him before the operation and not still love him now. If his wife had been blind and unable to see the age difference, would it have mattered to her then? If she were blind, would feeling his new body and hearing a different voice have made her love him less or not at all? Wasn't there at least something that would have enabled Andrew's wife to recognize her husband? Was she blind to who he really was? Cullen was sure that she herself would have known him intuitively from his "Andrewness." His brain may have been the transport that got him to another body, but what got transported was more than just intelligence, knowledge, and memory. Cullen felt certain there is something beyond the physical that creates a person's identity, that allows him to remain who he is. She was sure true love could always transcend such physical boundaries and recognize the beloved, sense his presence, know he is there. But then, Cullen was still young and not yet so cynical as to believe there is no such thing as unconditional love. From Cullen's point of view, regardless of which body Andrew was in, he was still the same lovable person. But she had to admit that Andrew in Tony's body was definitely the total package for her. And now he was gone.

Or was he? If anyone would know what could be done to help the situation it would be Walter. Cullen had grown rather close to Walter over the past several months. He always came along on the outings with Shawn. He had developed a favorite-uncle relationship with her. She knew Walter would help her if he could.

"Hello, Walter. It's Cullen. I need your advice."

"About Andrew, I'm guessing. You haven't heard from him since last Friday night, have you?"

"Oh, so you already know about that? Well, at least I don't have to go through the embarrassment of telling you. I don't know what to do, Walter. I have allowed myself to fall completely in love with Andrew, and I foolishly thought he might be close to falling in love with me. Am I totally mistaken? Is that just wishful thinking on my part?"

"No, Cullen, you're not necessarily wrong, but you've done a lot of damage to his already fragile ego. He's lost so much. His sense of self has become rather shaky. Although Tony's body has been Andrew's savior in one sense, it's also been his nemesis. No one sees Andrew as Andrew anymore. All they see is Tony. He is particularly sensitive to how you see him. Friday night you confirmed his worst fears."

"But it was an accident, Walter. I didn't mean it. I wasn't thinking of Tony; truly, I wasn't. It was just a slip of the tongue from a longtime habit."

"I know, and that's what I told him. But in his mind, the evidence suggests otherwise. He thinks you see Tony instead of him. He doesn't see how he can compete. He still thinks of himself as almost sixty-three years old. He thinks that he is too old for the dating game, too old for you. He is having trouble becoming thirty-three. His thinking and habits are still those of his former self. His body may be in its prime now, but his mind and spirit are still on the cusp of retirement."

"What can I do to fix it, Walter? How can I get him back?"

"His wife, Margaret, told him she had to leave because she could not love someone she couldn't see. Somehow, you must show him that you do see him. I know he cares about you. He may even be close to loving you—that is, if he's capable of loving anyone except Margaret. You have a decided advantage over his former wife because you are the present; Margaret is the past. It is hard to resist the euphoria of being in love here in the present when the alternative is a lingering, languishing past love. And while that euphoria may never completely eliminate the former love, it definitely relegates it to the archives over time. It's the indomitable human spirit at work, the human instinct for survival."

"So what do I do, Walter? Just pick up the phone and call him? What do I say? I can't use Shawn as an excuse. Shawn doesn't want to go out with Andrew anymore now that he knows the truth. He resents Andrew using his father's body. I can't reason with him. He's in that sullen preteen stage; at least that is what the psychologist says. He says I should give the subject a wide berth for now. So what's left? I can't invite him to dinner. He probably wouldn't come anyway."

"I just had a thought. Joshua Bell is giving a concert at Powell Symphony Hall next Saturday evening. The concert has been sold out for months, but I have four tickets. Why don't I invite you and Andrew to go with Rose and me? The couple we usually go with is going to be out of town. Andrew loves the violin. He's not going to turn down the opportunity to hear Joshua Bell, especially when he knows I always have excellent seats. I'll call him and set it up. I can be a buffer if there is any awkwardness."

"Oh, Walter, you're wonderful. Thank you so much. I knew I could count on you."

chapter 9

Argo

*A*ndrew was having trouble concentrating on his grant proposals. He looked out his office window at the beautiful fall day. The maple trees were in their full glory, and the weather was crisply perfect for a walk in Forest Park. He decided he had done enough for one day. The proposals could wait. He grabbed his jacket and headed for the park.

It was obvious Walter was playing matchmaker again. He seemed to relish this task, at least where Andrew and Cullen were concerned. After the concert, Andrew had asked Walter just whose interest he had at heart, Cullen's or his? Walter just smiled and said, "Both, actually. You two belong together. Cullen understands that. For an expert in vision and the brain, you sure are having a hard time making the connection. Open your eyes to reality, Andrew."

Cullen did look wonderful at the concert, but then she always looked wonderful. There was a difference this time, although he couldn't exactly put his finger on it. Was it because she had surrendered to him, that he had possessed her, that in some way she was now his? Over the past two weeks, he had replayed the scene a hundred times: the feel of her firm, youthful body, the scent of her hair and the silky auburn web it made across the pillow, the unbelievable sensation of entering her, the pleasure of it making him gasp as if it were his first ever experience with a woman, the way she held him to her with her smooth legs, her mouth seeking his, hungry for him, and then … He refused to go there again. He would forever edit out the way it ended.

Could Walter be right? Could Cullen actually be in love with him? Was it possible she really didn't love her husband? It would certainly answer the perplexing question he had asked himself all along about how she could have ended up with someone like Tony. And if that was true, it meant that she could in fact see him inside of Tony. It meant Cullen recognized the difference and loved who that difference was. Maybe Cullen looked particularly radiant at the concert because she was in love with him. Was that it? Or was he simply more attuned to her now that they had been intimate? Whichever, it didn't matter. Same difference, really. Andrew was getting a spring in his step. He was feeling a little lighthearted. He was almost happy as he shuffled through the deep orange and russet leaves, some of them the color of Cullen's hair.

By the time Andrew got home, he had convinced himself that Cullen really did love him. And while he wasn't in love with Cullen, he certainly had feelings for her that were more than casual. She was beautiful, intelligent, and interesting—reason enough to give the relationship another chance.

Andrew let Cullen's cell phone ring until voice mail picked up. He didn't want to leave a message, so he hung up, disappointed. Before he could get his phone back in his pocket, Cullen was calling him back.

"Hi, Andrew. I saw you were calling, but I had just come in the door with an armload of groceries and couldn't get to my phone soon enough."

"That was a good concert last Saturday night, wasn't it? I'm glad Walter invited us to go."

"Yes, I'm glad too, Andrew. I thoroughly enjoyed it. I kept the program so I could read about the pieces Mr. Bell played. I especially liked the Faure piece."

"Oh, you mean the 'Après un Reve.' You liked that? I used to play it in my former life. Can't now, of course, but maybe someday. It's slow going, but I'm working on it again. You don't hear him very often now, but Faure was the most influential composer in France at one time. He was the director of the Conservatoire, and Ravel was one of his students. Musicologists didn't pay much attention to him because his compositions weren't in the fashionable Wagnerian style. He wrote mostly small lyrical pieces for the piano, like those of Chopin. They tend to work well for the violin. I used to love to play them."

"I hope you will play some of them for me sometime, Andrew."

"I don't have enough dexterity yet, Cullen. It'll be a long time before I'll be back in practice. But enough about that. I'm calling because I thought it might be fun to take a ride out into the country for a picnic on Saturday. The leaves are at their peak right now, and the weather is supposed to be nice for the weekend. I have a farm about an hour down I-40 from here. It's up on a ridge, and you can see forever from there—well, at least twenty-five miles. The view is wonderful this time of year. Fall is my favorite time to be there. Shawn can bring a friend. There's a big walnut barn and lots of room to roam. Would you and Shawn like to go?"

"Sounds wonderful, Andrew. I'd love to go. Shawn won't be going, though, because he has an overnight Boy Scout camping trip down on the Current River. Did I tell you he's returned to his troop? His grades have improved too. The psychologist was right about what would help, but it was you, Andrew, who made it happen. Thank you again for that."

"I'm glad to hear things are getting back to normal for him. Shawn's a great kid, Cullen. You've done a good job raising him. Now about Saturday, why don't I pick you up at ten? Don't worry about the food; I'll bring everything. There's a good deli near my house. Just wear your jeans and old shoes. Better bring a wrap too. It could be a little chilly."

"Is there a house on the property?"

"Yes, a lovely old farmhouse, full of antiques we brought back from England some thirty years ago. I've always called the place my country house to annoy my English relatives. It was built sometime in the mid-1800s by a German master-carpenter who built it with the walnut and oak trees he cleared on the property. It's really a wonderful old place—a fireplace in every room, a large country kitchen, a swing on the front porch to sit and watch the birds settling down in the maples at dusk. You can sometimes hear the bucolic mooing of cows on the back forty I lease to a neighboring farmer."

"I can't wait to see it, Andrew. I'll be ready at ten."

They turned off the interstate and drove another five miles down a winding country road with farmland on both sides, working farms with cattle grazing and farmers baling hay. Cullen leaned forward the second the house came into view. "That's it, isn't it, Andrew? The pretty one with the four-board white fence?" There was a little excitement in her voice. "Hey, the signpost says Argo! That's the name of Jason's ship when he was looking for the golden fleece. I remember that from my high school Latin classes. Why did you name your place after a ship?"

"Well, I didn't actually. 'Argo' is also a corruption of the word 'ergo' that Shakespeare used. It means 'therefore.' Descartes made the word famous when he said, '*Cogito ergo sum*,' which means, 'I think therefore I am.' I thought the name was fitting because I have been coming here for almost twenty years to think, to get a different perspective on the theories I was hashing out in my research. It led to all my eureka moments. Could have named the place eureka, but that seemed a little too self-congratulatory. Ironically, Argo has an extremely fitting meaning for me now, since my brain is the only way I can tell I exist. In fact, it is the only part of my former self that does exist, unless the indelible marks christening and confirmation left on my soul transferred over as well. Funny how it has worked out. Anyway, here we are. Look around while I unload."

Cullen was gone for quite a while. When Andrew finished unloading, he saw her all the way past the barn and stable. She was walking back toward the house from the pond.

"Hey, Cullen, come on back. You haven't seen the inside yet. Come on in and make yourself at home."

"Oh, Andrew, I love this place. That walnut barn is so magnificent I could live in it, and the view across the valley and up the hills goes on forever. The leaves are gorgeous. No wonder this is your favorite time of year. Everything is so perfect. Who takes care of it for you?"

"There is a man and his wife, George and Edith, who have been looking after the place for me for years. George takes care of the outside, and Edith looks after the house. She also cooks for me when I want her to. I let them have half the produce from the garden and orchard, and the other half Edith cans or freezes for me. She will be harvesting the grapes next week and making the best grape jam you've ever eaten. I have a real weakness for her grape jam on peanut butter sandwiches. Over there on the counter is an apple pie she made us for dessert, and she left a note saying there is homemade ice cream in the freezer. Edith usually takes off a couple of days during the week if she knows I am coming so she can be here on the weekends for me. I let her have the rest of the day off today though. I didn't think we would need her."

After the picnic lunch on the patio, Andrew and Cullen took a walk through the fields down to the pond, full to the brim from recent rains. There was a weeping willow right where a landscaper would have placed it. There were cattails, and Jack-in-the-pulpits, a few ducks, and a big bullfrog that went *kerplunk* into the water as they reached its edge. Farther down on the property, in the valley, was a brisk spring-fed stream with a few boulders that made the water arabesque around them. Andrew held Cullen's hand as they step-stoned out across several of them to reach the big one in the middle. There they sat for a while and watched the fish making their way downstream. Andrew followed their struggle through the eddies and privately wondered where his own journey was taking him. The sun was beginning to sink. Darkness would follow pretty rapidly now.

"I'll race you back to the house. We still have an apple pie to eat. Edith will be miffed if we leave without having some of it—and the ice cream. Besides, it's beginning to get a little chilly. I don't know about you, but my shoes and socks are soaked. George left me a bunch of wood by the fireplaces. I'll build us a fire."

The fire in the family room was inviting after their long afternoon walk through the fields. They sat in front of the fire and concentrated on their desserts. Andrew was surprised at how much fun the day had been showing Cullen around. His spirits were high. Cullen's presence there was energizing. It was making him feel young again. He wondered if this was what becoming thirty-three felt like. He made some coffee and led her to the front porch.

"The tour isn't over until you have coffee on the porch swing and listen to the birds settling down and the tree frogs starting up. It's quite a concert. Then I will take you around to the back to see the star show. There are no town lights anywhere near here, so the stars you can see number in the millions."

It was dark now, the sky was clear, and as promised, the star show was spectacular. The farm was far enough away from the St. Louis city lights to expose a myriad of stars city dwellers never saw.

"The closest I've ever been to seeing a night sky like this was the show at the planetarium in Forest Park, but it couldn't hold a candle to this. Oh, look, Andrew! There's a falling star. See it? You're supposed to make a wish. Will it burn up completely or will a piece of it fall to earth? I would love to have a pocket full of stardust, as the song goes."

"Cullen, did you know the cosmologist Carl Sagan once said that 93 percent of our body mass is stardust? 'We are the stuff of stars.' Rather poetic for Sagan I think."

"What a lovely notion that is. Sounds like Shakespeare."

"Yes, when I first heard it, I thought he must have copped it from the old Bard, but I looked through all the Shakespeare concordances and couldn't find it. I guess it was just Sagan waxing eloquent on one of his programs. It's really getting chilly now. Let's get back to that fire."

The family room was filled with the glow of the fire. Andrew left the lights off. He didn't want to destroy the mood. Cullen sat down on the floor close to the warmth and motioned for Andrew to join her. He handed her a glass of red wine and a floor pillow, then sat down close enough to kiss her if he wanted. And he wanted that and much more. Andrew took another sip of wine and put his glass down. Cullen was leaning on one elbow gazing at the fire, the curve of her body outlined by the glow, her glorious hair falling to the side, revealing the nape of her neck. He leaned over and kissed it gently. She was incredibly sexy, and Andrew desired her with his whole body. He could not remember ever being this consumed with desire, but he didn't love her. He wondered if he would ever be able to love a woman other than Margaret.

"You're a beautiful woman, Cullen, but you're much more than that. It has been a long time since I have enjoyed being here this much. Thank you for today."

"I hope you will invite me back, Andrew. I have loved every minute of it."

With that, she turned to him and kissed him softly on his cheek, his neck, and his lips. She moved her hands slowly over his chest, feeling his strong, hard body beneath his shirt.

"Make love to me, Andrew. I want you to make love to me, right here on the floor in front of the fire. It will be the perfect ending to this special day."

And so he lost himself in her once again, and this time he would remember the ending for a long time to come.

chapter 10

Christmas

Cullen watched from the window as Shawn shoveled the snow off the walkway and front steps. She knew he hated to shovel snow, especially on Christmas Eve, but she also knew he was glad it was snowing. His dad had always loved for it to snow at Christmas. Cullen remembered how excited Shawn had been when he returned home from midnight mass the Christmas before his dad died. There was not a single flake of snow in sight when they went into the church, but his dad prayed it would snow anyway. When they came out, the world was magically white. He said his dad told him that if you pray hard enough, God will hear you. Cullen knew that Shawn had believed it then. She also knew he didn't believe it now. Nobody could have prayed harder for his dad to come back to life than he and his grandma. Cullen had to put aloe on both of their raw knees for months. She saw Shawn make one last hard scrape with the shovel and heave the snow as far as he could.

"You looked like you were freezing to death out there, Shawn. I've made you some hot chocolate. Come on in here in the kitchen where it's warm. You can take your shower before dinner. That will warm you up. We'll eat a little late tonight since I'm taking you and Louisa to midnight mass."

"You didn't used to go to mass with us when Daddy was alive, not even on Christmas Eve. Why didn't you? Father O'Rourke says it's a bad sin not to. You can go to hell for that."

"Well, that is what Father O'Rourke believes, but no one knows for sure if it is true. That's why it's called a belief and why people have to take it on faith. Anyway, I am going to church tonight to take you and your grandmother. I'm sure Father O'Rourke will be glad to see me back in the fold. Better get on with that shower now while I get dinner started. It'll take a while to cook."

Midnight mass was always a candlelight service with lovely flowers and beautiful music. Even though Cullen thought the Italian Catholic Church a little garish compared to the Irish neighborhood church of her youth, she found an unexpected comfort in the rituals of her former faith. There were still a few shreds of faith left in her after all; it just took a little distance from her disastrous marriage to gain some perspective. When her parents were senselessly killed in the accident, Cullen felt that God had abandoned her. Out of hurt, retaliation, and misunderstanding, she had abandoned God in return. She couldn't blame Him for her pregnancy though; she had to take responsibility for that. It had been so many years since Cullen had prayed she wasn't sure she could, but right now, right this minute, she was feeling full of happiness for her new prospects. She was full of gratitude for the chain of events that brought Andrew into her life. She needed to thank someone for that. Who else was there to thank but God? And once she bowed her head and started, an avalanche of pent-up emotions came tumbling out: anger, accusations, hurt, shame, sorrow, regret, contrition, remorse, and finally, thanks. Tears were flooding down Cullen's face. Shawn asked his mom what in the world had just happened to her. Cullen shook her head and fumbled for a Kleenex in her purse. She couldn't answer him. She truly didn't know.

When they came out of church, yesterday's snow was being painted over with a pristine layer of white. Shawn lifted his face up to the heavens and stuck out his tongue to catch some of the flakes. They landed on his lashes and nose instead. He gave a big sigh.

"I miss Daddy. Andrew isn't coming over for Christmas is he, Mom?"

"Yes, of course he is, Shawn. He said he has a special present for you."

"Why does he have to come? I don't want him to. It'll ruin my Christmas."

"You're being unreasonable, Shawn. Andrew is very fond of you. And besides, I want him to come. It makes Christmas special for me, and it makes Christmas special for your grandmother too."

"I don't care! I don't want him to come. Christmas was Daddy's special time."

"Let's not argue, Shawn. It's already Christmas. We are supposed to be happy and thankful and show our love for one another."

"How can I be thankful that my daddy's gone because Andrew has his body?"

"Shawn, nobody is to blame for your dad's death but your dad. Your dad would still be alive if he hadn't been showing off and ignoring the rules to stay away from the home plate when someone else was batting. He was always trying to be the big shot who didn't need to obey rules. That's why he got hit in the head with a thrown bat; that's why he's dead. Your dad was already dead when his body was given to Andrew."

"That's not what Grandma said. She said he wasn't dead, just in a coma, waiting for God to wake him up."

"Shawn, your dad was dead; his brain had no activity at all. What good would it have done to just let his body stay on life support for years on end or rot in the ground? This way, at least his senseless death enabled an important research doctor to continue his work."

"But every time I see Andrew, it reminds me of how much I wish he was Daddy and not Andrew. It hurts, Mom. It hurts. I shouldn't have to see him. It isn't fair."

"I'm sorry that it hurts, Shawn, but Andrew is a good friend of ours now. You have to admit that after almost three years it doesn't hurt as much as it did at first. It may still be a sharp pain right now, especially at Christmas, but time will wear away the edges until it doesn't hurt so much. It will just be a little ache in the back of your heart. Meanwhile, try to be nice to Andrew. Don't blame him. Andrew didn't choose to be in your father's body. Walter—Dr. Rubin, that is—chose your dad's body because it was young and healthy except for the brain being dead. And maybe it was God's will. Did you ever stop to think that maybe this was God's way of answering your prayers? Maybe, because God knew how much you missed him, He arranged for you to have your dad back in a different way. Think about that for a while. We're home now. Run on in and jump in bed. It's late."

⁓

By the time Andrew knocked on the door, it was two o'clock. Breakfast dishes had been washed, presents had been opened, the table had been set, and turkey dinner was about ready to come out of the oven. Louisa was waiting for him at the door.

"Merry Christmas, Tony. Give your Mama Louisa a big kiss."

"Merry Christmas, Louisa. I brought you a present. Let me get the door closed and my coat off, and I'll give it to you. Hi, Cullen. Merry Christmas. Where's Shawn? I have something for him too."

"He said he isn't feeling well, Andrew. He's still in his room. He told me to call him when dinner's ready. You can give him his present then, but please wait until after we eat. Let me take your coat. Open your present, Louisa. Let's see what Andrew got you."

Louisa gave a little squeal of delight when she saw the big present with beautiful blue and silver wrap and a huge silver bow. She tore into it like a child, unable to contain her excitement.

"Oh, what a beautiful coat! It feels so good. And it fits me perfectly! How did you know I needed a new coat, Tony? I have never had one this nice before. You must have saved all year to buy me this. You are such a wonderful son, Tony. See, Cullen, I told you Tony is a wonderful son."

"I'm glad you like it, Louisa. I had a little help from Cullen. She mentioned that you needed a new one and the size, but I did pick it out myself. I thought a pretty cashmere coat would be just the thing to keep you warm going to church."

"Cashmere! Mother Mary and Joseph, Tony! Cashmere! I will be the envy of the neighborhood. It is way too expensive, Tony. You shouldn't have. But thank you, my dear boy. I love it."

"I have a present for you too, Cullen. I would like to wait until later to give it to you, sometime after dinner, if that's all right. It takes some explanation."

"Then I'll wait to give you yours too. Besides, dinner's ready. You all get seated at the table, and I'll go see if Shawn feels well enough to come down."

Shawn came down at his mother's coaxing and politely said "Merry Christmas" to Andrew but nothing else during dinner. Afterwards, when he opened Andrew's present, his eyes widened with surprise.

"It's a guitar! It's one like Sister Mary Margaret has!"

"It comes with lessons, Shawn. There's a guitar teacher who's going to come to your house and give you lessons every Friday after school. You will be playing well by summer if you practice."

Shawn said thanks without even looking at Andrew. As he headed back up to his room, he mumbled to himself in a low voice, "Darn, why did Andrew have to be the one to give it to me?"

Cullen saw that Andrew had heard and blushed with embarrassment. "Christmas is a hard time for Shawn, Andrew. It's when he misses his dad the most. He really is thrilled with the guitar. It's the one present he has wanted ever since his teacher brought hers to school to play for his class. Shawn said Sister Mary Margaret told the class that playing music was the next best thing to praying. She said it was a way to express emotion, get rid of bad feelings and sad thoughts, make your heart happy, and praise God. I suspect Shawn has a lot of bad feelings and sad thoughts to get rid of, especially at this time of year. How in the world did you know what to get him?"

"Well, believe it or not, Cullen, I was a boy once myself, and playing music was the only way I could get my deep-down feelings out. I had my violin. I still have my violin, and although I can't play it nearly as well, it serves the same purpose for me even now. I thought the guitar would be a good instrument for Shawn to master quickly. He's still hurting, Cullen. That's easy enough to see. He needs an outlet. I hope this works for him."

"You never cease to amaze me, Andrew. I think you are the most sensitive and caring man I have ever known."

After coffee and another piece of Cullen's pecan pie, Louisa said good night, kissed Andrew on both cheeks, and went off to her bedroom carrying her beautiful new coat. Cullen turned on the gas logs in the small living room fireplace, and she and Andrew settled down on the sofa in front of the fire.

"This isn't nearly as nice a fire as the one you built at the farm, but it's the best I can do here. Okay, Andrew, what is this mysterious present you have for me that needs explanation? Wait, first let me give you yours."

Cullen walked over to the tree and picked up a small package with a beautiful big bow on it and handed it to Andrew.

"I couldn't think of anything to give you that you needed. You seem to have everything you could possibly want. But I thought maybe this could serve as a little memento of a very special time together. I hope you like it."

Andrew unwrapped the present. It was a small green leather picture album with a silver plaque on the cover with a single word engraved on it: Argo. Inside were twenty pictures Cullen had taken of his farm: the view from the road, the valley ablaze with fall color, the garden, the orchard, the barns, the stream, the water swirling around the stones, the front porch swing, and the fire ablaze in the family room fireplace. The only thing missing was the falling star show. Cullen had captured the entire first day they had spent at the farm. Inside the back cover, Cullen had written *Therefore, the Beginning!*

"What a wonderful, thoughtful gift, Cullen. This album and the pictures are lovely. I don't have any scenic pictures of the farm. It never occurred to me to take any. I only took pictures of guests when they visited. You couldn't have taken these the day we went out there. Where did you get them?"

"I took off from work the following Monday and went back out there. I hope you don't mind. I figured Edith would be there cleaning up and making jam, so I would be able to get into the house. I wish I could have stayed until evening to photograph the stars, but I'm sure my camera wouldn't have done them justice. Anyway, the day was so magical for me I wanted you to see it from my perspective. I'm glad you're pleased with my effort. Now tell me about this mysterious gift you have for me."

"Well, it's not something with a pretty bow you can unwrap, but I hope you will like it. You are not allowed to say a word until I finish my whole spiel. Understood?"

Cullen couldn't imagine what it could possibly be, but she dutifully nodded in agreement.

"Good. Cullen, I knew you confided in Walter about having to marry Tony and the circumstances surrounding it. I made him tell me everything he knew so I wouldn't have to embarrass you by asking direct questions. He told me that since childhood you have dreamt of becoming a doctor. He said you didn't even dare to dream of such a thing anymore because it just made you miserable to think about it. Anyway, I took the liberty of sending in your application to continue your premed studies at St. Louis University along with my glowing recommendation. You have been accepted for next semester, which starts in two weeks. At my urging, they have reinstated your full scholarship. I have arranged with my trust department to cover all book expenses and fees and to give you a monthly stipend equal to your current salary so you don't have to work. If you take an extra class each semester and three classes in the summer, you can finish premed in a year and a half. That's a heavy schedule, but I know you have the ability to handle it. Two Christmases from now, I'm sure you will be halfway through your first year of medical school."

When Andrew stopped for a minute and stared at the fire, Cullen thought he was finished and started to react. Andrew immediately hushed her up and continued.

"I have instructed my trust department to continue tuition and stipends until you have finished your MD. I have also arranged for Shawn to attend a good private school starting next fall. I guess I have covered everything except to tell you that this is an outright gift, not a loan. I can afford it, and it will give me great pleasure to help you achieve your goal. I want to make it absolutely clear to you that there are no strings, no requirements, and no expectations attached to this arrangement. Your life is your own, Cullen. I've told my trust department that this is an irrevocable gift. It was your willingness to give Tony's body to Walter that enabled me to have a new life. It is only fitting that I should return the favor and give you a new life too."

Cullen was dumbfounded, stunned. She just sat there with tears in her eyes, amazed at what she had just heard. It was unbelievable that after so many years adrift on a dark sea of heartache, a fresh wind was finally filling her sails, and she was being brought safely back to shore by this incredibly generous, lovable man. There could be no words to express her feelings. Cullen simply put her arms around Andrew's neck and held him to her. After a full minute or two, she said the uppermost thing in her heart. "I love you, Andrew. I am speechless. You have just made me the happiest, most fortunate, most grateful person in the world."

"Gratitude isn't necessary, Cullen, and neither is love. This gift is yours, free and clear. You are a beautiful young woman inside and out. You deserve to have an opportunity to make your dreams come true. Shakespeare may not have said that we are the stuff of stars, but, although he meant it in a different way, he did say we are the stuff of dreams."

chapter 11

Vail

*T*here were still ten days of winter vacation left before the beginning of second semester and the start of Cullen's new academic journey. Andrew thought it would be fun to take Cullen to Vail and introduce her to skiing before she got too busy and absorbed in her studies. He and Margaret used to go there almost every year for three weeks during Christmas—that is, until he had his accident. He had skied in Switzerland and the Italian Alps and on most of the slopes in Colorado, Utah, and Idaho, but for some reason Vail had always been his favorite. It was the first place he and Margaret had ever gone together; in fact, he had proposed to her there. Maybe he liked Vail best for sentimental reasons, although he had never stopped to analyze his preference. And it never occurred to Andrew that taking Cullen somewhere steeped in memories of Margaret was not a particularly smart move.

Anyway, he convinced Cullen to leave Shawn with Mama Louisa. He took her shopping for boots, two ski outfits, and luggage. Then he chartered a plane so they could fly directly in to the Vail Valley Airport and avoid the long trek from Denver. Cullen had never been on a plane before, never mind a private chartered jet. She told Andrew that stepping onto the plane felt like she was stepping into another world. But when the plane took off, Cullen turned pale and gripped the seat. It was a full five minutes before she let go and seemed to relax a bit. Along the way, they had some finger sandwiches and Brie from the well-stocked fridge and several glasses of good wine. Andrew enjoyed looking down at the snow clouds piling up like mashed potatoes, a pretty good sign that it had been snowing in the mountains and skiing conditions would be great. He thought it odd that Cullen wouldn't look out the window, but he chalked it up to nerves. It was her first flight after all. By the time they reached their destination, Andrew was ready to put on his ski boots.

Vail was beautiful. The snow was a perfect powder with a good base. Andrew offered to send Cullen to ski school or get her a private instructor, but Cullen said it wasn't necessary; she had been water skiing once with no problems. When Andrew warned her that snow skiing was very different, she shrugged and said she would be able to handle it just fine. Andrew had no idea she was terrified of heights, but it became apparent when he had to coax her onto the gondola in Beaver Creek. Andrew was a little exasperated. *Damn, why didn't she tell me she has acrophobia before I brought her skiing?* He held her hand and tried to reassure her she was safe. Andrew tried to get her to enjoy the magnificent view, but Cullen said the gondola seemed to be dangling by a thread, and she was too frightened to look out. By the time they reached the top, Cullen said she was exhausted from the ride, had a headache, and needed to rest before she put on her skis. Andrew offered again to send her to ski school. After he bought her some hot chocolate and sat with her for a few minutes, Cullen insisted he go about his own skiing. She insisted she was all right now and could manage. Andrew gave her some pointers, showed her the green slope, and told her he would meet her at the bottom. He took off slipping and sliding and tumbling down the black slope in Tony's body, once again surprised by the fact that it had no muscle memory for skiing. Frustrated and bruised, Andrew headed for the nearest spot to have a beer and wait for Cullen.

Andrew had a second beer, still waiting for Cullen to come down. The day so far had been a complete bust, not at all what he had envisioned. He was a beginner with skiing again, just like he was with his violin. And Cullen's acrophobia and timidity were a real disappointment as well. He had expected more camaraderie. He had envisioned a happy repetition of his times with Margaret, who had been both a good sport on skis and a great companion, always willing to tag along and try new things. Margaret had been far more adventuresome on her first ski trip. She had laughed at her ineptitude and made it to the bottom out of sheer determination. She had been proud of her accomplishment and wanted to head right back up and try again.

When Cullen finally arrived, she explained that she had lost her nerve. She simply couldn't summon the courage to try to ski down what seemed to her like a sheer cliff. So she sat down on her rear and scooted her way to the bottom, scared to death the whole time that some skier flying by would ski right over her in the process. Andrew offered again to send her to ski school, but Cullen declined, saying she had had all of this sport she wanted. She would rather spend the rest of the week walking around or reading by the fire in their condo. She would be happy enough by herself while Andrew skied. So Andrew contented himself with spending his days alone on the green and then the blue slopes, teaching his body the basics of skiing he had learned over forty years ago. Another real bummer for Andrew.

By the fourth day in Vail, Andrew was aware that his demeanor was changing. He was growing more impatient. He started complaining that the skiers were inconsiderate, whizzing past him right and left, almost knocking him over, that the wait for the ski lifts was way too long, that the snow conditions weren't good now, and that Vail was too crowded and not nearly as much fun as it had been when he and Margaret used to come here. That was the first time Andrew had ever mentioned Margaret in front of Cullen, and he saw her give a little jolt at the mention of Margaret's name.

"So your phantom wife is here at Vail along with my phantom husband. I hope I'm not being measured by a Margaret standard and falling short."

Andrew realized that was exactly what he was doing. He had let down his guard too much. He should never have mentioned Margaret. He really was going to have to be more careful.

"Of course not, Cullen. Why would you even think such a thing? I'm just tired from all the strenuous physical activity I'm not used to anymore."

Cullen didn't say much during dinner and acted like her feelings were hurt, but afterward they went to bed, and everything was forgiven.

Andrew woke to a horrendous headache the next day. He could hardly function. He was irritable and short with Cullen when she tried to help. He asked her to go have breakfast somewhere and give him some space.

Andrew didn't like the way he was acting, but he couldn't help himself. He knew exactly what the problem was, and it made him even more out of sorts. He was experiencing withdrawal symptoms from some of his drugs. He had not wanted Cullen to see him with a suitcase full of pills—twelve vials now, counting the antidepressant that had clearly stopped working. There were too many for him to hide them from Cullen and take surreptitiously. So, despite Walter's warnings, he had left all but the organ rejection one at home. He thought he could surely make it through one week without them. He figured he had enough strength of character and self-awareness to handle any situation that could arise in so short a time. He just needed to keep control. Two more days, and they would be back home. Surely he could manage two more days.

Andrew felt better when he got up to the top of the mountain in the fresh morning air. It had snowed again, and the world around him was really beautiful. There was a woman on the gondola who reminded him so much of Margaret she could have been her sister. This was enough to open all the floodgates of memory for Andrew. How he missed his beloved Margaret, ached for her. Now that he noticed, Vail was permeated with her spirit, her laughter, her smiles, the funny little things she had said and done, the angelic glow of her blonde hair haloed by the sun, the way she cuddled up to him to keep warm while they drank hot chocolate after several runs, the way she had looked at him as if he were the center of the universe when he had proposed, the joy she gave him just by being there. What a fool he had been to bring Cullen here. This was Margaret's place. Andrew now understood very well why Shawn didn't want to go to his dad's restaurant with him. That restaurant was no place for Andrew. Vail was no place for Cullen. He was getting madder by the minute at himself for not realizing this in advance. They were even staying in the same condo he and Margaret had always rented.

By four o'clock, Andrew was down the mountain and having a drink in one of the hotel bars. He thought about Cullen sitting back at Margaret's condo waiting for him to go to dinner, and that made him want another drink for fortification. He had a third one and then a fourth to procrastinate a little longer, and that was enough to make him completely inebriated. Cullen's welcoming smile disappeared the second he came in the door.

"Well, by the looks of it, I'd say you didn't have a very good day skiing."

"Quite the contrary, Cullen. I had a great day skiing. It reminded me of old times."

"I'm glad you enjoyed it. But it's getting late, and I'm starving. Can we go get dinner now?"

"I don't feel like eating right now. Why don't you go by yourself tonight?"

"I don't really like to eat alone, Andrew, especially in a strange place, and I ate breakfast by myself this morning. Please go with me."

"I said I don't feel like it, Cullen. Didn't you hear me? Don't you understand plain English? What's wrong with you?"

Andrew saw Cullen's spine stiffened, as if she were getting ready for a fight. He straightened his spine too, ready for it, if it came to that.

"What's wrong with me? What's wrong with you, Andrew? I have never seen you like this before. And you are obviously drunk. That may explain it, but it scares me. You are not the Andrew I know. You're behaving more like Tony, if you ask me."

"I'm not asking you, and how dare you compare me to Tony, Cullen. I am nothing like that uneducated, uncouth, violent husband of yours."

"Well, you're becoming more and more like him by the minute, Andrew, and I've had enough of Tony to last me several lifetimes. I'm going to dinner by myself now. Don't wait up."

———

Cullen quickly made her exit before she could hear Andrew say anything else to stir up her Irish dander. She was visibly shaking and very, very worried. What had she done to make him so upset? She scoured back over the past few days looking for a clue but couldn't find one. She was at a loss for something to say or do to make things better, put them back to normal. She was beginning to have that old churning in her stomach she used to have when things were bad with Tony. She hadn't felt that pain for three years now and was not happy to see it returning. In a matter of days, things had gone from the "died and gone to heaven" state to the "what in the hell is going on" state. Why was he acting like this? He said he was reminded of old times. He had to be thinking of Margaret and remembering when he had been here with her. Had her rejection of him become unbearable in this special setting? That didn't make a lot of sense since he was still living in the same house he and Margaret had shared and Cullen had been to the farm with him without a problem. No, it had to be something else. Missing Margaret couldn't possibly be the whole story. Not the way he was acting, cruel almost, like Tony. Cullen didn't know why Andrew was acting the way he was, but she definitely knew she didn't like it, not one bit.

Cullen couldn't tell you what she had for dinner, but she ate it very slowly, whatever it was. She wanted to make sure that Andrew was asleep when she returned. He was. She really needed to get to the bottom of this. It occurred to her that maybe Walter could help. She picked up her phone and went into the far bedroom where she couldn't be heard. Just in case.

"It's almost one o'clock in the morning here, Cullen. What's wrong?"

"I'm sorry to be calling so late and waking you up, Walter, but I have a big problem, and I don't know what to do. You seem to be my go-to person where Andrew is concerned."

"Acting a little irritable and impulsive, kind of like Tony?"

"Why, yes! But how did you know?"

"I was afraid this would happen. I warned Andrew not to stop taking his pills."

"What pills, Walter? I see him take his antirejection drug every morning."

"I'm talking about the pills he has to take every day to keep his personality stable."

Walter explained how the pills suppressed the influence of the piece of Tony's brain he had to leave in, and how that affected Andrew if he didn't take them.

"Andrew didn't want you to know he had to take all those drugs because he was afraid it would scare you. He thought he would be okay for a week. I warned him not to try it, but he was sure he could manage. Excessive alcohol exacerbates the situation even when he's on his meds. I can only imagine the effects if he's off them. Cullen, I am so sorry this had to happen, but it's nothing for you to worry about. As long as he takes the pills regularly and doesn't drink too much, he'll be fine. He will be his old self in a couple of days after he gets back."

Cullen couldn't help crying out in horror. "Oh no, Walter! Oh no!" She had no idea Andrew's personality was being artificially maintained and manipulated.

"Walter, do you mean to tell me that the only thing keeping Andrew from not turning into Tony is the concoction of drugs you give him?"

"Well, not exactly, Cullen. Andrew will never turn into Tony, as you put it. Without the meds, he may be irritable and moody sometimes, quarrelsome even, if he drinks too much or is stressed, but Andrew is a decent, nonviolent, generous human being with a loving spirit—soul, you might say. Those are hardwired qualities he brought with him: his habit of mind, his capacity for wisdom, his personhood, his 'Andrewness.' Tony's brain chemistry can't override those attributes. Andrew's brain will still dominate most of the time, and so will his personality. You needn't worry about him becoming Tony."

"But, Walter, what if you die and he can't get the drugs from someone else, or the formula gets lost, or they stop making the drugs? Or he gets to the point where he refuses to take them? What then? Andrew would be spending the rest of his life with an argumentative nature and that irritable edge in his voice I so despised in Tony. Not to be presumptuous, but I could be stuck with a miniversion of Tony on my hands. I don't think I could stand it, Walter."

"Cullen, you are getting unnecessarily worked up over things that are not irreversible. People get personality and behavioral problems just like they get heart problems and cancer. Psychiatrists can usually fix them. That's what psychiatrists do. There will always be drugs available that can help people get back to their normal selves. There's nothing wrong with using medication to keep the brain chemistry in better balance. Whether it's physical or mental, medications can usually take care of our problems or at least ameliorate them. People get worried about the mental aspects of health because they don't understand brains as well as they do bodies. I think most everyone identifies him or herself as a brain that is sacrosanct, the most personal part and not to be messed with. Well, it is the most personal part, but treating an illness or a chemical imbalance in the brain doesn't harm or touch a person's inner essence, that indefinable spark that establishes who a person is. There are exceptions, of course, but they don't apply here. Andrew's a very smart man, Cullen. I know he is aware of his actions and regrets not bringing his pills."

"Walter, you have no idea how frightening it was to see him like that. He turned into Tony before my very eyes."

"You can rest assured that he'll never make that mistake again, Cullen. But if you have concerns or fears about his dependence on pills, then he was correct to worry that you might think something was wrong with him and be alarmed if you saw him taking so many. I hope you can get past this. You've done wonders for Andrew's recovery. I'm aware that he has made arrangements for you to become a doctor, and I know they are not contingent upon your relationship with him. But Andrew's a very special person and a dear friend. I'd love to see the two of you together. Now, it's way past my bedtime. Sleep on all this, Cullen. Don't do anything rash. The effects of the alcohol will be gone by morning. I'm sure he will be much better when he wakes up. And, knowing Andrew, I'm sure he won't take another drink until he's back on his meds. Now I need to get back to my beauty rest. Feel free to call me anytime. Good night, Cullen."

"Good night, Walter. And thanks."

Cullen was relieved to know that the situation was not of her doing, but despite Walter's reassurances, she was more than concerned about Andrew's dependency on drugs to maintain his personality. She had now seen him off of them, and it wasn't something she thought she could or would be able to tolerate. She couldn't stand to see the person she loved so obliterated by Tony's crude behavior, especially when he'd been drinking. That was the worst! Had Andrew been in his former body, it would have been easier to see he was still Andrew, just drunk and out of sorts. But in Tony's body, all she could really see was Tony, or mostly Tony. It was hard to see Andrew in there when he was acting like this. Margaret had said she couldn't love someone she couldn't see. Cullen was beginning to understand what she meant by that.

❦

Andrew slept late. It was eleven o'clock! No wonder Cullen wasn't still in bed, but then, when he excavated the tape from his muddled memory of last night's shameful behavior, he figured she had slept in the other bedroom.

How could he blame her? He took a long shower, lecturing himself on not drinking anymore until he was back on his pills. Drinking destroyed his control. Andrew dressed and looked around the apartment for Cullen so he could apologize and take her to breakfast. He didn't find her, but he did find a letter on the table. *What's with the women in my life and their letters?* he wondered as he picked it up and opened it apprehensively.

My dearest Andrew,

By the time you read this letter, I will be on my way to the Denver airport and headed home. I hate to leave you like this without saying good-bye and thanking you for everything you have done for me, but I am afraid to have any further encounters with you in your current state. I talked to Walter last night, and he told me about your pills. That explains your behavior, which is a relief, but it doesn't fix the problem for me. I cannot begin to convey to you how horrifying it was to watch you turning into the very person I most wanted gone from my life. I couldn't sleep at all last night thinking about it. I don't think I could handle seeing you like that again. And despite Walter's reassurances, I don't think there are any guarantees it couldn't happen again for one reason or another. I know from this experience all too well I don't have the strength to handle vestiges of Tony anymore. I simply cannot take that chance. It could destroy me, and I do have my future and a son to think about.

I love you, Andrew, and I am sure I will never love anyone else, but I think it best to end our relationship now before I become so totally involved emotionally I can't walk away. You have to admit we're a very strange, improbable pair. Last night I couldn't see you anymore; I could only see Tony. Can you begin to imagine how that felt? If we were to continue, I would always live in fear that you could someday become so immune to your drugs you become some version of Tony. I might not be able to see the man I love at all.

It is heart-wrenching to write this letter. You will forever be in my thoughts and prayers.

All my love,

Cullen

Andrew took in a long, slow breath and let it out with a decisive sigh. "Serves me right," he said to himself. "I shouldn't have brought her to Vail. I shouldn't have been drinking so much. I shouldn't have left my pills at home. Cullen can't see me any more than Margaret could." He paced around the room a few minutes, thoughts flying through his head.

"That does it! Enough is enough!" He threw the letter on the table, put on his parka, got his skis, and went up the mountain. He thought he would try the difficult Back Bowls. Maybe he would end up in an avalanche or ski off a cliff. Either way, it was time to end Walter's experiment. God had rescued Job from the dung heap and given him back a wonderful life. Walter wasn't God.

chapter 12

The Gardens

*E*lizabeth read the note scribbled at the top of her manuscript. "I've reread your finished manuscript. Let's have coffee after class and discuss this. Dave." *Oh*, thought Elizabeth to herself, *Dave is it now! So it isn't just my imagination that Dr. Robbins has been subtly flirting with me in class. This could get interesting—and very complicated.*

"It's a perfect day out there, Elizabeth, what I call a Goldilocks day. Not too warm, not too cold, not too breezy. Just right. I'm sure you've never heard that one before, right? Let's walk over to the Duke Gardens. The azaleas are in full bloom, and we can grab a coffee there and take in the spring displays. You painted such a poetic picture of Argo, I thought you might enjoy what we have to offer in the way of beauty here at Duke. Have you been over to the Gardens yet?"

"No, but they're on my list of things to do. I'd love to see them in bloom."

"Well, you can't miss seeing them in bloom. There's a different display for every season. And there are so many different kinds of gardens: a wild garden, a rose garden, a lily pad garden, a Japanese garden, and azaleas of course. I'm sure I left something out. You'll be amazed at how big the place is, right here in the middle of everything. While we're walking, tell me a little about yourself. Your plot is highly unusual, not at all what I'd expect in a creative-writing class. You have a certain mystery about you,

Elizabeth. I don't think I've ever had a student quite like you before. Where are you from?"

"Boston. I mean St. Louis."

"Boston? St. Louis? I thought I was starting with an easy question. Which is it?"

"Well, I was born in Boston, but I've lived more years in St. Louis than anywhere else. I moved here from St. Louis."

"Where did you do your undergraduate work?"

"Radcliffe."

"The Radcliffe Institute for Advanced Studies? No offense meant, but somehow you don't seem like the Women's Studies type. Anyway, that's a graduate program. So, did you go to Harvard?"

"Yes, I meant Harvard. My mother was a graduate of Radcliffe when it was still a women's college, before Harvard went coed. I've always called it that for sentimental reasons."

"So you and your parents live in St. Louis now?"

"No. I mean yes."

"I tripped you up again with one of my hard questions. There has to be a story behind that answer, Elizabeth."

"I was born in Boston. My parents died a long time ago. I was adopted by a wonderful couple in St. Louis who lost their only child. I really don't like to talk about me. Let me keep a little of my mystery, as you call it. What's your history?"

"Well, I went to Yale—PhD in American lit. Thesis was on the twentieth-century American novel. Became more interested in writing than reading. Published a few things that got decent reviews. So here I am. Thirty-six years old. Not married. No significant other. No criminal record. Hate spectator sports. Love opera. That about sums it up. The little cafe I was talking about is right over there. You sit here in the gazebo and take it all in while I go get us some coffee."

Elizabeth was glad for a chance to get off the personal stuff. He was making her nervous, very uncomfortable. He was obviously a little nervous as well, trying too hard to be cute and casual. Elizabeth wondered why he should be nervous. After all, he was the professor; she was just a graduate student. She realized she could have a problem on her hands if he asked her out. She knew it wasn't a good idea to get involved with your professor, at least not before the semester was over, but if he wanted a date, why not? The only person she was really interested in didn't even know she existed. And besides that, he was taken already. She absorbed the beautiful vista from the gazebo overlooking flowers cascading down the tiered garden to the pond. She saw one man lounging on the grass on the far side. She was surprised more people weren't out enjoying it.

"Thanks for the coffee, Dr. Robbins."

"Dave, please. Call me Dave. Let's sit on that bench over there in the shade. Get out your manuscript. I have a few places marked I would like to discuss. Okay. One thing that I find a little unrealistic about your characters is that you've made them all superlative types. They are all brilliant, fabulous, beautiful people for the most part, all fairy-tale princesses and knights in shining armor. There are no ordinary people riding mules. Is this your real experience in life?"

"Well, just how many people with mules do you know, Mr. Yale PhD, Duke professor, and opera lover? Were you first exposed to bel canto living in the projects?"

"Ouch! You bite hard, lady. Rather defensive, aren't you? But point taken. I guess you can't write convincingly about what you haven't been exposed to, but surely you have known some smart ugly ducklings or some pretty, dumb blondes. There are plenty of them running around this campus. Not everyone made straight eight hundreds on their college boards."

"First of all, the story takes place in the rarified air of two first-class universities, Washington University in St. Louis and Duke. Maybe not all the students are exceptional, but the faculties are quite strong. Nobel laureates, etcetera. Brilliance and extraordinary pulchritude are both essential to my characters. Walter would not be pioneering brain transplants if he had been a C student. Being a brilliant neuroscientist makes Andrew's demotion in professional status more troublesome for him and also makes him a perfect candidate for analyzing the effects of his brain transplant on his sense of self. Because Andrew still loved Margaret, it would have taken an especially beautiful woman to get his attention. By the way, I did say Margaret was attractive, not beautiful, creative and talented but not brilliant. The fact that Andrew could not love Cullen despite her beauty says something about the nature of love. True love is not fickle. The kind of love I deem valuable is love that makes no comparisons, that has no reference point beyond the beloved. The lovers don't even see the surface anymore. They focus on and bond with what is inside. That is why Cullen could fall in love with Andrew. That is why Andrew can't love anyone but Margaret. My explanation isn't perfect, but you get the drift."

"You have strong opinions and a very aesthetic, poetic sense of what love is. If that's the kind of love you're offering to some lucky man, I want to be first in line or at least on the waiting list."

He smiled and looked at Elizabeth as if he were trying to judge her reaction to what he just said. Elizabeth couldn't help but smile back. He really was cute.

"Now back to your manuscript. You need to do a little rewrite in places. The dialogue is good, but in some places there is too much and in other places not enough of it. I want you to show me more and tell me less. Let the dialogue reflect more of the action. A good example of dialogue is your use of Walter. You've made him your Greek chorus. Every time Walter comes into the picture, he throws some clarity on the situation. The chapter on Argo is one of my favorites, one little spot of pure joy. Rather poetic in spots. In fact, now that I think about it, I see poetic descriptions quite often in your writing. You must have a drawer full of poetry you have written over the years. You have a poet's sensitivity."

"Thank you, Dave. I'll take that as a compliment."

Dave flashed another big smile and continued.

"I do like the way you've made the events flow so naturally into one another. That love scene was by far the most vivid I have ever read from a student. And from a man's point of view! You handled it quite deftly. There just wasn't enough of it. If you want to get published, you need more sex, and it needs to be more explicit. That's what readers expect these days, and they tend to be a little disappointed if they don't get it."

"I'm interested in the quality of love, not that the quality of sex is unimportant. I just prefer to approach sex a little more obliquely. I think the power of suggestion fires the imagination, and the sex becomes whatever a person's fantasy dictates, rather like Salome in her seven veils, shedding them one by one, down to the last but not the last. Tantalizing, but something left to the imagination."

Dave was gazing at Elizabeth with a quizzical look.

"Your comments are rather mature for someone your age. How old are you anyway?"

"About twenty-four or twenty-five. I took a break after Harvard for a few years. I lose track."

"You certainly write with more maturity than your age would suggest. Anyway, where was I? Oh yes, the Christmas gift chapter. It sets up a contrast between Shawn's disillusionment with prayer and his mother's new need for it and the cathartic release it brings her. Nice touch. Now we get to the Vail chapter. This is where we run into problems. Interior monologues here are okay, even though you have to change points of view several times. It does allow us to learn more about Andrew and Cullen. The problem here is I don't think the conflict over Andrew's change in personality is motivation enough for Cullen to walk out. It's not realistic. A woman in her situation would not give up her opportunity for a better life so easily, especially if she loves Andrew as much as you imply. Walter tried to assure her she had nothing to worry about. Shouldn't the kind of love you were talking about a few minutes ago accommodate whatever is required? Once again you have terminated your story without coming to a resolution acceptable to the reader. You end it at a dark moment, and yet it isn't as dark as each of them has experienced and overcome before. I refuse to let you have it just fizzle out like this prematurely. You have built Cullen and Andrew into characters we care about. You can't just let Cullen run away and Andrew ski off into oblivion. The ending needs to be more definitive, inevitable, not to say predictable. I feel the major themes of the story are lost, like they didn't really matter."

"I disagree that they are lost. Andrew has been confronted at every turn, especially in the Vail chapter, with the fact that his emotional make-up is not totally controlled by his brain. He can think all he wants and reason all he wants, but his emotions and his behavior are subject to influences beyond his control. His physical presentation in the world is at odds with how he perceives himself. Instead of embracing his new body and his new life, he has remained separate from them. His reference point is always Margaret and his former life, the way things used to be. It is his false expectation to resume his old life that causes his problems. Andrew has underestimated his new life and has failed to value it. Even though he hasn't articulated it to us, he does realize that he isn't the same person he was before the accident. He can't accept the person he now is, and the women he cares about can't accept that person either. This is why he is through with it. If he were just his brain as he has always contended, he shouldn't be having such a problem. At least that's how I see it and what I'm trying to convey."

Elizabeth realized that Dave seemed to have his mind elsewhere; he was looking at her, but she had the impression what she was saying wasn't registering. Was he daydreaming? Elizabeth was trying to make an important point, so she started speaking a little louder. He snapped to.

"And as for Cullen, Dave, maybe your problem with her decision to leave Andrew shows your own romantic bias that love conquers all. Cullen is a smart woman with a strong sense of self-preservation even though she has a heart. She would not divorce Tony even though he beat her because of Shawn's relationship with his dad. It was a conscious sacrifice she was willing to make for her son's sake. She was abused by Louisa, but she would not leave her out of pity, her sense of humanity. Louisa had Alzheimer's and no one left to care for her. It was a conscious sacrifice she was willing to make because she has some compassion for helpless human beings. Andrew, on the other hand, is neither helpless nor in love with her. In his case, the sacrifice was too great because she wasn't making it for anyone but herself. She also has a new sense of herself as headed toward her dream of being a doctor. Although Andrew is the only man Cullen has ever loved, she does not trust her ability to love him unconditionally when he presents himself as her former husband whom she loathed. She is afraid she would not be able to see that 'Andrewness' she was blaming Margaret of not being able to see. She said that if he were in his own body, she could see him as just drunk and out of sorts, but in Tony's body with Tony-like behavior, all she could see was Tony. And that gets us back to the nature of love. Does love have as much to do with the self as with the other? Does it depend on time and circumstances? Can it be unconditional? Can you love someone you cannot see? Cullen has reached the same conclusion as Margaret, it seems. So the story has come full circle and ends."

"You're pretty good at defending your position, Elizabeth, but I don't think what you have said is all that clear in your story as written. I'm not going to let you off the hook that easily. First of all, I don't think you have adequately shown that Andrew realizes that he is not just his brain or that he has really rejected the person he now is. I want more story. I want you to explore other aspects of these themes. Walter had suggested that Andrew go to Duke or somewhere he is unknown except by reputation. I want to know what happens if he does that. If he is in a place where the whole package, as you put it, is what he presents walking in the door, and no one is freaked out because he's in a different body or the father's body or the husband's body. He will not have to have the bifurcated life he hates. He can just be who he now is. Does he embrace his new self in the new environment? I don't mean to be hard on you here, but see, there is still a lot to explore."

"I'm really ready to be through with this story, Dave. I've been working on it all semester. I want to write about something entirely different. Please let me quit and start something else. If I continue, it could get really complicated. I may not be able to think of an ending that works for you. You seem to want everything to be all wrapped up neatly and end happily ever after. I told you before, life most often falls short, disappoints. Despite all planning, all hoping, all trying, all best efforts, most lives have less than happy endings, especially if measured from the distance of early promise and potential."

"My, my, so pessimistic at such an early age. You sound like some older woman who has had more than her fair share of disappointments in life. Don't be so cynical, Elizabeth. Life can be beautiful and wonderful and joyous."

"Is that why you're age thirty-six and without a significant other right now, because life is so wonderful and joyous?"

"That's two zingers in a row, Elizabeth. Sarcasm is unbecoming and unwarranted. It is also unkind. You're paying tuition for my opinions and feedback. I'm not trying to be a jerk. You're the best student I've had here. I'm setting high standards for you because I want to help you develop into a real star. How about calling a truce and letting me take you to dinner Friday night? Not to be presumptuous, but maybe we can start working on the joyous part together. I know a little Italian restaurant not too far from here that actually has ricotta pie on the menu. Will you allow me to take you there?"

"My better judgment tells me not to, but I absolutely adore ricotta pie."

chapter 13

Time to Go

"Good morning, Andrew. Got the coffee on? I stopped by the deli and picked up some bagels and lox and cream cheese. I figured you would be in no shape to run."

Andrew showed Walter into the den and went to the kitchen for plates and coffee.

"Do you want the lecture now or later, Andrew? You must never stop taking your pills again. I tried to warn you. Don't even stop them for one day. Don't even think about stopping them for one day. Doctor's orders. Have you got that now?"

"Aw, cut me some slack, Walter. But I was right about the possibility of Cullen being freaked out about the pills. I'm going to frighten away every woman I ever date when she sees me popping twelve pills. Can't you combine a few things and make it three or four? Even six or seven, maybe? Better yet, Walter, let me out of our stupid agreement. I'm really fed up with this experiment. Just let me put an end to my misery. This is not a life I want to live. I have no reason to continue this charade of being me. Without Margaret, without my life before the accident, my former life, I can't find any purpose to continue except to validate your experiment. I don't want to be your research project anymore. What difference does it really make if my brain continues to age at the old rate or resets itself in a younger body with a younger chemical environment? At the very least, you have enabled a person to continue living a life unhampered by a disabled body. I almost went skiing into the sunset in Vail. Given the emotional state I was in, I don't know why I didn't. Something stopped me at the last minute. I guess I felt I owed it to you not to ruin your experiment. That's a really pathetic reason to continue living. If you weren't my very best friend, I would have ended it right then and there, now that I can do it on my own, unlike before."

"Of course it matters if the brain resets! You know the implications of that as well as I do. And did you hear yourself say that at the least I have enabled a person to continue living unhampered by a disabled body? The operative phrase there is 'to continue living,' Andrew, not to commit suicide after all we have been through. And all because you don't think you have anything left to live for, to contribute to life? You think the only possible you is the former you? You think that you have lost all your authenticity? Really? If you are only your brain as you contend, how is that possible? If you have no ideas left worth exploring in your field of research, why did you bother to write a new grant proposal? Why did you allow your name to be placed in contention for a position at Duke, and why did they offer you the position, a named professorship at that, if you aren't worth having, if you have no further potential? If you have nothing left to enjoy in life, why are you still practicing your violin so much? If you don't think you can ever love anyone but Margaret, why have you been courting Cullen? Don't say you aren't really interested in her. I know better. All those actions imply a future. You are a brilliant man, Andrew. You have built a fabulous career with spectacular results because you have always said, 'What if.' Why can't you apply that method of exploration to your new life? Where is your sense of intellectual adventure and spirit? Why aren't you curious about what kind of life might be possible for you? What kind of life might you be able to create that *is* worth living if you only give yourself the opportunity to do so?"

"You always make it sound so simple, Walter, but you aren't the one having to live it."

"Oh for God's sake, Andrew, quit your bellyaching! Accept the job at Duke and get out of St. Louis. Start over. You'll meet a whole new world of people, some who may know that you had a body transplant, but they don't know what you looked like before, so it doesn't matter. You can just be who you are, and everyone will accept you as you are. I wish I were in your shoes, with another thirty or forty years left to work and see the results of my efforts take hold and turn into a useful reality. Just think what good your own research can produce. And you have the luxury of time to see it all come to fruition. Besides that, Andrew, the psychological problems you are having are worth analyzing to see how they could be ameliorated in future transplants if I ever get another opportunity to do one. No one can analyze that better than you. Only you can know what could be done differently to improve your outcome or ability to adjust."

"Well, one thing I can tell you for sure right now! If it's always going to be necessary to retain a small portion of the right anterior frontal lobe, then the body donor should be from the same socioeconomic class and the same ethnicity, and the same education and temperament more or less, if possible. The closer those demographics match the brain donor, the less need for so many pills to maintain personality, and therefore less psychological conflict. Tony was just too far removed from me in every way."

"So I am supposed to find a WASP with a PhD, born with a silver spoon in his mouth, who is a good violinist and tennis player and who is contemplative and well mannered. Is that all? Do you even know how lucky I was to find anyone at all with a young, healthy body who was brain-dead and available, Andrew? I could have searched the rest of my life without coming across someone who fit your demographics. But I see your point, and I agree that, given a choice, I would choose the closer match. It would indeed make the transition easier. For everyone."

Walter stopped lecturing to take a few bites of his bagel and sip some coffee. Andrew went to the kitchen to brew some more. He needed a little time to process some of the things Walter was saying. Walter didn't waste any time continuing as soon as Andrew reappeared.

"Dare I mention Cullen? She called me from the airport to tell me about the note she left you. She was worried that it was too strong and didn't show enough appreciation for what you have done for her. She was afraid that you would think her ungrateful and callous. She even mentioned that maybe she should turn down your gift, but I know she wasn't serious because she went on to say that she was excited about starting classes. I told her that what happened between you two was totally separate from the gift, that what would hurt you most would be for her not to allow you the privilege of helping her and Shawn. She seemed to accept my comment a little too quickly, so I'm almost positive she had no intentions of turning it down. It was just a gesture she thought she should make. I wished her luck in her studies and told her to feel free to call Uncle Walter anytime. I thought you might like to know about that."

"Thanks, Walter. I couldn't have handled it better myself. It's probably for the best that it ended, though, for her sake as well as mine. I'm not sure I could have given her the love she deserves. I just hate that it ended the way it did. On the other hand, if it hadn't been something like that, it probably wouldn't have ended, and I would be left in the untenable position of always being one pill away from Tony in her eyes. And I would forever be reminded of being in Tony's body. At least at Duke, there will be no Tony reference. I will just be me on a bad day, if it comes to that."

"All right then, Andrew, get on with it. Call Duke tomorrow. No, call today. Accept the job and ask the secretary to find suitable temporary housing for you. You can contact a realtor to look for a home in Durham or Chapel Hill when you get there. Have Charles take care of selling the house and the farm. All you have to do is pack. I don't want you to think I'm trying to get rid of you, Andrew, but the sooner you leave the faster you can move on to your new life. Too many ghosts here and too much heartache."

Andrew was silent for a few minutes, envisioning his new life, masquerading around in Tony's body but without the stigma and baggage of Tony attached. He felt the enormous burden he had been carrying around since the operation fall away. He would no longer be a freak. He would no longer be somebody's son, somebody's daddy, somebody's phantom husband. He would simply be himself, different from his old self but himself just the same.

"Okay, Walter, you've convinced me. I'll go. I'll do it now but with one caveat: I'm not selling Argo. I did some of my best thinking there and made some of my best memories there, so I have a strong attachment to it. I don't need the money, so I don't need to sell it right now, and George and Edith do need employment. I want to keep them on as caretakers. Besides, Margaret loves the farm too. I left the title in both of our names because she may want to come back and visit her old friends sometime after I leave. You and Rose might even enjoy going out for a day in the country once in a while. It'll also give me a base of operation if I come back to visit you. I'm just making up excuses now because I'm emotionally unprepared to sell it. I may never come back to St. Louis; in fact, I probably won't. I'm through with St. Louis. You're going to have to come to Duke if you want to see me. But I still want to keep Argo for now. If I find a wonderful property in North Carolina to take its place, then I will have Charles check with Margaret to see if she wants to keep it or wants to sell. If Margaret doesn't want it, I might give it to George and Edith or talk them into moving to North Carolina to take care of my new place. Who knows?"

chapter 14

Duke

The Doris Duke Gardens were in their full spring glory when Andrew walked over from the medical school and sat down on the grass near the pond. Watching the koi was something he always found relaxing after a morning in the lab. Andrew had been coming here ever since he arrived at Duke over three years ago and never tired of basking in the beauty these gardens provided, no matter the season. Walter had been right about Duke. He was accepted without reservations by his colleagues and postdocs. He no longer felt besieged or defensive. Once in a while, he would get asked at a faculty party how hard it was to adjust to being in another person's body, but the questions were purely scientific curiosity and not judgmental. It had now been over six years since the operation, so he could be a little more objective about the experience. At last he could let down his guard and just be Dr. Andrew Hamilton, holder of an endowed chair in the neurosciences, with the entire litany of accomplishments implied by that title. He was beginning to settle into his new life, beginning to be more comfortable in his new skin. His violin practice was even improving. Sitting here with the azaleas blooming and the daffodils and tulips cascading down the tiered levels from the gazebo across the pond, Andrew was reminded of the glorious spring greetings he used to get out at Argo, the whole hillside full of daffodils and lilacs. It was a magnificent sight! Edith would fill every vase at the farm with the daffodils, and Margaret would gather a whole tub full of lilac blossoms to take back to the city. Their fragrance permeated the house as strongly as Margaret's love and personality permeated his life. Oh, how he missed her still. Andrew drew in a deep breath and released it in a sigh. *Ah, Margaret, if only you were here with me now. Life would be almost perfect.*

Andrew checked his iPhone for messages. One was from Walter giving him an update on Cullen, who was now finishing her second year of med school and doing well. Shawn was making straight As at his private school. Louisa had died after a long illness. Cullen said she probably would have died a lot sooner, but she was trying to hang on for Tony to return. Finally her heart just gave out. He and Rose had been out to the farm several times. Everything seemed to be fine there. The last time they were there, Edith had made them a splendid fried chicken dinner with all the trimmings and a lemon meringue pie. He now understood why Andrew was reluctant to sell the farm and why he wanted to keep George and Edith around. More pills were in the mail. He'd finally been able to combine several of them, so there were now only nine, still a lot but better. Walter kept strict control over the medications and personally saw to their formulation, working directly with the manufacturers. He was not going to let anything derail Andrew's brain chemistry through accident or negligence. He even had Charles put a copy of the formulas with names of the manufacturers in his law firm's vault with his patents and will so they would always be available if something happened to him. *That's Walter for you*, thought Andrew, *meticulous to the last tiny detail.* And Mama Louisa? Andrew could imagine her on her deathbed, unable to understand why he'd left and hadn't returned when she was dying, hoping to the very end that he would. Andrew wondered if he would have gone back to see her if Cullen had told him Louisa was dying. He really didn't know the answer to that but probably not. He could imagine the deathbed scene, and it would have been excruciating for him. He hadn't dealt with being Tony since he got to Duke and had no interest in making a return appearance in that role. He also didn't know how he would feel if he saw Cullen again. She had been a refreshing, rejuvenating breeze at a time he most needed to move on from his stagnant past, to be freed from his old life. But that was three years ago. Life was becalmed again but in a better place. Andrew liked it here.

Right now it was a soft sunny day in the Gardens with the faintest of breezes and a strikingly good-looking blonde sitting just across the pond from him, talking in animated fashion on her cell phone. Andrew only noticed her because she reminded him of Margaret forty-five years ago when he was at Harvard and she was at Radcliffe. They were in a play together, and it had been love at first sight.

"Hello, Dr. Hamilton. I thought I recognized you sitting here. I could never forget a handsome young man like you. I'm Sarah Brenner. We met briefly over at the faculty club several weeks ago. Mind if I sit here and enjoy the sunshine with you?" The voice belonged to a reasonably attractive woman who looked to be in her fifties. Andrew was having trouble placing her.

"By all means, have a seat. Call me Andrew, by the way. I have to leave shortly to get back to the lab, but I still have a couple of minutes."

"I'm actually through for the day. Just finished teaching my graduate seminar in epistemology. You know, that knowing about knowing stuff. I recall someone saying you're a neuroscientist, so I guess we have something in common. Sometimes I deal with the brain, though I must say my approach is different from yours. You look under the hood to see how it works. When I deal with it, I'm looking out the windshield to see where it goes."

Andrew wondered what drug she was on. Her search for commonality was a real stretch that required imagination, but then stretching the imagination was what philosophy did. He really didn't know how to respond to her casual shop chatter, so he simply nodded and let her continue.

"I'm having one of my little music nights at my house next weekend, something I do every once in a while. Several of us have retrieved our old instruments out of mothballs and enjoy making a lot of noise and a little music together. Nothing serious. No one is in the least professional, but we have fun. I'm the pianist for the group. Do you have an old instrument gathering dust in the closet that you could take out and join us? We have a great time, lots of food and drink, and I would love to have an interesting, handsome man to add to the group."

Spontaneity was not Andrew's long suit. He hesitated for a minute, not knowing how to respond to an invitation from someone he didn't know. But then, what harm could come of it? She was on the humanities faculty and not from the medical school, and it was a music affair. He could always give an excuse at the last minute if he changed his mind later.

"Well, I do enjoy music, and I have an old violin. I'm truly not very good. I don't have a lot of dexterity anymore. Why don't I come and be your audience. After I see your level of play, I will decide if I can comfortably join you and not embarrass myself."

"Believe me, Andrew, we park all our musical exegesis and better judgment outside the front door. It truly is a safe haven for mediocrity. I don't know what our students would think if they could hear how bad we sound. They would probably laugh till they peed in their pants. Fortunately, this is a faculty-only gathering, just not for anyone from the Music Department. Come and bring your violin. I promise you will be playing with us before the night is over. Seven o'clock sharp this coming Saturday. I will send you my address and directions through the campus mail."

"Thanks for the invitation. It actually sounds like fun. Can I bring anything?"

"Yes, your violin."

Andrew had only been to a few faculty parties since he arrived, mostly medical school functions. He was beginning to feel comfortable enough to branch out a little, and this invitation struck his fancy as something that might get him back into playing his violin in public again. He really had worked hard to regain some proficiency. He wasn't back all the way to his former level of play, but he wasn't that bad either. At least it would be worth one evening of his time to see if he fit. But Sarah was a piece of work. He remembered all the leading comments and propositions he got back before his accident from neglected faculty wives and bold graduate students. He knew a woman on the make when he saw one: the body language, the looks, the offhanded comments. Sarah had them all down pat, plus a directness that normally would have sent him running in the opposite direction. Something appealed to him about her. Her self-confidence. Her maturity. She had a take-charge manner about her that reminded him of Margaret. It had been a very long time since Andrew had had a conversation with a woman near his own psychological age, no one really since Margaret left, unless one insisted on counting Mama Louisa.

⁓

Sarah answered the door in a skintight jumpsuit with a martini in her hand. "Come on in, handsome. Hey, everyone, this is Andrew and his violin. Introduce yourselves and make him feel at home. What are you drinking tonight, handsome? I have everything you could possibly want."

"A little red wine if you have some open. Otherwise a weak scotch and water, with an emphasis on the weak. I usually don't drink much."

"Well, while I get your red wine, grab a violin score over there on the piano and find a spot to settle down. We are going to murder some Mozart tonight. 'Eine Kleine Nachtmusik,' to be exact."

Sarah had not been kidding. As promised, they did murder Mozart. But it was fun to be playing in a group again and not be self-conscious about technique. He was actually better than most of the players. He hesitated calling them musicians. Sarah was a passable pianist—that is, when she wasn't trying to catch up with the cellos, who were racing toward the end of a section so they could have another drink. All in all, it was a surprisingly enjoyable evening. Walter would be proud of him. He would have to send Walter a text: "Acted almost thirty-six tonight." Andrew was glad he had come.

"Thanks for an entertaining evening, Sarah. I'm glad you ran into me in the Gardens."

"My dear Andrew, that was no accident. I have been looking for you ever since I saw you at the faculty club. Someone told me you often go over to the Gardens late mornings or early afternoons. Our Department of Defense and Homeland Security should study the efficiency of our communication system around here. Everyone knows everything about everybody. Nothing stays secret on this campus for very long. I also know you aren't married. More importantly, I know that you are actually older than I am. Tucked away inside that fabulous body of yours is a sixty-six-year-old brain. You are someone I definitely want to know better, much better. And you play the violin extremely well. I think we should play some real music together, maybe some violin and piano sonatas. I have an extensive library of scores for piano and violin. My late husband and I spent many wonderful hours playing duets. How about next Friday night? Around six? I cook better than I play. I'll fix something simple for an early dinner, and we can play as late as you want. I won't take no for an answer. I'm battling cancer. Time is of the essence. *Tempus* is *fugiting.* Carpe diem and all that. See you next Friday, Andrew."

chapter 15

Margaret

"Margaret, how wonderful to hear from you! What a pleasant surprise! Where are you?"

"I'm here in St. Louis, Walter. I need some medical tests done, so instead of driving all the way down to San Francisco, I decided to fly back here to see my old internist at Barnes Hospital and visit some of my friends while I'm waiting for results."

"What are you doing for lunch tomorrow? I'd love to see you and catch up on things. It's been at least five years."

"I know. Seems longer than that. I can do a late lunch tomorrow, say around one thirty if that works for you. I have tests all morning."

"That'll be fine. I'll meet you at Trattoria Alfredo in Clayton. One thirty."

"Trattoria Alfredo? That's one of Andrew's favorite haunts. It will be great to see you, Walter. I look forward to it."

Walter hung up the phone. He was indeed surprised that she had returned. One of her old friends must have told her that Andrew had moved away and the house had been sold, or else Charles did. He wondered what kind of tests Margaret was having. She was always very athletic and the picture of health. Of course, stress could take a real toll on the healthiest of persons, and Margaret was under severe stress throughout the years following Andrew's accident and then surgery and rehab, not to mention the crazy media frenzy afterward and the divorce. Walter remembered their long talks about the right course of action, given Andrew's new physical age. He was moved by Margaret's extreme anguish over the fact that she would need to end their marriage. He envied the strength of her love.

———

Walter was already seated in the far corner of the restaurant when Margaret arrived. She was smartly dressed in a St. John suit, and her lovely, still-blonde hair was neatly pulled back to the nape of her neck. She looked more like a corporate executive or financial advisor than a … than a what? Grieving widow? Bitter divorced woman? Walter couldn't put his finger on how he had pictured Margaret in his mind. He knew she was smart, creative, strong-willed, and self-confident. He had even bought and read her book of poetry that came out several years ago. Her poems exposed a certain vulnerability, a sensitivity he had not expected. It was a collection of previously published works from *The New Yorker* and various poetry magazines. Walter had always thought her attractive, almost beautiful when she was smiling. As she approached his table, he rose to greet her. He didn't see any evidence of stress in her face. She certainly didn't look sixty-six.

"Margaret, you look wonderful. I would say California has been treating you well. I remember that you like their veal piccata, so I took the liberty of ordering for us. How were your tests this morning, and, more importantly, why were you having them, if I may ask as an old friend?"

"I've been having swollen lymph nodes for some time now and finally decided I should get them checked. They suspect some sort of cancer, Walter. I shouldn't have waited so long. You know I had endometrial cancer thirty years ago and had to have a radical hysterectomy along with radiation and chemo. I guess I suspected it might be cancer again, and I just didn't want to face all that a second time. Anyway, the tests are to confirm what kind it is and what stage. That will take a while. Andrew didn't sell the farm, so I'm staying out there most of the time while I'm waiting. Argo is so lovely. I have always found it an inspiration for my poetry. I haven't written much lately though. Just haven't been in the right frame of mind since losing Andrew."

"You didn't lose Andrew, Margaret; you left him, remember?"

"Oh, Walter, let's not fight about that again. You of all people know how hard that was for me to do. I should have won an Academy Award for my convincing performance. Only my deep love for Andrew enabled me to act the way I did and write that letter. You and I both agreed that it had to end at some point, for Andrew's sake, because of the age difference. We just disagreed about what would be the best way for Andrew. You thought we should string it out until it eventually disintegrated. I was unwilling to watch our wonderful marriage unravel thread by thread until all that was left was a heart-wrenching, guilt-ridden pile of recriminations and regret. I know Andrew well enough to know he would never have forgiven himself for walking away from me, even though it was the only answer. He would have considered it selfish, disloyal, and reprehensible. So I made it my fault and left him. '*The coward does it with a kiss, the brave man with a sword.*' I forget who said it, but he was right on. Whatever pain has to be inflicted, swiftly is better than the daily dread of the inevitable. I'm sure, in retrospect, that I did the right thing. It enabled him to move on with his new life. Charles tells me that he is in love. With Costello's wife, no less. That's a very big surprise. Did she move to Duke with him?"

"Charles told you that? He must not have been talking with Andrew about anything personal for some time. He's way behind the curve. That relationship ended over three years ago. No need to go into details. She approached him. Andrew was infatuated with her looks but still ambivalent about the relationship. He wasn't really in love with her, Margaret; she didn't measure up to you. That is why he didn't pursue her when it ended. And to my knowledge, he's still in love with you. Part of his problem all along has been his inability to let go of his former life. You were and are the centerpiece of that life."

"Well, I so much wanted him to find someone to love and marry and start a family. Still do. After all he has been through, he deserves another chance at a happy life."

"What about you, Margaret? Have you found the happy life you deserve? Are you seeing anyone? You still have too much life left not to be sharing it with someone."

"Heavens no, Walter! Andrew's too hard an act to follow. No one could ever measure up. Besides, Walter, I'm an incurable romantic; I'll never stop loving him. We'll be together again in the afterlife. Of that I'm sure. I may have to search through every level of Dante's hell to find him, but I will, and I'll take him up to heaven with me, where he belongs, agnostic or not."

"Margaret, I don't mean to play devil's advocate here, but what if he still looks like Tony then or has no form at all? What if he is just his mind, invisible but conscious? Or just his soul? You still won't be able to see Andrew. How would you find him then? Tell me, truthfully, Margaret, did you just make up that bit about not being able to see him, of not being able to love someone you cannot see? Was there any tiny smidgen of Andrew you could detect after the surgery?"

"Well, after I managed to get over the enormous shock of seeing him for the first time, and it was unbelievably shocking, I did search for clues that he was indeed Andrew and not some imposter. Of course, I knew it was Andrew. I could see all the old familiar facial expressions and gestures, and as a poet I recognized his use of language, syntax, vocabulary, and also his sense of humor, habits of mind, sensitivity, preferences, memory, and things like that. So there were many remnants of Andrew I could see, yes, especially when his personality drugs were working right. But he wasn't the same Andrew; he wasn't my Andrew."

"The things you have just named all emanate from Andrew's brain; it's what remains of Andrew, who he is and all he is. His self, his essence. He's the same candy, just housed in a different wrapper, Margaret."

"It's too different a wrapper, Walter. Way too young."

"Then, if he had received a body more his own age, even if it were an older version of Anthony Costello, would you have been able to accept him as the husband you love? Would you have resumed your life as his wife? Think about it before you answer, Margaret. This is not a frivolous question I'm asking. It's important in terms of my research. Andrew told me the body donor needed to be more like him in age, ethnicity, and socioeconomic status. That of course was impossible, and for the purpose of my research, I needed it to be a young, healthy body in order to determine age's effect on the brain. But in the future, when we are beyond the research phase, I need to know if a significant age difference alone is the marriage breaker or if it is more than that."

"I'm not sure how to answer that question, Walter. I do think Andrew is right about the age issue, for cultural as well as physiological reasons. If Andrew had been in Iraq or Afghanistan and had come back badly burned and disfigured in the face with several limbs missing, I would have welcomed him home with open arms. And I know that my love would be strong enough to accept this new version of my husband, strong enough not to recoil at the sight of him, no matter how disfigured. He would still be my beloved husband on the inside. I would just have to get used to him again. And if he were later able to have a face transplant or a body transplant from someone the same age, he would certainly look like a totally different person, but he would still be my husband. On the inside, I would hope him to still be the same person I had always loved, acknowledging of course that he couldn't be completely the same. One likes to think that one's love is strong enough to meet those kinds of challenges, that one's humanity and compassion would take over while adjusting to the new reality. One thing is for certain though; it would not be an easy transition. A weak marriage would never make it. There could be a lot of emotional debris left in the wake of destroyed relationships, married or not."

"That's definitely something to consider when determining if a person is a suitable prospect for such surgery. But you didn't really answer my specific question, Margaret. You said in your letter to Andrew, at least in the draft you gave me, that you could not love someone you could not see. Yet you told me a few minutes ago you could see many remnants of Andrew. Was that a reason you made up for Andrew's sake, or did you really mean it? I've never known a couple with a stronger marriage than you and Andrew had, so it is very important to know. Would you have loved Andrew and remained happily married to him if he'd been put into the body of a sixty-year-old version of Anthony Costello?"

"I believe I would. I would certainly hope I could. I would try my best to make it work. I would will it. But in truth, Walter, I don't really know. I don't think anyone could possibly know how she would feel and what she would do until she's in the situation."

"Margaret! So much for romantic love. So much for searching through every level of hell to find Andrew in the afterlife if you aren't sure you could embrace him here on earth unless he looked like his former self. The body is just the shell, Margaret. Just the cover on the book. Andrew would still be there. Even you, by your own admission, could see the important pieces of him. Surely you don't have to see all of him to love him. Surely you would love him still. All it requires is getting used to the difference. You still have all the shared bibliography of experience, a history that doesn't require explanation about what you mean when you say something. Is that not worth the effort?

"You're being awfully hard on me, Walter. Here's our food. Let's eat before it gets cold. No wine?"

"I'm still a working man, Margaret. I can't drink in the middle of a workday. I ordered us both tea because I seem to remember you never like to drink alone."

"That's very thoughtful of you, Walter. Are you still mad about my leaving Andrew abruptly instead of inching away like you wanted me to?"

"No, no. We're way past that. I'm just disappointed that you aren't certain you could stay with Andrew under those circumstances. If your marriage couldn't successfully make the transition, I don't think anyone's could. This means a terribly disabled veteran would have to decide which is more important: keeping a marriage or gaining a usable body again. No one should have to make that kind of decision. Keeping the person you love and getting a new lease on life should not be mutually exclusive options."

"My impression is that very often marriages can't survive the hardship caused by those extreme injuries, so they would be over long before any surgery could be arranged anyway. Others would fail because they are based on the need to be needed, which is not a strong foundation for a marriage either. It would be interesting to know if studies have been done and what the findings were. I personally think most women would feel honor bound to stay in the marriage initially, but I think many of the marriages would tank under the strain eventually. Half of all marriages in this country tank even when there aren't these kinds of problems. You have been married three times yourself, Walter. I wouldn't think you would be so concerned about a few marriages failing."

"I'm not concerned personally, but I would be remiss not to consider it as a surgeon scientist looking for good outcomes. I would have to make sure the candidates were emotionally strong enough to handle the consequences. Otherwise they would end up committing suicide and wasting a perfectly good and not often available healthy brain-dead body. Even Andrew, as strong as he is, has contemplated suicide several times. Only our agreement and friendship has kept him from going through with it."

"Oh no, Walter, not Andrew! Don't tell me that! Really? Why in the world would he do that? He should be grateful for his new life. He should be embracing it like a child with a room full of new toys."

"Even a child in a room full of new goodies sometimes misses and cries for his favorite old comforting teddy bear. Although Andrew understands it all intellectually, he doesn't appreciate or value the opportunities his new life affords. And he still thinks like a sixty-six-year-old. He's too mature for his age. And he's burnished his memories of his former life. He feels that he has lost everything that had any meaning for him, although his research is going well again. Thank God for at least that! He's doing a lot better now that he's at Duke. He's no longer confronted with old friends and colleagues shunning him because they can't deal with his physical transformation. You know, I haven't had the least problem with that. I wonder why that is. You would think that it would have affected me a little. But, believe it or not, I still see him as Andrew. Who he was is who he is to me. I thought you would be able to see him too, Margaret. You lived with him for over thirty years. He's still the person you loved."

"Are you sure he's still the same person, Walter? Is he really the same person? Hasn't this extraordinary experience changed who he is at least a little? If ever there was what is called a life-changing experience, this had to be it. I have never believed a person is only the brain, a soup of chemicals and a network of neurons and synapses. God's magnificent creation surely doesn't reduce to that!"

"That brain, from my perspective, is the most wondrous and mysterious creation God could possibly have imagined. It is that part of Him that He has put in all of us."

"Spoken like a true Jewish atheist, Walter."

"Well, I'm trying to bridge the gap and put it in terms you would understand and accept. You do happen to be hacking away at my most sacred cow. Oh, I have to run now. I have an appointment in twenty minutes. I'll pay the tab on the way out. You sit here and finish your tea. Keep in touch, Margaret. I want to know how things turn out. Let's get together again before you leave. Maybe we can continue our discussion."

"Then it needs to be dinner next time, Walter. Wine would be a big plus. This tea isn't nearly strong enough for this kind of discussion."

chapter 16

Sarah

*S*arah answered the door wearing a white frilly blouse and a full, ankle-length black flamenco skirt. She had on stiletto heels. There was a big red rose in her hair. Andrew thought she looked a little old for the role of Carmen, but all she needed were some castanets. The menu must be Spanish.

"Hello, handsome. We're having paella tonight. The Rioja is doing some heavy breathing in the kitchen. Come on in and have some."

"I haven't had paella in a very long time. I love it."

"Well, I hope it's as good as the last one you remember. By the way, speaking of memory, I want to correct something I said to you last weekend. I told you I was battling cancer. That isn't true. I'm tilting a dragon, but it isn't cancer; it's early onset of dementia. Since your brain is all that's physically left of your former self, I figured you're pretty sensitive about brains. I didn't want to frighten you away right off the bat by telling you that I'm in the process of losing mine."

Andrew smiled. Something about Sarah always made him smile. Her playfulness?

"Well, you had enough presence of mind to lie about it, Sarah, so it must not be too bad yet."

Sarah laughed.

"I've decided to make the most of the situation, handsome. As an epistemologist, I am finding the process quite interesting from a professional point of view. I have decided to document how my mind changes my reality as my brain deteriorates, at least as long as I lucidly can. Maybe even beyond lucidity, if I don't kill myself first. Of course, I'm assuming I'll in fact be able to recognize that it has or is changing. One of my star graduate students will use my notes for her doctoral dissertation somewhere down the line. One of the reasons I sought you out, Andrew, is to learn something about self-awareness from your unique perspective. But not now. And that certainly isn't the only reason I want to know you."

Dinner was delicious, followed by over an hour of piano and violin duets. Sarah did cook better than she played. Despite Sarah's mistakes, Andrew still found it enjoyable playing some serious duets again.

After opening a bottle of vintage port, Sarah and Andrew sat down in the den with port glasses full enough to promise this was not going to be a short discussion. Andrew was glad he had already had several glasses of Rioja. He didn't know what to expect from this conversation, although it could be interesting to see where she took it. Sarah was nothing if not straightforward and to the point.

"Andrew, how do you know who you are?"

"That's easy. Cogito, ergo sum. That's how Descartes put it."

"Descartes also brought renewed focus on the old mind-body problem, which is more to the point of this conversation. Seriously, Andrew, you are being too simplistic. I didn't ask how you know you exist; I asked how do you know for sure you are the same person now that you were before your operation? Do you think your mind would be able to detect the difference if you have changed?"

"But it hasn't changed, Sarah. I have full continuity of memory from before, and I still have the same habits of mind, the same feelings, language use, and so forth. I see the world in the same way. That is precisely how I know I am still me."

"But would you really know for sure if in fact you are different? Would a mind produced by a rewired brain in your new body be able to know it is different from your old mind? Everything you have said is self-referential."

"What else would I reference if not myself, Sarah? My brain is the only thing that was transplanted, but here I am."

"You are talking as though your brain and your mind are one and the same. They aren't, of course. As I slowly lose my mind, my brain will still be there physically, but it will be producing thoughts with less and less quality control and become less and less efficient and reliable as it becomes more and more diseased. What I know and how I know will change. As my brain disease progresses, I will misremember or not remember at all. I will become confused, misinterpret reality. I will lose my sense of self. How will I even know when I do? Eventually, toward the end, living in the moment will be all I can do because there will be no past, no knowledge, no reference point. I won't know anything. Each moment will be different and new to me. It will be as though I am watching an endless cacophony of images going across the screen, unconnected, meaningless, confusing, disturbing, frightening. As one who has made her living off of thinking about knowing, this is a very scary future to contemplate. There will be no self left to reference, but my diseased physical brain will still be there for some neuroscientist to take out and study at my death. My mind will have been long gone by then."

"You paint a grim picture, Sarah. I'm sorry you will have to endure this process, especially at such an early age. I'm afraid we will all suffer this fate if we live long enough. If it's any consolation, the brain usually shuts the body functions down as it deteriorates, and, if you're lucky, you'll die before your mind is in the end state. It would be far preferable, I would think."

"What I am trying to figure out, Andrew, is how I will know when I am not me anymore. So often you hear someone say 'Mother isn't really there anymore' or 'Mother has been gone for over a year. That isn't really her there sitting in the chair.' Is she still in there somewhere? Does she still know who she is? Is she constantly becoming a different self as her brain atrophies and her mind becomes disconnected to context and is eventually nonexistent? So, do you see what I mean by referencing yourself? If your mind could look at itself, it would be like looking in a mirror; all it could see is itself at a particular moment. If your mind were able to look at a picture of itself taken before the operation and compare it with what it sees in the mirror now, then it would have a reference point that might have some validity. It either is what it was or it isn't. Of course, since the mind is not physical, it couldn't look in the mirror to begin with, but you get my drift."

"Look, Sarah, my mind is the product of my brain. Producing it is what my brain does, so they go hand in hand. My operation was successful because, after surgery, my brain still functions, and my mind still works. Walter, my surgeon, was careful, absolutely meticulous, so my brain did not get rewired. Same brain, same mind. Yes, technically one is physical, and one is not, but for all practical purposes they are one and the same. And to throw a monkey wrench into the argument for you, in some sense our thoughts are material too and visible now, thanks to MRIs. When we think certain kinds of thoughts, our brains light up in the areas where those thoughts occur. This is the methodology being used now to map the brain, the Connectome Project, similar to the way we did our genome."

"All you are seeing on an MRI, Andrew, is brain activity, not thoughts."

"I don't agree. We are seeing traces of the thoughts. We know they are there the same way we know the Higgs boson, the so-called God particle, exists, even though it took the Supercollider to find it. It leaves a trace of its existence. Something totally immaterial can't leave a trace."

"Oh no? What about a split personality? Would that be a counterargument? You wouldn't be able to see physical evidence in the brain or in an MRI of a person's split personality, but you would certainly see traces of it in real life. Such a phenomenon indeed exists. Really, Andrew, you are trying to make the mind physical. That's a real stretch. It can't be. You scientists want to reduce everything down to its tiniest physical, quantitative property until there is nothing left that resembles in the slightest the way we experience it in reality. I subscribe to an emergence principle that allows things to interact, build up, and become more than they were separately, something that can be actually experienced."

"I think you just lost me there, Sarah. What do you mean? Give me an example."

"Okay. You scientists see water and break it down into two hydrogen atoms and one oxygen atom, and then break that down further into electrons, neutron, protons, and further still, all the way to bosons. I see what emerges from bosons on up the chain through protons and electrons to when two hydrogen atoms and one oxygen atom combine to form a substance we can swim in, that quenches our thirst and makes grass grow. I see the mind as what emerges from all the brain functions when they are working together synergistically like the instruments of an orchestra that together can play a Beethoven symphony. You are musician enough to know that music cannot be reduced to a bunch of notes. Even the written score for one instrument cannot enable you to hear the whole symphony. But enough of this chatter for tonight. We can come back to it another time. Besides, it's time to get to the important business."

"The important business? I thought this was the important business, Sarah."

"I'm surprised at you, handsome. Here we are alone after a good meal, a good session with Beethoven, a good conversation, a good port, and you haven't made the first move toward the bedroom. I want us to be friends, Andrew, good friends. Not lovers—it's too late for me for that. But good friends with privileges. We are both single adults. We both have sexual needs. We can take care of each other as friends until you become involved with someone in a serious way. I'm not much to look at, but I happen to know how to please a man, and I am dying to get my hands on this fabulous body of yours. You won't be sorry."

———

"Wow!" said Andrew as he lay there on Sarah's bed after a nonstop marathon session of sexual pleasure. "You weren't kidding, were you? It would be ungentlemanly of me to ask how you learned all that, but where did you?"

"My late husband, Harry, was a sex therapist. Don't laugh! No joke! He taught me all kinds of stuff. He was the love of my life. We had a great time. I miss him every day. We were married for thirty-one years. Couldn't have children, so we clung all the closer to each other. We were just one unit in this world. I was the one who always had my head in a book of hypotheticals. He was able to pull me away and make me see the real world, go for a walk at sunset, sit on the back porch and watch it rain, smell the fresh spring air, and feel life as it was being lived. I adored him. Still do, and he has been dead almost five years now."

"Amazingly, you have almost described my marriage with Margaret, my former wife, only she was the one who created the magic in my life, which was more like yours."

"Then why is she your former wife? Did she die too?"

"No, she divorced me after I had my body transplant."

Andrew gave Sarah an abbreviated version of his painful loss. *Will this always be the story of my life,* he wondered, *telling it over and over again? I feel like the ancient mariner.*

"That's really tough, Andrew. But she must have loved you incredibly much to make that kind of personal sacrifice for you. And I think you owe it to her to find that new someone. You must miss her terribly."

"Every day, Sarah. Although she always insisted that we are kindred souls, I had no idea how completely she has permeated my world. It took me a while to realize she is the standard by which I automatically measure anyone I would consider dating. It will be a rare woman who will measure up. She held my life afloat and kept me on course. Without her, I have been rudderless and far from shore."

"I know what you mean, Andrew. Sometimes I find myself talking to Harry about this and that, imagining how he would answer. Sometimes I see someone in the distance who walks like him or dresses like him, and for a brief moment my heart leaps up, and I thank God for giving me that tiny little rare moment of pure joy. I find myself talking to God a lot too, especially now. I don't really believe in God, but I don't disbelieve in Him either. That kind of knowing is way above my pay grade. I'm just an agnostic. Atheist seems too harsh a label for me. Atheism claims as much certainty as theism does. Given the shape the world is in right now, though, I don't think anyone up there is paying much attention to us. That might give the atheists a bit of an edge."

Andrew laughed and propped his pillow up a little.

"Believe it or not, Andrew, I hope there is a God, a personal one, one who is more magnanimous and forgiving than most man-made religions would have us believe. One who will sit us down at the end of time and explain what the game plan was and how we managed to get it right, what this wonderful, crazy, beautiful, painful existence here on earth was all about. The ultimate knowing—that is what I would like. But I have trouble figuring out just how we could possibly participate in an afterlife in any meaningful way. Would we be bodily raised from the dead as some believe? If so, what age would we be? Surely not the age we died, especially if we were babies. And where would we be raised to? Would we be visible or invisible spirits floating around? Would our souls just be absorbed back into God's being from whence they came? Would we even be aware of it and have any separate identity or be able to find our loved ones again?

In God's great love, would our earthly loves be so insignificant that we would not want or miss them? My husband sure thought this life is all we get. Before he died, he would tell me the very worst part about dying was having to leave me. These are all things I think about sometimes. How about you, Andrew? Do you believe in God?"

"I consider myself a very friendly agnostic, like you. I seem to be unable to have that 'willing suspension of disbelief' William James talked about. I have my doubts. I suspect many religious people have their doubts too sometimes; they just prefer to seek God from the inside instead of from the outside of organized religion. I sometimes wonder if the pope believes 100 percent all the time, or if he prays that he can conquer his moments of unbelief in order to guide his massive flock safely to heaven's gate. Margaret doesn't have doubts. She's very religious, an Episcopalian who definitely believes in souls and an afterlife. But she is a poet and perceives things through an aesthetic lens of her own making. Anyway, this is a topic for another day. I need to be going. It's quite late."

"Why leave now, Andrew? It's not like you have someone waiting for you at home. Be a good boy and don't argue. Just pull the covers up and sleep here with me tonight. No one is going to notice or care if you leave here in the morning."

"I can't stay here, Sarah. I don't even have my toothbrush or shaving kit."

"I've already thought of those objections and have them covered. New toothbrush and shaving stuff on the second shelf of the medicine cabinet."

"You're a riot. Truly amazing, Sarah. I have never met anyone like you before."

"And I've never met anyone with a brain transplant before, so we're even."

"Body transplant, Sarah."

"Okay, body transplant. Good night, handsome. It has been a very stimulating evening, in every sense of the word. My guess is that you will be back next weekend, and not just for the music and my cooking."

chapter 17

The Diagnosis

*W*alter saw Margaret was on the line and picked up the phone. It had been two weeks since their lunch, so he assumed this would be about the report. He had a special place in his heart for Margaret. He hoped the news wasn't bad.

"Well, hello, Margaret. Are you ready for our dinner?" He thought he would let her bring up the subject.

"Maybe so, Walter. I'd rather not have this discussion over the phone. Can you get away this evening? About six o'clock? Can we go back to Trattoria Alfredo? I want some comfort food: really good wine, veal piccata, and ricotta pie."

"Sure, Margaret. I'll call Rose and let her know she's on her own tonight."

Margaret arrived in a cheerful, pink cashmere sweater, but she was not wearing her usual radiant smile. Walter knew immediately her test results were not good. He ordered the best bottle of pinot noir in the house. When it was poured, Margaret gave him the news.

"I have what is called a cancer of unknown primary, Walter. Stage four, but at least it hasn't reached my brain yet. That's one small thing to be thankful for. With luck, I'll have about six months to live. There is no curative treatment at this stage of the game. I waited too long."

"Oh my God, Margaret, that's horrible! What are you going to do?"

"Well, I've been thinking about it for almost a week now. I found out last Friday. I don't really have anything or anyone to live for now, Walter. With Andrew gone and no children, I have no reason to put up the good fight to prolong life a few months. Anyway, there is only a 4 percent chance of survival at twelve months with the current treatment options. If Andrew were still in his wheelchair and needed me, I would fight like hell to stay alive for as long as possible. As it is, I think I would like to stay out at the farm and let Edith take care of me until it's over. I figure you can get me the painkillers I need—morphine, whatever—and instruct Edith in what to do. When I asked Charles if it would be okay for me to stay there, he said it's still half-mine anyway. Andrew left his only two keys, so there would be no chance that anyone could use the farm without getting a key from Charles."

"Of course I can and will do everything necessary to make sure you're comfortable, Margaret, but are you absolutely certain this is what you want to do? Wouldn't hospice be a better solution? There's one here that is beautiful and has excellent care. The farm is too far out for homecare. Should I call Andrew? I know he would come, Margaret. I know he would want to come. He still loves you. There is no one else in his life."

"No, Walter. As much as I would love to be with Andrew these last few months, I am not going to interrupt his new life at this point, his research and his emotional state. It would be very selfish of me. I can't do it. And I would rather remember him as he was."

"Margaret, I think you need to rethink this thing. Andrew would never forgive me for not telling him. You are staying out at the farm. He would know you'd contact me if you came back to St. Louis. He'd consider it a total breach of friendship. Besides, you shouldn't have to spend this precious little time alone."

"I won't be alone, Walter. Edith will be there. You have to respect my privacy. I don't want Andrew to know. I will leave him a final note absolving you, if that is what you're worried about."

"It isn't just that, Margaret. We've been friends for over twenty years. I care about you. I don't want your last days on this earth to be so lonely. I have seen lots of people die in my lifetime. It is not something to do alone."

"Everyone dies alone, Walter, no matter how many loved ones are in the room. It's a solitary sport."

"But it's a lot easier, I would think, if someone you care about is holding your hand."

"God will be holding my hand, Walter. You forget I have God. He will help me through this final journey back to Him. I have absolute faith that He will take care of me."

"Margaret, are you absolutely positive this is the way you want to leave this world, you the poet who has chronicled all the harbingers of spring, the dew on spider webs glinting in the morning sun, and little hummingbird eggs? All your poetry is about beginnings. Endings are not something you have contemplated. They aren't pretty, Margaret."

"You really have read my poetry, Walter. I always thought you were just saying you did to be polite. Anyway, I see death as another kind of beginning. I'm not saying I am looking forward to the dying process, but I trust what has been promised on the other side."

"Think for a moment, Margaret, about Andrew. Don't you realize how much it would mean to him if you were to tell him you needed him now, that he was still Andrew to you? He told me that without you he feels like his only purpose in life now is to prove whether or not his brain age has reset. You would be giving him a real purpose to continue to live, and you would be reaffirming his worth. Couldn't you consider asking him to come? Couldn't you try to deal with his transformation here at the end?"

"Walter, I have been thinking a lot about our last conversation concerning Andrew. I have come to the conclusion that I would be able to love him because, if I had met him in a physically different body back at Harvard when we were young, I would have still fallen in love with the wonderful person he is. So, if I could magically wave a wand and become a young woman again, I would run to Duke as fast as I could and find the man I have always loved inside of who Andrew is now. But to ask him to come to my deathbed would be like asking him to watch his mother die all over again. Dying is not a spectator sport. It was horrible watching my own parents die: the labored breathing as though they were about to suffocate, the hallucinations, the nails turning blue, the little white ring around the mouth that got whiter the closer death came. You are wrong about my not having contemplated endings. There was a time when I was bombarded with too many of them. You forget about all my miscarriages. That is precisely why my poetry has always been about the beauty and promise of being alive in this world. There is nothing beautiful about death."

"Well, I hope you will allow Rose and me to keep an eye on you. We will do our best to see that you have what you need and don't suffer. You also need to give me your burial instructions and who needs to be contacted when the time comes."

"Of course you and Rose can come out to the farm. I would love for you to. It will be good to see Rose again. It's been a long time. Just be sure to bring the morphine with you. As far as the rest goes, I have given Charles all the instructions. He's still my attorney too. He also has been sworn to secrecy."

"What about your sister? I just remembered you were living with her out in California. Shouldn't she come to be with you?"

"No, she broke her hip in a fall and hasn't been very well since. I think the anesthesia from the surgery caused some permanent mental fog. I got her settled in an assisted-living place before I left and set up a small trust to handle her end-of-life needs. Her daughter can see to her care.

"To change the subject a bit, Walter, please tell me about the woman Andrew was dating here. I am quite curious to know what kind of person he was attracted to. In the old days, I always assumed if something happened to me, one of those brilliant grad students would latch onto him. I was never in Andrew's league intellectually and worried about it a lot. Faculty parties were very hard for me. Once in a while, one of my poems would appear in *The New Yorker*, and someone would talk to me about it. Except for the few professional ones, most of the faculty wives spent their time gossiping or talking about their children, none of which interested me. Andrew always had to come to my rescue. So I thought he probably wished he had married someone who could hold her own with the professionals and that he would choose to do so now that he has the chance."

"The last thing a research scientist wants when he comes home at night is more shoptalk, Margaret. I speak from experience with three wives, so I am an expert on the subject. My first wife, Barbara, was a woman I met when we were doing our residencies at Johns Hopkins. She was as obsessed as I am with brain surgery and as competitive. Shoptalk was nonstop. It didn't work at all. My second wife, Shirley, was a malpractice lawyer. Big mistake. Most of the time, she was quizzing me about medical protocols and information to help her with her cases. It lasted long enough to have three kids, but we led separate lives and split the day after the last kid left home. Now my third wife, Rose, is a keeper. She paints a little, plays the piano a little, cooks a lot, and makes love to me often enough. We talk about books we are reading, movies we want to see, places we want to visit, stuff like that. In other words, we share a real home life, a love life, a fun life. When I come home, I'm just Walter. And that's what Andrew had with you. You gave him a real life. He got it right the first time."

"But you haven't told me about the woman he dated. What's she like, Walter?"

"Cullen? She's a strikingly pretty young woman somewhere around thirty-three or -four, I think. Smart, auburn hair, green eyes, great figure. She's had a lousy life. Turns out Tony was an abusive husband with very average intelligence and a drinking problem. No love there on either side. She married him because she was pregnant."

"Does anyone do that anymore? Marry someone because she's pregnant? You can have children today without being married. It seems to be the big thing now. Everyone's doing it. You certainly couldn't get away with it back when we were young. Abortions are also legal now, although I personally oppose them. So why did she marry him?"

Walter gave her the short version and hoped it was enough to satisfy Margaret. He felt uncomfortable talking to her about Cullen.

"That's a sad story, Walter. Poor girl. But how did she and Andrew get together? It seems so weird that she would want to date someone who looks like her deceased husband she didn't love. How did they meet?"

"It's too long a story for now, Margaret. I promise to give you all the details the next time I'm out at the farm visiting. I frankly encouraged the relationship because I thought it would be good for Andrew. Although he wasn't in love with her, he found her very appealing and welcomed her company as a diversion while he was trying to get his new life going."

"So why didn't it work? What went wrong?"

"It might have eventually worked. Who knows? But the truth is it didn't work because she wasn't you. No more questions, Margaret. Seriously, I will give you the whole story when I come out to the farm. The important takeaway, for you, is the fact that Andrew has never loved anyone but you, and I don't believe he ever will. I personally think that's sad because it means he's going to have a lot of less-than-happy years ahead of him."

Margaret stopped asking questions and returned to her ricotta pie. He could tell she was mulling this point.

"Walter, I really will search through all levels of Dante's hell to find Andrew, whatever shape or nonshape he's in. Like your Rose, he's definitely a keeper."

"I hate to rush you, Margaret, but it's getting late, and I have an important meeting first thing in the morning. There's a twenty-three-year-old girl in Barnes Hospital with severe brain trauma. She's an only child, and the distraught parents want me to take a look at her to see if I can save her. Because of all the publicity over my surgery with Andrew, people seem to think I'm the only one to call for anything concerning the brain. Last month an elderly man came to see me, wanting to know if there was some way I could cut out his wife's dementia. Anyway, it keeps wine on the table and concert tickets in my pocket. Shall I walk you to your car?"

"No, Walter, I think I will just sit here for a while and enjoy the rest of this good bottle of pinot noir. I need to practice not rushing through what's left of my life. I want to savor every minute I can."

"We should all start doing that, Margaret. The world would be a better place. Good night. I'll call you soon. Meanwhile, if you need anything, you call me."

chapter 18

The Stuarts

*W*alter knocked softly and opened the door to the room in the private wing of the hospital. The morning sun was creating a shifting mosaic on the floor as it found its way through the trees outside the window. The room's cheerfulness belied the reason for his visit. There were a number of orchids and roses on the tabletops and several stuffed animals tucked here and there along with cards. In the bed lay a young woman barely out of college, hooked to an IV and breathing equipment. He was surprised that Mr. and Mrs. Stuart were not in the room, but he was a few minutes early. He skimmed down her chart that was at the foot of the bed and, nodding his head, wondered to himself why they had called him to come save her. Their daughter was clearly brain-dead.

Mr. and Mrs. Stuart came into the room apologizing for not being there when Walter arrived. Mr. Stuart had on business attire. He was wearing an expensive watch, and his shoes were buffed to a high shine. Walter noticed things like that. Mrs. Stuart looked like she had just thrown herself together in a hurry to get there, although Walter knew she had paid over five hundred dollars for the sweater she was wearing. He had bought Rose one just like it.

"Dr. Rubin, thank you so much for coming. I'm Allen Stuart, and this is my wife, Deborah. As you can see, our daughter is nonresponsive. She's been like this for nine days now. My wife has practically lived here by her side since the accident, and I've been here as much as I can and still keep my investment company running."

"It's a pleasure to meet you both, although I am sorry for the circumstances that brought us together. You said your daughter was in an accident. Was it a car accident?"

"No, according to the friend she was biking with, she swerved to miss a little boy chasing his ball out into the road. Her front tire hit a curb and catapulted her headfirst over the handlebars. She was going pretty fast at the time. Unfortunately, her head slammed into a tree. Except for a broken collarbone, nothing else was damaged except her brain. She was wearing a helmet. If that tree hadn't been right there, she'd probably be okay. The doctors here have told us that there's nothing more to be done and that we should consider removing her life support. She is our only child, Dr. Rubin. We can't lose her. Because of your reputation, we decided to see if you can save her for us."

"I looked at her chart before you came in, Mr. Stuart. This isn't what you want to hear, but there really isn't anything I can do for her either. No brain operation is going to make her brain function again. I'm truly sorry."

"Dr. Rubin, we know you can't restore her brain. We wanted to see you because we want you to give us back our daughter by giving her a new brain. We want you to give her a brain transplant. But we don't want the donor to keep her own identity the way that doctor did. We want her to still be our daughter. Money isn't a problem. We will pay whatever you ask if only you will do this for us."

"Oh. I see." Walter looked down at the floor, shifted his weight, and looked back at the young woman in the bed before he spoke. "Well, Mr. Stuart, I'm sorry to say I'm not sure I can help you there either. Finding a woman who wants her brain transplanted could take years, and since I have only performed one of these operations, and it was over five years ago, I cannot promise that the operation would be successful, even if I were able to find a donor."

"But we could leave our daughter on life support for a long time while you are looking for someone. Maybe you can find a young woman who has come back from one of the wars in Iraq or Afghanistan who is paralyzed and wants a new life. I remember back when you were on Fox News talking about the good your operation could do for veterans. As far as the operation being successful, we have every confidence in you."

"No two operations are exactly the same, Mrs. Stuart. There is a strong possibility it wouldn't work. I wouldn't want to give you or the brain donor false hopes. And I would not relish having to deal with all the media coverage if the operation failed. The various interest groups would have a field day."

"Oh, Allen and I specifically don't want any publicity, Dr. Rubin. In fact, we want no one to know that she's even had a brain transplant. We want it to be kept secret permanently. The brain donor has to agree to be our daughter and not reveal her former identity. We will tell everyone she has finally come out of her coma. There was so much commotion over that doctor whose brain you transplanted. We don't want people thinking she's weird or anything. We just want her to be her normal self again, the daughter we love."

"It is obvious that you love your daughter very much, Mrs. Stuart. Tell me a little about her."

"Dr. Rubin, you would love her. She's such a wonderful, sweet, girl. Very bright, quick-witted. She graduated from Harvard this past June and was taking a year off to think about what she really wants to do before going to grad school. She is so creative, so talented. Sometimes a little sarcastic and edgy when she's challenged, pushing the boundaries a little, but that goes along with her creative temperament. She's quite sensitive, a romantic really. We have saved several drawers full of stories and poems she has written. Allen wants her to go to Wharton for an MBA and come into his business. I personally think she doesn't want to get an MBA. I think she took the year off because she really wants to be a writer, and she's stalling because she doesn't want to admit it and disappoint her father. She hates confrontation with her father and is always trying to please. She got into biking while she was at college and rides every day for exercise. And of course, that's what she was doing when she had the accident. I've always worried about her riding a bike where we live in Ladue. There really isn't a good place to ride."

"First of all, Mrs. Stuart, you misunderstand the nature of the operation if you think your daughter will be her normal self. That's impossible. The donor brain would dominate. Even if some aspects of your daughter's personality remain, the mind will belong to the donor, along with thoughts, beliefs, emotions to a certain extent, creativity, memories and, most importantly, her sense of self. The identity would belong to the donor, not your daughter."

"What if we said the donor could keep her identity as long as she keeps our daughter's name and never reveals her real name and past and accepts us as her parents and stays in our lives?"

"I'm afraid you're being naive, Mrs. Stuart. You are asking way too much of the brain donor. That donor most likely would already have parents or a family and a career. Her motivation for undergoing the brain transplant in the first place would be to continue her life as she knows it, even though she will find out, as Dr. Hamilton did, that her life will never be the same. You are asking that the donor give your daughter her brain, and at the same time you want her to stop being who she is. That's impossible. Why would anyone want to do that even if she could? Why would she be willing to allow your daughter's personality to become dominant instead of her own? She would be giving up some of her own sense of self, a piece of herself that she couldn't control. I know from Dr. Hamilton's experience that it is very disconcerting when the medication dosage is wrong and the other personality takes over to some degree. Trust me, when the donor brain is not in control, it can cause big problems. You have imposed conditions that just wouldn't work, Mrs. Stuart, even in a best-case scenario. No sane donor, or at least only a very rare one, would ever agree to your conditions. Nor could she conform to your expectations."

"Then what if we said the donor wouldn't have to give up her personality or anything. She could pursue her own interests and live her life as she sees fit as long as she is willing to use our daughter's name and accept us as her parents. That shouldn't be so hard. We are nice people, and we would continue to love her as we always have. Can anyone have too many people loving them? And if she has parents, we can be a second set, like families who have divorced parents who have both remarried. If she is married and has children, we could take them into our hearts too. We just want our daughter in our lives, and progeny, grandchildren someday. We can't lose her, Dr. Rubin. She's all we've got. We are both only children. Our DNA will cease to be if we can't have her back. You are our only hope. We will pay you for all your time searching for a donor. In addition to paying whatever fees you ask, we will make a generous donation to your research effort. Dr. Rubin, please. Please help us."

"Mrs. Stuart, it isn't a question of the money. I know the money is there. But even if I by some fluke can find a female donor, I doubt seriously that I can find a donor who would agree to your conditions. You would be sending me on an horrendously expensive wild goose chase for nothing."

Walter was about to end the discussion when something came to mind. "Wait a minute. One possibility does occur to me, but it's a real long shot, and I can't promise anything. Let me think about it and get back to you in a few weeks, after Thanksgiving. Meanwhile, leave your daughter on life support until you hear from me. By the way, you haven't mentioned your daughter's name. What is it?"

"Elizabeth, Dr. Rubin. Her name is Elizabeth."

chapter 19

Margaret Alone

*M*argaret watched the dark clouds gathering over the distant mountains. They would be rolling into Argo soon. The birds were already hunkered down somewhere, and the world had gone quiet, not even a sound in the pastures beyond the stream. This was going to be a big one.

How many years had it been since she and Andrew sat under the shelter of the walnut barn and watched the rain come in over the ridge? Twelve? How many times had they been caught in an October downpour out in the orchard at apple-picking time? She remembered one October when it rained every Saturday afternoon and left a rainbow perfectly painted over the horizon. Margaret loved the rain, but she equally loved the sun and the snow at the farm. She found something wondrous about every month at Argo, and she had written poems about them all. But Octobers were special. It was the month that invigorated Andrew the most. He came most alive with the maples in their glory and the mornings crisp. For eighteen Octobers here at Argo, she and Andrew had watched the drama of each year shedding its mantle in preparation for the two-month journey toward the end. Margaret wondered how many months her own journey would be. This was certainly her very last October.

Novembers were special for Margaret too. Every Thanksgiving, she and Andrew had invited friends with their children to come to the farm for a traditional holiday feast. About twenty people usually came. Edith worked all week making corn pudding and green bean casseroles, mashed potatoes and sweet potatoes every way possible, cranberry sauce with her secret ingredient, cornbread dressing with homegrown soft-shelled hickory nuts, a big plump turkey plucked from a neighbor's farm, and pies of every kind. After the food settled and the children had gone off exploring, the adults would go out in the field beyond the pond and cut volunteer cedar and juniper evergreens to take home for old-fashion Christmas trees. Andrew would help them tie the trees down on the tops of their cars and give each family a bunch of mistletoe he had shot out of the maples. It was an especially wonderful time Margaret tucked away in her memory. She had taken pictures and written poems to put on her Christmas cards each year. All those friends and children made her feel like she and Andrew were part of a big family, a family that she and he didn't have. Holidays were otherwise difficult for Margaret. It was the time she felt the most bereft. Margaret missed having a family, always wanted a family, and needed one even now. Especially now.

The house was dark when Margaret went inside. Edith had left a nice pot roast cooking in the oven with potatoes and carrots and onions around it. The delicious aroma filled the kitchen. There was one of Edith's granny smith apple pies cooling on the counter. What a prize Edith was.

George had already laid the wood for a fire. All Margaret had to do was turn on the gas starter to light the kindling, which she did as soon as she entered the den. Watching the flames dance up and down and in and out between the logs was mesmerizing. *Why is it*, she wondered, *that everyone enjoys gazing at the fire? In some ways, our fascination with it seems to be part of our DNA. Would the first humans to witness fire have been in such fear and awe that they worshiped it as a god?* Margaret was reminded of her old college course on the role of fate and free will in Aeschylus's tragedy *Prometheus Bound*. The Titan Prometheus took pity on mere mortals and stole the fire from the gods to benefit mankind, knowing he would be punished by Zeus. He was nailed to a rock for his effort and tortured mightily for stealing the goods. He knew his fate but exercised his free will to steal the fire anyway. Margaret knew when she sacrificed her marriage to set Andrew free that her fate would be to live out her days warmed by happy memories but equally burned to her very core with longing. *So fire is a double-faced god, both benevolent and malevolent. It is an agent of death as well as life: volcanic eruptions, lightning strikes, burnings at the stake, holocausts, atomic explosions, hell. Desire. Fire brought the world into existence with the big bang, the first cosmic explosion, and fire will bring it to an end, the final act of our dying sun's supernova. Creator and destroyer like the God of the Old Testament. Maybe the gentle God of the New Testament will loosen our gravity and let this beautiful world of ours just float away with the rest of the expanding universe into the forever—that is, if man doesn't incinerate it first with nuclear war. The fire again.*

Margaret must have fallen asleep and been dreaming. Something about Prometheus and fire? *What was that all about?* Looking at the fire now, she noticed it had died down a little, and a nice pile of embers was glowing beneath the burning logs. They were just right for roasting marshmallows, something she and Andrew often did after dinner for dessert. Andrew loved to set out a plate with Hershey's chocolate bars and graham crackers and make s'mores with extra-large marshmallows toasted to a golden brown. Margaret wondered if Andrew had made any s'mores since they were last here together.

After dinner, Margaret put on a heavy sweater, poured herself a cup of coffee, and went out to the front porch swing to watch the rain, which was still coming down hard. Sitting out there in the evenings was a ritual the two of them had established right after they bought the place. Andrew loved the porch swing because it reminded him of his childhood summers on the Cape. His parents had owned a grand old lady of a place overlooking the ocean. It had a big porch swing where Andrew would read and daydream, watching the sailboats and the seagulls. It was also where she and Andrew spent one memorable night kissing passionately and declaring undying love until dawn. He often said he should have kept it after his mother died, but it was a long trip, and they had no children, so he let it go. Argo had no ocean or seagulls, but the stream with its sitting rocks provided four seasons of pleasure. Wild turkeys visited the fields from time to time, and birds twittered in the yellow maples a large part of the year. Other than that, what Argo offered was peace and quiet and sounds one at a time. Margaret missed Andrew.

She had come back to the farm to die because it was the place she felt most at home. How much poetry had she written and read here? How much of her poetry was directly inspired by Argo? More than any other place, she felt closest to Andrew here at the farm. There was something magical about it, something spiritual. Margaret spent many hours over the years meditating and thinking up here, giving herself Sermons on the Ridge, as she called them. She had brought her prayers of thanks and songs of praise for every tiny blessing given to her, and she equally laid out her disappointments for God to explain His reasoning and justice. Why had she had endometrial cancer surgery that robbed her of children, especially when the treatment now didn't leave one sterile? Why had He allowed Andrew to become paralyzed? Why had He allowed her beloved husband to be transplanted into a body too young for her, ruining their marriage, their happiness? And why at the early age of sixty-seven was she dying of cancer? Margaret believed in a loving God, a just God. She knew God had good reasons for what had happened in her life; she just wanted to know what they were. He needed to explain them to her.

Margaret was not ready to leave this world. She loved life. She loved Argo. She could feel God's presence at Argo stronger than anywhere else, even more strongly than in the magnificent cathedrals of Europe she had visited. She didn't just believe in God; the relationship was lifelong and personal. And she talked to Him now like the old friend and confidant He had always been.

"God, if you want me to die, why haven't You at least made me more willing to go, more ready? If You plan to work a miracle and let me live, why are You putting me through all this to begin with? I have always believed in the efficacy of prayer, but You have never come through for me in any way I can recognize. I prayed so hard for a child. I prayed so hard that if Andrew survived the transplant, he would be in a body that would give me back my husband. What am I missing? What have You been trying to tell me? What alternate plan have You had for me? More to the point, if You have a plan for me, why haven't You told me what it is so I can do my part willingly? I have certainly prayed for Your guidance."

Margaret could feel the tears welling up. Her emotions were flowing freely now.

"What trace of me will be left in this world but a few poems that will quickly be forgotten? Where is the ripple effect of my existence? How can I leave this world in a better way than I found it? I have nothing of significance to point to in the way of accomplishments. I wanted to be more, do more. I have taken the calculus of my lived life: what was well spent, what was wasted, what is left, what is hoped, what is believed, what is valued, what is loved. When I add it all up, multiply, subtract, and take the derivative, I find myself to be more fortunate than most, but I don't have anything to show for it. I have squandered my opportunities and privilege. To my shame and regret, I have been a very ordinary person in this world. I do have one special gift though. I have an extraordinary ability to love very deeply and unconditionally. You know this, of course, but Andrew doesn't. Poor Andrew. God, please look after him. Let him through heaven's gate. He is a good man, a caring man, a gentle man. Can't You open his heart to the possibility that one can believe without offending the intellect? Save him for me, God. At least do that for me. Please!"

chapter 20

Thanksgiving

*I*t was the day before Thanksgiving, and the rain was practically coming down sideways with the strong north wind blowing over the ridge. Margaret curled up in front of the fire with her laptop. She had set aside today to write to her sister and several friends to give them the news and explain her decision to stay at Argo. Since coming back, Margaret had spent much of her time reminiscing over her life, editing out the low points in favor of the highlights: her relatively happy childhood back in Boston, her years at Radcliffe, her big, beautiful wedding to Andrew the day after graduation, their honeymoon in Tuscany, their fascinating trip to India and China, the unforgettable hot air balloon ride in the African desert at sunset, and the many other travels and adventures over their thirty-five years together. It all seemed so distant now. She knew her life had been a privileged one, and she was thankful for that. But Margaret certainly wasn't feeling very thankful right now. Although she had told Edith not to bother with turkey and the trimmings just for her this year, Edith insisted on doing it anyway. She would make enough for herself and George and still leave plenty of leftovers for the weekend. Edith had been busy all morning making apple, pecan, and pumpkin pies.

Margaret was dreading being alone during the holidays, especially this final year. She wished that, unbeknownst to her, Andrew would somehow find out that she was dying and realize how much she loved him and come running to her side. She yearned so much to be with him through these final months, no matter whose body he was in. But she could not summon him herself. To undo what she had sacrificed to give him would be unconscionable here at the end. Still, how wonderful it would be to die in his arms.

It was hard to contemplate that this would be her last Thanksgiving, her last Christmas, her last ringing in the New Year. It would be more like a knelling for her. Would she start counting the days, striking each off as though she were a schoolgirl eagerly awaiting her sixteenth birthday and the keys to the car? No, Margaret was not eager, even though the keys were to heaven. Which day would be her last? Would she make it until Easter? It wasn't so very far away. Would she live to see the lilacs bloom again? Would the summer roses outside her bedroom window be her last glimpse before she closed her eyes forever? Would she be so drugged up on morphine that she wouldn't even notice or care? Tears were blurring her vision at this point. She was reaching for a Kleenex when her phone rang.

"Margaret, it's Walter. How are you doing?"

"You called just in time, Walter. I was sitting here in front of the fire having myself a pity party, and it was beginning to get too dramatic and maudlin even for me. It's good to hear your cheerful voice."

"I could hear your deep sighs all the way back here in the city, so I thought I better call and perk you up. Actually, I was calling because the kids have all gone to their in-laws for Thanksgiving, and Rose and I were wondering if we could come out to the farm and have an old-fashioned Thanksgiving with you. We have really missed all those great feasts you used to have. Besides, we don't want to be alone on Thanksgiving. It's our very favorite holiday."

"Walter, you are such a dear, trying to make me feel like I'm doing you a favor, when in reality you don't want me to be alone on Thanksgiving. Of course you can come. Edith is cooking more than plenty."

"I know. I spoke with her yesterday just to make sure she would. Forgive me for being so presumptuous. You know how detail oriented I always am. We'll see you about noon. I'll bring a couple of good pinots."

⁓

Thanksgiving dinner was a sumptuous feast. Edith really outdid herself. Although the rain had stopped, it was cold and raw outside, so Walter and Rose settled down in the family room. Margaret brought in some well-aged port from the wine cellar and espresso coffee and set them down on the coffee table in front of the fire.

"Well, tell me what's going on with you, Walter. After our dinner, you were scurrying off because you had an early-morning appointment to save someone's only child. How did that go?"

"It was an interesting meeting, Margaret. The girl, Elizabeth, was brain-dead. She was only twenty-three years old. Harvard graduate, smart, blonde, athletic, wrote poetry. Such a shame. The parents are absolutely devastated."

"What a horrible loss! But if she was brain-dead, why were they calling for you to save her?"

"They want me to do a brain transplant for her so they can have their daughter back. Not only do they want me to find a donor, they want the donor to be willing to be their daughter, take her name, keep as much of her personality as possible, and be in their lives. I tried to explain to them that it doesn't work that way. Anyone willing to be a brain donor, even if I can find one, will already have parents and families and a career. She won't want to be their daughter."

"How sad for them. It must be pure agony to lose a child. I remember my miscarriages and how grief-stricken I was each time, but I had not spent years loving and nurturing them and watching them grow up. Did you encourage them to donate her organs?"

"Not yet. They are such nice people and such loving parents. I couldn't just walk away. Like a soft old fool, I promised I would spend a little time looking to see if I can find a donor. I told them it would be next to impossible. I know I can't."

"Walter Rubin! You didn't really come here for Thanksgiving dinner. You came here to talk me into being your donor! Blonde, Harvard, poet, athletic, loving parents. Rose, how can you live with this man? Have you ever known anyone more manipulative?"

"Actually, yes, my first husband. Walter's a pussycat compared to Sam. But I'm staying out of this conversation. I'm just along for the ride, a mouse in the corner."

"Hold on, Margaret. Hear me out. Of course it occurred to me that, since your life expectancy is only a few months now and your mind is still good, you might be an ideal candidate for the transplant. There are some other advantages I can think of. You have been through this once already with Andrew, so you know the drill and what to expect. Except for age, you have similar demographics to Elizabeth, a fact that Andrew insisted would make a huge difference in the adjustment period. You have always wanted a family, and this girl's young, fertile body will give you that opportunity. Dare I mention again that Andrew is still in love with you? He keeps looking for someone like you. It would be a chance for you to have Andrew back without searching through Dante's hell to find him."

"Walter, you're terrible! Have you no shame? How can you approach me when I'm dying and dangle heaven on earth in front of me? How can you use my love for Andrew and the possibility of a having a child as bait to reel me in? What are you going to do, call Andrew and say, 'Wait, put everything on hold for a year or so. Margaret is coming back to you, and you are going to have children.' You are being totally unrealistic, Walter. Life doesn't happen that way. Anyway, I thought you weren't interested in any more publicity in the press."

"I'm not, and it is a condition of this operation that it not be made public ever, but I think I can negotiate that down some. 'Ever' isn't helpful to the scientific community. I'm going to insist on ten years. Their point being that they don't want people looking at their daughter like something out of science fiction. They plan to tell everyone that Elizabeth has finally come out of her coma."

"So Andrew wouldn't even know I'm Elizabeth? He would have to fall in love with me without knowing I'm Margaret? What if he isn't attracted to the new me? What if he can't see me inside her body, Walter? This whole idea is patently ridiculous. I couldn't do this even if I wanted to."

"Why not, Margaret? What do you really have to lose? If the operation succeeds, you really will be able to start your life all over again with Andrew. You told me not too long ago you would have fallen in love with Andrew back at Harvard no matter what body he was in. I know Andrew will fall in love with you even in Elizabeth's body. If the surgery fails, and that's a possibility, you will only be losing several months of life, some of them drugged up to mask the pain. So, it really is worth taking the chance. And you will make four miserable persons very happy: Mr. And Mrs. Stuart, Andrew, and yourself."

"Walter, I have been spending this time here preparing my soul to meet my death with courage and the conviction that I have tried to make myself worthy of God's love and grace. I can't be derailed at this late date. I can't go against God's plan for me."

"What is God's plan for you, Margaret? To die here alone at the early age of sixty-seven? Why would a loving, merciful God do that to someone like you? How can you be so sure that is His plan? Is it possible that God is giving you another chance at life? What if becoming Elizabeth is God's plan? What if He gave you an aggressive form of cancer because He knew you would never commit voluntary euthanasia like Andrew was willing to do? And since you are dying anyway, it should be easier for you to accept my offer. The whole situation seems made to order to me, but what do I know about God?"

"Oh, Walter, you have always been supportive and understanding. Such badgering seems out of character for you. It seems like you're trying to put doubts in my head. I feel like God has sent you here to test my faith."

"That's nonsense, Margaret. My take is that He has sent me to give you the opportunity to have a new life. He is practically handing it to you on a silver platter. Maybe He heard you tell me recently that if you had a magic wand and could be a young woman again, you would run to Duke and find Andrew. Maybe this opportunity is the magic wand. Maybe He isn't through with you yet. Maybe He has another role for you to play. If He doesn't, the surgery won't be a success, and He will take you anyway. Surely He won't mind if you simply exchange dying on the operating table for dying full of morphine here at Argo."

Margaret was on the verge on tears. Her emotions were in turmoil contemplating the possibility of having a second chance to live life with Andrew. She sipped her port and tried to envision their new life together, this time with children.

"Look, Margaret, I am not trying to badger you into doing this. Well, yes, maybe I am. For your sake and for Andrew's sake. Still, you are the only one who can make this decision, and you don't have to do it here right now. Just say you will think about it for a few days. If you do decide to become Elizabeth, we must move quickly before any of the cancer gets to your brain. Will you at least give it some thought?"

"This is all so sudden and confusing, Walter. And you of all people talking about God and His plan for me. I will pray about it. I will ask God to guide me to the right decision. I will ask Him if you are the devil incarnate, Walter, tempting my soul to hell."

"Well, if you are already there, it will make it a lot easier for you to find Andrew when he arrives."

chapter 21

Walter's News

*S*arah answered the door barefooted, wearing a saffron silk sari and gold bracelets on both arms. The red dot on her forehead, the bindi, was slightly off. Andrew wondered if she always wore costumes to match her cooking or if this was for his amusement only. The geisha outfit she wore for her teriyaki dinner three weeks ago when he was there last was a real stand out, lots of intricate embroidery on satin. She even had the chopsticks or whatever they were in her piled-up hair. Sarah said it was authentic geisha dressing she had picked up while she and Harry were in Japan. They loved to travel. Took a trip every year. In bits and pieces, they had managed to make their way around the world several times during their marriage. She said she made it a point to buy some traditional clothing almost everywhere they went. Andrew thought her closets must be amazing, wondrous troves to behold. The Smithsonian would probably have a heyday with her stuff.

"It's got to be curry tonight, Sarah. Am I right? Or are you giving a sitar performance this evening?"

"It's curry, handsome. Come on in out of the cold so I can close the door before I freeze my tits off. I shouldn't try to wear this gossamer outfit in December. Looks like we are getting an early winter this year. I thought curry would warm us up. Come on in the kitchen. I'm having trouble getting the top off the curry powder."

"The top doesn't come off of this, Sarah. It's one of those twist-and-grind pepper containers. Where do you keep your spices? I'll find the curry powder for you."

"Oops, glad you were here to catch my mistake, handsome. The spice rack is up in the cabinet by the stove."

After dinner, Andrew and Sarah stumbled their way through some Beethoven, and then Andrew serenaded her with several pieces he had been working on at home. His bowing and finger work were getting better. His Guarneri violin was sounding sweeter and stronger all the time. He wished Margaret could hear him now.

"Well, handsome, I hope your week was better than mine. I spent the better part of a half hour looking for my car in the faculty club parking lot last Friday night after the happy hour. I only had one drink, and, as you know, the parking lot isn't all that big. Either I am not paying enough attention or my memory is getting exasperatingly lax."

"I really haven't noticed any problems until tonight, Sarah. Surely these problems didn't just start since I was here three weeks ago."

"I started noticing little things a number of years ago, forgetting names, where I put my keys—you know, the usual stuff that makes people laugh and call you an absentminded professor. But it was happening too much. It became worrisome, so I went over to neurology to get checked out. As you certainly know, medicine here at Duke is first rate, and it still took the doctors almost three years to diagnose my problem. It's hard to get an early diagnosis. It isn't the first or second thing that comes to mind because, until recently, early onset was considered relatively rare. Average life expectancy after diagnosis for Alzheimer's is eight to ten years. I'm four years in now. No one can say for sure how long I will last, but I can tell that I am getting worse. I have been reasonably successful in hiding my symptoms up till now. But now the problems are becoming obvious. I'm noticing some trouble remembering words giving my lectures, I'm losing my train of thought in seminars, and I'm beginning to find ordinary tasks more confusing and difficult. For example, I have difficulty making choices. That's why I always have you order for me when we go out to eat. So I have made the decision to resign at the end of the semester. I'll sell my house and give away all my belongings. I'm going to spend whatever time I have left to be independent living in Tuscany, painting bad landscapes and eating my favorite cuisine."

"But, Sarah, surely you aren't going to try to live in Italy by yourself in your condition, are you?"

"My favorite graduate assistant is going with me to help with my journal and play caregiver. She will be using my information to write her doctoral dissertation, so her time won't be wasted, and I will be paying her well. Don't worry. I'll be okay; she'll take good care of me. Enough about the wretched future, handsome. Let's concentrate on the present. I haven't forgotten any of my bedroom tricks yet, and there are still a few you haven't seen. Isn't it about time we headed that way?"

Andrew was used to Sarah's rituals now. He let her undress him slowly, massaging him as she went along to increase anticipation. After dropping her sari quickly to the floor, revealing her nude body underneath, she escorted him into the shower and oiled him up and down all over and massaged his back and chest and groin areas far longer than necessary as the fine warm spray of the shower glided over the two of them. Next came the big, heated Turkish towels and a soothing body lotion. Finally, they lay down on her freshly washed and ironed eight hundred thread-count sheets.

"Now I want you to just spread out and make yourself comfy, handsome. I am going to have my way with you tonight."

And she did.

Andrew left before Sarah got up and headed for the Washington Duke Inn, which was on his way from her place to the office. It was a stately yet friendly place he frequented for lunches, drinks, or a bad round of golf. He loved the breakfasts there, especially the mushroom omelet and French toast, and he was in the mood for a big breakfast after last night. He had never met anyone like Sarah before. Despite her intellectual accomplishments, as evidenced by two shelves of books she had published by leading university presses, Sarah had an offhanded manner unusual for an academic. She was uninhibited, brazen even, kooky, flamboyant, outrageous sometimes, certainly not the kind of person Andrew would ever have imagined wanting to spend time with. But she was amusing, spontaneous, lively, and unpredictable, all things Andrew needed to brighten his life right now. He was comfortable with her. He could forget himself for a little while. Actually, he felt absolutely normal when he was with her. She could make him laugh. And she was spectacular in bed. He wondered just how long she would still be the same interesting person he had grown to care about. It made him sad to imagine her living in Italy trying to chronicle the progression of her illness as long as she could, a sad diary of mental decline. Her last publication.

While he was having a second cup of coffee, Andrew noticed he had an e-mail on his iPhone. It was from Walter. "You'll never guess what! After all these years, I have decided to do another transplant, only this time it is to be a brain transplant and not a body transplant like you had, and it's on females. The donor brain has agreed to take the identity of the recipient body and to allow as much of the recipient personality to dominate as occurs naturally. Can you believe it? What good luck to be able to observe how this alternative transplant works. And there will be absolutely no publicity for ten years. The parties involved want total secrecy. So in the event that the operation is a failure, no one will ever have to know. The body is a twenty-three-year-old only child. The parents want the brain donor to be willing to accept the girl's name, the girl's personality to the extent possible, and continue to be their daughter. I thought their conditions would make it impossible to find a donor, but miracle of miracles, I have actually found someone without a family who is willing. More interestingly, except for age, the parties have similar demographics, so I hope to be able to test your theory that similarity will make an easier transition to another body, and this time no drugs will be necessary to maintain personality. If the perspective donor goes through with it, the operation will take place at my clinic next week. Wish me luck. I'll keep you posted, but obviously this is privileged info that can't be breathed to a soul. By the way, Cullen is doing well in her third year of med school, and Shawn is still hanging on to his good grades. Hope all is well at your end."

A female brain transplant. That's an interesting development. Andrew wondered where Walter could have found a donor willing to give up that much of herself, or more likely, what devilry he used to convince her to do it. If it worked, he hoped the poor donor knew what she was in for.

chapter 22

Ashes

*A*ndrew was glad to have the holidays over and the new semester underway. He usually went into a deep depression during the winter break and hibernated until the start of classes in January. It was his protection against the memories of happier Christmases past with Margaret. His inability to find a compatible jogging and coffee buddy like Walter made this time of year even lonelier. With all the faculty and students dispersed during the holidays, the main campus seemed like a deserted movie set or a relic, as if all the students had decided to get their degrees online. The emptiness reinforced his state of mind. Except for one rousing music night and several evenings with Sarah, there was nothing very thankful or merry about November or December.

It had been an especially cold, dreary winter so far, and there were still a couple of months to go. Andrew bundled up against the elements and headed home. He would work on his never-ending grant proposals sitting in his favorite green chair in front of the fire with a warm cup of tea. They never had the heat up enough in his office. Except for the newer buildings, the whole medical school was downright cold during the winter. If the government kept cutting the research budgets, they could turn off the heat altogether and the lights as well.

No sooner had Andrew settled into his chair than the doorbell rang. FedEx had a rather heavy package he had to sign for. He hadn't ordered anything and couldn't imagine who would be sending him something. He checked the label. It was from the Charles Wilson Law Firm. Andrew opened the package and found a letter from Charles on top of a large, sturdy cardboard box with an envelope attached to the top that said "For Andrew." It was Margaret's handwriting. Puzzled, Andrew picked up Charles's letter, sat down in his chair by the fire, and read:

Dear Andrew,

I am very sorry to have to tell you that Margaret passed away and was cremated on the ninth of December. She had been diagnosed with an aggressive cancer. She spent her last days out at Argo. She told me she wanted to stay there to die because Argo was the place she felt closest to you. Edith took care of her, and in recognition of her service over the years, Margaret has left her entire estate to her, including her half of Argo. She hoped you will give Edith your half as well. As Margaret's executor, I was given instructions to have her cremated remains mixed with yours, which she had kept these past years for that purpose. It was her wish that you decide on the place to bury or disperse them. You will find them in this box. Margaret wrote a letter, which she asked me to give to you along with the ashes. It is taped to the box. I know this sad news comes as a shock to you. I understand from Walter that Margaret is the only woman you have ever loved. If there is

*anything I can do to help you through this terrible
loss, I would be honored to do so.*

Charles

Andrew just sat there and stared at the letter for a long time. A deep
sadness overwhelmed him. He thought of her out at Argo all alone, dying
without him beside her. Why didn't someone tell him? Why didn't Walter?
Why didn't Charles? He would have been there. He would have taken a
leave from Duke and stayed with her until the end. He loved her. Surely
she knew he still loved her. Why didn't she call him to come? He didn't
get to say good-bye, again. Hard tears began to fall. Andrew just put his
head down in his hands and sobbed. He had not cried since he was a boy
and never this hard or this long.

The room had darkened with the setting sun. Andrew finally got up,
turned the lamp on, poked the ashes, and put several more logs on the fire.
Ashes. Margaret had saved his ashes to add to hers. Margaret the poet to
the very end. The poem of loss she had written after his operation, called
"Vines," had the lines "Like tangled vines they bloom as one / 'til winter's
frost and then are gone." Ashes instead of vines. Death instead of life. *Oh,
Margaret! How could your God let such a tragedy happen to our lives? We
were happy, a marriage made in heaven, kindred souls you always said. These
twelve years since my accident have been pure hell for the both of us. I had
dreams that somehow, someday, we would magically be together again. Your
God could have done that for us.*

Andrew looked at the box with the envelope attached. He decided
he needed something stronger than tea before he read it. He kept some
eighteen-year-old single-malt scotch in the fridge. He liked sipping it neat
and cold. He poured a full glass and hoped his meds could handle it. He
had an eight o'clock seminar in the morning. Maybe he would cancel. Yes.
He would call one of his postdocs right now to handle everything for the
rest of the week. Death in the family.

Andrew sat down with Margaret's envelope, carefully opened it,
and unfolded the letter as if it was something precious and fragile. Her
handwriting was always a perfect Palmer script. What a shame that no one
learned Palmer handwriting anymore. He noticed that she had written the

letter with her Mont Blanc fountain pen he had given her many decades ago. He could tell from the special nib marks it made.

My dearest, dearest Andrew,

I never expected to be writing you again. I thought it would be best for you if I just disappeared for good and left you to find a new path for yourself, hoping you would find the happiness that has been absent from your life for so long now. But Walter assured me your love still belongs to me and that I would be remiss not to write you this one last time. He begged me to have you come to Argo, but as much as I wanted to be with you, I thought it would be best for you if I didn't.

Isn't it strange how life zigs and zags? When you think you have life settled and know where it's going, it surprises you and changes directions. I have always believed that God works His will in mysterious ways. Still, given all we have been through, I am hard-pressed to understand what He has wanted from me and from us. Despite all my efforts to be obedient to what I believed His will to be, I have no idea whether or not I have in fact complied. I hope intent counts.

Do you remember the first time we met? It was junior year at Harvard, and you and I were starting our first rehearsal as the leads in Ibsen's A Doll's House. *I fell trying to hide the Christmas tree in the closet and twisted my ankle. You rushed over and lifted me off the floor and carried me over to the sofa. Then you lost your balance putting me down and fell right on top of me. Everyone laughed. You were so embarrassed and apologetic. I think I fell in love with you right then and there. You couldn't remember my name, so you kept calling me Nora. Whenever I wanted to tease you, I would call you Torvalt. Can you imagine anyone ever saddling a baby with that horrible name? You asked me out to dinner that weekend, and we were together ever after.*

I remember going with you to your summerhouse on the Cape to meet your mother and spend the weekend. She put me in the bedroom on the first floor so we would be properly separated, but you came tiptoeing down after she went to bed. We sat out on the front porch overlooking the ocean and made out until dawn. You told me that night that you were going to marry me the day after graduation. We had to show up for breakfast looking all bright-eyed and bushy-tailed and ready to go sailing with your mom. I don't think I have ever been so tired and sleepy and so happy. Funny how all those wonderful old memories come flooding back.

Andrew, I have never stopped loving you, and I will for all eternity. I know that you have loved me measure for measure. I also know that it would not diminish your love for me in the least if you were to find happiness with someone else now. Love is not a lake. It is a river that flows on and on. Your generous heart can carry both me and a new love. Please, I beg you to scatter your broken old life along with our ashes and start a new life, a different life but a robust one worthy of the unique opportunity God has given you.

My deepest regret has been my inability to say or do the magic thing that would turn your agnosticism into belief. You have always tried to approach God empirically with your mind. If you would only try to approach Him spiritually with your soul, I am sure you would find Him, Andrew. Can you not maybe be an agnostic intellectually but a believer spiritually? I have prayed all these years for God to help you find your way to Him. It is my fervent wish that He will spare you and let you be with me in heaven someday.

Oh, Andrew, I hate to bring this sad, short letter to an end, for when you read it, I will be gone. If God would stay my execution as long as I could tell you all the wonderful moments I remember of our life together, I would be Scheherazade and spend a thousand nights more telling you stories. If only I had the time to do so. Had I the magic to be in your arms one last time and kiss you farewell, I

*could more willingly leave this world. My heart is
full to overflowing. I am saddened beyond words
to express. I dare not say more.*

Good-bye, my love.

Your Margaret

Andrew read the letter several times before folding it carefully and
putting it back in the envelope. He walked over to his desk and placed it
in the drawer with the charred remains of his other letter from Margaret.
He was exhausted. He was cried out. He went to bed.

chapter 23

Cullen's Problem

$\mathcal{W}$alter had been very busy since the second week of December working with his new transplant patient. The operation was more difficult, but the surgery was a success, and Elizabeth seemed to be doing fine now. She was in an induced coma for longer than Andrew, but rehab had started. Walter was happy with the results so far. Having a truly motivated patient whose adjustment was less problematic helped enormously. Andrew had been right about closer demographics making a difference.

When his cell phone rang, Walter was surprised to see that it was Cullen. He called her every few months just to check in, but Cullen had not initiated any calls to him since Andrew left. He went into his office to take the call in private.

"Good to hear from you, Cullen. What's up? Is everything all right?"

"No, Walter. I have a terrible problem. It's Shawn. He was in a bad accident and had some internal injuries. He was on the back of a friend's motorcycle. The MRI showed Shawn has only one kidney, and it's badly damaged. I didn't know it, but apparently some people are born with only one kidney. It's relatively rare though. He's barely sixteen. How can this be happening, Walter? This is the last thing I needed right now. I'm not a match. The hospital has been searching for over a month, but so far no luck. I need your help."

"Is he on dialysis?"

"Yes. And he hates it. I can't stand the thought of spending months and months taking him to be hooked up to a machine."

"I know that's tough, but a suitable kidney will show up, Cullen. It may take a little while, but sooner or later one will be available."

"Oh, Walter, you can help me. Please help me."

"Just what is it you want me to do for you, Cullen? I can't get you a match from the transplant agency any sooner than your doctors at the med school can."

"Walter, I know you have all of Tony's information from the transplant for Andrew. Tony—I mean Andrew—could be a match for Shawn. If he is, I need him to give Shawn one of his kidneys. I'm desperate, Walter. Will you help me convince Andrew to do it?"

"What? The short answer is absolutely not, Cullen. Andrew could be a match, but Shawn is not in danger of dying. I don't want to take the risk of putting Andrew's brain through general anesthesia for an operation that isn't absolutely necessary. A good-enough match will show up eventually."

"Walter, a mediocre match will leave him on antirejection drugs. I don't want him to spend the rest of his life on drugs. Andrew could be a really good match. Please, Walter, check it out for me. Please."

"I don't want you to involve Andrew in this, Cullen. Even a small risk to Andrew's brain from the anesthesia isn't worth taking from my point of view. You have other options. I really don't want you to use Andrew. Besides, he may not be a match. Frankly, I hope he isn't."

"Oh, Walter, please check for me, and if Andrew is a match, please ask him for me. Given the way I left him, he probably won't even want to talk to me, and besides, I'd feel funny asking him to make such a sacrifice for Shawn when Shawn treated him so badly."

"So why you are willing to have him make the sacrifice? I'm sorry, Cullen, but this is one time Uncle Walter is not coming to the rescue. I will check it for you, but if he is, you, my dear, are on your own to contact Andrew. Knowing Andrew, my guess is he will feel obligated and honor bound to do it. Please don't press him too hard, Cullen. The well-being of his brain is still of major importance to me, and Andrew is not your only option. Like I said, a match will eventually be found for Shawn, even if it takes a while."

"Walter, do you know how hard it is for me to deal with a sixteen-year-old boy unable to play sports and be one of the guys in high school? He could be on dialysis for a long time before a match shows up. He is becoming more depressed by the day. His grades are going down, and his temper is getting out of hand. He inherited that from his dad. This situation is very difficult to manage with me still in med school. I need some relief from this as soon as I can get it."

"Sounds like the problem's more yours than his. Listen, Cullen, we have been through this before when Andrew showed up in his dad's body. You need to take him back to the psychologist. I'm sure you have enough money from Andrew's trust to pay for some therapy sessions. It worked last time. I would like to see you try some alternative solutions before you get Andrew involved in this. I would hate to have him all mixed up in the Tony stuff again, especially since he is still struggling with Margaret's death."

"Oh, Margaret died? I know Andrew still loved her. That was always clear to me. I left before I got her relegated to the archives, as you put it. So, I guess it hit him pretty hard. How did she die? She was still young. Was she in an accident?"

"No, she had an aggressive cancer. I'd rather not talk about it. Back to the issue at hand. Cullen, it's only the first of April. School doesn't let out until the first of June, so you have two more months before Andrew and Shawn would be able to have the surgery anyway without both missing classes. That gives you time to get some help, and who knows, a match could show up by then. Have the doctor send me Shawn's info. I will check for a match in case Shawn's status becomes critical, but I'm not going to tell you the result until June. So, you might as well try the psychologist first. If Andrew isn't a match, you will still need to get Shawn some help."

"Okay, Walter, I'll take him to see Chris, but I'm not sure how much good it will do. Since Shawn reached puberty, his personality has become more and more like Tony's. I hate his angry outbursts. I'm not sure he will agree to go see Chris again. He's too big for me to physically make him."

"Chris? Who's Chris?"

"Chris is the psychologist I used to take Shawn to see. He'd been trying to date me ever since. Finally, after I got through my first year of med school, I relented because I felt the need to have a man in my life. We've been dating for about a year and a half. Nothing serious, Walter. I don't know if I will ever love anyone else enough to marry him. Andrew is always there in the background. Chris knows and understands, but he wants to marry me anyway. He says I will grow to love him over time. Where have I heard that before! Still, I do enjoy his company—and who knows what life has in store."

"Well, life moves on, Cullen. That's a good thing. Andrew is best gone from your life now. He's adjusted very well to his new circumstances. His research is going well, and he's getting his life together. Occasionally I hear him mention someone by the name of Sarah, on the Philosophy faculty, I believe. I don't know how serious it is, but I hope he has found a suitable companion now. Anyway, let's not interrupt his life if we don't have to."

"Gee, Walter, there was a time when you encouraged me to go back to Andrew. You've really changed your tune. Why the shift now? Do you think that Sarah woman is a better match?"

"You are very tied up with med school, and there is the geography issue. I just think your lives are going in different directions now. I've never met Sarah. I don't really know much about her, but I do know Andrew enjoys not being reminded that he is in Tony's body. The people at Duke haven't known him in another body, so he's just himself to them. He told me that he'd always feel that he was just one pill away from being Tony to you."

"I know you well enough, Walter, to know when you are hedging and just making excuses. What's the real reason?"

"You are beginning to sound like my wife, Cullen. I don't know why I don't think it's a good idea anymore. I just don't think it will work now. Neither of you is in the same place you were four and a half years ago. Too much life has occurred, for both of you. Better to leave it alone. You need a husband that doesn't remind you of Tony. Andrew needs a wife that doesn't remind him of Tony."

"Okay, Walter, but I still feel like you are holding something back. I can see I'm not going to pry it out of you. I guess I'd better get back to the hospital. It's time for afternoon rounds."

"Bring Chris over for dinner sometime, Cullen. I want to meet this guy you're dating. He needs Uncle Walter's approval if he's dating my very favorite niece."

"Sometime, Walter, if it gets serious. Thanks. I'll have Shawn's info sent right away. Don't forget to check for me. It will be good to know even if we don't need Andrew."

Walter was glad to be through with that conversation. He wished he was a religious man so he could pray that a kidney would become available in the next two months. Andrew didn't need to return to St. Louis, especially not now. He went back into the clinic with Elizabeth.

"Sorry for the interruption, Elizabeth. Now where were we? Ah, yes. Muscle exercises."

chapter 24

Elizabeth and Dave

*E*lizabeth handed in most of the next installment of chapters she had been working on, but she was not quite ready for Dave to see the last few chapters she had written after much deliberation. They had been going out for dinner and afternoon coffee regularly for over a month now, and Elizabeth suspected Dave was getting serious. She enjoyed his company very much. He was refreshingly funny and had an endearingly optimistic approach to life. And he was also a romantic. So far he had taken her subtle hints and not even tried to kiss her, but she could sense that was about to change.

Elizabeth had very mixed feelings about the relationship and where it was headed. Dave was lovable, and his charm was having an effect on her. She could tell that her feelings for him were growing stronger in spite of herself. She tried to reconcile her religious beliefs with her new emotional needs and physical yearnings. Her emotions and intellect were constantly at war where Dave was concerned. Her new personality seemed to have a mind of its own, which she was always struggling to rein in. It bothered her that her beliefs were more intellectual now. She wasn't as emotionally connected to them as she used to be. She still considered herself spiritual but no longer felt tethered to her Episcopalian roots. The "thou shalt nots" didn't seem as commanding anymore.

The truth of the matter was Elizabeth was feeling very lonely. Like most twenty-five-year-old unattached women, she was aching to be loved in a tangible, satisfying way. It had been so long since Elizabeth had been in a man's arms and kissed him passionately she could hardly remember how it felt. Physically, she was still a virgin, and while that was unusual nowadays for a twenty-five-year-old, more unusual was the fact that psychologically she was not. She was quite frankly eager for a sexual relationship. Dave was a sweet, kind, gentle man, yet she could detect the strong sexual energy in his body; she often could feel him possessing her with just the longing in his eyes. Quite aside from the religious, moral question, there was the purely ethical one. Dave was playing for keeps; he wanted love, a home, a family, a lifelong companion, and Elizabeth knew he wanted it with her even though he had not yet said so. She yearned for those same things, but she knew she probably would not be able to give Dave all the love he deserved. Still, she couldn't help wanting as much of him as was possible without having to make a forever-after commitment. Was it fair? Who's to say? If circumstances stayed the same, maybe it would last, but if things should ever change, she might someday break his heart. She felt she had no control over her future. It was in someone else's hands, God's she hoped. But what if God had given her Dave? What if it had been His intentions all along? What then? How would she know if she didn't pursue the relationship to see? If God did intend for her to marry Dave, He had His work cut out for Him. There was already someone ensconced in her heart, lodged deeply in her soul, embedded in her psyche. But he had another life now. God seemed not to have chosen to give him to her. Elizabeth wanted to know why.

"You seem awfully pensive this evening, Elizabeth. Is anything wrong?" They were sitting in the Bull Durham Bar at the Washington Duke Inn having burgers and fries on the patio. Elizabeth was nursing the last of her beer. She loved this place in the evening. The landscape lights had come on, and the beautiful view across the golf course was almost invisible. She could still hear an occasional laugh from a nearby table, but the night sounds were becoming more muffled as the dew began to settle.

"I'm sorry, Dave. I was just thinking that the semester is coming to an end soon, and I need to decide if I'm going to take another class this summer or get a job. I have to go see my parents at some point. I haven't been to see them since Christmas."

"You seem to be very close to them. That's wonderful. My parents are divorced. I'm close to my mom. Dad remarried and moved to France. I haven't seen him in almost fifteen years, but we talk and catch up from time to time. He has another whole family now. He married one of his students, a French girl twenty years his junior. Mom is really my only family now. Mom has always said family is the very most important thing. Family is the bedrock upon which everything else has to be built. She's told me more times than I can count that I should never marry a girl who isn't close to her family."

Elizabeth saw Dave looking at her quizzically for a moment, probably trying to discern her reaction to that comment. He often did that. It was clear to her that he was trying to decide whether or not to take the next step.

"It's still early. Let's go back to my place and watch a movie or one of my operas. May I interest you in an opera? I have Zeffirelli's film version of *La Traviata*. It's wonderful. Very romantic. You'll love the music. Would you mind watching it with me? I would love to share it with you."

"Actually, I would enjoy seeing it, Dave. I had some exposure to opera at Harvard because my roommate was an opera nut, but she was into German opera and played Wagner loud and often. Quite frankly, all that bellowing above the orchestra by a ten-ton Brunnhilde was more than I could take. I was so turned off I never bothered to explore opera any further than the little bit I had in a history of music elective one semester. I remember liking the Italian bel canto period, but I don't remember much except that one was by Bellini. I remembered his name only because my roommate's last name was Bell. You'll have to explain what's happening though. I don't understand Italian."

"The film has English subtitles, but if I tell you the plot, you can just relax and enjoy the beautiful music and not bother with the script. The action is pretty self-explanatory. I can promise you won't be disappointed."

Dave had not been kidding about the opera. It was actually filmed on location, not on the stage. The music was indeed lyrical and passionate. Elizabeth fell in love with Violetta. She understood the personal cost of her sacrifice in giving up her beloved Alfredo at his father's behest. Elizabeth's eyes were brimming with tears. They started running down her cheeks. At the end, when Violetta was dying and Alfredo, who now understood why she had left, came rushing to her bedside in time for her to die in his arms, Elizabeth was crying uncontrollably. Dave gave her his handkerchief and put his arm around her. Fortunately, to Elizabeth's relief, he didn't say anything, but the way he held her to him said volumes. He seemed to know instinctively how to comfort her.

"I'm so sorry, Dave. I don't know what came over me. It was so beautiful and so sad."

"Yes, it was. I am moved every time I watch it. Violetta's love for Alfredo was rather like your Margaret character's love for Andrew. Did you notice the similarity? I was hoping you would see the connection. After I read your story, I immediately thought of this opera. I've wanted to show it to you for some time."

Elizabeth started tearing up all over again. This time Dave stood up and raised Elizabeth to him. He enfolded her in his arms and held her as closely as he could and buried her head against his shoulder. He stroked her long, soft hair and kissed it over and over. Finally, he ever so gently raised her head and kissed her, softly at first, then with the thirst of a man dying for water. Without saying a word, Dave took her hand and led her to the bedroom. He carefully unbuttoned her blouse and slid it off along with her skirt. He ran his hands gently over her smooth torso before sending her bra and panties to the floor. Then he swiftly removed his clothing and kissed her again, skin to skin. Elizabeth could feel him hard against her. Dave lifted her onto the bed. Elizabeth didn't stop him.

The morning sun was streaming through the open bedroom window when Elizabeth opened her eyes. She didn't remember that the window was open last night. What time was it anyway? Eight thirty! She never slept that late. There was some noise coming from the kitchen and the smell of coffee. Dave appeared in the doorway dressed for the classroom with a mug in his hand.

"Good morning, sunshine. You were sleeping so soundly I didn't have the heart to wake you. Here's some joe to get you started. Breakfast in ten minutes, so don't dally."

Elizabeth took a few sips and headed for the shower. It was a rather strange morning-after feeling to be perfectly comfortable waking up in

Dave's bed and being handed her morning coffee with milk, no sugar, and a sprinkle of cinnamon, just like she liked it, as if they were an old married couple grooved into a routine. How natural it all seemed. After the initial pain of entry, the sex had been great. And Dave? It was clear to her that he wasn't having sex. He was making love to her. He may have wanted to plunge right in, but he took it slow and easy, giving her pleasure and exciting her until she pulled him to her. He made up for the wait.

Dave placed a perfectly done omelet on her plate as soon as she entered the kitchen.

"Don't start getting any ideas, Elizabeth. This is the only thing I know how to cook. So unless you want an omelet or cold cereal every morning this summer, you are going to have to pick up a potholder or two. In a few weeks when the semester ends, you will need a place to live for the summer, especially since you are going to do a graduate seminar with me and finish your novel. This arrangement will make it more convenient for both of us."

"Oh, this is probably the smoothest invitation to live together anyone has ever received. It was that good last night, huh? I passed the test to be this summer's live-in? I think I detected a supposition in there somewhere that I'd accept and that I'd be taking a seminar with you instead of getting a job."

"Well, I thought I would solve your housing problem for you, and if you stay here, it makes sense for us to be working together, hence the seminar. As for being this summer's live-in, I haven't had a summer live-in before. The only woman I have ever lived with is my former wife, who left me four years ago because she found life in academia insular and boring. She moved back to New York to take a job with Sotheby's. She has a doctorate in art history. We met at Yale. We were young. So now you know the story of my life. Not once since then have I asked someone to come live with me until now. Not once."

"You didn't exactly ask me."

"I know. I was afraid if I asked you might say no. It's been on my mind for a while. After last night, I thought you might be willing if I kept it casual enough. No commitments or anything like that. You will accept, won't you, Elizabeth? I think we're very compatible, and I know we'll have a good time together. I will always respect your privacy when you want it. I'll never assume that I have a right to your body just because you're in my bed. I'll always be sensitive to your wishes. I'll even turn my desk in my study over to you for your writing. I can do my writing at the office. And, wait, wait—that's not all, folks. This offer continues for the fall semester as well, if you feel comfortable enough to continue our living arrangements after you have spent the next three months with me."

"Well, how can a girl say no to all that? But I don't want to take your writing desk. I always do my writing on my iPad, usually in the library or a coffee shop, or on a bench in the Gardens, now that you've introduced me to them. You can even play your opera, as long as it isn't German. But, really, Dave, I have no idea how this is going to work out, and you don't either. I'm a rather complicated person; you don't really know me."

"You're wrong, Elizabeth. I do know you. I know all I need to know to love you. The details will come with time. I can't imagine anything that you could ever say or do to change my heart. Your Margaret character isn't the only one who knows how to love unconditionally."

"Dave, you're a wonderfully sweet romantic, but I thought you said you were going to keep this casual with no commitments. Let's enjoy the summer, but let's not expect too much of each other. At least, please don't expect too much of me. That way no one gets disappointed or hurt."

chapter 25

Cullen's Dilemma

*C*ullen was aggravated and exhausted from dealing with her son. She had shared her anxiety over Shawn's kidney failure and depression with Chris, but she had been reluctant to admit to herself and him that she almost couldn't stand being around Shawn anymore; he had turned into a teenage version of Tony. Now, at Walter's urging, she told Chris that Shawn was exhibiting the same overtly aggressive personality that Tony had. His teachers were concerned about his belligerence, and given his size now, Cullen was a little afraid of Shawn herself. He was obviously a kid who acted out his frustrations. She needed Chris's help once again to get Shawn under control. Chris told Cullen being a sixteen-year-old boy wasn't easy when there weren't medical problems and a missing father. He told her not to worry so much; time would fix most of this. Cullen doubted it.

In reality, if anyone needed counseling right now, it was Cullen. She was spinning out of control. After an unfortunate traumatic incident during her second year of med school that practically derailed her prospects for a career in medicine, she had completely transformed herself into an obsessed, strong-willed woman, determined to be at the top of her class no matter the cost. Even being at the top of her class wasn't good enough. She needed to be seen as exceptional by the faculty. She needed to prove to herself and everyone else that she was worthy of the second chance she had been given to complete her medical education. She needed more than ever to be somebody important, someone admired for more than her looks. She also wanted to prove to Meghan, who came to her defense that fateful night, that it was worth the risk she took to do so. To that end, she had developed a veritable fortress against any obstacle that could tumble her ambitions, and she was ready to do battle with anyone who stood in her way.

Controlling her emotions was her biggest challenge now. She still loved and wanted Andrew. He was the goal, the brass ring to reach for. But she had wandered off script; she also loved Chris. And she still loved the vulnerable little boy who was buried somewhere inside of her son. Shawn's behavior and medical problems were further complicating her life, adding extra stress and pressure. She knew that he really needed much more of his mother right now and that she could make a difference in the direction of his life if she gave him more of her time. Cullen could detect small cracks in her resolve; her plans were in danger of crumbling. She struggled with her conflicting feelings of love, guilt, and ambition, but ultimately ambition won out. She was not going to let Shawn or Walter or Chris stand in her way.

With only months left to make her specialty decision, Cullen was now confused about her choice. Ever since her discussion with Walter four plus years ago about Andrew's personality drugs, Cullen had been determined to become a psychiatrist so she could take charge of Andrew's formula and make adjustments as needed. Having control over his personality would erase her fears about Andrew becoming Tony, thereby enabling her to marry him. Cullen's dilemma was caused by one simple fact: she didn't really like psychiatry and had no natural affinity for it. It wasn't even her second or third choice of specialty. And too, Walter was signaling her to back off. His words: "a lot of life has happened since Vail." Did she really want to go into psychiatry for Andrew's sake if his life and her life were going in different directions now? If Andrew were out of the picture, what kind of medicine would she really like to practice? Walter was hiding something from her that could help make her decision. He was giving her the signal to move on. She interpreted it to mean Andrew was not an option anymore. She wondered why Walter thought he wasn't. Andrew was living inside the body she gave him. Andrew was hers; he belonged to her.

And Cullen was sure she could take care of anything that could possibly get in her way of having him, even if it meant breaking up a marriage.

Cullen's relationship with Chris was another matter. Because she enjoyed the comfort and convenience of having Chris around to depend on for whatever, Cullen had allowed the relationship to become more serious than Cullen had initially planned. While they weren't living together because of Shawn, their sex life was quite active. On more than one occasion, Chris had asked her to marry him. Walter had certainly been right about the intensity of a present love overshadowing a love languishing in the background. Cullen had thought she would never love anyone but Andrew, that her love for him was permanent, exclusive, and inviolate. But Chris was Irish and had her dad's red hair and green eyes, and with an infectious smile not unlike her dad's, he had unexpectedly found his way into her heart. The fact that he was good in bed didn't hurt. But Cullen had no intention of being the wife of an unknown clinical psychologist when she could have a world-renowned doctor for a husband. She was not about to relegate Andrew to those archives Cullen had once hoped Margaret would inhabit someday. And now Margaret was dead. Did this new revelation change anything for Cullen? With the competition gone, it could be easier to get Andrew back in her life. But how exactly? That was all part of what she had to figure out.

"Earth to Cullen! Hey, I asked you a question. And your coffee is getting cold. I don't blame you for not drinking it though. The coffee here in the hospital cafeteria is not the best. Come back down out of the clouds. What are you thinking so hard about? I asked if you would like to go out to dinner tonight."

"Sorry, Chris, can't tonight. I have to work."

"I thought you were off duty."

"I am, but I don't know what I'm going to do for my residency, and I can't stand not knowing what comes next and planning it out. Between you and Shawn, I don't get much alone time to think. I need to sit down and do some hard thinking."

"I don't see why it has to be decided tonight, but if you're set on it, come do your thinking over at my place. It's quieter there than at your place with Shawn and his friends playing their guitars and banging on the drums. Nobody can think with all the noise. Besides, I can help you work your way through the thought process. I'll order us a pizza or two, and we'll go at it."

"That's what I'm afraid of, Chris. We'll end up going at it, and I'll not get a thing accomplished."

"Hey, I'm an honorable man. I can keep my hands off you for a few hours. Please come. Let me help you. I need to look after my own interests in this process. I want to lobby for staying here in St. Louis and making Washington U your first choice. With your grades, I know you'll get your first choice no matter where it is."

"The specialty I choose should dictate where I apply, not where my boyfriend lives."

"Your boyfriend? Since when have I been downgraded to the status of boyfriend? I may not be the love of your life yet, but I am at the very least your significant other. I would readily be your spouse if you would just say the word."

"Chris, this isn't the time to bring marriage into the equation. Deciding my specialty is a serious matter. After I've settled on a specialty, you can help me decide where."

"Just for the record, Cullen, love and marriage are serious matters too. Besides, I thought you'd already decided. You've been telling me you're going to be a psychiatrist for the past two years. What's making you rethink it at this late date? I thought it was settled long ago."

"That's the problem; it was settled long ago. That was then, and this is now. Things have changed a bit. Duty has been guiding me to psychiatry, not passion."

"You mean Andrew. When are you ever going to stop fixating on Andrew? Andrew this, Andrew that. Andrew has always been your driving force. Everything you have done, excluding dating yours truly, has been done for Andrew. At what point do you think you will have done enough for this man who has been out of your life for almost five years? At what point will you decide to put yourself first, to do what you have a passion for, to love someone who adores you and is here with you now? For God's sake, Cullen, you gave the man his life back when you gave him Tony's body. Why do you think you have to give him your life too? Your conscience should be clear about taking the money. He told you your life is your own."

Chris was on his soapbox again. This wasn't the first time Cullen had heard this.

"I'd like to think that our relationship has something to do with your rethinking process, Cullen. I'd like to think that you're not discounting our relationship as something you can easily toss aside as if it has meant nothing more than a convenient way to have a little sex and pass the time while you're getting trained to take care of Andrew. I was beginning to think my love was having some impact on you. Don't just stand there mute, Cullen. Tell me I matter to you and I'm at least a consideration in your decision-making process. I'm totally in love with you. Andrew has never loved you. You told me yourself he loved his wife and probably still does. Why should he matter more than I do?"

"You do matter to me, Chris. That's the problem. Deciding not to be a psychiatrist is the same as choosing to forget about Andrew and his future needs if something happens to Walter. I have felt obligated to Andrew and have wanted to be in his life ever since I've known him. My self-esteem was so beaten down by Tony, that beyond Shawn, I had no sense of purpose in life. Andrew became my raison d'être. Being with him some day has been my goal for so long I have accepted it without question. My mind has been closed to any other possibility. I thought my heart was closed too. That's why I have refused to marry you. Walter recently told me Andrew's wife died. Now that she is dead, there could be a real chance he would eventually marry me. Instead of discussing options, I should be packing my bags and rushing to Duke to do psychiatry. But my direction has become less clear. My feelings for you have complicated the situation. My heart has put me on pause. You've become far more important to me than I realized, Chris. I'm very dependent on you emotionally. I'm beginning to think I love you. Besides, you remind me of my dad, and you are the only person I know who can make me laugh."

"Then stay in St. Louis with me. Marry me, Cullen. Go to Washington U and specialize in something you enjoy. Andrew has managed to get along for five years without you. He can manage the next forty just as well. And if you don't ever have to deal with him again, what difference would it make if he does turn into Tony?"

"It would matter to Andrew. The last thing he would want is to be stuck with Tony's personality for the rest of his life. Let's not discuss this anymore now, Chris. I have to get back to the hospital. Afterward, I'll come have pizza with you, but I won't stay. These are decisions I need to make on my own with a clear head, without pressure from you or anyone else. After all, it's my life. There are lots of angles to consider. I have to do what's best for my career, what's best for me."

Chris slowly nodded his head. "Why, out of all the women who have been interested in me, did I have to fall in love with someone so peculiarly ambivalent? You have me hooked on the bait, but you seem totally uninterested in reeling me in. I feel like a plaything, Cullen."

Cullen ignored his comment. "See you at six, Chris." And with that, she walked out of the cafeteria.

———

After pizza with Chris, Cullen decided to drive over to her favorite coffee shop in Clayton for a latte and a little solitude before heading back to her noisy house. This time of evening, she could always count on a quiet table being available. Most everyone there was alone with a laptop. Cullen detoured past Andrew's old house on the way. The brick had been painted taupe by the new owners, and the beautiful boxwoods edging the walkway had been cut down. It looked entirely different now, just like its previous occupant. If she hadn't known the address, she would never have recognized it.

Cullen got her latte and found a comfortable seat in the corner. It was a quiet night with the usual laptops glowing. Cullen's iPhone lit up. Meghan was calling to touch base like she often did.

"You need to keep me in the loop, Cullen. I've thought of another reason you shouldn't be doing your residency in psychiatry. You're a high-energy person, and psychiatry is a slow profession, sometimes rather boring, dispensing medicine mostly. I can't see you spending all your time dealing with other people's mental and emotional problems. You don't seem to have enough patience to deal with your own and Shawn's. Isn't there any area that has captured your heart or engaged your attention? Surely you've had a rotation that you liked best."

"Well, to be honest, I really enjoyed pediatric oncology, of all things. If I were to pick something I really find interesting and challenging, that's what I think I would want to do. Working on the cancer ward at St. Louis Children's was particularly gratifying. Everyone is so grateful for anything you do, no matter how small. If you are able to really help, the parents treat you like a god. What do you think, Meghan? You're a nurse. You've been on that ward before. Is it a fit? Do you think I would be good with the kids?"

"Well, I'm sure being treated like a god appeals to you. Seriously though, there are pluses and minuses. You can be a reasonably compassionate person when you want to be. You're usually patient with small children, and your voice is soft and sweet. Children respond to beauty, so that part works, and I think you have a personality children would find comforting. You'd be good at it medically, but you may not have the emotional stamina to handle it in the long run. I can see you getting burned out rather quickly. There's a lot of heartache. The little ones have to endure so much, and they don't understand why. And some of them don't make it. It's really hard, Cullen. And sometimes, when a child doesn't make it, the parents blame you because they have to blame someone, and they can't blame God. You might have some trouble handling that kind of hostility. You don't take criticism or abuse well. Also, you get attached. Anyway, I can't imagine you changing directions at this late date. Something must have happened to make you question going into psychiatry for Andrew. Is Chris beginning to talk some sense into your head? Are you going to stay here in St. Louis? That would be wonderful, Cullen. I've been worried about your quixotic notion of sallying forth to Duke to save the great Dr. Hamilton, especially when he probably doesn't want or need to be saved. I've told you a million times what craziness I think that is. Barnes-Jewish and St. Louis Children's are both in the top twenty hospitals in the country. You'll get good training. Are you thinking about marrying Chris? Tell me, Cullen, why the sudden possible change?"

"Well, I haven't decided anything for sure yet. I'm just taking a last look at my options. I need to make a decision soon so I can start planning my future. I know it's still early, but you know how anxious I get when I can't see around the next curve."

"Cullen, it seems simple enough to me. Even though you've always said you would never marry anyone who isn't a medical doctor, and Chris is only a psychologist, he does have a PhD, and he's a wonderful man. He loves you and wants to marry you despite your obsession with Andrew. You've told me you love being with him. Did you love the last time you were with Andrew, in Vail? How did that work out? When was the last time Andrew said he loved you? Never! Not once, ever! You don't even know if he has found someone he can love now. By the time you finish your residency, he could be married to a professor or a student or someone he met at a party. He may already be married for all you know. You don't really know anything about his life over the past five years beyond what little Walter has told you. Why is this so hard? Stay in St. Louis. Do your residency in pediatric oncology or internal medicine or anything other than psychiatry. Swallow your false pride about marrying an MD and marry Chris. After all, you will have enough prestige being a doctor yourself. Ta da! Dilemma solved."

"Okay, Meghan, slow down. I'll sleep on it."

"Look, Cullen, with your grades and recommendations, you will get your first choice even if it's Johns Hopkins. If you have to leave town, I would rather see you go there or anywhere but Duke. Forget Andrew. He doesn't deserve you, and you don't need to be constantly reminded of Tony."

"That's the third time I've heard that in the past seven days. Walter told me it was time to move on last week. Chris told me that this afternoon."

"Three times in one week sounds like your guardian angel is looking after you, Cullen. How many more signs do you need?"

"All right, Meghan. Like I said, I'll sleep on it. Gotta go now. My latte's getting cold."

"Okay, Cullen, but one more quick thing. I've been thinking about what you told me not long ago about Shawn's behavior, and it occurred to me that part of Shawn's problem with his attitude toward you could be plain jealousy of Chris and the amount of time you spend with him."

"He still doesn't know I've been dating Chris. My hours are so erratic I've been able to keep it from him. He's been in such a bad place psychologically since his kidney problems started I've been reluctant to say something that might make him worse. After the resentment he's carried for Andrew, I don't want to introduce another man into his life unless I'm sure I'm marrying him. Besides, Chris is going to do some more counseling with him. It wouldn't be a good thing for him to know right now. I really do have to go. Talk to you when I've made my decision. Good night."

By the time Cullen drank her latte and left the coffee shop, she knew exactly what she was going to do. She would hedge her bets—stay in St. Louis for now to be with Chris, but she would do her residency in psychiatry. She was sure she would eventually have Andrew back in her life. Meanwhile, Chris would do just fine.

chapter 26

Andrew and Sarah Again

$\mathscr{A}$ndrew was glad to see the end of the spring semester. It had seemed almost interminable to him. Not even the glorious riot of color in the Gardens could coax him out of his mourning mode. He tried to tell himself Margaret had removed herself from his life years ago, so it shouldn't really make any difference now that she was dead. But it did. Her letter tore him to pieces. She had loved him until the very end. She had wanted him there with her. Once again she had sacrificed her own needs to do what she thought was best for him. He ached for her. He fervently hoped there was a heaven for Margaret's sake. He would invent one for her if he could, just so she wouldn't be disappointed. Andrew certainly understood now why almost all religions subscribe to an afterlife: it is too painful to believe a person one has cherished simply disintegrates and is gone, that love cannot protect the one adored from permanent, irreversible death. Love should confer immortality. Religions make that possible.

Andrew needed a change of scenery to get himself out of his depression. He was tired of his research, tired of his lab, tired of academia, but mostly tired of himself. Andrew needed another dose of Sarah. He could always count on her to cheer him up. He felt comfortably himself in her presence. Despite her increasing concerns over her degenerative medical condition, she still managed to keep her spirits up, especially when he was around. He also needed a diversion, a change of scenery. He'd always wanted to take the coast-to-coast walk across northern England, ninety miles of English summer, from sea to sea across the moors, through the Lake District, staying in little villages, eating in local pubs, perfect for two weeks of forgetting everything else. This would be a good time to do that, and he would ask Sarah to go with him. She loved to travel, and Andrew knew she had never taken a walking trip. It could be a perfect sendoff for her new life in retirement.

"Well, hello, handsome. It certainly didn't take you any time to get here. That horny, huh? I barely had time to hang up the phone and put my happy face on. Want your usual? Drink, that is."

"You're in a jovial mood, Sarah. I came to take you out to dinner and make you a proposition."

"You're going to proposition me, lover boy? That's a role reversal! Let me grab my purse. I can't wait to hear what it is. Oops, I forgot my jacket. They turn the air-conditioning on in the restaurants around here way too early. It's usually too cold for me. Be back in a sec, handsome, or follow me into the bedroom if you dare."

"I'll wait out here, Sarah. If I come in the bedroom, knowing you, we may never get to dinner."

By the time dessert came, Andrew had convinced Sarah to take a trip with him and let Charles handle getting her house sold while they were gone. It didn't take much persuading. Then he told her about his plan to take her walking across the "waist" of northern England.

"That sounds like a wonderful trip, handsome, and I'd love to go, but I let my passport expire, and I just applied for a new one to get ready for Italy. This is the busiest time, with all the teachers and students going abroad for the summer. I'm sorry to say you will have to go without me. It can't possibly get here in time. What a bummer! I would have had two glorious weeks with you scandalizing the prudish English."

"Well, I guess I'll have to think of something stateside because half the fun of that trip was going to be taking it with you. So, if there's any place in the country you'd like to go, name it, and if I haven't been there with Margaret, we'll go."

"Hmm, let me think. You know, there's a place I used to go every summer for several weeks when I was a little girl. We rented one of the cottages on the grounds. I used to hike, horseback ride, play tennis, and go skeet shooting with Papa. Haven't been back there since I was fifteen. I don't know why Harry and I never went. I'd love to go back there one last time."

"Okay, Sarah, but you haven't said where it is."

"It's a wonderful old resort called the Greenbrier, in West Virginia of all places. About a six-hour drive from here. At one time it was a place presidents went in the summer. It even has deep underground chambers for government operations if our country comes under attack. I'm sure the resort has changed a lot in the past forty years, but from what I hear, it's still a beautiful place. I hope you haven't been there with Margaret. I'd really like to go."

"Haven't been there, Sarah. You're in luck. I'll make reservations for the next two weeks. I'll even reserve one of the cottages. We'll leave Sunday."

"Oh, this is going to be so much fun, handsome. Two whole weeks with you. I can't wait to get you back home to show you how excited I am. Get the check and let's go."

———

Sunday came quickly. Sarah was standing on the doorstep with a ton of luggage. "All that luggage, Sarah. Didn't know you were moving today. I thought we were going on a trip."

"It's just a few of my favorite costumes, handsome. Figured this is my last chance to wear them. I couldn't decide which ones to bring, so I brought them all. Hope I won't embarrass you too much."

"Not a chance, Sarah. I'll just pretend I don't know you if it comes to that."

Andrew loaded the car and started down I-85 toward I-77.

"You know, Andrew, you've become very important to me. I've never had a close male friend before, except for Harry, of course. I want you to know how much your friendship has meant to me. Will you come see me once in a while in Tuscany?"

"Of course I will, Sarah. You've become equally important to me, helped me make the transition to my new life and helped me get back to my violin. Besides that, you've spoiled me rotten. Where will I ever get such a good lay again?"

"Well, at some point I hope you fall in love with someone. You need more than sex and friendship with a woman twenty years your senior. Haven't you found anyone yet? You've been here five years now. You never talk about other women, but you aren't with me every weekend. Surely you've met someone who's a possibility."

"You forget. I'm eleven years older, not twenty years younger. Don't let the body fool you. And I've had a few dates with several professors and grad students, but they're all so young and energetic. They wear me out. I just can't get interested in them. They're so optimistic and unrealistic, shallow seeming even when they aren't. They like crowds and noise and Facebook, they drink too much, and they're incessantly playing with their cell phones. They're like butterflies and hummingbirds, a sip of this, a sip of that, never staying still for more than a millisecond."

"But that's one of the glories of being young and being with the young, Andrew. Everything is still possible; the world is fixable. They want to make a difference. Their energy is contagious. Doesn't it lift your spirits a little? Have you become that bogged down in life? Boarded up the windows and taken down your sign? Really, Andrew, don't be such an old soul! Did spending all those years in a wheelchair wither away all your expectations about life? You can't spend the next forty or fifty years mourning the loss of Margaret. You mustn't fritter your life away regretting what isn't possible. Margaret would want you to take advantage of this second chance to live your life. It's a gift, a miracle really. I wish I had a second chance, especially knowing what I know now."

"People say if they had it to do over again, they would live their lives differently, but I don't see it that way. I'd want to do it the same, except for my accident of course. Otherwise, it was perfect."

"Oh, come on, Andrew! Nobody's life is perfect. You have a selective memory. The good parts are what you want to remember. You told me you always wanted children. Not having any was less than perfect, just to name the first thing that comes to mind. You have become mired in a past that has been severely edited, romanticized. In fact, you've been acting more like a widower in his eighties, his life's work finished, his love buried, and his mind shuttered against the future. While you're jogging around campus from time to time, you need to jog your mind into a younger way of thinking. Get some more of those thirty-something juices in your body flowing up there to hit the restart button. We'll start at that place we're going—the, the, you know, the Greenbrier. Yes, that's it. I'm going to show you a good time, lover boy. We're going to have some crazy fun."

chapter 27

The Greenbrier

It was a lovely ride up through the Shenandoah Valley to White Sulphur Springs, an area Andrew had never seen. The dogwoods and rhododendron were still blooming, dotting the woodlands and meadows along the way. The profusion of azaleas and flowers on display when they arrived at the Greenbrier made it high season for spring all over again. Andrew decided right away that he was going to like this place.

While Sarah was unpacking and dressing for dinner, Andrew walked over to the main building to have a look around. When Sarah finally arrived, she was wearing a beautiful Viennese ball gown, complete with powdered wig and a beauty mark on her right cheek.

"So this is why I had to help you into a corset. Aren't you a little overdressed for Sunday evening dinner, Sarah, or is this place that formal? You didn't tell me I needed to bring my tux."

"You always look well dressed to me, especially when you aren't wearing anything. We're going dancing tonight, handsome. The ballroom is this way. Hope you know how to waltz."

"Wouldn't you like to have dinner first, Sarah? I'm starving. Besides, it's Sunday night. Most places don't have an orchestra on Sundays."

"Who needs an orchestra? We'll dance to our own music. A waltz is a waltz."

"Did you know that the waltz was considered indecent when it was first introduced? Respectable people condemned such closeness as inappropriate for young ladies. But then it was fun and it caught on, so the elites took it over, and it became all the rage. May I escort Madame into the dining room? I need some energy if I'm going to dance the night away."

The days went quickly for Andrew and Sarah, filled as they were with riding, bad tennis, worse golf, and hiking. Sarah wanted to go bowling too, but Andrew drew the line there and managed to talk her out of it. Each day for dinner, Sarah wore one of the many costumes she brought with her. Andrew had to help her into a lot of them. It was fun to see her so lively and delighted with ordinary things that she managed to make extraordinary. She was almost a kid again, and Andrew could imagine how much fun she and Harry must have had all those years traveling together, uninhibited by what was expected. He was almost sorry that he and Margaret had always played it so straight, a second less-than-perfect thing about his former life.

One morning Sarah joined Andrew for breakfast wearing her safari outfit from Kenya.

"What's on for today, Sarah? Big game hunting?"

"I thought we'd go up to Kate's Mountain Lodge and shoot some skeet like I used to do with Papa. Do you mind?"

"No, of course not. I must warn you. I've had a lot of practice shooting mistletoe out of trees, but I've never tried to shoot a moving target."

"Great! You need lots of new experiences. We need to juice up that brain of yours a bit more. Dancing without music was a start. You did pretty well, considering. Teaching you to Charleston the night I wore my red flapper dress was great fun. Wish I could have taken pictures to remember it. I've never seen you laugh so hard. You were hilarious."

By the time Andrew and Sarah got up to the Mountain Lodge and were fitted with guns and coached on how to aim ahead of moving targets, it started to rain. So they went back down the mountain to their cottage and never came back out. Room service brought champagne and dinner. Room service brought champagne and breakfast.

"Enough, Sarah, enough! Please no more. I've had so many climaxes in the last twenty-four hours, I'm sure it qualifies for the *Guinness Book of World Records*."

"Aw, lover boy, I'm just getting started."

"No, Sarah, no! I mean it! Please, please, no, no, ooh …"

Every day was a new adventure with Sarah. Andrew was relaxed; he smiled more than he had in a long time. Sarah was good medicine. People sometimes stared at her as she walked into the dining room. Others just enjoyed the show, eager to see what she would be wearing next. Sarah was having the time of her life. Andrew was so glad he had brought her here for a last hoorah.

———

On their day of departure, Andrew was taking a long walk around the grounds while Sarah packed. The old familiar ringtone on his iPhone startled him. Cullen? Could it be a mistake? After all these years? His sunny day began to darken. He put himself in neutral and took his cell out of his pocket and answered.

"Cullen? This is a surprise. It's been a long time. You're getting ready to start your final year of med school, aren't you?"

"Yes, my last year starts in another month, thanks to you. It's going well. Look, Andrew, this is an awkward call for me to make. I'm really sorry to bother you, but I have a huge problem with Shawn, and you are the only person who can help me with it."

"I seem to remember your using that line on me once before, Cullen. I don't mean to be unkind, but it didn't end very well last time. I'm rather out of practice playing the Tony role. Can't say that I've missed it."

"I know, Andrew. I know. I was afraid you wouldn't be particularly pleased to hear from me after the way I left you in Vail. That's why this call is so awkward. I had hoped to find a solution without getting you involved, honestly, but I have no alternative. And I asked Walter to make the call for me, and he wouldn't do it. So I had no choice."

"Well, if Walter wouldn't make the call for you, he must disapprove. What's your problem with Shawn this time, Cullen?"

Cullen described the situation as dramatically as she could.

"Poor boy! Is he on the list for a kidney?"

"Yes, but it's been four months, and they haven't found a match yet. It's almost impossible to juggle his dialysis and my schedule and put up with his frustration and depression. Life will be so much easier for both of us once he has the new kidney."

"Cullen, I'm sorry you are having such a hard time, but why do you need me? What can I possibly do for you that the doctors there aren't already doing?"

"Well, I can't think of an easy way to say it, Andrew, so I'll just tell you straight out. I want you to give Shawn one of Tony's kidneys. Walter checked the information in Tony's files. He said you're a match. I'm asking you to give Shawn one of his father's kidneys."

Andrew knew that Cullen had obviously spent some time figuring out just which button to press to put the most pressure on him, make him feel obliged. He could feel that Tony anger rising in him. He waited until he had it enough under control to speak in a reasonable tone.

"What? Oh, I see. I like the way you put it, Cullen. Not one of my kidneys, one of Tony's! That's a rather large request, don't you think? Is Shawn in a critical state and can't wait for a match to show up?"

"No, not exactly, but I'm in a critical state and need the problem to go away."

"So, let me guess. Walter didn't want you to ask me because it isn't medically critical and he doesn't want to chance how the anesthesia might affect my brain. Did I get it right?"

"Yes, Andrew, you know Walter all too well, but I really need you to do it for me. I don't have time to wait for a match. Shawn is unmanageable. He's becoming more and more like Tony every day. I can't stand the turmoil. I need to concentrate and do well this last year. You know how important the fourth year is. I have my career to think of. I want to get a good residency."

"So it isn't so much your concern for Shawn as your concern for yourself? I would really be doing this for you, not Shawn? That sounds more than a little callous. What happened to the soft, gentle Cullen I used to know before Vail? You seem harder now, more self-centered. Has med school changed you that much?"

"I'm just stressed out, Andrew. Being a single mom in med school is hard with a son at home like Shawn. You were able to see some of those personality traits as he started reaching puberty. Now he is full-blown Tony, especially since he started dialysis. You certainly know how strongly I react to that."

"Rather hard to forget, Cullen. I still have your letter."

"Well, will you do it for me, Andrew? Walter was being overly protective about your brain. I talked to the surgeon here who said it could be done microscopically and that it wouldn't hurt your brain in the slightest. He said you would be under no more than an hour and a half at most. You would be up and out in a couple of days and back to your normal activities and exercise in three or four weeks max."

"You make it sound so simple, Cullen. I'm not thrilled with the prospect of another operation. Pardon my saying so, but it's rather bold of you to ask when it isn't medically necessary as a last resort. Why don't you call me back in six months if you haven't found a donor and it's critical?"

"But it's critical for me now, Andrew. I can't wait six months. It needs to be now, and I don't have time for you to think about it. It's already scheduled for next Thursday. At Barnes. Dr. Lathem is doing the surgery. He says he knows you."

Andrew's blood pressure hit the ceiling. He was livid. He could feel Tony taking over in earnest. He was about ready to explode through the phone.

"What? You set it up before you even asked me? That takes a lot of nerve even for you, Cullen. You think I'm that easy to manipulate? Well, you can call Dr. Lathem and cancel it, Cullen. Just because you gave me your deceased husband's body doesn't mean you have a right to take back parts of it whenever you want and on your own timetable. It's my body now, Cullen. It houses me."

"Walter said you would do it if I asked, that you would feel obligated under the circumstances. I scheduled the surgery because I was sure you'd do it, you'd come to Shawn's rescue. You're that kind of generous, caring person. You will do it, won't you, Andrew? For me?"

"No, Cullen, I won't. I don't like this one bit, and I particularly don't like the way you have insinuated it's my obligatory duty. I said cancel the surgery and call me back in six months."

With that, Andrew shut off his phone. He was fuming. He started walking, and the madder he got the faster he walked. By the time he was back in control of his emotions, he was practically jogging. He slowed down and took a couple of deep breaths. How could Cullen have changed so much in less than five years since Vail? Something had to have happened to cause such a dramatic shift in her behavior. Andrew could not think of a single hint of indifference or hardness in her character back when they were dating. How could she be so callous now about her own son's suffering? What kind of a mother did that? He could remember how deeply concerned she was about Shawn when they first met. She was the perfect mother back then. *Poor Shawn. He's never recovered from his father's death, and he's never recovered from seeing Andrew in his dad's body.* Andrew started feeling guilty, knowing that he was partially responsible for Shawn's suffering. The more he thought about it rationally, now that he had cooled off, the more he was inclined to reconsider. If he did give Shawn one of his father's kidneys, Shawn maybe would find some comfort in knowing at least a little of his dad would always be with him. Yes, thought Andrew, maybe that was the answer. He really should agree to the transplant, not for Cullen's sake, but for Shawn's. He took out his phone and called Cullen back.

"All right, Cullen, I'll do it but not next Thursday. You'll have to reschedule. Set it up with Lathem for the end of the month. I have some important things I need to do over the next couple of weeks. And for the record, I'm not doing it for you. I'm doing it for Shawn. Tony's death left a big crater inside of that boy. With my kidney, Tony's kidney, as you so delicately reminded me, Shawn will have a piece of his father back to carry with him for the rest of his life. Maybe that will give him some comfort."

"Oh, Andrew, thank you so much. I can't tell you how grateful I am, for this and for everything else." Cullen said it in that soft, sweet voice she used on Andrew whenever they had made love. It calmed him down, made him remember the Cullen of his dreams, the one he fantasized about when he masturbated or had sex with Sarah. He took a deep breath.

"And it will be so good to see you again, Andrew. Shall I pick you up at the airport?"

"No, that won't be necessary, Cullen. Charles will get me. I want to go out to Argo."

"Argo! Oh, I'll take you out to Argo, Andrew. I have fond memories of our times out there together. You remember those times too, don't you?"

"That was a lifetime ago, Cullen. Thanks for the offer but no thanks. I have something I need to do out there. I was going to have to make a trip to St. Louis eventually. You just pushed my timetable forward a year or so."

"You sound mad. You aren't mad at me are you, Andrew? I can't stand the thought of your being mad."

"If that's the case, Cullen, you should have considered it a distinct possibility before you called. I need to go now. I'm meeting someone in a few minutes. You can give Walter the details. I'll get them from him. Good-bye, Cullen." He shut off his phone before she could reply.

Andrew started walking back to the cottage, still mad at Cullen and upset with himself for letting her manipulate him into agreeing to the operation. He didn't want to have this surgery, he didn't want to be back in St. Louis right now, and he definitely didn't want to see Cullen. There were some good memories, but he tried not to think of them since the ending had almost sent him over the edge. It took him a long time to recover from her total rejection as a potential Tony knockoff and to regain his sense of self and his sense of self-worth.

Left with the responsibility of dispersing Margaret's and his ashes made him realize there was only one place to scatter them. They belonged at Argo, the place they had enjoyed their most wonderful times together. He knew he would have to return to St. Louis sometime to take them to the farm. He simply wasn't ready to face it yet. Cullen just changed all that for him.

Sarah was waiting with her baggage on the porch of the cottage when Andrew got back. She was back in her traveling clothes. Her big smile when she saw Andrew brightened his spirits. The last vestiges of his Tony mood disappeared.

"Can we have lunch down at the tennis club before we leave, handsome? I'm famished."

"Of course, Sarah. We have the long drive back, and there isn't really any place convenient to stop. By the way, I forgot to tell you that Charles called yesterday and said someone has made an acceptable offer on your house and wants to close in three weeks."

"Three weeks? Oh my God, Andrew, how can I get rid of all my stuff that fast, and where will I stay while I'm waiting for my passport?"

"I can come over and help you sort through things you want to keep and give away to various friends or organizations and institutions. The leftovers can be sold in an estate sale. I'll have Charles set that up for you. Don't fret. It'll be fine. As for a place to stay, you can come over to my place until you are ready to leave for Italy. You can have your own bedroom, or maybe I can persuade you to sleep with me. I have to make a trip to St. Louis at the end of the month. I'll be gone for three or four weeks, so you will have the place to yourself while I'm gone."

"St. Louis? I thought you said you never wanted to go back there. Why now?"

"I have Margaret's and my ashes to scatter. I decided Argo is the best place to do it. I thought I might as well spend a little time there as long as I'm going. The lab is covered, so it's not a problem. Don't worry; I'll be back before you leave. I wouldn't let you go without a send-off night of hot sex. I want to make sure you remember me for a little while anyway, at least until you find a new Italian boy toy."

"You needn't worry about that, handsome. I will hold on to my memory of you about as tightly as I hold on to Harry. Well, not quite as tightly but almost."

chapter 28

Becoming Tony

*W*hen Andrew got home, he immediately put in a call to Walter. "So you're going to do it, aren't you, Andrew? I told Cullen that I knew you would, but I practically begged her not to get you involved in her life again. She was absolutely determined. I told her it might hurt your brain, which of course wasn't true. I just don't want her back in your life, Andrew. You're in a good place now. You don't need the stress of being reminded of Tony and the past. But there was no dissuading her. I don't know what's gotten into her. She's changed, Andrew."

"I've noticed a big change in her too, Walter, but I always had the idea that you wanted to see us back together. What changed your mind? You seem to be rather passionate about us not getting together now."

"I don't know, Andrew. It's just a visceral feeling. I don't know what's gotten into her or what happened. Several years ago, she called me in the middle of the night from the hospital ER, crying hysterically and asking me to come down, but I was in bed with the flu, and she didn't want Rose to come. She never told me what was wrong, but I did notice a certain coolness in her demeanor after that and a change of attitude in general. Cullen's a different woman now. And not for the better. She seems to have become very strong willed, driven almost. And a little too self-centered, if you ask me, given her feelings of being inconvenienced by her son's illness. I've heard some rumors among my colleagues at the med school that she's learned how to use her beauty to get what she wants. I'm pretty sure what she wants now is you, Andrew. You need to keep away from her."

"You needn't worry about that, Walter. I got a good dose of what you're talking about when she called me. I made it clear that I'm doing it for Shawn, not for her. Now, about the surgery, Lathem told her an hour and a half under would be max. If that's the case, it shouldn't be a problem, should it?"

"No, I called Lathem myself because I didn't trust Cullen on this point. He assured me it probably wouldn't take nearly that much time. He does these all day long, over two hundred a year. The sticking point for you is that you'll have to be off your drugs for the full two weeks prior to surgery, so you couldn't have had surgery next Thursday even if you wanted. But it does mean you have to stop taking them right now. I suggest you take half a dose of everything for the next two days and then stop altogether. You will just have to hole up at home and deal with Tony's personality until the operation, but for God's sake, Andrew, don't drink. You've been there before; you know what it does to you. Anyway, I'll schedule surgery with Lathem for the afternoon so you can have the pre-op blood work that morning. You needn't come any earlier than a couple of days before. The usual tests can be done one day prior to surgery."

Andrew spent the next several days helping Sarah sort through her things. She invited her graduate students to come over and take whatever furniture and odds and ends they wanted. She insisted Andrew take her favorite painting, a Miro aquatint Harry had purchased for her on their honeymoon in Paris. She decided to donate all of her costumes to the Smithsonian and her extensive music collection and piano to the Duke Music Department. The rest, including her car, would be sold at auction and the proceeds given to Meals on Wheels, a charity that Sarah felt provided a much-needed service more efficiently than most. By the end of the week, Sarah was moved into Andrew's house, and her house was ready for new occupants.

"Well, handsome, I could never have accomplished all that so quickly without you. You really put in some long days. I think you overdid it a bit though; you seem a little edgy and off your game."

"No, Sarah, that isn't the problem. It's something else. I'll be all right. Don't worry."

"What is it? You can tell me. Maybe I can help."

"There really isn't anything you can do, Sarah. I might as well tell you now as later though, because it's only going to get worse. You know that bag full of drugs I have to take every morning to regulate my personality? Well, I've had to stop taking them. I'm going to donate a kidney to the son of my body donor. Sounds odd, doesn't it? My body donor! Anyway, that is the real reason I'm going to St. Louis."

"Oh, so that explains it. I was worried that I was beginning to get on your nerves. Why do you have to donate your kidney? I thought that's what organ banks are for."

"It's a long story, but suffice it to say I'm a match, and I feel like I owe it to the son to give him back a piece of his dead father."

"I think that's very generous and thoughtful of you, handsome. So, help me understand. Without your drugs, your personality is going to become more like that of the donor body? What was he like?"

"Not someone I care to be. I struggle with his abrasiveness and dark moods every time I have a little too much to drink. That's why I never have more than two or three drinks when we're together. Even though my mental capacities are still my own, the piece of his right frontal lobe that was left in asserts itself when my brain chemicals are out of balance. They make me prone to strong, negative emotions, especially in stressful situations. The extra adrenalin throws my drug chemistry out of kilter as much as alcohol does. Put them together, and I can be a holy terror."

"That must be terribly disturbing, handsome, almost schizophrenic."

"You're right about that, Sarah. Maybe I should volunteer to be a psychiatric study subject for multiple personalities: who I am now, who I was before, and who I am struggling not to be. Seems like I am always in a transitional phase, becoming and unbecoming who I am."

"You told me once you have no doubts about who you are. Whether or not you realize it, handsome, you have just admitted to me that you are not just your brain. You change with the circumstances."

"No, Sarah, my personality changes with chemical compositional changes, but my brain stays the same. It is the constant by which I know when I am behaving differently. I'm always aware when these changes come over me. I just can't control them very well."

"Really, handsome, I think you're begging the question, mixing brain and mind again. Your personality is part of who you are. It is the you that you present to me, to your colleagues, to the world. Personality is the zest of being, the emotional context that adorns your thought process, that makes you interesting and sexy. But mind has to be dressed, made presentable. Otherwise you might as well be cold text read off the page. And your brain, handsome, is no more than the circuit system. The mind can't run without electricity, but it creates all manner of wondrous things when the lights are on. Your personality gives those things dimension and flavor, so to speak. But I've never even heard you mention your self, Andrew, just your brain."

"Now you're really splitting philosophical hairs, Sarah. My brain is my self."

"No, it isn't. There is a part of you that knows when your personality is changing, when your emotions are changing, and when your mind isn't as clear or as sharp. Your self is the underlying constant against which all these changes are measured, not your brain as you claim."

"I have to hand it to you, Sarah. For a person who can't remember what she had for dinner yesterday, you still manage to defend your philosophical positions rather passionately. And cogently, I might add. If I weren't feeling so Tonyish tonight, I might be halfway inclined to concede your points."

"And I might be halfway ready to give Tony an outlet for some of those strong emotions. Shall we, handsome?"

"Well, if you like these emotions, Sarah, just wait till I'm ready to leave for St. Louis. I'll be about as full-blown Tony by then as it gets. One small side benefit—I was told he could be great in bed when he was in a good mood."

"I don't think I'll have any problems keeping you in a good mood, lover boy. You're in good hands with me."

chapter 29

Andrew at Argo

*A*ndrew was fidgety. He couldn't get comfortable, even though he was sitting in first class and no one was sitting next to him. It was too warm. He turned his air up, and then he was too cold and turned it down again. This flight to St. Louis seemed to be taking forever, not that he was in any hurry to get there. All the old memories were crowding in on him, reminding him once again of what he had lost, first with Margaret, then with Cullen. And here he was going back, having to face his past again, having to face strewing Margaret's and his ashes at Argo before he was emotionally ready and having to face Cullen. Andrew decided to have one scotch on the rocks to take the edge off. Then he figured he could manage a second one without any problem. Pretty soon the edge was almost gone. Andrew decided on a third one for good measure.

When the plane hit the runway in St. Louis, Andrew was soused. He was irritated when he didn't see Charles waiting for him in baggage claim as agreed. A few minutes later, he felt a tap on his shoulder. When he spun around, there stood Cullen.

"Welcome home, Andrew." Cullen gave him a big hug and a peck on the cheek.

Andrew's mood made a mercurial rise to high dudgeon. He didn't try to hide his temper. He waved her away from him and grabbed his bag.

"Why are you here, Cullen? Charles was supposed to meet me."

"I told him I would pick you up. I told him you and I had a lot to discuss. Aren't you glad to see me? I told you I would love to take you to Argo."

Andrew was in a full-blown fury now. Walter was right. This new Cullen was a very strong-willed woman. Well, he would show her what a strong-willed man was like!

"You have a lot of nerve changing my plans without consulting me first, Cullen. Isn't taking my kidney enough? Do you think you also have a right to the rest of me at your beck and call? What's gotten into you, anyway?"

"Calm down, Andrew. You're off your drugs and acting like Tony again. And you're drunk, just like the last time I saw you."

"You don't need to remind me of Vail, Cullen. And don't you dare mention Tony to me again, or I'll take my kidney and go back to Durham. You knew I'd be off the drugs when I got here. You knew I'd probably be like this. So why in the hell did you come?"

"Because I was anxious to see you, Andrew. I've missed you, and I didn't want our first time together since forever to be at the hospital with Walter. I didn't know you'd be drinking."

"Well, I have been, and if you'll excuse me, I need to catch a cab to Charles's office."

"Don't be silly, Andrew. I'll take you."

"I don't want to talk to you; I just want you to leave me in peace. I'm taking a taxi. Good-bye, Cullen." And with that, Andrew walked out of the terminal and left Cullen standing there.

By the time Charles reached Argo, Andrew had had several cups of coffee and a snooze. The edginess was gone, and so were the effects of the scotch. Andrew smiled when he saw the hillside of lilacs blooming as Charles drove him through the gate. He had called to alert Edith he was coming. Although she now owned half the farm, she said she didn't feel right about moving in and calling it home unless it was all hers. Andrew hadn't given her his half yet, but Charles told her he probably would.

Dinner was still warm in the oven when they arrived, and strawberry shortcake was sitting on the counter. The June crop was in, and a large bowl of berries was washed and ready for breakfast. Andrew wrote himself a mental note to have his half of the farm deeded over to Edith as soon as he left St. Louis, this time definitely for good.

How comfortable it felt to be back where he belonged—where he used to belong, he corrected himself. Being here brought home just how content, intellectually and emotionally, he had been with his old life before the accident. For the last seven years, he had simply been treading water by comparison. The transplant had taken away at least as much as it had given him. The accident had paralyzed his body and had broken his momentum, but the transplant had paralyzed his emotions and completely disoriented him. He could no longer find his true north. He was beginning to suspect that Sarah was right, that his magnetic field had shifted, that he was not completely the same person he had been in his former life. Sarah had insisted that even if his brain was the same, his mind wasn't and couldn't be. It had plasticity and its own way of changing, adjusting and adapting to whatever realities were presented. She told him he needed to stop fighting the difference and start embracing his new life and his new self. He knew Sarah was right, but he wasn't quite sure how he was supposed to do that. He still considered himself to be the same person in spite of all the evidence to the contrary.

After dinner, Charles and Andrew took their coffee out on the front porch to watch the birds settle for the night. The last time Andrew sat there, he was with Cullen. He remembered how high his spirits were that day, showing her the place, sitting in the stream, watching the stars fall out back. He had been the closest to happy he had felt since his accident all those many years ago. Andrew thought he had found his new life. He should have known better. He tossed his coffee out of his cup over into the shrubs and went back inside.

"Hey, what was that all about, Andrew? I think the coffee's good. If you don't mind, I'll finish mine before I go back out to the car and bring the ashes in. It's hard to believe those are actually your ashes in there with Margaret's. UPS just delivered them back to my office this week. I was afraid they wouldn't arrive before you got here. If I'd known you were coming back here to distribute them, I wouldn't have bothered to send them to you in the first place."

Early the next morning, Andrew left Charles reading an old *Scientific American* mag in the den and went out back with the ashes. He opened the box, gave them another big stir with his fingers, and sprinkled a handful of them in the lilacs, a few around the maple trees, and another handful in the gardens and pond. He went down the hill and stepped out onto his favorite rock. There he strewed the rest of the ashes a little at a time into the stream. He and Margaret would be carried away together wherever the water took them, gone without a trace but together. Andrew watched as the love of his life and his former self swirled in the eddies for a while before working their way downstream. Andrew then placed the empty box gently in the water and sent it sailing after them. *You said love is an ever-flowing river, Margaret, but all my love is flowing away with you; there is nothing left behind. My old self, the one you loved, will be your steadfast companion on the long journey to the ocean and beyond. You were my life, Margaret. I have no life now. I am empty.*

Andrew wasn't sure how long he had been sitting there on the rock tearfully reminiscing about the twists and turns of their life together, but eventually the noonday sun glinting on the water got his attention. He wished he could have stayed in that spot forever, but he knew Charles was sitting back at the house waiting to take him to the city. Charles had argued that it made more sense to stay in town and go to Argo after surgery, but Andrew felt he needed to disperse the ashes before surgery just in case something went wrong. He reluctantly allowed his reveries to evaporate with his tears, and, returning to the present, he slowly made his way back to the house.

"I'm ready to go to the hospital for pre-op tests now, Charles. I don't know why they couldn't wait until tomorrow morning and do all the tests at the same time. Except for an overnight bag to stay at your house tonight, I might as well leave my luggage here. I will be in hospital gowns for three days. I can wear what I have on coming back."

———

When Andrew arrived at the hospital on the day of surgery, Cullen was there waiting for him. She seemed softer, more beautiful than when she met him at the airport, more stunning than Andrew could remember. And, in spite of himself, here was that old automatic reaction again, damn it. Luckily, Walter was with her and immediately gave Andrew a distracting bear hug.

"Hello, Andrew. Welcome back. Did you have a good trip? Charles told me you came two days early so you could spend some time at Argo. I don't know why you didn't take up my offer to stay with me. Charles said you spent last night at his house. I thought you would want me here for moral support. Besides, I do have a vested interest in this process. And I thought it might make things less awkward if I were here. Cullen told me about the incident at the airport."

"Hello, Andrew. I'm happy to see you in better spirits today. A dose of Argo worked wonders on you." Cullen leaned in to him as she gave him a big hug and kissed him on the cheek again.

"Save the theatrics, Cullen. It's my kidney you are happy to see, not me."

"Oh, Andrew, be fair. Play nice. It's both you and the kidney."

"Okay, kids, save the reunion for another day. I've seen your pre-op lab results, Andrew. They look good. The paper work's done. You're preregistered. I'll go with you. I want to talk to Lathem and the anesthesiologist this morning. Surgery isn't until two o'clock. Cullen, you go on to Shawn's room. I'll catch up with you in the waiting room this afternoon. All right, Andrew, come with me."

"Shouldn't I go see Shawn before we go into surgery?"

"No, the sight of his dad might upset him. Not a good idea. Better for you to wait a day or so after the surgery."

Surgery went as expected with no complications, and recovery was coming along nicely. After several days in the hospital, Charles drove Andrew back to Argo and placed him under Edith's care. Andrew had wanted Walter to come out for a few days, but he said he was tied up with his new brain transplant and couldn't get away for more than a few hours at a time. Just driving out to Argo and back would use it all up. Andrew was certainly in good hands with Edith though. She clucked over him like a mother hen. Andrew knew she had taken equally good care of Margaret during her final days, but every time he tried to broach the topic with her, she just shook her head and said she couldn't talk about it. Andrew figured it had all been very hard on her emotionally, especially the end.

———

Toward the end of the fourth week, Andrew was feeling quite vigorous again. He was feeling so good he sent Edith home for a few days of rest. After all, she had been going nonstop every day since he got out of the hospital; she needed the rest more than he did. Besides, he felt like fending for himself and spending some time alone.

Andrew had seen Shawn the day after surgery and told him why he had wanted to give him a piece of his dad. It had brought tears to Shawn's eyes. It was the very first time Andrew had ever seen Shawn genuinely grateful. It made Andrew very happy with his decision to do it. He was surprised that Cullen hadn't called to say how Shawn was doing now that he was out of the hospital and back to his regular activities. Andrew thought maybe she had finally gotten the message that their relationship was over. He toyed momentarily with the idea of calling her to check on him and just as quickly decided against it. He had seen Shawn's vulnerable side and wished him well. He certainly didn't want to give any encouragement to Cullen by calling. She didn't need much. He was debating the pros and cons over an afternoon glass of Malbec on the front porch when a car turned into his driveway and stopped halfway up. He stood to walk out and see who it was when the car door opened and out stepped Cullen, dressed in a white lacey dress, looking ever so much like a special offering to the gods. Andrew felt those same familiar stirrings he always felt when he saw her. Tony's pheromones were at work again; at least that is what he told himself. He almost always fantasized about her while having sex, even though there had been a few graduate students who were stiff competition. He realized now why he had never been able to completely erase her from his mind. She was breathtaking. And she had been his!

"Well, hello, Cullen. Believe it or not, I was about to give you a call to see how Shawn is doing."

"He's doing beautifully. That's why I came out. I wanted to thank you."

"Oh, you needn't have come all the way out here for that, Cullen. You could've just called."

"That's what Walter said. He didn't want me to come. I'm not sure why. But I wanted to thank you in person for what you have done for Shawn, and for me too. I can't tell you how much I appreciate it. I know I sort of forced it on you, but you still could have said no."

"Ancient history at this point, Cullen. Why don't you sit down here in the swing? I'll get you a drink. I'm having Malbec. What can I get you?"

"I'd really like to have a glass of white wine, Andrew. It's rather warm today. Hmm, it's been a long time since I sat in this swing, but I remember the first time really well. It was one of the happiest days I ever spent with you, Andrew. Magical really. Did you feel the same way I did that day? Was it special for you too?"

"I don't really want to talk about that, Cullen."

"Oh, come on, Andrew. There's nothing wrong in two friends talking over old times. It really was a special day. Admit it."

"I said I'd rather not talk about old times, Cullen. Those days are long gone."

"Really, Andrew, there's no harm in admitting to me that it was a very special day. You remember it as special, don't you?" It was that soft, seductive voice again.

"Please, Cullen, can we talk about something else? Let's just sit here and enjoy our drinks and talk about the weather or med school or something. I'm not interested in discussing anything personal." Cullen was stirring up old memories of their time together at Argo, images of her glorious hair backlit by the fire while he held her in his arms and her beautiful body shimmering in the firelight when they made love. As he looked at her now, smiling at him in a flirtatious way, Andrew knew she was still his for the taking. He could feel his resolve melting. Despite himself, he still thought she was the sexiest, most beautiful woman he had ever known. He needed to get up and busy himself getting another drink.

"While you're up, may I have some more wine, Andrew? I didn't realize how thirsty I was. This one is almost gone."

Cullen followed him into the house with her glass. "Do you still have the little album of pictures I gave you about that day, Andrew?"

"Yes, it's come in handy over the years. Every once in a while, I get homesick for Argo, and I take the album out and look at the pictures." He immediately wished he hadn't said that.

"Does it remind you of me, Andrew, and how totally in love with you I was? Still am, really. I have to confess that's the real reason I came to the airport and why I wanted to come out here to see you. I couldn't pass up the opportunity to see if there's any possibility that we could still have a life together."

"A life together? Are you kidding, Cullen? No, I don't think so. Besides, Walter said you already have a significant other, that psychologist who said I needed to spend some time with Shawn."

"I've been dating him for several years, but he knows how I feel about you. Walter said you've been dating a professor at Duke. Is that a serious relationship? I'm surprised you're still single. Surely there have been plenty of interesting women to choose from."

"No, I haven't found anyone who interests me that way. Sarah's just a good friend, and she's moving to Italy soon. As for the two of us getting together again, Cullen, I'm afraid Vail put an end to that possibility. It took me a long time to get over your rejection. I wouldn't want to ever go through something like that again. Thanks to Tony, I don't deal with extreme emotions very well."

"In all fairness, Andrew, you are the one who didn't take your pills and started acting like Tony. Can you really blame me for leaving you under those circumstances? I was really scared. And when Walter told me about all the pills, I was even more afraid. The only thing keeping you from turning into Tony again is the concoction Walter has formulated to subdue Tony's personality."

"Then why are you here, Cullen? Why are you trying to stir up this whole mess of a situation again? I'm just getting comfortable being who I am in this body. I have worked hard to achieve a kind of peace with myself. I'm happy not to have anyone reminding me that I'm a bit of a freak. If my pills are off balance, it's just me on a bad day, not me turning into Tony."

"I'm here because I'm not afraid anymore, Andrew. I've discovered a way to take care of any problems in the future. Actually, Walter is the one who gave me the idea. Until recently, about six or seven months ago, he was advocating that I try to renew our relationship. Then, all of a sudden, he didn't seem to think it was a good idea anymore. I don't know what changed his mind. Anyway, I have decided to do my residency in psychiatry so I can monitor your drugs for you and see to it that you always have what you need. I don't have to worry about you becoming Tony again, and neither do you. I will be in control of your personality, so I will always be able to see you as Andrew. You are still the only man I have ever really loved."

"Cullen, are you crazy? That's insane! You're going into psychiatry for me, to preserve me? How could you even assume that I would allow you back in my life? I can see us over the dinner table now: 'I noticed a little bit of Tony in your tone of voice today, dear; time to change your formula again.' Do you think for one minute that I could spend the rest of my life having you constantly reminding me how I'm doing against the Tony index? It's impossible, Cullen. It won't work. I can't live like that. When I marry, it will be on a 'what you see is what you get' basis. There will be no warning label on the package, no instructions."

"But what happens when Walter dies or the formula gets lost or needs to be changed as you get older? You won't want to live the rest of your life with Tony's personality. You will be miserable if that happens. You need me to be there for you."

"I have the formula. Charles has a copy of the formula in his vault. If they all get lost or the formula becomes ineffective and I can't find a psychiatrist to handle it, Cullen, I will definitely kill myself. End of problem. You don't need to feel obligated to look after me. I definitely don't want you to look after me. Look, stop playing the martyr, if that's what you're doing. I told you a long time ago when I gave you the gift that your life is your own. No obligations. You have your whole life ahead of you. Go marry your psychologist friend and do your residency in something you really enjoy. Duty does not beget a long-lasting passion, anyway."

"But my passion has always been to be with you someday, Andrew. As I told you before, I'm still in love with you. What am I supposed to do? Doesn't it matter to you? You were almost in love with me once. Isn't there some residual spark worth fanning?"

"Cullen, we are both five years down the road from where we were. Circumstances have changed us both to some degree. It isn't that easy to just pick up where we left off, and where we left off is definitely not a place I wish to begin again."

"You still haven't answered my question, Andrew. Do you not still have some feelings for me? Could we not start over? Isn't it at least worth a try?"

The alcohol was beginning to have its mellowing effect on Andrew. There she was looking at him that way again.

"No, I don't really think so, Cullen. Of course I still have some feelings for you. How could I not? But never once have I entertained our being together again as an option these last five years. As far as I'm concerned, Vail shut the door on any future for us. I frankly think it'd be a disastrous mistake to try to resurrect our relationship. Too complicated. Too risky for me. I can't trust your staying power. Let's face it: I'm too old for this, too old for you. I don't have the emotional stamina to even try."

"Andrew, you're not too old for me. You're only thirty-eight. I'm thirty-five, almost thirty-six. As for your mature mind, I happen to be partial to your older-generation gentlemanly ways. I still love you after all these years apart. That sounds like staying power to me. Listen, Andrew, I'm off for the next two days. I was hoping I could spend them here with you. I brought my jeans. I have my overnight bag in the car. Please, can't we at least just enjoy this time together and see where it takes us? If it's nothing more than a last hurrah, it will make for a better ending than Vail. May I stay? Please?" It was that soft, seductive voice again.

"No, Cullen. That isn't a good idea. If you came out here to weaken my resolve about a possible future together, you might as well leave right now. I have no intentions of allowing my identity to be compromised again. I am not Tony, and I refuse to be held responsible for your discomfort if I remind you of him from time to time. I can't help that I look like him. The bodily reminder is always going to be there. That's just the way it is."

Cullen put her glass down and moved up close to Andrew, almost touching. He could smell the fragrance she always wore with him. She put her arms around his neck and kissed him softly on the lips and let her tongue tease its way in. He was hard now, and she was leaning against him.

"But I have missed you so much, Andrew. Can't we just enjoy each other while you're here? No strings, no expectations, just some good wine and good sex for old times' sake? What harm can it do? May I please stay?"

She was using that voice again.

"Okay, Cullen, putting it that way, I would be crazy to turn down such an offer from an irresistibly beautiful woman. But I want to go on record as saying this is sheer madness. I have no intention of changing my mind. As long as you truly understand that, I'll help you get your things out of the car. Shall we have lunch on the patio?"

chapter 30

Elizabeth's Final Chapter

*I*t was the second week of August when Andrew returned to Duke. He hadn't meant to stay the extra two weeks in St. Louis, but Cullen had her special way of persuading him. After a few weekends of fabulous sex and good-spirited camaraderie, she convinced him to stay a little longer. Surely it wouldn't hurt to examine the possibility of a future together one last time. Walter had been out several times. He opposed the idea flat out. He was adamant about not wanting Andrew involved with Cullen again, but his arguments were uncharacteristically vague.

Walter was also evasive about his new patient, Elizabeth. When Andrew offered to come by the lab and talk to her about what to expect and what coping strategies worked for him, Walter said it wasn't time yet for that kind of conversation, even though it had been eight months already. Andrew thought maybe Walter was just plain worn out from coaching his patient through the grueling recovery process. Maybe he needed to retire and let his protégés take over. He was in his seventies now and didn't have the energy he had seven years ago. Maybe that was why he seemed disagreeable and out of sorts. Walter said it was especially important to see this one through. Besides, it would only be a few more months before the patient would be ready to rejoin the world. Her parents were happy with her progress. She would be home for Christmas.

Walter needn't have worried about Andrew going back to Cullen.

Falling in love with her was out of the question. She wasn't really the same sensitive woman he used to know. Although she was on her best behavior and he still found her to be beautiful and extremely sexy, she had lost much of her softness and therefore much of her appeal. When he first met her, she had a sweet vulnerability about her. He had felt a need to protect her. Now she radiated a strident confidence he found a little overbearing. The other big drawback was the old Tony baggage that came with her. Andrew hated being constantly reminded of Tony. There was no getting beyond it. She would always be Tony's widow to him, and he would always be Tony's body to her. After many long, tiresome, and sometimes heated conversations, Andrew thought he had finally put the issue to rest, that he had persuaded her it wouldn't work. As for her specialty, Walter took charge of reaffirming that she needn't do her residency in psychiatry for Andrew. He told her it was ridiculous for her to think he had been so careless as to not make provisions for Andrew in his absence. Any good psychiatrist could manage his situation when it became necessary. Cullen didn't need to worry about Andrew. Andrew would be fine. She could take up a specialty better suited to her interests, stay in St. Louis, and marry Chris.

The rug had been pulled out from under Cullen's plan. She and Andrew kissed a brief good-bye at the airport and wished each other a happy and fulfilling life. Cullen couldn't keep her tears of bitter disappointment from falling as she watched the main star of her many dreams take wing and vanish into thin air.

Sarah was all smiles when Andrew returned. She said she was beginning to worry he wouldn't make it back before she left. Her rental in Italy was scheduled to start the middle of September. Her flight to Florence was scheduled to leave in three weeks. All of her possessions had now been given away or sold, including her car. Charles had come over for the house closing and had done a good job of seeing that everything was taken care of. Her bank account was full, and to help her manage her affairs as her illness progressed, he set up automatic payments for her monthly rental fees, monthly medical insurance premium, and a weekly living allowance in euros for as long as she lived. At her death, any residual amount would be given to the Duke Department of Philosophy for fellowships in her name.

Andrew and Sarah spent their last few weeks together like two lovers on furlough, cherishing every minute, afraid they would never see each other again. It was clear to both of them that what they had given to each other was a rare, special kind of friendship, love really. They gave each other validation, they felt each other's deep sense of loss, and they shared the music that nourished their souls, that enabled them to express the inexpressible. They showed each other they still mattered in this world. Andrew knew Sarah had saved him more than once from giving up. And Sarah credited Andrew for making her want to live out what was left of her life, to relish being alive to the very end.

"Well, handsome, I'm all set. God, I'm going to miss you! It's been such fun. Hope I can find a good-looking Italian gigolo to take your place. I know it won't be easy, but I'll try my best. Promise me you'll come over to visit before I forget who you are. I hope you'll bring a wife with you. Seriously, Andrew, nothing would please me more. I have to admit I'm glad things didn't work out with Cullen, but you do need a wife, one who will make you happy in your new life. Go find her."

"I'll miss you too, Sarah, in more ways than one. You take care of yourself. Keep in touch. Let me know if you need anything. And I will start looking for a wife. I promise. If I find one, you'll be the first to know. I'll have to send her over to you for some training."

Sarah laughed and gave Andrew a good-bye peck on the cheek. Andrew watched her board the plane and waved good-bye to this most unlikely, extraordinary, dear friend. Yes, he would miss her. He already did.

The house seemed quiet and lifeless with Sarah gone. He hadn't fully appreciated until now how her laughter had filled the house for the short time she was there, furnished it with energy and warmth. The emptiness was palatable. He nibbled at his meals and took long walks in the evenings to fill his time. He called her several times a week just to hear her voice and make sure she was settled and okay. He really missed Sarah.

———

By the time October rolled around, Andrew was back into his research. He was happy to be busy working with the new postdocs who had come on board. He didn't have time to dwell on his loneliness. His life was getting back to a well-greased hum when his phone rang during one of his usual afternoon breaks sitting in the Gardens. Cullen again! What now?

"Hello, Cullen. Is something wrong? Is Shawn's new kidney being rejected?"

"No, no, it's not that, Andrew. Shawn is fine. Are you sitting down?"

"Yes, what's wrong, Cullen? Has something happened to Walter?"

"No, no, it's not that either."

"Well, what is it then?"

"I have some rather interesting news, Andrew. I'm pregnant."

"Pregnant? You're pregnant? So you two decided to settle down and start a family. I'm a little surprised you didn't want to wait until you finished med school next May, but congratulations. I'm very happy for you, Cullen. I'm sure Chris is thrilled. He knows you will definitely marry him now that you're carrying his child. Have you set a date?"

"Andrew, Chris isn't the father. You are."

"I am? You're kidding, of course."

"No, I'm not, Andrew. It's your baby."

"What kind of joke is this, Cullen? I'm not finding it very funny."

"This isn't a joke, Andrew. I'm serious; it's yours."

"How can you be so sure? I don't mean to be indelicate, but how do you know I'm the father and not Chris?"

"I'm sure, Andrew. Chris was so upset I was spending all my free time with you he wouldn't have sex with me until two weeks ago. You were the only person I was with during July and August. You're definitely the father."

"This is hard to believe, Cullen. I don't understand. I thought you were on the pill. You were before, so I just assumed you still were."

"Well, I was and I am, but I forgot to bring them out to Argo with me a few times. I really didn't think missing a few days here and there would make a difference. Obviously, I was wrong."

"My God, Cullen, you've almost finished medical school, and you didn't know what every woman in America with three kids knows?"

"Well, I must have missed that particular fine point in my OB-GYN rotation. Anyway, I can't believe this is really happening to me, especially after all our conversations out at Argo. It's more than embarrassing. I'm in my last year of med school, which is bad enough, but given your feelings about any future relationship, this is absolutely horrible. What should I do, Andrew? What do you want me to do? My first instinct was to have an abortion, but since you've always wanted a child, and I've always wanted to give you one, I felt we should at least discuss the matter before I do anything. Chris doesn't know yet, and if I have an abortion, he need never know."

"Do you love Chris, Cullen?"

"In a way, yes. He's a good man, Andrew. I love him, but I'm not in love with him the way I love you. Still, he'll be devastated when I tell him. I certainly don't want to hurt him unnecessarily. If you don't want me to have your child and be in your life, then just say so, Andrew, and I'll get rid of it."

Andrew was reeling with conflicting emotions. A child. Cullen was carrying his child. How could something so wonderful, a child, and something so terrible, the prospect of marrying Cullen, come wrapped so tightly in the same package? How was he supposed to respond? How could he respond? He was speechless.

"When you put it that way, it sounds horrible, Cullen. What's the huge hurry? Why do I have to make a decision right this minute? I haven't had time to even absorb this news yet, much less make a decision. I'm not some cold, unfeeling person who can nonchalantly tell you to go ahead and get rid of it. You know how much I have wanted a child. I need some time to think it over, Cullen. Is that too much to ask? Several days?"

"I'm at eight weeks, Andrew. If I'm going to have an abortion, I need to get it done now. What's so hard to decide? When I found out I was pregnant, I was thrilled. I knew immediately I wanted to have your baby—but only, of course, if you wanted it and me. Am I so very hard to live with and love? I know you didn't want to continue our relationship when we were together this summer, but doesn't this change the equation for you? Don't you want me now that I'm carrying your baby?"

"It's all such a surprise, Cullen. I do still have some feelings for you, but I don't want the specter of your former husband shadowing me for the rest of my life. As I told you when I was there, I have enjoyed the past five years living my life free of references to Tony. But I have to admit, your pregnancy does change things. I don't know how I can possibly tell you to destroy my child."

"Then are you saying you want me to have the baby and you want me to be your wife? Are you? Is that what you're saying, Andrew? Are you sure about this?"

"This is all quite surreal, Cullen. And so sudden I'm not thinking very clearly. But yes, I guess that's what I'm saying. I can't imagine that thinking about it for a week will bring me to a different conclusion. I can't tell you to destroy my child. Are you absolutely certain this is what you want, Cullen?"

"Andrew, why do you think I spent all that time with you out at the farm? I'm in love with you. I want to have your baby. I want to be your wife. If I didn't, I wouldn't have told you. I would've had an abortion, and that would've been the end of it. You would never have known."

"Then I guess that settles it. I suppose we should get married, Cullen. I want our child to be legitimate and have a proper home."

"We don't have to decide all the details right now, Andrew. I just hope the baby doesn't come until I'm through with this final year. End of May. It'll be close. There is another complication. Chris convinced me to make St. Louis Children's and Barnes my first choice for a residency in pediatric oncology. It's too late to change. I'll have to wait until next fall to apply for a transfer to Duke. That means it will be almost two years before we are together."

"Two years? Why two years? That's a long time. I would miss the whole first year of the baby's life except for a few holiday visits. You should take next year off so we can get settled into our new life in Durham. You can spend all your time the first year with the baby to give it a good start. We could get married right away to make the baby legitimate."

"My, you really are behind the times, Andrew. No one cares anymore whether or not the parents are married when the baby is born. As for assuming that I should quit my career path for a year to come to Duke to be with you, that isn't an option. And it's a very selfish, sexist position for you to take. Why don't you quit or take a sabbatical for a year and come here?"

"You know I can't move back to St. Louis, Cullen. It would spiral me right back into a deep depression to be with all those painful memories again. And I gave Argo to Edith, so I don't have the farm to escape to either. Besides, I'm in the middle of a major research project. I just received another multimillion-dollar grant. Coming back to St. Louis is out of the question. Be reasonable, Cullen. If I'm going to have a wife and child, they should be here with me. I thought you said you were partial to my old-fashioned, gentlemanly ways."

"Andrew, you are the one being unreasonable. If you won't come here to be with me while I do my first year of residency, you'll just have to wait until I can get there. I have worked too hard to get where I am to stop now. I don't want to lose my momentum."

"But what about the baby? Your schedule will be hectic that first year. The baby won't see either of us enough to know it has a mother and father. That can't be good. Please come here as soon as you finish this year and marry me. Let's start a home for the child."

"Listen, Andrew, you seem to be a lot more concerned about the child than about me. I've been a stay-at-home mom once already. It isn't all it's cracked up to be. I don't have the temperament for it now. My primary interest is my career in medicine."

"I thought you just said a few minutes ago that you love me and you want to have my baby and live your life with me. Do you or don't you, Cullen? I'm getting confused."

"Yes, I do, Andrew, but on my own timetable. Look, if you are so concerned about missing the first year with the baby, why don't I bring the baby to you in Durham. You can be the single parent the first year, hire a nanny, and enjoy walking the floor with a colicky infant and having sleepless nights. That would actually work well for me, now that I think of it. You forget I already have one child to tend to. Thank goodness he's driving now and can take himself to school, but still, he isn't easy to manage. Another good reason to wait. Shawn will be finished with high school in two years and headed for college. You won't have to deal with him much again."

"Are you serious, Cullen? You would bring the baby here and leave it with me? Are you really willing to do that? I don't know anything about babies. I don't even know how to change a diaper. Don't babies need their mothers? What about nursing and all that?"

"I'm totally serious, Andrew, and the more I think about it, the more I think it is the right answer. Lots of working mothers don't nurse their babies. There are infant formulas for that, and I can teach you how to hold a baby and change its diaper in a day. Just hire a good nanny. You'll do fine."

"You don't sound like you're all that interested in having the baby or in marrying me, Cullen. Perhaps we should rethink this. Maybe this isn't a good idea after all. Are you absolutely sure you want to go through with this?"

"Of course I am, Andrew. I love you. Ever since I met you, I have prayed that someday, somehow, all the things that were problematic about our relationship could be resolved so we could be together. God works in mysterious, roundabout ways, but here we are at last. Funny, it just occurred to me that I'm getting married for the second time because I'm pregnant, and neither time has my future husband ever mentioned the word love."

"I'm not Tony, Cullen. I will be good to you. I will honor you, and I will grow to love you in my own fashion. I just need a little time to get used to this. Give me a little time. I promise you that I will be a good husband and father. We will have a good life raising our family. We will be happy together, Cullen. At least happy enough."

chapter 31

The Proposal

*D*ave put the manuscript down on the kitchen table and poured himself another cup of coffee. Then he sat down across from Elizabeth, who was busy working the Sunday *Times* crossword puzzle. It was a Sunday ritual. They took turns with it until last week when they got two Sunday papers so they could have a contest to see who finished first. All ink. No strikeovers. They were pretty evenly matched. Today Dave finished first because there were a lot of television program clues. Elizabeth was not a big TV watcher, so he had the edge on her. He reread the ending to Elizabeth's book while he was waiting for her to finish. She finally threw her pen down in exasperation, complaining about all the pop culture stuff they now put in the puzzle. She saw that Dave had her manuscript and was ready to give his appraisal.

"So, Elizabeth, you've found a halfway happy ending after all. I'd like to think that living with me these past two months has almost made an optimist out of you. What are you going to call it? Have you come up with a title yet?"

"Not really, Dave. I've played around with a number of ideas—*The Transplants, Tangled Vines, Second Chances*—but none of them seems right."

"What about something like *The Inside Man* or *The Second Time Around*? Or maybe something intriguing like *Mind Sight*? Actually, I think the title should be romantic and poetic, but if you include something too romantic in the title, it might be mistaken for a romance."

"It's more than just a romance. It's about the kind of love and choices that really matter in life. But the title isn't important, Dave. I don't ever expect to get it published."

"I don't know why you say that. It's a good story, which reminds me of a point I've been wanting to discuss with you. There's one bothersome weakness in the book. I think it's kind of fun that you named the brain-dead girl Elizabeth after yourself, but I also think she is superfluous to your story. You ought to eliminate her because she doesn't really serve a purpose or add anything. You suggest that maybe she is Margaret, but then Andrew gets back with Cullen, who gets pregnant, and that's the end of it. They live almost happily ever after, or happily enough. At least that is the assumption. If Elizabeth was really Margaret, the story wouldn't make any sense unless she and Andrew got back together. That would be an entirely different story. It's not the one you're telling. No need to bring any suggestion of Margaret back in. Just let Margaret die and skip the Elizabeth character all together. It'll make for a stronger story."

"Maybe you're right, Dave. Maybe Margaret should have just died. Elizabeth really is irrelevant—superfluous, as you say."

"I think so. Hope you aren't upset with my suggestion. It's an easy fix. The rest of the novel is very good. Aren't you glad I encouraged you to keep writing?"

"Yes, I suppose so. But I am worn out with writing right now. I think I need a break."

"Not from me, I hope. Elizabeth, we have been living together for two and a half months now. We are very compatible. Don't you think we've had enough time to know we belong together? You've never said you're in love with me, but you know I absolutely adore you. Will you please make an honest man of me? Marry me, Elizabeth. I love you. I will cherish you all of my days."

"You're a very dear man, Dave, and I have grown to love you. I just worry that my love is defective in some way. I'm afraid I may not be able to love you totally and unconditionally like Margaret loved Andrew. Maybe love like that is so rare it's unrealistic to expect it. Maybe I just got caught up in my own story and have become too much of a romantic."

"Don't say no, Elizabeth. The way you love is enough for me. I know what you are capable of giving me. It is enough, Elizabeth. More than enough. I want you. I want our children. Please be my wife."

"I need a little more time, Dave. I need to get things clear in my head. Just give me a little more time. It's only the first of August. Let me go home for a week or two. I need to spend some time with my parents. I'm all they have. They'll be very disappointed if I don't stay in St. Louis at least a week. I'll think about it while I'm gone. I'll pray about it. But please don't call me. I don't want to communicate with you because I could be influenced by your arguments. I need to come to this decision on my own. I'll try to figure out if this is right for me, for us. I'll ask God to let me know if we should be married. We'll see."

———

Elizabeth's parents were excited to have her back home. Elizabeth was happy to see them. It was wonderful to have such a warm, loving family. Elizabeth and Deborah quickly settled down to a comfortable routine of tennis in the afternoon and dinner at the club, with Allen joining them when he wasn't working late. Deborah suggested that maybe they should invite Walter and his wife to dine with them one night. They wanted Walter to see how well Elizabeth was doing now, and they would have the opportunity to thank him again for giving them back their daughter. Elizabeth froze at the suggestion.

Walter had sent an e-mail to Elizabeth in March asking her to call him sometime when she could have a private conversation. Elizabeth could not imagine what it could be about. She was glad to hear from him though because she was anxious to tell him that she had seen Andrew in the Gardens several times but hadn't thought of a way yet to accidentally meet him or be introduced. She wanted to ask Walter for suggestions on how to get Andrew to notice her and be interested. Walter had stopped her short. Cullen had called to tell Walter that she was pregnant with Andrew's baby and that she was due at the end of May. Andrew would keep the baby the first year while Cullen finished her first year of residency. After that, she would transfer to Duke, and they would be married. There was a long silence at Elizabeth's end of the connection. She couldn't understand how this could have happened. Andrew would have had to be with Cullen while Elizabeth was still recovering in Walter's lab. Walter told her about the kidney transplant and that he had done what he could to try to keep Cullen away from Andrew, but Cullen was determined. Walter apologized for keeping this information from Elizabeth, but he explained that it would have been detrimental to her recovery process if she had known. Elizabeth couldn't breathe. She clutched her stomach to keep from throwing up. She had to steady herself against the tree she was standing under. As she felt her world coming apart, she screamed at Walter. How could he have talked her into becoming Elizabeth? She blamed him, unfairly she knew, but nevertheless he was the closest target and the bearer of the bad news. How could she have been so foolish to believe God was giving her a second chance with Andrew? She accused Walter of being the devil after all and hung up.

It had taken Elizabeth weeks to calm down. She wouldn't go walking in the Gardens. She didn't go to class. She just sat around her apartment. Dave had even called her several times to make sure that his best student, as he put it, was okay. This was before they started dating. Finally things got back to normal and Elizabeth returned to class, but she still wouldn't go to the Gardens at the time of day she knew Andrew was usually there.

And now she was going to be having dinner with Walter and Rose as if nothing had ever happened, as if she had not screamed at him and blamed him for everything. Had he not said he tried to stop Cullen from seeing Andrew? It was Cullen's fault really. Not Walter's and certainly not Andrew's. She had told Andrew to marry and have children. Could she blame him for having sex with a beautiful, intelligent woman like Cullen? Of course not. Could she blame Andrew for asking her to marry him when she became pregnant? No, Andrew would never neglect what he considered to be his duty. Elizabeth hoped that Walter would realize that she didn't mean what she had said to him in the heat of the moment. It had been the pain of her heart breaking that had made her scream. But she couldn't apologize to Walter with her parents there. She hoped he understood that too.

chapter 32

The Reckoning

$\mathcal{B}$ecoming Elizabeth was not a difficult transition for Margaret. She and her donor body were sufficiently similar that giving up her old Margaret personality and taking on Elizabeth's only became a problem when her mental life and emotional life came into conflict with each other. She rather liked being less inhibited and more of a free spirit, and she more often than not gave into these new tendencies.

What Elizabeth was finding difficult was reconciling her religious beliefs with what had happened to her. She went back to services at her old church of St. Michael and St. George to pray for guidance and clarity. Why had God blocked her plans by allowing Cullen and Andrew to get back together? Why had God let Cullen have Andrew's baby when, according to Walter, nothing else in the world would have made him want to marry her? Walter, who gave Elizabeth an update in June, told her the baby was born the last week of May, and Cullen was planning on taking it to Andrew the last week of August. It was hard to imagine Andrew trying to care for a three-month-old baby by himself.

Elizabeth tried to make sense of all these events. The only explanation that made any real sense to her was that she had been operating under false assumptions. God must not have saved her for Andrew. Maybe she had been given a second chance at life because He was giving her to Dave. They certainly were very compatible, probably better suited emotionally and intellectually to each other than she and Andrew. She never felt intellectually inferior in Dave's presence, and Dave didn't need a violin to express himself. He loved her in a way she could readily absorb.

By the time Elizabeth returned to Durham, she had convinced herself that marrying Dave was what God wanted. It was the right answer. She decided to come back a few days early and surprise him. When he got home from the office, she would have a lovely candlelight dinner and champagne ready for them to celebrate their engagement. She was actually getting excited about seeing him. She could just imagine the joy in his eyes as he took her in his arms and kissed her over and over again. Dave was a wonderful man. After his failed first marriage, he deserved to be happy. He deserved to have his love returned full measure. She would do her very best.

Dave was indeed surprised to see Elizabeth, but there was no joy in his eyes. He didn't gather her into his arms and give her the big movie screen reunion she had expected.

"What's the matter, Dave? I thought you would be happy to see me."

"If you had come back two days ago, I would have been."

"I did come back early. Why wasn't that soon enough? What's wrong? What could possibly have happened to make you not happy to see me? Don't you love me anymore?"

Dave was obviously agitated. Elizabeth had never seen him like this, pacing back and forth, waving his arms up and down, and practically shouting at her.

"Love you? Love you? I don't even know who the hell you are! My heart has exploded. Pieces are flying everywhere. I can hardly breathe. And you can stand there innocently asking me what could possibly be wrong?"

"Dave, I don't know what's come over you, but believe me, please. I have no idea what you're talking about." Elizabeth was fighting back tears.

"Believe you? What is it that you want me to believe, Elizabeth? That you are the girl of my dreams? That you're the sweet, adorable woman who has shared my bed for over two months, to whom I've made love night after night, dreaming of the day you will be my wife? The woman I would have lain down my life for?"

"Stop! Stop it, Dave! I don't understand. Please tell me why you are saying these things." Elizabeth was crying now.

"I guess you thought your secret was safe. I guess you thought I would never figure it out. Were you ever going to tell me, Elizabeth, or Margaret, or whoever the hell you are?"

"What? Margaret? What are you saying? When was I going to tell you what?"

"Oh, you think I don't know? I know all right. Like the dunce you figured me for, I sent your novel off to my publisher. I thought with my recommendation she might be willing to accept it for publication. I asked her to put a rush on it so I could surprise you when you returned. But guess what? I was the one who got the big surprise. She told me your story wasn't fiction. Eight years ago there was a successful brain transplant. Interestingly enough, the brain belonged to a doctor whose name just happens to be Andrew Hamilton. It was big news in all the major papers. I should have known, only I was in Bali for six months with my wife working on a novel. So I missed it and got played for a chump by a student of mine that I thought I knew and fell in love with. That's what's wrong. That's what I learned yesterday. That's what's changed. My whole world—that's all." Dave had tears in his eyes. His voice was quieter now. "Elizabeth, how could you do this to me? I have loved you with all my heart. I thought you loved me too. I thought you were God's answer to my prayers."

"Oh, Dave, I am so sorry. I truly am so sorry. Please don't judge me too harshly. It never occurred to me that you didn't know about Dr. Hamilton's transplant because it was on the front page or the cover of almost every paper and magazine in existence. Like the book says, I really had been sworn to secrecy by a ten-year contractual agreement with Walter and the Stuarts. I gave my solemn pledge to the Stuarts. I shouldn't have written that first class assignment because it wasn't fiction, but my creative juices weren't flowing. I had no intention of continuing it. When you kept referring to my story as unusual and kept emphasizing how imaginative it was and how you had never heard of anything like it, I thought you were letting me know that you knew better and you were giving me a pass as a way of flirting with me. You were the one insisting that I continue writing it. I did try to end it a number of times. I certainly had no intention of it ever being published. In fact, I would have been prohibited from publishing it. When we became intimate, I deliberately broke my oath, at least partially, by including Elizabeth in the story to try to let you know who I am. It was the only way I could without breaking my oath completely. But it didn't work. You just thought Elizabeth was irrelevant. I even warned you early on to keep it casual because you didn't really know me. I wasn't expecting our relationship to go this far. Elizabeth's needs and desires silenced Margaret's conscience. Things got out of control. Feelings and circumstances took over. I wasn't trying to play you, Dave. I am still human. My feelings are real. I have loved you honestly in my own way. These past few months have been wonderful. I did a lot of thinking and praying in St. Louis, and I came back here convinced that God had saved my life to be with you. Now I know He saved it to punish me for my hubris. I didn't steal fire from Him; much worse, I stole my soul. He obviously wants to tear my heart out over and over again. He wants to make me live my hell on earth."

Elizabeth's obvious pain softened Dave's anguish. He paused for a few moments and continued in a quiet voice, choking back his tears.

"I went back and reread your book last night, Elizabeth, only this time I understood it as autobiography, that you were Margaret and in fact still are, at least mostly. The tears were falling so fast I could hardly see the pages. Your love for Andrew is so beautifully moving, complete, and self-sacrificing. And you love him so much you were even willing to risk your soul to be back with him. It became clear to me that, no matter what happens, you will never stop loving Andrew and that you will never love me as deeply. I could accept less love from someone I thought incapable of loving like that, but I cannot accept less love from you, Elizabeth. I am not a consolation prize. I cannot be a distant second to your first-place love."

No one said anything else. There really wasn't anything else to say.

chapter 33

The Nanny

*E*lizabeth spent the week getting settled in her new condo. She knew her parents were disappointed to hear that she and Dave had called things off. The way Elizabeth was talking when she left St. Louis, they were expecting a wedding soon and grandchildren. She didn't volunteer any information, and they didn't dare ask her what had happened. When she declined their invitation to return to St. Louis, they replenished her bank account so she could buy her own place and decorate it properly. Elizabeth chose some comfortable furnishings in soft pale green and heather. Then she treated herself to a Sonos music system, which she promptly loaded with lots of Chopin and Bach. She needed a beautiful, calm, quiet cocoon in which to hibernate for a while after all she had been through.

Elizabeth was emotionally exhausted. She decided to drop her classes and rethink her new life. When she and Andrew were married fifty years ago, life decisions were easy. Andrew and his career set the agenda, and that was pretty much that. She couldn't remember if she chose writing poetry because it was her passion or because it fit into their lifestyle. Either way it had been a successful, emotionally rewarding career. But poetry was totally out of the question for her now. If she submitted anything for publication in the future, it would be rejected as too derivative, too close in style to the work of the deceased poet Margaret Hamilton. *How ironic is that!* And Dave was the head of the creative-writing department, so she was definitely through with writing. She had dabbled in paint a little in her former life. Maybe she could take up painting again or go to law school or get an MBA like her father wanted and become a partner in his business. Without Andrew or Dave to set the agenda for her now, Elizabeth would have to join other twenty-first-century women in searching for a purposeful life of her own. She could pray to God for guidance again, but after all that had just happened, she certainly didn't expect His help. It was obvious to her that God had no intention of helping her.

Thumbing through the local paper on Sunday, the name Cullen Costello caught Elizabeth's eye. It was part of an oversized ad right next to the Sunday crossword puzzle she usually worked after she finished the one in the *New York Times*: "Wanted, full-time nanny to care for infant. Experience and references required. Competitive salary. Full benefits. Call Dr. Cullen Costello for an interview today or tomorrow. Employment to start immediately." Elizabeth's heart started beating a little harder. Cullen! That's right. Cullen was bringing the baby to Andrew. End of August, Walter had said. Today was the twenty-seventh. Elizabeth had zero interest in being a nanny, but the temptation to check Cullen out was too much to resist. The impulse to go for an interview was overwhelming. What could be the harm? With no experience or references, there was no chance that she would be offered the job. She could be certain of that. It could even be amusing, since she would have the advantage of knowing what she knew, and Cullen wouldn't have a clue.

Elizabeth had always been curious about Cullen. Walter had gone on and on about how beautiful she was, a real femme fatale. Maybe she would get to see Andrew's baby. She hoped she would not see Andrew. But then, if she did, he would not be able to recognize her because she was in her Elizabeth *tarnhelm*, like the invisible shield that Siegfried used to disguise himself from Brünnhilde in Wagner's *Ring*. Andrew had a tarnhelm too, but he wasn't invisible to Elizabeth. She knew what his disguise looked like. Before she had time to think of the possible consequences and lose her nerve, Elizabeth picked up her phone and called. She managed to get an appointment.

A housekeeper answered the door and ushered Elizabeth into the living room and asked her to sit on a loveseat, one of the many pieces in the room Elizabeth recognized from her old house in St. Louis. Several chairs had been reupholstered, but the tables and the pair of block front chests were arranged just as she had them before. What a creature of habit Andrew was. She bet the master bed still had the same duvet cover and pillows. She wondered if Cullen was sleeping on Margaret's old sheets. The thought made her smile.

Cullen walked in carrying a little bundle with bright red hair sticking out. Elizabeth took one look at Cullen and understood how Andrew would have found it nearly impossible to resist her. She really was exceptionally beautiful with her pale skin, green eyes, and auburn hair. She was obviously of Irish descent. The baby must take after someone on her side of the family. No one on Andrew's side had red hair. *Oh, wait—the baby wouldn't have Andrew's genes anyway. It would have Tony's.* Still, the baby didn't look Italian either.

"Hello. I'm Dr. Cullen Costello. You must be Elizabeth Stuart. As you can see, this is the little boy in question. His name is James, but I call him Jamey. Tell me about yourself, Elizabeth. Are you a local girl? Did you go to college? Are you married? Do you have children of your own?"

"Well, I'm a graduate of Harvard. I came to Duke for an MFA in creative writing, but after one semester and a summer, I decided it wasn't for me. I like the area though, so I'm staying here instead of going back home to St. Louis."

"St. Louis? What a coincidence. That's where I'm from. In fact, I'm doing my residency at Barnes now in pediatric oncology. That's why I need a nanny. Jamey is going to be staying here alone with his father for a year until I can get my residency transferred to Duke. Jamey's father is an important neuroscientist and needs his mind free of worries about the child's care. So it's very important that I have someone unencumbered and very dependable who will be willing occasionally to stay after five and sometimes work on Sunday. Otherwise, Sunday will be your day off. The housekeeper, Maria, is here Monday through Saturday and will see to the cleaning, laundry, and meals. Your sole job will be taking care of Jamey and overseeing his progress. While he naps, you may read or do something in his room. There is a comfortable upholstered rocker in his bedroom for that purpose as well as to rock him to sleep. I'm sorry there's no TV, but then you probably have Netflix or Amazon on your laptop or smartphone, so that won't really be a problem for you. What is your experience with children?"

Elizabeth felt very uncomfortable now. Embarrassingly awkward, actually. She had to admit that she had no experience or references but that she loved small children and really wanted to be a nanny. Was she convincing enough?

"Well, Elizabeth, I must say I'm rather surprised that someone with a Harvard degree wants to be a nanny instead of using that good brain you must have. Tell me why you aren't pursuing something intellectually challenging? Don't you have any dreams or aspirations?"

Now Elizabeth felt ridiculously stupid. Just as she was trying to cobble up something to say, Andrew walked in. Elizabeth stopped breathing. Her heart was pounding so hard she was afraid they could hear it. She practically fainted. Good thing she was sitting down.

"Elizabeth, this is Jamey's father, Dr. Hamilton. Andrew, this is Elizabeth Stuart. She's from St. Louis and is a graduate of your alma mater. I was just telling her that I'm surprised that a Harvard graduate is applying for a job as a nanny. She was about to tell me her long-term goals when you came in."

"My guess is that she's applying for this job because she hasn't formulated her long-term goals yet, Cullen. Not every young woman is as driven and independent as you are. Am I right, Elizabeth?" Andrew was smiling with a certain sense of scoring a point. He had anticipated her discomfort at this personal probe and had let her off the hook. That was so Andrew!

"Yes, Dr. Hamilton. My father has an investment firm and wants me to get an MBA and become a partner in his business. I'm taking a year off to reassess my life. I'm stalling, to be honest, because finance is the last thing I want to do. I love my father, but he's used to having his way. Saying no will be difficult unless I have a sufficiently passionate reason. I am giving myself this year to discover just what that passion is."

"Smart girl! Finance is a brain drain in my opinion. It steals too many good minds away from more important endeavors. Well, I'll leave you two to finish the details. I need to get over to my lab to help one of my postdocs with a problem she's having. Nice to meet you, Elizabeth. I look forward to having you here to take care of Jamey. It will be a real plus to have someone of your acumen handling his development. Research shows the first year is the most important for molding a baby's brain."

"Well, Elizabeth, even though I have four more applicants to interview, it looks like Dr. Hamilton has already made the decision for us. I am concerned that you have no experience, but I guess this is a skill that comes naturally enough to women. After all, the human race manages to thrive in spite of inexperienced young mothers. Can you start early tomorrow? I need to get back to St. Louis. I can show you the routine and answer your questions and take the late-afternoon flight back."

Elizabeth just sat there. This was a totally unexpected turn of events. What was she supposed to say now, that she really wasn't interested in the job? Andrew would certainly wonder why she applied. Running into him somewhere later might be particularly uncomfortable if she turned them down. Still, she certainly didn't like the idea of being tied down with a baby six days a week when it wasn't her own. On the other hand, it was Andrew's baby, and she would be in close proximity to him on a daily basis. Maybe over time he would begin to see who she really was. Maybe he would recognize her "Margaretness." But what could possibly come of it beyond heartache? Andrew was honor bound to marry Cullen, and besides that, Cullen radiated the confidence of a woman who got what she wanted one way or another.

"Elizabeth, forgive me. How can you possibly accept when I haven't even discussed financial arrangements? I am prepared to offer you two hundred dollars a day; that's twelve hundred dollars a week Monday through Saturday, plus fifty an hour for overtime and Sundays. All medical will be covered, and two weeks of paid vacation to be taken over holidays. Is that suitable with you?"

"Well, uh, I need to think about it, Dr. Costello. May I call you this evening?"

"Really, Elizabeth, what do you need to think about? The salary is more than fair, but to make sure I'm pricing you out of other markets, I'm willing to raise it to two hundred fifty a day; that's fifteen hundred a week. Even a Harvard degree is worth only so much without experience. That's my final offer."

Elizabeth realized that she had gotten herself cornered. At that level of compensation, she was not going to be able to come up with a good reason to turn the job down. She would just have to find some excuse to quit later. She accepted the offer, shook hands with Cullen, and promised to be there at 8:00 sharp the next morning. What had she just allowed to happen? Either Elizabeth needed to have her head examined or else she needed to seek a workable peace with the Almighty. God seemed to have declared all-out war on Margaret, or Elizabeth, or both.

chapter 34

The Poet

"Good morning, Elizabeth. Maria called in sick today, so I am fixing myself some coffee. Jamey's still sleeping. Won't you join me? I've made extra."

"Oh, good morning, Dr. Hamilton. Actually, coffee sounds good. I was running late and didn't take the time to make any."

"Have a seat then, and I'll fix it for you. How do you like it?"

"A little milk with a sprinkle of cinnamon, if you have it."

"A sprinkle of cinnamon? I haven't heard that expression in a long time. That's the same way my wife used to have her coffee. In fact, she used the same words, a sprinkle of cinnamon."

"I didn't know you had a wife, Dr. Hamilton."

"Please, call me Andrew. My wife died almost two years ago. It's hard to believe. She was a wonderful person and a well-respected poet."

Andrew studied Elizabeth while she sipped on her coffee.

"You know, Elizabeth, there's something about you that reminds me of her. I can't put my finger on it, but certain facial expressions, certain comments, the way you use words. Have you ever written poetry?"

"Oh, I've dabbled in it from time to time. I've read a lot of poetry. The first book of poetry I ever received was a volume of Emily Dickinson on my sixteenth birthday. The second was the *Complete Works of T. S. Eliot*. I was hooked. Since then I have read almost all the more important poets in the English language. I wrote my senior thesis on twentieth- and twenty-first-century American poets. Wait, was your wife Margaret Hamilton?"

"Why, yes. You know her work?"

"I love her work! Some of her poems come so close in feeling to my own temperament I even memorized them."

"Really? That's quite remarkable. Is there one in particular that's your favorite?"

Elizabeth looked past Andrew and out the window as if she were trying hard to decide. Then a smile flashed across her face. "I think my favorite one is 'Vines.'"

"Amazing that you would choose that one. It happens to be my favorite too, mainly because it was the last one she wrote. But that is a peculiar choice for a young unmarried woman. Margaret was very sad and disillusioned when she wrote it. The poem starts out optimistically but then denies that love can last, even for lovers with kindred souls. But I associate her image of tangled vines with lovers who have loved each other so long and so well that they have become just one unit in this world."

"I think, based on her other poems, she really did believe that love can be eternal, Andrew. Her other poems certainly refer to never-ending, unconditional love. Anyway, it's the kind of love I would like to have someday, although I'll probably have to settle for a lesser version. You don't seem old enough to have really experienced it either."

"I'm a lot older than I look, Elizabeth. I'm the doctor who had my sixty year old brain put in this younger body. I assumed you knew that."

"You're the one! I remember someone saying that he was here at Duke. And it's you! Of course. I don't know how I thought anyone is supposed to be able to tell who has had a transplant. It isn't the first thing that comes to mind when you meet someone."

"Well, that operation put an end to our wonderful marriage. Although it turns out that she didn't mean it. At the time, she was trying to convince me to go find a new life without her. That's why her poem was so pessimistic. Our marriage wasn't viable anymore, mainly because of the thirty-year age difference. Funny how a man can marry a woman thirty years younger, but the reverse isn't really accepted, except under very special circumstances, among the rich and famous. The transplant separated us, ended our marriage, but it couldn't end our love. Only death can do that."

"Maybe death isn't the end. Maybe love can survive for all eternity."

"That's what Margaret believed. I wish it were so. I'm afraid I'm one of those friendly agnostics who can't believe and can't disbelieve. It makes no sense to me intellectually."

"Maybe you can be a nonbeliever intellectually and still be a believer emotionally."

"That's exactly what Margaret always said. I wished for her sake that it was possible. But so far no such luck."

"Oops, sorry Andrew. I hear Jamey. Got to go. Thanks for the coffee. I enjoyed our conversation."

"I enjoyed it too, Elizabeth. Let's do it again soon. I don't like eating alone. Perhaps you would like to start coming a little earlier and having breakfast here with me. Maria makes great omelets and oatmeal. French toast too. I took her over to the Washington Duke Inn to have their challah French toast so that she could duplicate it. Hers isn't quite as good but good enough. Will you join me?"

"I'd love to. Thank you, Andrew. Jamey's really getting upset. Excuse me."

Andrew watched Elizabeth as she left the dining room and turned down the hall. He finished his coffee and headed toward his office, walking as usual. It was a crisp October morning, a little foggy still, and the soft Turneresque sun glowing through the haze felt good against his cheeks. It reminded him of Argo mornings with the clouds of fog lifting from the valley below to the east. Margaret had written a beautiful poem about it. Margaret. What a coincidence that Elizabeth's favorite poem was the same as his. For that matter, how interesting that Elizabeth had read Margaret's poetry. There was something a little unsettling to Andrew about Elizabeth. He was too comfortable around her. He seemed to be able to anticipate a lot of her reactions and comments. Her expressions were very readable, and her perspective on things seemed more like his, too mature for a twenty-five-year-old. Of course she was very bright. Maybe that explained it all. Still, it was unsettling a bit. How lucky though that they were able to find her for Jamey. Andrew thought on this a little longer and then said out loud to make it official, "Elizabeth is a real prize."

chapter 35

The Baby

"Cullen, why in the world would you want to leave Barnes to go marry a man who doesn't even love you when Chris is still head over heels? I know you love Chris too, unless you're only sleeping with him for the sex. That redheaded baby is probably his anyway. Have you even had a paternity test done?"

"Oh, Meghan! You are forever lobbying for me to marry Chris, and you've never even met him. Does he have you on his payroll? And no, I haven't had a paternity test. I don't want to know if it's not Andrew's. He thinks it's his. That's all that matters."

"Are you serious, Cullen? Are you absolutely out of your mind? I know you don't hesitate to lie occasionally, but this isn't just a lie. This is positively unscrupulous! How could you have Andrew raising a child that isn't his? How could you in good conscience give a child away if it rightly belongs to Chris?"

"You are making too much of a fuss out of it, Meghan. I'm not some horrible person. It's not really as bad as you think. Andrew has always wanted a child, and I thought it would be a wonderful gift if I could give him one. He has done so much for me. That's why I went off the pill while he was here. I figured there would be a good chance that one of them would get me pregnant. Since I didn't have a paternity test, I haven't actually lied. There's a fifty-fifty chance that Andrew is the father. Of course, I did tell Andrew a little fib. I told him I hadn't slept with Chris while he was in St.

Louis. Anyway, Andrew has no reason to think it isn't his, and now I'm going to be his wife. So you were wrong about him being too big a stretch for me, Meghan. He's mine."

"Through subterfuge, which hardly counts in my book. And by getting pregnant! You must want to marry him awfully desperately to get pregnant. I thought you said you were through with raising kids after all the problems you've had with Shawn."

"Well, I did say that. I'm not interested in raising another child. I have wanted to be a doctor all my life, and despite all my missteps, now I am one. I love pediatric oncology. It fills my life, Meghan. With all those beautiful children needing my help, I don't really need anything more or anyone else. But Andrew really wanted a child, and so does Chris, for that matter. So I was stuck with having another child regardless of which one I married. If Andrew had turned me down, which I was pretty certain he wouldn't, I would have told Chris it was his and married him. It really wouldn't matter too much which one I married. Sex is sex."

"Well, you get enough of that without marriage. And if you really mean that, Cullen, why don't you just marry Chris and be done with it? At least you'd be married to someone who loves you. Why all the obsession with Andrew if he doesn't matter that much?"

"Oh, he still matters, just not as much as he did at first. I was very young and lonely when I met him, and I was flattered that a distinguished neuroscientist could possibly be interested in me. My ego was so beaten down from Tony. I had no future that I could see. Andrew was a real lifeline for me at the time. I grabbed it, and I guess I just haven't ever let go. He's been my security blanket. And I did miss Tony's sexy body. That has always been a problem for me. But I have to admit that things are different now. I'm really a different person from the one that fell in love with Andrew seven years ago. After what happened to me that night I called you to come to the hospital, how could I not have changed? I had to fight like crazy for it, but I'm not vulnerable now. I'm finally actualizing my potential. Having a distinguished neuroscientist as a husband can't hurt my career either. The baby seals the deal. I have Andrew to thank for a lot of things. That's reason enough to give him the baby. Is that really so bad, Meghan?"

"You want my honest opinion, Cullen? It's worse than calculating and unscrupulous. If you really care about Andrew, I can't believe that you would deliberately deceive him into thinking the baby is his if it isn't and deprive him of whatever life he would otherwise find for himself. He had already turned you down for marriage when he was here. What you are doing is outrageous in my book. He's only marrying you because he thinks that baby is his. You've told me a hundred times that he will never stop loving his wife, even if she's deceased. If you want to look at it from a selfish point of view, think about how miserable you will be married to a man who doesn't love you, one you won't be able to manipulate when you start losing your looks. If you marry him, Cullen, you'll live to regret it, maybe not at first, but eventually you'll be sorry. Medicine is new to you now. It gets a little old over time. You'll want more. Everyone eventually wants more. I know that from personal experience, given all the doctors at the hospital who are always hitting on me. Why would you want to play second fiddle to a dead woman, anyway, especially if you can be the whole orchestra to a man like Chris?"

"Meghan, I wasn't thinking far enough ahead at the time. I did it on impulse because I was thinking how overjoyed Andrew would be to have a child. I figured he wouldn't object to having me come along with it."

"That argument won't work on me, Cullen. You knew exactly what you were doing."

"Well, anyway, how can I just hand Andrew the baby and tell him it's all his, that I don't want it?"

"How can you marry him and pretend you do? You'll have both a baby you don't really want and a husband who doesn't really want you. At least with Chris you'll be with someone you care for that doesn't remind you of your former miserable life. And if it's Chris's baby, is it fair to give it to Andrew? He and his first wife didn't have children either. Cullen, I know you aren't religious, but I'll give you the benefit of a doubt and say that your motive isn't all selfish. Let's say you're doing this also out of gratitude and want it to be seen as a noble sacrifice. But what you are doing is very immoral in the eyes of God, and it's extremely unethical by any standard. Andrew won't even be aware that you are making this so-called sacrifice. How many times do I have to tell you that you don't owe Andrew anything? He's still using Tony's body. If anything, he still owes you. Give up this crazy idea of yours. Give it up, Cullen. Promise me that you'll at least have the paternity test before you make any irreversible decisions."

"Okay, Meghan, I get your point, but we both know me well enough to know I'm not going to do it. It's easy enough for you to make judgments and tell me what to do, but you aren't standing in my shoes. I don't know why you've stuck by me all these years. You're such a straight arrow, and I'm always doing things that don't meet with your approval. You've been my best friend since grade school, my only friend, really. God knows I've needed one over all these years. What would I have done without you when my parents were killed in that accident? What would I have done without you when I got pregnant and had to marry Tony? And, most importantly, what would I have done if you hadn't come to the hospital that night to help me? If I've never thanked you for always being there, I'm thanking you now."

"You're stuck with me, Cullen. Somebody has to be your conscience; you certainly don't own one. Just kidding, but not really. I've always tried to be a good friend, Cullen, but I almost never get to see you anymore. This is the first time we've met for coffee or lunch in a long time. The last time I saw you, I would never have known you were pregnant if you hadn't told me. You weren't showing at all. That baby must have been tiny when it was born."

"It was. I gained very little weight. Now it's time for me to get back to the hospital. I'm glad we could meet for coffee. Let's get together again soon. I have next weekend off, and I'm flying over to see Andrew and Jamey. Andrew says the nanny is working out fine, thank God. I won't have to deal with finding someone else this late in the year."

"Tell Andrew hello for me. And think about what I said. You can get the baby's sample while you're there and have it run when you get back. Also, for the record, I'm not your only friend, Cullen. Chris is definitely your friend too. I've never met him, but why else would he still be around when you are planning on marrying Andrew next summer? I know he hopes he can talk you out of it."

"Yes, I know. He told me the other night that he would be willing to adopt Andrew's baby if I would marry him. And Shawn too. I know Shawn likes him. Chris has helped him a lot, and they have spent a lot of time together, going to ballgames and bowling."

"Well, Cullen, you just gave yourself another reason why you should quit this nonsense with Andrew and marry Chris."

"Okay, okay. Bye. I'm going to be late if I don't leave now."

chapter 36

Dave

The end of October was glorious in the Gardens, a canvas of reds and oranges and sienna against the evergreens and the bright blue sky. Elizabeth loved to take Jamey for strolls there. At five months, he was alert and babbling, but mostly he slept while Elizabeth sat on a bench overlooking the lake, reading and sipping an afternoon coffee.

"Hello, Elizabeth. I was hoping I would find you here. May I sit down?"

"Dave! Yes, of course."

"What are you doing with yourself? Where'd you get the baby?"

"I dropped out of school, Dave. Thought I ought to take a breather and figure out what I want to be when I grow up. I've taken a job as a nanny for a little while."

"That's about the last thing I would have expected you to do, not that I don't think you would be wonderful with children. It just isn't very intellectually challenging."

"I don't feel much like being challenged these days. I've had enough challenge recently."

"Look, Elizabeth, I'm sorry about the way I reacted. I was hurting beyond belief. I wish I hadn't sent your manuscript off to my publisher. I had no right to do it. I would much rather have learned the truth from you."

"You have nothing to apologize for, Dave. It was my fault. I shouldn't have let my feelings get out of hand. I shouldn't have allowed our relationship to happen. But there you were, such a wonderful person, such a dear, lovable man, and I was a lonely, miserable lost soul. Still am. Do you remember back in March when I was so upset I didn't come to class for weeks on end? That's when I found out from Walter that Cullen was pregnant and Andrew was marrying her."

"No wonder you were so distressed! It had to be horrendously painful for you, especially after all you had gone through to be with him."

"Yes, of course it was. Very. It was clear to me that God must not have saved me for Andrew. The only logical conclusion I could draw was that He had saved me for you instead. I was really happy and confident to be coming back to you. That only lasted until you walked in the door, of course. It became abundantly clear that God didn't save me for you either. I think He has abandoned me altogether."

"I think you're being too rough on yourself, Elizabeth. So, Andrew and Cullen are married now and living in St. Louis?"

"No, Andrew is here at Duke. That's why I came here in the first place. Cullen is going to transfer here in May after her first year of residency. They will be married at the end of May. Meanwhile, Andrew has the baby here. And I'm the nanny. How ridiculously pitiful is that!"

"Does Andrew know? Have you told him?"

"No, I can't do that, for the same reason I couldn't tell you. And I wouldn't now anyway. He has the child he always wanted."

"Does Andrew love Cullen?"

"No, that's the worst part. I have breakfast with him most mornings before the baby wakes. He never mentions Cullen. All he talks about is how much he still loves his deceased wife and what a wonderful poet she was."

"After you left, I bought several volumes of Margaret Hamilton's poetry. You're a first-rate poet, Elizabeth. That's what you need to be doing."

"The crazy thing is I would be accused of imitating Margaret's style. I've been writing some anyway because that's the way I've always processed my thoughts. The difference is now, instead of sending them off to the *New Yorker*, I put them in my desk drawer."

"Well, when your ten years are up, you can dig them out of your drawer and publish several volumes under your real name. Only eight more to go. Look, Elizabeth, if Andrew and Cullen aren't married yet, why can't you ask your parents for a reprieve so you can at least tell Andrew? He can be trusted to keep the secret. If he loves you half as much as I still do, he would want to know before he marries her. As much as he wants a child, I know he would choose you instead. He would much rather have a child with the woman he loves. I know I would."

"Dave, how sweet of you to be so concerned about me. I don't deserve your kindness."

"Elizabeth, love doesn't have a spigot you can just turn off when you want. I do still love you. It will be a long time before I can relegate you to the archives, as you put it. And because I care about you, I care about your happiness. You belong with Andrew. If there is any God who cares about the sanctity of love and marriage, He will make that happen. As much as I have wanted you for my wife, since that can't be, I want you to be Andrew's wife. According to your story, Cullen seems to be ambivalent about which man she marries anyway, Chris or Andrew. Let her marry Chris. Chris has red hair. The baby will fit right in. By the way, I assume a paternity test was done to prove the baby is Andrew's."

"I don't know. You would think so. Otherwise Andrew would not feel obliged to marry Cullen. I must say she doesn't seem to have a lot of interest in Jamey. She has only been here once in the past six weeks. I know she's busy, but still. I certainly wouldn't go off and leave my own child for six weeks at a time. And Jamey is a very sweet little baby. He probably thinks I'm his mother."

"By the way, Elizabeth, the publisher sent your manuscript back when I told her you didn't want to publish it. Assuming you don't need it right away, would you mind if I keep it a while?"

"I don't want it back, Dave. It chronicled the loss of Andrew and my soul. It ruined any possibility of happiness with you. Burn it. Build a fire in your fireplace and burn it chapter by chapter. It needs to be destroyed."

"I'm not sure I can do that, Elizabeth, at least not right away. It's all I have left of you, that and a few small volumes of your poetry. I will get rid of it my own way when I'm ready but not right this minute. I'm leaving on sabbatical right before Christmas. I want to spend the holidays in Paris before going on to Tuscany. I'll get rid of it before then. I promise."

"Okay, but do get rid of it. It's getting a little chilly. I should probably get Jamey back home now. Thanks for seeking me out, Dave. Have a great year in Tuscany. Italy's a romantic country. Maybe you will fall in love with someone there. Good-bye, Dave. It's been great seeing you. I'll always carry you in a special place in my heart. As you said, love can't be turned off like a spigot."

chapter 37

Margo

"Elizabeth, I've finally found a country place to replace Argo, the farm I had outside St. Louis. The old house needs some work, but most of the essentials are there. It's a gorgeous day. Let's have Maria pack us a picnic lunch, and we'll take Jamey and drive out. I want to show it to you. The house isn't as large as my other one, and there isn't as much land, but it has a patio overlooking a pond, and the land gently slopes down to a stream. And there are some great big, old maple trees with glorious golden foliage and lots of evergreens. Only forty acres but plenty enough for privacy and a sense of space. Argo was up on a high ridge. The land here is more rolling, but it's caught my imagination. I think it will be just fine when it is finished."

"It sounds wonderful, Andrew. How far is it from here?"

"Only about thirty minutes or so, if you take the back country roads. They're narrow and curvy, but it makes for a much shorter trip. I'll watch Jamey while you go home and change. You'll want to wear your jeans and some boots or walking shoes. It might be muddy in the fields. We'll leave as soon as you get back."

During their trip out, Elizabeth couldn't keep her mind off Argo. She had memorized every square inch of it and had written poems about so many of its features and moods: misty mornings, rainy afternoons, thick fogs closing in, glorious night skies with millions of stars, dappled moonlight through the maples, swirling eddies in the stream, daffodils and lilacs. The memories were bittersweet. She and Andrew had been so happy there. This new place couldn't possibly measure up, but Andrew seemed excited to have found it and eager to share it with her. She told herself that she would have to act excited too.

"Don't you think so, Elizabeth?"

"Uh, I'm sorry, Andrew, my mind must have wandered off a minute. I didn't hear what you said."

"I said once we get the place fixed up, it will be fun to spend the weekends out here with Jamey. Don't you think that's a good idea?"

"Well, yes, I guess so, if that's what you'd like to do."

"Yes, of course it is. Margaret and I always spent our weekends out at Argo. I'm asking you if it's all right with you. Would you like to bring Jamey out here and spend the weekends with me?"

Elizabeth wasn't sure what exactly that meant, but it was probably innocent enough. The house was bound to have several bedrooms. Then again, Andrew was lonely with Cullen gone from the scene, and he wasn't married yet, and she and Andrew had become rather close over three months of breakfasts. Elizabeth decided she'd take it as it came. He was her former husband, after all.

"I think that would be lovely, Andrew. Maybe we can even start a winter garden. It should be about time to get the cold weather crops in, and daffodils for the spring."

"That's a great idea, Elizabeth. I had a garden at Argo, and we had daffodils covering one whole hillside. I think I saw a tiller in the barn. Did I tell you it has a big barn? It's not a walnut barn like Argo has, but it's picturesque and well situated away from the house. If the weather is nice next weekend, maybe we can get it tilled and start a plot. I'll buy some daffodil bulbs. You can decide where to plant them. We can have this place shaped up in no time. I'm looking for a caretaker. I'll never be able to find a couple as wonderful as the ones I had at Argo, but there has to be someone nearby who can cook and clean and someone who can work around the place."

When they arrived, Elizabeth had to smile. She could see immediately what had drawn Andrew to the place. The house resembled his old one in some respects, and there was a big, wide front porch with a swing, overlooking a yard full of maples for the birds.

"Oh, look, Andrew! There's a porch swing. I love porch swings."

"So do I. After dinner, Margaret and I used to take our coffee out on the front porch and watch the birds settle down. It's such a peaceful time of day. Wait till you see the inside. It needs to be fixed up, painted, and decorated. I'm not really good at that sort of thing. I was hoping you might be willing to give it a woman's touch."

"Andrew, don't you think Cullen is going to want to do that?"

"Cullen seems to be too busy to even come for a day or two to see her son. I don't think she's going to be interested in decorating some old farmhouse."

"Well, I'd love to do it. Give me a budget and some time to shop for colors and fabric and furnishings. I'll get it done for you before Christmas. You and Cullen and Jamey can have your Christmas out here. You can cut down one of the evergreens. They make wonderful Christmas trees."

"Margaret and I always had Christmas at the farm with one of the cedars cut from our land. But we won't be doing it this year. Cullen has already said not to count on her for Christmas. She's coming for Thanksgiving and will have to work Christmas."

"That's terrible. She'll miss Jamey's first Christmas. That's very sad. I can try to have things finished for Thanksgiving, but it will be hard. Still, I can try."

"Don't worry about it. We can have Thanksgiving in town. You'll be back in St. Louis with your parents for the holiday. I may let Maria off as well and just have Thanksgiving dinner at the Washington Duke Inn. I know Cullen isn't going to want to spend her short time here in the kitchen cooking."

Andrew led Elizabeth through the house. His enthusiasm reminded her of the first time he saw Argo. They were taking the back roads from a camping trip and saw a For Sale sign in the yard of a grand old property that had seen its better days. He bought it on the spot. Andrew was so excited he almost couldn't contain himself. Elizabeth cherished that old memory. They were so happy then.

"Sorry, I'm just rattling on. Forgive me. But do you see the possibilities? Do you think you can make it comfortable and homey? I do want it to be homey. Beautiful but homey. Margaret had a real gift for that."

Elizabeth had to smile. Margaret again. It was always Margaret.

"Yes, I definitely see the possibilities, Andrew. And I'll do my best to make it warm and friendly. I may not be able to match Margaret's level of taste, but I will do my very best. You still have to give me a budget though."

"No budget, Elizabeth. Just do what needs to be done. I'll hire a practical nurse to care for Jamey several afternoons a week so you can get things going. This is going to be great fun. I will work with a landscape architect to site the gardens and orchard and work on the entrance to the property while you do the inside. We'll create another Argo. Argo Two, Argo Too, East Argo, Argo East. What do you think, Elizabeth? What would you name it?"

"What about Margo? In memory of your wife? Perhaps that's not a good idea. Cullen will object."

"No, I think that's a brilliant idea. It'll be our secret. When I put the sign up, I'll tell her the painter misunderstood and made an error. I'll just never get around to having it fixed."

"That's not a very nice joke to play on your new wife, Andrew. You don't sound like you're really in love with her. Do you realize how much you talk about Margaret? You must have loved her very much."

"I still do, Elizabeth. And I always will. You remind me of her in so many ways. Sometimes, like showing you this place, I forget momentarily that you aren't Margaret. You'll have to forgive me when I do that. I care about Cullen but not in the same way. I'm not in love with her. I wouldn't admit this to anyone else, but I certainly wouldn't be marrying her if I weren't the father of her child. When I first met her, she was very sweet and vulnerable. Beautiful too, of course. Now she has become an overly strong-willed, independent woman, a little insensitive and hardened around the edges, yet she has an attachment to me still that I don't fully understand. Maybe it's misplaced gratitude for sending her through medical school. You would think she would not like to be reminded of her former husband whom she despised, except occasionally in bed. Excuse me for that comment."

"Forgive my asking, but you are certain you're the father of her child, right? I only ask because I haven't been able to see any likeness. I sometimes wonder if she's his mother; she seems so disinterested."

"That thought's crossed my mind, Elizabeth, but Cullen wouldn't lie to me about something so serious. I'm sure she had a paternity test before she told me. And she said it couldn't be anyone else during that time frame. How did we get on this subject? I'm hungry, and Jamey's beginning to get heavy in his carrier. Let's go have our picnic on the patio. Then I'll show you the rest of the place. Wait till you see the pond and the stream."

chapter 38

Thanksgiving

"Margo?" Cullen was looking at the name on the entrance gate as they drove through. "What kind of a name is that?"

"Oh, I guess they made a mistake and added the *m*. I'll have to get it changed sometime. But look at the house, Cullen. It isn't finished yet, but it's coming along. Don't you like that big front porch?"

"It's okay. It sort of reminds me of Argo. But that's the only thing that does. The house is so much smaller and needs painting badly. Those shutters look rotten. They really have to go."

Andrew was already beginning to be sorry he brought Cullen out to see it.

"It takes time, Cullen. I've only had the place a few weeks. It's a work in progress."

"It looks to me like a tear-down. When you said you had bought a wonderful old place, I thought it would be ready to move into, not a work in progress. I hope you aren't expecting me to spend a lot of my time out here working on it. I won't have time for that—or the interest. You're on your own. Hire someone to make it a turnkey operation, Andrew. Maybe it can be ready by summer."

"You don't need to do a thing, Cullen. Elizabeth is handling it. I asked her to help me."

"Elizabeth? I hired her to take care of Jamey, Andrew. Who is watching him while she's out here playing house?"

"Most of the time, Jamey's with her. I've hired a practical nurse to take care of him several afternoons a week when she has to go into Raleigh shopping."

"Into Raleigh shopping? I'm paying her fifteen hundred a week to go into Raleigh shopping?"

"No, Cullen. I'm paying her fifteen hundred a week to go into Raleigh shopping. She needs to find furnishings and fabrics. You've already said you aren't willing to do that."

"Well, I don't like it. Hire a decorator. I haven't even seen this practical nurse you have taking care of my son."

Andrew was really getting irritated with her. She almost never came over to Durham, but when she did, she was like the commander coming to review the troops. Why did she have to be so negative and suck the joy out of everything?

"Our son, Cullen. And since when have you become so interested in what's going on with Jamey? You seem to be perfectly comfortable with the way I'm raising him. This is only the second time you've bothered to come to see him."

"Don't put it like that, Andrew, not in that Tony tone of voice. You know how hard things are for me right now, juggling first-year residency and Shawn's senior year. That doesn't mean I don't care what's going on here. I do call you once a week to check on him."

"Most weeks, anyway. Look, you are only here for two days. Let's not argue. I thought you would enjoy seeing the place. My mistake. No point in even going in. It's still a mess inside. Let's get back to Durham. They have two seatings for Thanksgiving. Our dinner reservations are for three o'clock. I have the nurse coming at two thirty to look after Jamey for a few hours. You'll get a chance to meet her. She is perfectly capable of handling Jamey. She works part-time on the maternity ward at the hospital."

"The maternity ward? Why didn't you say so? That piece of information makes a difference. In fact, why don't you hire her full-time? It'll be a lot less expensive."

"Not necessarily. Besides that, Jamey has become very attached to Elizabeth. I'm not going to have her suddenly disappear from his life at this point."

"Better sooner than later when he becomes even more attached. She isn't planning on staying here long anyway, and Jamey will have me here at the end of May."

"We'll cross that bridge when we come to it, Cullen. Until you get here, I hope I can persuade Elizabeth to stay. Jamey needs her right now."

"Jamey needs her, or you need her to work on your farmhouse? Really, Andrew, hire a decorator and save the money on a nanny. Jamey will be fine. He has you, and I will be here shortly."

"The first year is the most important for developing the brain. Elizabeth plays games with him and has activities that are really good for cognitive development, and she talks to him constantly, not in baby talk but in intelligent language. The nurse is just a babysitter, Cullen. What Elizabeth brings to his life is very important right now. You aren't here to do it. Remember, I did ask you to take off a year and spend the necessary time to get him off to a good start. So don't get upset now that someone else is doing it."

"I'm not upset, Andrew. I just don't like her playing mommy with my son and house with my husband."

"Our son, Cullen. And I'm not your husband yet. Elizabeth stays for now. Let's drop the subject. We're home, and the nurse will be here in an hour. We need to get dressed for dinner. Jamey's been asleep in the back the whole time. The nurse will probably have her hands full while we're gone."

⁓

Elizabeth asked Walter to meet her for lunch at their favorite Clayton restaurant the Friday after Thanksgiving. She could never get enough of their veal piccata.

"I'm so glad you came home, Elizabeth. I need to keep an eye on you. How are you getting along? I had dinner with your parents again in September. I was sorry to hear things didn't work out with Dave. They are very concerned that you're wasting your time being a nanny. Why are you taking care of babies now instead of trying to prepare for a career?"

"Don't judge me, Walter. It's Andrew's baby."

"What! Are you crazy or just a glutton for punishment? For heaven's sake, Elizabeth, why would you want to put yourself through this? I know you would do just about anything to be with Andrew, but this is totally absurd! You are going to get attached to that kid, and then Cullen is going to kick you out when she gets there. I know Cullen. Andrew's not good at hiding his feelings, and he's bound to recognize the Margaret in you by then and become attached. She will need to eliminate the competition. It's going to be heartbreak all over again."

"I know, Walter. And Andrew is already beginning to see me as Margaret sometimes. He says I remind him so much of her. As for Cullen, she doesn't seem to care whether she sees her son or not. She doesn't even seem to care if she sees Andrew, for that matter. I don't understand her at all."

"Well, every once in a while I run into Cullen in some restaurant or other with that redheaded psychologist, Chris. She was dating him when Andrew came back for the kidney transplant. That may explain some of it."

"Redheaded psychologist? Walter, the baby has bright red hair. And it doesn't look like Andrew in the slightest. It doesn't look anything like Cullen either, for that matter. Could it possibly be that this child is not Andrew's? But if it's this man's, why would he let her give it to Andrew, and why wouldn't he marry her?"

"That's an interesting question, Elizabeth. Maybe it ought to be investigated. I really don't believe Andrew would marry her if he knew the baby wasn't his."

"He told me as much, Walter. When I asked him if he knew for sure the baby was his, he said Cullen wouldn't lie to him about something that important."

Walter gave a little fake laugh.

"Andrew has a lot more faith in Cullen than I do. I wouldn't put anything past her, especially when it concerns Andrew."

"Well, I'm not so sure either, so I brought some of the baby's hair with me. That's one of the reasons I called you to have lunch. You have Andrew's new DNA. I want you to run a paternity test for me. I want to know the truth, and if it isn't a match, someone will have to tell Andrew, and it can't be me."

"I guess I would have to tell Cullen I'm on to her and force her to tell Andrew. Of course, she's going to want to know how I got the baby's sample, but let's not worry about that unless it becomes an issue."

Elizabeth took the little Ziploc bag with the lock of red hair out of her purse and gave it to Walter.

"Well, it certainly looks to be about the color of Chris's hair. I'll run it right away and let you know. Don't get your hopes up though, Elizabeth. I don't know how this is going to play out, but it could be very messy before it's over. We'll just have to let things take their course and see how it all unfolds."

Elizabeth's heart began to beat a little faster. Maybe she could be with Andrew after all.

"Oh, Walter, wouldn't it be wonderful if Cullen is lying and the baby isn't Andrew's."

"Now, don't get your hopes up yet. This ruse seems a little too extreme even for Cullen. But you never know. I've been proven wrong before. You may get Andrew yet, Elizabeth. You just may get him yet."

chapter 39

Elizabeth and Andrew

By the end of the first week of December, Elizabeth had the house at Margo in pretty good shape. The outside had been painted a friendly custard with white trim. New black shutters to match the roof had been added as well as new white railings on the front porch in a classic design. The porch swing had been replaced, and two rocking chairs had been added to balance the other side. The new front door had full-length shutters on either side. Elizabeth had made a beautiful wreath of evergreens and holly from the side yard and put it on the front door with a big red bow.

The inside had been painted in soft neutral colors for the most part, and the furniture was perfectly scaled and comfortable. Elizabeth couldn't resist buying pieces, most of them antiques that were similar in feel to the ones at Argo, and arranging them approximately the same way. She wanted it to feel familiar to Andrew when he walked in. The fabrics had just the right touches of color to make the rooms beautiful and cozy. The kitchen was another matter. Elizabeth decided to make it the real hearth of the home, with an oversized fireplace and a farmhouse table made out of a thick, solid piece of hand-planed cherry with breadboards on the end to keep it from warping. It held the place of honor over by the sunny windows in the alcove, with benches on either side. She bought all high-end appliances, but they were hidden behind or surrounded by warm, rich cherry paneling. There were handmade pie cupboards and a huge farm sink. The floors were wide-board cherry too. Ferns and airplane plants hung on macramé hangers from the ten-foot ceiling. It was a stunning creation. The only things left to get were pillows to be thrown here and there and a few special paintings, watercolors mostly, to sprinkle throughout the house.

Elizabeth had asked Andrew not to come out while the house was being painted and all the furnishings were being delivered and arranged. She wanted to surprise him. This restoration was a happy time for Elizabeth. So many of her memories of Argo were coming to life again at Margo. It was almost like magic. She was transported back in time to those early years creating Argo when she was about the same age she was now. It was a strange feeling but an exhilarating one.

Christmas was coming in another two and a half weeks. She had promised Andrew it would be through by then. The pillows were being made and promised for delivery three days before Christmas. The paintings were being brought down from New York galleries for her to choose the ones she wanted. She had paid one of the art history professors to go up to New York and find a good-quality John Marin and Mary Cassatt. She promised to have Andrew donate them to the gallery someday. She left the rest to his discretion. They were due in a day or two, so she would have time to place and hang them before the twenty-fifth.

Elizabeth had decided that she would not go home for Christmas. She wanted to stay and make Christmas for Andrew and Jamey at Margo. She had not told Andrew yet. That was part of her surprise. Her parents were disappointed, but Elizabeth promised to come sometime in January. She knew Andrew would let her off then. She had looked online for just the right toys for Jamey's development. She also had a beautiful rocking horse designed and made for him as a special present. That would be a surprise for Andrew too.

Elizabeth and Andrew were due to go out to the farm on Friday. She had already bought ornaments and hidden them in the hall closet. It was her plan to tell him then that she was staying. She wanted to go out into the field and cut down the perfect tree. Jamey's first Christmas would be special after all. The only thing bothering her right now was that she still hadn't heard from Walter yet about the paternity test. It normally only took a week. Why was it taking so long? She thought about calling but decided to wait. Walter would call her when he was satisfied with the results. Walter was nothing if not thorough.

⁓

Friday came, and the weather was bright and crisp, perfect for the farm. Andrew had decided to take off so they could spend the next two weeks at Margo before Elizabeth had to fly back home for Christmas. As they approached the house, Andrew marveled at the transformation.

"Elizabeth, how in the world did you manage to get the house painted and the shutters up and new porch railings in one week? I can't believe the difference it makes. It looks great."

"It took a lot of planning and coordination; that's how. The shutters were ordered weeks ago. They were hiding in the barn. The railings and swing were measured and made off-site. The painters started last Monday and worked hard all week. There are a couple of little touch-ups for them to do next week, but basically it's finished. I can't wait for you to see the inside."

Andrew had not formulated what he thought the inside was going to look like. He knew he had to keep an open mind and not look disappointed in front of Elizabeth. She had worked so hard and seemed so enthusiastic; it reminded him of Margaret when she was refurbishing Argo. Her spirits were high, there was a little more color in her cheeks, and she would gaze right into his eyes and wave her hands around while she talked, just like Margaret used to do when she was excited. Sometimes Andrew had to do a double take just to make sure it wasn't Margaret. But he had concluded a little time ago that if she wasn't Margaret, she was the next best thing. He didn't know what he could or would do about it, but it was clear to him that Elizabeth belonged in his life. He had truly fallen in love with her.

When Andrew walked through the front door, he stood there for a moment dumbfounded. He simply could not believe his eyes. The living room and dining room looked so much like Argo it was amazing to him. What kind of magic had Elizabeth performed? Except for a few pillows and pictures, it was near perfect.

"Elizabeth, it is absolutely beautiful—the colors, the furniture, the arrangement, every single thing. It is both elegant and friendly at the same time, a perfect balance. Margaret could not have done a better job, and that's a real compliment."

"Thank you for that, Andrew. You have to see the kitchen. That's where a good bit of the money went."

Andrew stopped dead in his tracks. He didn't know what to say. It was something out of a storybook, a make-believe room for the family to live in. Except for sleeping, there was no need to go anywhere else. Big chairs were pulled up to the fireplace, stools flanked the large island, and there in the window alcove was a magnificent table for eating and reading and playing scrabble. It was the most wonderful room Andrew had ever been in. It fit his temperament completely.

"Elizabeth, how did you ever come up with this?"

"I hope that means you like it. I designed it just for you, Andrew. I created a room where I thought you would be content, comfortable any time of day, any time of year. I tried to envision you happy. This is what I saw."

"It's a masterpiece, Elizabeth. I love it. I truly love it."

"I have another surprise for you, Andrew. I'm staying here with you and Jamey for Christmas. I thought we would cut a tree this weekend and decorate it. It would be a shame to have such a wonderful country place and not celebrate Christmas in it. It needs a memory."

"That is the best surprise of all, Elizabeth, having you here with Jamey and me for Christmas. I couldn't be happier. Let me get Jamey down for his nap, so we can have lunch. After naptime, we can go foraging for our tree. I wish we had some ornaments so we could decorate it."

"We do, Andrew. They're in the hall closet."

After dinner was finished and Jamey was down for the night, Andrew built a fire in the living room fireplace and put the tree up in one of the windows facing the front of the house. He opened a bottle of wine he had brought and poured himself and Elizabeth a glass.

"It's been a big day, Elizabeth. Let's just sit here in front of the fire and relax for a while. We can decorate the tree tomorrow. I propose a toast to the most creative, talented nanny in all of Christendom. To you, my dear Elizabeth. You have earned all the praise I can think to give you."

They drank their wine in silence, basking in the warmth of the fire. Andrew felt at home sitting there with Elizabeth. He almost felt like his old self when Margaret was by his side. He sensed that something had permanently changed in their relationship, and he knew full well what was going to happen upstairs when the last of the wine was drained from their glasses.

chapter 40

Caught

"Chris, this is Walter Rubin. I know it's Christmas week, but I wonder if you would mind if I come by your office for a few minutes. Do you have any time today?"

"Dr. Rubin! Why, yes. Cullen has told me so much about you. It will be a pleasure to have a chance to actually talk to you. So far we have simply exchanged a few pleasantries in restaurants. What about eleven o'clock? I'm meeting Cullen at twelve for lunch. We're making our final plans for our trip to the islands for Christmas. Would you like to join us?"

"No, Chris, I would like to see you alone. If it's all right, I'll keep the eleven o'clock slot. See you then."

Walter had thought the situation through very carefully. He didn't dare approach Cullen without first talking to Chris. He hoped he wasn't stepping into the middle of a situation he couldn't handle, but he had to do something. Andrew's future was at stake, and so was Elizabeth's. He had a vested interest in the outcome. He had every reason to become involved.

"Come in, come in. It's so nice to see you, Dr. Rubin. What can I do for you?"

"It's good to see you too, Chris. I wish it were under better circumstances."

"Why? What's wrong? What's happened?"

"I don't know exactly how to approach this matter, Chris, so please forgive me if it's wrong. I have a mystery to solve. It concerns Cullen's baby."

"Cullen's baby? What baby? Cullen doesn't have a baby."

"Yes, I'm afraid she does. He's seven months old now. I'm sorry to tell you that she spent a lot of time with Andrew when he was here for Shawn's kidney transplant and became pregnant. The baby was born in May, and she told Andrew it was his. He is caring for it until she can transfer to Duke next summer. They will be getting married then."

"Dr. Rubin, that's ridiculous! I have no idea what you are talking about. Your information is wrong. Cullen didn't have a baby. She couldn't have. I've been with Cullen two or three times a week for the past two years, including at least once a week while Andrew was here. She told me she had to discuss her medical school funding with him a few times to straighten out some problems, but she told me unequivocally that they didn't have sex. If Cullen had become pregnant during that period, I would be the father. But Cullen wasn't ever pregnant. She couldn't have been without my knowing it. I was with her every week except one this past July when she went on a trip with her friend Meghan for a few days."

"July? That's when Cullen took the baby to Andrew."

"This doesn't make any sense. I know for a fact that Cullen didn't have a baby. And if she told Andrew it was his, she had to be lying to me about not having sex with him."

"Well, that answers one big puzzle and brings us to my mystery. I didn't have Cullen's DNA, but I did have Shawn's. Cullen had sent it to me to see if Andrew was a match for the kidney. So I ran the baby's DNA against Shawn's to get an approximation. It turns out that Shawn is the father. You are Shawn's psychologist. How do you explain this?"

"It isn't possible that Shawn's this baby's father. He can't be."

"Why can't he be, Chris?"

"Because Cullen wouldn't … I really can't discuss this with you. Doctor-patient privacy restrictions."

"Look, Chris. Andrew is taking care of a baby that isn't his that was brought to him by Cullen, who you say couldn't possibly be the mother. And the paternity test matched the baby to Shawn, and you want to hide behind doctor-patient privilege? What's going on here? Cullen's lying to you. Cullen's lying to Andrew, and he's planning on marrying her this coming May, not because he loves her, which he doesn't, but because he thinks the baby is his."

"Cullen's going to marry me! She's very grateful for all Andrew's done for her, but she's never once mentioned wanting to marry him. I don't understand any of this! None of it makes sense to me. I'm not a gullible man, Dr. Rubin, and I have known and loved Cullen for years. How could she have pulled something like this off so convincingly? I still can't believe she could possibly do something so deceitful. This isn't the Cullen I know. There must be an acceptable explanation for this. I'm sure she could clear things up if she were here. I simply can't believe what you are telling me."

"Well, it's going on twelve o'clock. You were going to meet her for lunch, so she's free right now. Why don't you call her to come over here? I can ask her my questions directly. We can both hear what she has to say."

It took about fifteen uncomfortable minutes in Chris's office for Cullen to arrive. She walked in and gave Chris a big kiss.

"Hello, darling, what's up? Walter! What are you doing here? I haven't seen you in forever."

"Yes, it has been a long time. I don't believe we have even talked since you called to tell me you were pregnant with Andrew's baby."

"Pregnant? Andrew's baby? Walter, what are you saying? Chris, what is he saying? Walter!"

"This cruel, bizarre game is over, Cullen. I don't know what kind of explanation you can possibly give for having Andrew taking care of a baby that he thinks is his when it isn't even yours. Worse, Shawn's the father! It's your eighteen-year-old wild child's baby. When were you going to tell Andrew? Before or after the wedding? Or were you ever going to tell him, Cullen?"

"How did you know it was Shawn's? Chris, did you tell Walter?"

"No, I didn't tell him about Shawn. I couldn't. But I am beginning to see a side of you I didn't know existed, Cullen. You told me the baby had been given up for adoption. You told me that you hadn't had sex with Andrew when he was here. You told me you were going to marry me. For God's sake, Cullen, when did you become this lying, cheating, heartless ballbuster who has no regard for the men in your life?"

"It isn't like that, Chris! Honestly, it isn't. I can explain."

"Well, it better be good, Cullen. Right now I am feeling like a stupid jackass. I don't know how I could have fallen in love with a woman capable of what you appear to have done."

"Chris, you already know part of the story. Walter, Shawn has been a problem for some time now, a lot like Tony without any of the charm. He got a thirteen-year-old girl pregnant last year when he was out on one of his wild drinking nights. After the girl's parents found out she was pregnant, the girl claimed he raped her. It's unclear whether she was raped or not, but the parents were very angry and confronted me. When I tried to calm them down and suggested she have an abortion, they looked at me like I was the devil incarnate. They are fundamentalist Christians. They said they were going to press charges and ruin Shawn's life the way he had ruined their little girl's life, and they were also going to tell the head of my pediatric oncology department, who happens to go to their church, what a lousy mother I am and that I wanted their child to have an abortion. They were going to try to ruin my life too. The only way I could stop them from going through with their threats was to promise them that I would raise the child as my own and that I would pay all expenses for their daughter to go away and have the baby. I also promised to pay for her therapy and her education, through college, as compensation for what my son had done to her."

"My God, Cullen. Why didn't you tell me this? We could have married and raised the child. He does have red hair like mine."

"And like my father's. If you remember, Chris, it is one of the things that first attracted me to you. But let me finish. I knew that if you and I had the baby here in St. Louis, Shawn would not be able to resist letting the child know at some point that he was the real father. It could end up causing all kinds of problems. I also knew that the expenses that I had just taken on would be a burden on you. It will still be a number of years before I will be making any money. I knew Andrew has always wanted a child. He's wealthy and can easily take care of any future obligations. As much as I love you, Chris, I was willing to sacrifice my happiness and marry Andrew to take care of the situation. You have to believe me, Chris. It's the truth. I swear it. Walter, what can I do? I can't let Andrew know. He will think I'm some horrible person and not marry me. Then what will I do?"

"Cullen, if you don't tell Andrew, I will. I'm not going to allow you to ruin Andrew's life for your own secret purposes. He doesn't love you,

Cullen. He was marrying you to make an honest woman of you. That's rather ironic now that I think of it. You would be living a lie. The truly sad thing is that if you had told Andrew the circumstances you just described, he probably would have volunteered to take the child and raise it. Then you would not have started all this subterfuge. Andrew would have a child, you would have Chris, and the poor fundamentalist girl would have her education and therapy. Win, win, win. The truth is always the simplest answer, Cullen. It's less messy."

"But you are forgetting the most important part, Walter. I gave my solemn promise that I would raise the child as my own. That is why I'm going to marry Andrew. I couldn't just give him the baby. I have to be part of the package."

"You could have married me, Cullen. We would have made it work one way or another. You know how much I love you. I can't believe you were willing to break my heart and not even give me the slightest say about it. And when were you actually going to tell me that you were transferring to Duke and marrying Andrew? I had no idea."

"I'm so sorry, Chris. I truly am. I hated to tell you and hurt you so much; I simply couldn't make myself do it. Maybe now that the truth is out, you and I can get married after all."

"No, I don't think so, Cullen. The woman I have loved would not have done this. And she would not have lied to me or to Andrew about such basic things, nor would she have had sex with Andrew one night and me the next and lied about that too. No, the woman I love evidently doesn't exist except in my imagination."

Cullen had tears in her eyes now.

"Walter, help me. You aren't going to tell Andrew, are you? I'm sure he is very attached to Jamey at this point. It would be cruel to take the child away from him now."

"It's rather ridiculous for you to be talking about something being cruel, Cullen. From my point of view, everything you have done so far has been cruel."

"Given all the ramifications of the situation, I was honestly trying to do the best thing I could think of for everyone. I didn't mean to hurt anyone. If anyone was getting shortchanged, it was me."

"Really? Let's examine that premise, Cullen. The parents could not have pressed charges against Shawn because he was still a minor at the time and the girl was riding around on the back of his motorcycle, kissing and feeling him up in public and bragging to her friends that she was having sex with Shawn—that is, until her parents found out she was pregnant. Under the circumstances, he wouldn't have been charged as a sex offender or anything else. As for your reputation with the medical faculty, your real concern was the head of pediatric oncology, who might not look on you so favorably if he found out that you had helped the girl get an abortion. And so, even though she begged for your help to get one before her parents even knew about the situation, you wouldn't do it. I think you were more interested in Cullen than anything else. You weren't going to allow anything to stand in the way of your success."

"How did you know all that, Walter?"

"As you know, I have an excellent lawyer, Charles, who can manage to find out just about anything, especially if it impacts his friend and mine, Andrew. So even now you are still spinning your story. Abortion was never discussed with the parents. Nor did they tell you that you personally had to raise the child. They just wanted you to pay for her therapy and education. The parents' threat of making a fuss about what a bad absentee parent you are is true. How much of the rest of it have you spun, Cullen? Let me tell you. Even though you perhaps love Chris, ever since you figured out that you could control Andrew's drugs by becoming a psychiatrist, you've wanted to marry Andrew because his status will bring credit to you. You ensnared Andrew. Against my wishes, instead of waiting for a match for Shawn, you persuaded Andrew to come here and give Shawn his kidney. The recuperation time would give you another crack at catching him. You went out to Argo for the sole purpose of having sex with him. After your attempt to get him to fall in love with you at Argo failed, you decided to use the old standby ploy, pregnancy. You knew he's an old-fashioned gentleman who would offer to marry you under such circumstances. I can clearly see now that was your intention all along. If Shawn hadn't gotten that girl pregnant, Cullen, just how would you have managed it? I'm sure you would've thought of something. Meanwhile, Chris was a convenient companion. He was just someone to coo over you while you figured it all out—collateral damage, as they say. You would never have married someone you think of as an unknown psychologist when you could have

Andrew. It is difficult for me to believe that the smart, beautiful young woman I used to think of as my niece, that I encouraged to marry my special friend, Andrew, could in six short years turn into such a conniving, morally bankrupt egoist. Did being married to Tony all those years warp your understanding of the human heart? Do you think that becoming a doctor gives you license to play God with other people's lives? Have you no better use for all your beauty and brains than to play the men in your life like pawns on a chessboard? You had better become one of the best pediatric oncologists that ever lived, Cullen. That's all you'll have left to possibly commend you in my book."

Cullen was sobbing now.

"What I want to know is who gave you the baby's sample. I don't think Andrew would have done that. He had no reason to disbelieve me. Who was it? That nanny? Was she the one? I knew from the start she was nothing but trouble. I wanted to get rid of her, but Andrew wouldn't let me."

"Good thing you didn't, Cullen. He is going to need her."

"What do you mean?"

"Because he has Tony's body, Andrew is the baby's biological grandfather. Charles has already talked to the girl's parents about Andrew adopting the baby if he wants to keep it. He will need Elizabeth to help him take care of it."

"You mean until I get there. So he still plans to marry me? You didn't tell him?"

"No, Cullen, I didn't. You're going to call him here right now and tell him that you lied to him. Tell him the whole truth. Tell him you're not applying to Duke and you're not going to marry him. Tell him you're sorry, but don't tell him you love him. That would be another lie, Cullen. You only love yourself."

chapter 41

Therefore

Sunday was another beautiful, crisp day at Margo. Elizabeth and Andrew decorated the tree and planned the winter garden. Andrew tilled up the spot on a small rise inside the gate so that Elizabeth could plant a host of daffodils reminiscent of the ones Margaret had planted out at Argo some forty years ago. Forty years! Had it really been that long? Margaret was the same age then that Elizabeth was now.

Time collapsed, and the world evaporated. Andrew was happily, miserably, hopelessly in love. Neither he nor Elizabeth had verbalized their feelings, but the truth was there in every look, every touch, every kiss, every night in bed. He could tell that Elizabeth loved him as desperately as he loved her. Andrew dared not name the force that fused their souls, set their passions aflame, intensified their longing. He simply held her close, feeling their heartbeats and breathing synchronized, as if they were just one unit in the world, old vines already, somehow.

On the Monday morning before Christmas, Andrew decided they should stay at the farm through New Year's Day. There was no reason for them to return to the real world. He had not been this content, this settled, and this happy since before his accident over twelve years ago. He was reluctant to break the illusion of a happy married life with Elizabeth. And Elizabeth seemed equally happy puttering around the place. They would need more food though and something special for Christmas dinner and New Year's Eve. Andrew would call in an order of groceries to Maria in the morning and would run into town to pick them up around noon. He also wanted to get his violin. He had not played for Elizabeth yet. He hadn't been able to express his deepest feelings for her. He thought it was time to do so.

When Andrew arrived, Maria was busy in the kitchen unloading the groceries from the bags and getting them ready to take to the farm.

"Oh, Dr. Hamilton, some man came by the house about an hour ago and left a Christmas present for you. He said there was a note attached for you to read before opening it. I put it on the table by your big chair. I'm getting the groceries packed in the ice chest for you now. It'll only take me a few more minutes."

"That's fine, Maria. Thank you. When you finish, you can leave and take the rest of the holidays off. I won't be needing you. I'm staying at the farm."

Andrew went into his den and sat down. There on the table was a box, neatly gift wrapped, with a note card tied to the ribbon. Andrew could not imagine what man would be giving him a Christmas present. He opened the note card quizzically.

Dear Dr. Hamilton,

I was Elizabeth's creative-writing professor here at Duke for the spring and summer semester. She is one of the most talented and fascinating students I have ever had the pleasure of knowing. She left behind a remarkable book she had written during that period. When I offered to send it to her, she requested that I burn it, but I could not bring myself to destroy such an accomplished piece of writing. I understand that she is in your employ as a nanny. I thought for that reason you might find her book especially interesting.

Dave Robbins, PhD

That's very strange. How could this man have known I might be interested in something Elizabeth had written, and why would she have wanted him to burn a book that her professor thought had merit? Andrew unwrapped the box and slowly opened it. Inside was a book that had been handsomely hand bound in a beautiful, deep russet-colored leather. Andrew was certain that Dr. Robbins himself had it bound before he brought it over. Elizabeth would not have gone to that much trouble and expense if she didn't want to keep it. Dr. Robbins obviously thought a lot of the book. His choice of a fine-grained leather for the cover with gold-leaf arabesque borders and print said volumes about his feelings for the book and, perhaps, for the author as well. It had the look of a labor of love.

All That Really Mattered by Elizabeth Stuart. Andrew repeated it out loud several times. What an unusual title. When he opened it, the end papers had been hand painted in a beautiful, delicate curvilinear pattern. All the colors were soft muted yellows and oranges and greens on an ivory background. The whole presentation was stunning. It conveyed the message that this book was very important, a treasure. He couldn't read it now, of course, but his curiosity was piqued. He would quickly scan the first few pages before he headed back to Margo. Just as Andrew was turning the page to the prologue, his cell phone rang. Andrew closed the book and fished his cell phone out of his pocket. He didn't recognize the number when he answered.

"Hello, Andrew. It's Cullen. I'm standing here in Chris's office and calling you on his speakerphone. Walter is here too. He wanted me to call you."

"What's going on, Cullen? Why are you on a speakerphone? Why doesn't Walter call me himself?"

"Because he is insisting that I be the one to tell you."

"Tell me what, Cullen?"

There was a long pause. He could hear Cullen taking a deep breath.

"Andrew, the baby isn't yours."

Dead silence. It took a full minute for the news to sink in, and as it did, Andrew's emotions began rising to the surface. This didn't make any sense.

"What are you saying, Cullen? I've had Jamey for five months. What do you mean he isn't mine?"

"Jamey isn't your son, Andrew. You aren't Jamey's father."

"I've been rocking and burping and bonding with someone else's son for five months, and you are just now telling me he isn't mine? Whose son is he then? Chris's? Why would you give me Chris's baby to raise? Why would Chris let you give me his baby? And how did Chris get you pregnant when you said he wouldn't sleep with you while I was there because he was mad? You said you were certain that I'm the father, that I was the only person who could have gotten you pregnant."

"I didn't get pregnant, Andrew. The baby isn't mine."

"What? Are you crazy, Cullen? The baby isn't yours, and I'm not the father? Then where the hell did this baby come from, and why did you tell me it was ours?"

Andrew was shouting now. He could feel the adrenalin dumping into his system, the anger engulfing him. He was beginning to shake. Normally, he would try to fight strong emotions, but these were beyond his control. He was drowning. He couldn't suppress his outrage now even if he wanted to. Tony's anger had taken over. It was going full throttle.

"Please don't shout like that, Andrew. You're getting that Tony voice again."

"You haven't heard anything yet, Cullen. I'm going to totally explode here in a minute. Where the hell did this baby come from, Cullen? Answer me. Where?"

"It's Shawn's."

"Shawn's! Shawn is the father of a child you have pawned off on me?"

"Please calm down, Andrew. You're frightening me. I'm sorry. I made a mistake."

"You made a mistake?" Andrew was shouting with such force he almost couldn't get the words out fast enough. "Good God, Cullen, is that the best you can do? If you weren't pregnant, how could you possibly have made this mistake? It wasn't a mistake, Cullen. It was on purpose. It was entrapment! When I refused to consider marrying you out at Argo, you decided you would find a way to change my mind. So you dangled Shawn's illegitimate offspring as bait, knowing how much I wanted a child. How could you stoop that low, Cullen?" Andrew drew a deep breath. He felt ready to burst. "Why would you do something so despicable to someone who has treated you with kindness, who has paid your way through medical school so you could make your dreams a reality? Have you no shame at all? No conscience? Don't ever talk about how horrible Tony was again, Cullen. He had a temper, yes, and was physically violent sometimes, yes, but nothing you have ever told me about him is as monstrous as what you have done, as heartless as how you have treated me. His transgressions pale in comparison to yours." Andrew literally spit these last sentences out.

"Please calm down, Andrew. Control yourself. You're letting Tony's chemicals take over."

"Shut up, Cullen. I'll do as I damn well please. I'm through with this conversation, and I'm definitely through with you."

Andrew threw the phone across the room. He heard her say "Wait, Andrew" before it hit the wall and went dead. He was beside himself. He paced the room for a while. He turned on the gas logs in the fireplace and sat down. Then he jumped back up and went over to the bar fridge, pulled out his single-malt scotch, and poured a glass full to the brim, no ice, neat. He belted it down and poured another one, and then another one. He got up and staggered over to the bar to fill his glass again. Time collapsed. He dozed a little in his chair and woke with a start. His head was pounding. He threw a little cold water from the bar sink on his face and got himself another drink. Then he remembered the phone call. How the hell could this have happened to him? Why did it happen to him? He had spent the last fourteen months of his life depressed over his unfortunate entanglement with Cullen and dreading his upcoming marriage. The only good thing to come out of it so far was the pleasure little Jamey gave him, and of course, without him, he would never have met Elizabeth. Elizabeth! She was waiting for him to come back to the farm. He had gotten so worked up over Cullen's call he had forgotten what he was supposed to be doing. It was almost six o'clock and dark already. He searched around on his hands and knees for his phone and finally found it under the sofa. He grabbed his violin and the ice chest full of groceries and headed for the car, slipping and sliding. Snow! It was coming down hard. When the hell did it start snowing? The sun was shining when he left Margo six hours ago. He didn't remember seeing snow in the forecast. *Must be a good two inches now.*

Andrew backed out of his driveway and lurched forward. He finally got some traction and sped off down the highway, turning off onto the country road toward Margo and Elizabeth. He realized he was free now, free to marry Elizabeth. Elizabeth, his Margaret, at least near enough. He drove faster and faster, exhilarated to have found at last the new life he'd been waiting for, to have that wonderful feeling of being so completely, so deeply in love again. He never saw the truck coming.

chapter 42

Epilogue 1

"So tell me again how this happened?"

"Well, Officer, this guy was driving down the middle of the road, lickety-split. Had to be going ninety miles an hour. Can you believe it? On this narrow country road with it snowing like this? Must have been drunk or crazy. Anyway, I slammed on my brakes and tried to move my truck over, but with that big gulley there, I could only do so much. The poor bastard didn't even see me, I guess, until the last second or two. He swerved hard to the right, and that's when his car turned over and rolled down the bank. I called 911 and ran to see if I could help anyone. It was just him, slumped over the steering wheel, pinned in. Blood everywhere. He was still alive then 'cuz I heard him say 'Elizabeth' once or twice, but he didn't say no more after that."

"Hey, Jake, I just found his cell phone. There's food scattered everywhere and what looks like parts of an ice chest. There's also a violin, knocked right out of its case. Too bad the neck's broken. It was kind of pretty."

"Bring me that phone, Bob. I checked the license plate. The car, or what's left of it, is registered to the man driving, Dr. Andrew Hamilton. There's a Duke faculty sticker dangling from the broken windshield. Must be a professor there. Truck driver said the man muttered the name Elizabeth a few times. Wonder if that's his wife. I'll look to see if there's an ICE number. Yep, a Walter Rubin with a 314 area code. I better call and give him the bad news."

"What! Oh, my God! No! When? Is he still alive? Oh, my God, No! Rose, call that private jet service we use sometimes. Charles and I need to get to Durham tonight. Then get me a limo to the airport. Andrew's dead. Car accident. Call Charles. Have him meet me at the airport. I better call Elizabeth."

"Noooooooooooooooo! Nooooooooooooooo! Nooooooooooooooo!" Elizabeth let out several more primal screams and started sobbing uncontrollably.

"Elizabeth, listen to me. I will call the Durham police and ask them to send a car out to get you and take you back to Andrew's house. I'll meet you there as soon as I can. What did you say? Try to stop crying long enough for me to understand what you're saying, Elizabeth. Oh, Jamey. You've got the nurse's number who sometimes takes care of him. Call her now. Have her meet you at the house. She can take the baby home with her. Did you hear what I said? Elizabeth, get control of yourself. Call her now. I'll see you in a few hours."

Charles and Walter had three hours on the plane to make plans.

"Andrew wanted to be cremated and have his ashes scattered at Argo where he scattered Margaret's ashes and his own. That sounds weird, doesn't it? Scattered his own ashes."

"I think you should keep them for a year or so. No hurry. I can always do it later if Elizabeth doesn't want to."

"How does that affect your experiment, Walter? How will you ever know if the brain rejuvenated?"

"I'll have to get permission to take the brain back for examination. You'll have to arrange it, Charles. Besides, I still have Elizabeth."

"Oh, yes. I almost forgot. Margaret. Things haven't worked out too well for her, have they? They've worked out well for Cullen though. Andrew's baby's future is certainly secure. After Cullen got pregnant, Andrew changed his will. He made a provision that if he had offspring, born or unborn, half of his estate would go to his issue. Otherwise it would go to the Duke Department of Neurosciences for fellowships. The other half, of course, goes to your research."

"Jamey isn't Andrew's baby, Charles. Cullen called him this afternoon to tell him. Andrew was terribly upset. You know how his chemistry gets out of balance when all that adrenalin dumps into his system. Tony's temper takes over. If only I had thought to adjust his meds while he was in St. Louis. I'm afraid I'm to blame, Charles. His death is my fault. I should never have insisted Cullen call him. I should have come over to Durham and told him myself in a gentler way. But I was so damned incensed at Cullen's deception my temper got the best of me. I wanted her to take the consequences of her actions. I'm sure he drank himself silly in a rage and then calmed down and realized he was a free man. Charles, I have a feeling Andrew died happy. I knew Andrew well enough to think he was racing back to his farm to tell Elizabeth he loved her and wanted to marry her. That's where Elizabeth was when I called. They had been there for the past two weeks. Andrew had just gone back to town to pick up more groceries. The most tragic part is the two of them had reconnected. Elizabeth said she thought he was in love with her, that he could see beneath the surface and recognize Margaret. She took it really hard. Poor Margaret. The only reason she was willing to have the transplant in the first place was for the chance to be with Andrew again. I told her that maybe getting back to Andrew was God's plan for her."

"Well, evidently, it wasn't His plan. Wait a minute, Walter. What were you doing talking about God's plan anyway? I can't believe you said that."

"Well, it worked. She had a perfectly good brain that was about to go to waste, and I had a great young woman's body to put it in. I don't think that was so bad. Win-win, if you ask me."

"If Elizabeth was staying up at the farm with Andrew, I doubt they were sleeping in separate bedrooms. I think I should take my time settling the estate. Andrew may have an offspring after all."

"Wouldn't that be wonderful for Elizabeth? Margaret always wanted a child."

chapter 43

Epilogue 2

*A*pril was Elizabeth's favorite time in the Gardens, maybe because the azaleas were in full bloom the first time she went there. Had she only been in Durham two and a half years? It seemed like a lifetime ago that she arrived looking for Andrew. So much had happened since then. After Andrew died and Walter took Jamey back to Cullen, Elizabeth was left drowning in the cold, unforgiving misery of loss and loneliness. She was numb with grief. She blamed herself, she blamed Walter, and she blamed God. She could understand why God might still want to punish her, but why would he kill Andrew in order to do so? It didn't make sense to her. She had heard priests and rabbis and anchormen on television ask survivors what they thought God was telling them or saving them for, but surely, despite the story of Job, God didn't really sacrifice some people to test the faith of others or to teach them lessons or tell them something. Why would He place the burden of being special or needing to live a special life on some individuals because through some fluke of fate or physics they managed to survive a catastrophe that others did not? Elizabeth did not consider herself worthy of surviving Andrew. Why didn't God kill her instead? Maybe God wasn't through with her. Maybe He had a plan for her after all. Maybe Andrew's actions killed Andrew. Maybe Tony's chemistry killed Andrew. *Maybe the real answer is God doesn't break His own laws that He established to run His universe. Drunk drivers going ninety miles an* *hour down a narrow, winding road in the snow at night are likely to crash. If they survive, is it a miracle or the result of particulars according to the laws of physics?* Elizabeth's God was still an inscrutable God, but she believed Him to be a loving, evenhanded God, not a God who played favorites with miracles. She came down on the side of physics.

It had been almost a year and a half since Andrew died. Elizabeth had finally made peace with herself and God. Her overwhelming grief had receded down into some safe corner of her heart. She had a reason to live again. Elizabeth looked lovingly at her beautiful little seven-month-old son in the pram. After leaving Dave, Elizabeth had stopped taking birth control pills because she wasn't planning on dating anyone else, and she certainly didn't think she would be having sex with Andrew. *Strange how when one door closes, another one opens. Does God do that for us or have we just learned over the millennia to interpret and accept any lucky thing as compensation or a blessing? A survival positive technique, maybe?* Even though her beloved Andrew had been taken from her, she had been given the child she had wanted so badly in her other life. Fair enough? Who was she to judge? Elizabeth wasn't going to do the calculus.

Dave had thought about Elizabeth constantly while he was away on sabbatical. He dated a number of Italian women and had a six-month affair with a truly beautiful woman who wanted to marry him, but nothing ever came of it because he simply could not relegate Elizabeth to the archives. What a useful metaphor that had become for him.

Dave didn't learn of Andrew's death until he returned to Duke. It took him a while to discover that Elizabeth was still in town, living in Andrew's old house. Although he had her cell phone number, he knew instinctively that he shouldn't call. It would be more respectful to wait until he could see her face-to-face. He had a lot on his mind and in his heart that he wanted to say to her. Dave knew that, ever since he had first taken her to the Gardens, it had been one of her favorite places to go, so he knew that when the time was right, he would find her there.

"Hello, Elizabeth. I was hoping I would find you here."

"Dave! I haven't seen you in forever. How have you been?"

"Biding my time, Elizabeth. Are you still playing nanny? I thought Cullen would have taken her son back to St. Louis by now."

"This isn't Cullen's baby, Dave. It's mine and Andrew's."

"Oh, really? So you and Andrew did find each other before he died. I'm so happy you did. I was worried that he would marry Cullen before he knew who you were. That's why I sent the novel to him. I hope you aren't upset with me. I was only trying to make you happy, Elizabeth."

"I know that, Dave. I only had to take one look at that beautiful binding and the lovely end papers to know that it was done out of love. I found it lying on the table beside his chair. He hadn't had a chance to read it. Your note was on the floor nearby. I'm saving it for our son, Drew. Someday, when he is an adult and has lived and loved enough to better understand the challenges his father and I faced, I will give him the book. So I thank you for not destroying it, Dave. I thank you for preserving it in such a lovely way."

Dave sat down on the bench beside Elizabeth and pondered how he should begin to say all the things in his heart.

"Elizabeth, I have done a lot of thinking since you left. I have wanted to talk to you ever since I heard about Andrew's accident. I hope I have waited a respectful period of time."

Dave put his hand on top of hers and smiled at her. They had been lovers, after all, and at one time Elizabeth had told him she thought it was God's plan for her to marry him. It occurred to Dave that maybe it still was.

"Elizabeth, I can't tell you how often I have read and reread your poetry, especially the poem 'Vines.' Those were old vines that had grown all wound together. It took them many years to get so intertwined they seemed like one. It brought home to me a very important lesson about the nature of love. I realize now that, as wonderful a feeling as it was, falling in love with you was just the beginning, an awakening of my heart, the 'sweet cry of kindred souls,' as you put it. It made me feel euphoric, more alive. But no matter how powerful the feelings, they were still fragile and shallow until the roots had time to take hold and start to grow. One cannot expect to experience the depth of love starting out that develops over many years of being together. It was a foolish mistake for me to require that you love me as much as Andrew after so short a time together. I was just devastated. I really wasn't thinking rationally."

"Well, Dave, if you hadn't taken that position, I wouldn't have had the opportunity to be with Andrew again. You and I both would have always felt a silent 'what if,' keeping one little door in each of our minds locked with a Do Not Open sign on it."

"You're probably right about that, Elizabeth. Neither of us would have wanted any closed doors in our marriage. All the doors and windows in a marriage need to be open with sunlight and fresh air blowing through."

Dave put his other hand over hers and hesitated a moment before he continued. "This brings me to the reason I've come here today. I have never stopped loving you, Elizabeth. I want a chance for us to grow old together. I want you to be my wife. I have never wanted anything as much as I want to live my life with you. I know it's probably too soon for you to think about marriage, but I can wait until you're ready, Elizabeth. Please give me a second chance to win your heart."

Dave looked longingly at Elizabeth, at how beautiful she was with the sun's glow forming a halo around her hair. He leaned over and kissed her ever so gently, as if she were almost too holy and fragile to touch. He truly adored her.

"You once said that love is not a lake, confined and finite, but an ever-flowing river that can carry more than one. I don't have to replace Andrew. You can carry me in your heart along with him, Elizabeth. Whatever love you can give me now will be enough. I know beyond any doubt that someday you and I will be old vines too."

Acknowledgements

The idea for this novel grew out of many delightful "what if" conversations over the years with my lifelong friend Dr. Sandra B. Rosenthal, an internationally acclaimed Epistemologist. She played philosophical advisor to my whimsical musings in the story. To her I am most indebted.

I must also give special recognition to my dear friend Beverley K. Whitten for her enthusiastic support and helpful suggestions over many long breakfasts. I am also indebted to her for her perseverance in proofing the entire manuscript three times.

The world's best brother-in-law, Larry K. Granville, read my book as it was being written and acted as my barometer for male interest in the story. His comments and encouragement were extremely helpful to me.

My medical advisors, Dr. Ernest Lathem and Dr. Douglas Kennemore were generous with their time discussing various medical issues and speculating how this impossible, implausible operation could have occurred and how the personality of the body donor could have had any influence on the brain donor. They were both good sports in their imaginative hypothesizing.

A number of friends read the first draft of the manuscript. Many of their suggestions were incorporated into the novel. (It takes a village…) Most notable among them was my legal advisor and tireless cheerleader, Carol Simpson, Esq., who read and reacted to every chapter has it was being written. I also want to thank my dear friends Virginia Norris Green, Debra and Len Rubin, Nancy Stewart, and Laurie Greenway for their many helpful comments and encouragement.

My lovely and perceptive daughter-in-law, Alicia Barker, read a later version of the manuscript and pointed out several important things that needed to be deleted, changed or expanded. I am indebted to her for her insightful suggestions that helped strengthen the story.

My biggest supporter was my wonderful, sweet husband, Dr. James D. Koerner, who taught me everything I ever needed to know about unconditional love. He is greatly missed.

The impetus for writing a novel in the first place came from my son, John H. Barker, to whom this book is dedicated. Many years ago, when he was too young to know better, he told me that someday he wanted a painting on his wall that I had painted, a novel on his bookshelf that I had written, and some music on his piano that I had composed. Well, John, you have the painting. Here is the book. And maybe instead of that piano composition you will settle for another novel.

Printed in the United States
By Bookmasters